MW01598772

茶花女

LA DAME AUX, CAMELIAS

欧 洲 文 学 卷

[法] 小仲马 著
Alexandre Dumas fils

盛世教育西方名著翻译委员会 译

盛世教育西方名著翻译委员会
主　　任：黎小说　高民芳　杜　毅
本册委员：孙　怡　张云燕　贺金云
　　　　　黄碧鑫　张梦荣　张　雪
　　　　　孙利锋　刘　刚　程　娜

世界图书出版公司
上海·西安·北京·广州

图书在版编目（CIP）数据

茶花女：中英对照全译本/（法）小仲马（Dumas, A.）著；盛世教育西方名著翻译委员会译. —上海：上海世界图书出版公司，2011.5（2013.1 重印）

ISBN 978-7-5100-3237-0

Ⅰ. ①茶… Ⅱ. ①小… ②盛… Ⅲ. ①英语－汉语－对照读物 ②长篇小说－法国－近代 Ⅳ.①H319.4：I

中国版本图书馆 CIP 数据核字(2011)第 028063 号

茶花女

[法] 小仲马 著

盛世教育西方名著翻译委员会 译

上海世界图书出版公司 出版发行

上海市广中路 88 号

邮政编码 200083

北京兴鹏印刷有限公司印刷

如发现印刷质量问题，请与印刷厂联系

（质检科电话：010-84897777）

各地新华书店经销

开本：880×1230　1/32　印张：10.25　字数：356 000

2013 年 1 月第 1 版第 2 次印刷

ISBN 978-7-5100-3237-0 /H · 1103

定价：18.80 元

http://www.wpcsh.com.cn

http://www.wpcsh.com

前　言

　　通过阅读文学名著学语言，是掌握英语的绝佳方法。既可接触原汁原味的英语，又能享受文学之美，一举两得，何乐不为？

　　对于喜欢阅读名著的读者，这是一个最好的时代，因为有成千上万的书可以选择；这又是一个不好的时代，因为在浩繁的卷帙中，很难找到适合自己的好书。

　　然而，你手中的这套丛书，值得你来信赖。

　　这套精选的中英对照名著全译丛书，未改编改写、未删节削减，且配有权威注释、部分书中还添加了精美插图。

　　要学语言、读好书，当读名著原文。如习武者切磋交流，同高手过招方能渐明其间奥妙，若一味在低端徘徊，终难登堂入室。积年流传的名著，就是书中"高手"。然而这个"高手"，却有真假之分。初读书时，常遇到一些挂了名著名家之名改写改编的版本，虽有助于了解基本情节，然而所得只是皮毛，你何曾真的就读过了那名著呢？一边是窖藏了50年的女儿红，一边是贴了女儿红标签的薄酒，那滋味，怎能一样？"朝闻道，夕死可矣。"人生短如朝露，当努力追求真正的美。

　　本套丛书的英文版本，是根据外文原版书精心挑选而来；对应的中文译文以直译为主，以方便中英文对照学习，译文经反复推敲，对忠实理解原著极有助益；在涉及到重要文化习俗之处，添加了精当的注释，以解疑惑。

　　读过本套丛书的原文全译，相信你会得书之真意、语言之精髓。

　　送君"开卷有益"之书，愿成文采斐然之人。

CONTENTS
目 录

CHAPTER 1

第一章

In my opinion, it is impossible to create characters until one has spent a long time in studying men, as it is impossible to speak a language until it has been seriously acquired. Not being old enough to invent, I content myself with narrating, and I beg the reader to assure himself of the truth of a story in which all the characters, with the exception of the heroine, are still alive. Eye-witnesses of the greater part of the facts which I have collected are to be found in Paris, and I might call upon them to confirm me if my testimony is not enough. And, thanks to a particular circumstance, I alone can write these things, for I alone am able to give the final details, without which it would have been impossible to make the story at once interesting and complete.

This is how these details came to my knowledge. On the 12th of March, 1847, I saw in the Rue Lafitte a great yellow placard announcing a sale of furniture and curiosities. The sale was to take place on account of the death of the owner. The

我认为只有通过对周围人的长期的观察，才能成功塑造人物，正如只有在认真学习后，才能讲一种语言。我年纪尚轻，还没有能力创造，只好叙述一个故事。在此我希望读者相信这是个真实的故事，除了女主人公外，故事里所有的人都还在世。此外，在巴黎还有其他人见证了我所记录的大部分事实。如果我的一面之词还不足为信的话，他们可以为我作证。由于情况特殊，只有我才能把这个故事写出来，因为只有我才了解事情的来龙去脉，因而才能写出一个完整而吸引人的故事。

接下来就说说我是如何知道事情始末的。1847 年 3 月 12 日，我在拉菲特街看到一张拍卖家具和古董的黄色巨幅广告。因为物主去世，拍卖会才举行的。广告上没写明物主的姓名，只提到拍卖将在 16 日中

owner's name was not mentioned, but the sale was to be held at 9, Rue d'Antin, on the 16th, from 12 to 5. The placard further announced that the rooms and furniture could be seen on the 13th and 14th.

I have always been very fond of curiosities, and I made up my mind not to miss the occasion, if not of buying some, at all events of seeing them. Next day I called at 9, Rue d'Antin.

It was early in the day, and yet there were already a number of visitors, both men and women, and the women, though they were dressed in cashmere and velvet, and had their carriages waiting for them at the door, gazed with astonishment and admiration at the luxury which they saw before them.

I was not long in discovering the reason of this astonishment and admiration, for, having begun to examine things a little carefully, I discovered without difficulty that I was in the house of a kept woman. Now, if there is one thing which women in society would like to see (and there were society women there), it is the home of those women whose carriages splash their own carriages day by day, who, like them, side by side with them, have their boxes at the Opera and at the Italiens, and who

午 12 点到下午 5 点在昂坦街 9 号举行。广告上还通知，13 日和 14 日可以参观房子和家具。

我一直喜爱古董。心想这回可一定不能错过机会，就算不买，也得去看看。于是第二天，我去了昂坦街 9 号。

时间还早，可是已经有人在房子里了，男女都有。虽然这些女宾着装华贵——丝绒衣服、开司米披肩，还有在门外恭候的华丽马车，但是却都注视着她们眼前的豪华摆设，眼里充满了惊讶和赞赏。

不久，我就知道她们为什么赞赏和惊讶了。我仔细地环视了四周，很快发现这是一个高级妓女[1]的房间。如果说上流社会的女人（这里正有一些）对什么感兴趣的话，便是看看这种女人的闺房。这种女人出门后风光总是盖过这些贵妇；这种女人像她们一样，出入于歌剧院，在包厢里跟她们并肩而坐；这种女人厚颜无耻地在巴黎街头炫耀自己的姿色和珠宝，传扬自己的"风流韵事"。

---

[1] 高级妓女，这里指外室，靠男人供养的情妇。

parade in Paris the opulent insolence of their beauty, their diamonds, and their scandal.

This one was dead, so the most virtuous of women could enter even her bedroom. Death had purified the air of this abode of splendid foulness, and if more excuse were needed, they had the excuse that they had merely come to a sale, they knew not whose. They had read the placards, they wished to see what the placards had announced, and to make their choice beforehand. What could be more natural? Yet, all the same, in the midst of all these beautiful things, they could not help looking about for some traces of this courtesan's life, of which they had heard, no doubt, strange enough stories.

Unfortunately the mystery had vanished with the goddess, and, for all their endeavours, they discovered only what was on sale since the owner's decease, and nothing of what had been on sale during her lifetime. For the rest, there were plenty of things worth buying. The furniture was superb; there were rosewood and buff cabinets and tables, Sevres and Chinese vases, Saxe statuettes, satin, velvet, lace; there was nothing lacking.

住在这儿的妓女已经死了，所以，现在连最有操守的女人都能进入她的卧室。死亡已经净化了这个华丽而肮脏的住所的空气。如果说还有其他的理由，她们可以说是为了拍卖才来的，根本不知道主人是什么样的人。她们看到了广告，想亲眼看看广告上介绍的东西，提前挑选一下，没有比这更顺理成章的了。然而她们还是情不自禁地想从这些精致的摆设里寻找这个妓女的生活痕迹。毫无疑问，她们已经听闻过有关她的离奇故事了。

遗憾的是，那份神秘已经随着这位女神一起消逝了。不管这些贵妇人怎样努力，她们也只能看着死者留下的要拍卖的东西，却看不出她生前是过着什么样的生活。不过，有不少东西值得买。房间里的摆设极尽奢华，有玫瑰木的橱柜和软皮家具，塞夫勒[1]和中国的花瓶、萨克森[2]的微型塑像、绸缎、天鹅绒，还有蕾丝边，琳琅满目，应有尽有。

---

[1] 塞夫勒，法国巴黎西南郊城市，盛产精致瓷器。
2 萨克森，德国一地区，是瓷器工业中心。

I sauntered through the rooms, following the inquisitive ladies of distinction. They entered a room with Persian hangings, and I was just going to enter in turn, when they came out again almost immediately, smiling, and as if ashamed of their own curiosity. I was all the more eager to see the room. It was the dressing-room, laid out with all the articles of toilet, in which the dead woman's extravagance seemed to be seen at its height.

On a large table against the wall, a table three feet in width and six in length, glittered all the treasures of Aucoc and Odiot. It was a magnificent collection, and there was not one of those thousand little things so necessary to the toilet of a woman of the kind which was not in gold or silver. Such a collection could only have been got together little by little, and the same lover had certainly not begun and ended it.

Not being shocked at the sight of a kept woman's dressing-room, I amused myself with examining every detail, and I discovered that these magnificently chiselled objects bore different initials and different coronets. I looked at one after another, each recalling a separate shame, and I said that God had been merciful to

我随着那些好奇的贵妇人们信步走过一个个房间。她们走进了一间挂着波斯帘子的房间，正当我要进去的时候，她们却马上面带微笑着退了出来，似乎为自己的好奇而感到羞愧，我却更想进去看看。原来这是梳妆间，陈列着各式各样的梳妆用品，通过这些用品似乎可以看出死者生前的穷奢极侈。

在靠墙的一张宽 3 英尺、长 6 尺的桌子上放着欧克和奥迪欧[1]制造的各种各样的珍宝，闪闪发光，光彩夺目。这上千的小饰品，对女主人来说都是梳妆不可或缺的，而且都是用黄金或白银打造的。然而这么多的饰品只可能是一件件收集起来的，而且也不可能全部是某个情夫一个人送与的。

看到了一个妓女的梳妆间，我并不感到厌恶，而是饶有兴趣地观赏每一件东西。我发现所有这些做工精细的用品上都镌刻着不同的人名首字母和各种纹章。我一件件地看过去，每一件都使我联想到一次耻辱的交易。我想，上帝对那可怜的孩子还算仁慈，使她免遭通常的

---

[1] 欧克和奥迪欧，金银器制造业的著名品牌，是"法国式"奢华的象征。

the poor child, in not having left her to pay the ordinary penalty, but rather to die in the midst of her beauty and luxury, before the coming of old age, the courtesan's first death.

Is there anything sadder in the world than the old age of vice, especially in woman? She preserves no dignity, she inspires no interest. The everlasting repentance, not of the evil ways followed, but of the plans that have miscarried, the money that has been spent in vain, is as saddening a thing as one can well meet with. I knew an aged woman who had once been "gay," whose only link with the past was a daughter almost as beautiful as she herself had been. This poor creature to whom her mother had never said, "You are my child," except to bid her nourish her old age as she herself had nourished her youth, was called Louise, and, being obedient to her mother, she abandoned herself without volition, without passion, without pleasure, as she would have worked at any other profession that might have been taught her.

The constant sight of dissipation, precocious dissipation, in addition to her constant sickly state, had extinguished in her mind all the knowledge of good and evil that God had perhaps given her, but

那种惩罚，让她在衰老之前，带着她的美貌，在奢华的生活中死去。对于妓女来说，容颜老去就是她们的第一次死亡。

还有什么比放荡生活后的晚年，尤其是女人的，更悲惨的呢？这种晚年活得完全没有尊严，不能引起他人的半点同情，她们并不追悔曾经误入歧途，而是悔恨计划不能如愿实现，浪费了金钱，为此而抱恨终生，这是我们能遇到的最悲惨的事情了。我认识一位曾经风流一时的老妇人，过去的生活只留给她一个女儿。她女儿长得几乎和她年轻时一样美丽。她母亲未曾对这可怜的女孩说"你是我的女儿"，只是要她赡养，就像她自己曾把她抚养成人一样。这可怜的孩子叫路易丝。她顺从了母亲的意愿，甘于堕落，变得麻木不仁，没有意志，没有情欲，没有快乐，就像对待其他任何一种职业一样，有人教她，之后她便去从事。

一直以来目睹的都是荒淫的堕落生活，而且是从早年就开始了的堕落生活，加上这个姑娘长期以来羸弱多病，消磨了她分辨是非的才智。上帝可能也曾赋予她这种才智，

that no one had ever thought of developing. I shall always remember her, as she passed along the boulevards almost every day at the same hour, accompanied by her mother as assiduously as a real mother might have accompanied her daughter. I was very young then, and ready to accept for myself the easy morality of the age. I remember, however, the contempt and disgust which awoke in me at the sight of this scandalous chaperoning. Her face, too, was inexpressibly virginal in its expression of innocence and of melancholy suffering. She was like a figure of Resignation.

One day the girl's face was transfigured. In the midst of all the debauches mapped out by her mother, it seemed to her as if God had left over for her one happiness. And why indeed should God, who had made her without strength, have left her without consolation, under the sorrowful burden of her life? One day, then, she realized that she was to have a child, and all that remained to her of chastity leaped for joy. The soul has strange refuges. Louise ran to tell the good news to her mother. It is a shameful thing to speak of, but we are not telling tales of pleasant sins; we are telling of true facts, which it would be better, no doubt, to pass over in silence,

却从来没有人想过要使它得到施展。我永远都不会忘记这位姑娘，在母亲的陪同下，每天几乎都在同一时间走过大街。她母亲就像其他真正的母亲一样，不辞辛劳地陪伴着女儿。那时候我年纪还轻，很容易接受那个时代淡薄的道德观，但是我仍旧记得，一见到这种丑恶的监护行为，我便感到轻蔑和厌恶。姑娘脸上流露出的无辜、忧郁和痛苦的表情，使得她看上去无比纯洁，难以言表。她就像是委屈女郎[1]的化身。

　　一天，这个姑娘的脸突然一扫往日的忧郁。在她看来，在母亲一手安排的堕落生活里，上帝似乎还留下了一点儿幸福。上帝已经赐予了她软弱的性格，那么在她承受悲苦生活的重负时，为什么就不能给予一点儿安慰呢？一天，她意识到自己有身孕了，她思想中还残存的那点纯洁的意识，使她开心得全身颤抖。人的灵魂有它不可理解的庇护所。路易丝连忙跑去告诉她母亲自己的发现。这事让人难以启齿。但是，我们并不是在瞎编乱造什么"风流韵事"，而是在讲述一个事实。这种事，如果我们认为没有必要经常公开提起这些女人的苦难，

---

[1] 委屈女郎，指巴黎圣厄斯塔什教堂里一座由大理石雕成的神情哀怨的妇女头像。

if we did not believe that it is needful from time to time to reveal the martyrdom of those who are condemned without bearing, scorned without judging; shameful it is, but this mother answered the daughter that they had already scarce enough for two, and would certainly not have enough for three; that such children are useless, and a lying-in is so much time lost.

Next day a midwife, of whom all we will say is that she was a friend of the mother, visited Louise, who remained in bed for a few days, and then got up paler and feebler than before.

Three months afterward a man took pity on her and tried to heal her, morally and physically; but the last shock had been too violent, and Louise died of it. The mother still lives; how? God knows.

The story returned to my mind while I looked at the silver toilet things, and a certain space of time must have elapsed during these reflections, for no one was left in the room but myself and an attendant, who, standing near the door, was carefully watching me to see that I did not pocket anything.

I went up to the man, to whom I was causing so much anxiety. "Sir," I said, "can you tell me the name of the person who formerly lived here?"

毫无疑问最好还是保持沉默。人们谴责这种女人却对她们的申诉置若罔闻，人们蔑视她们却又对她们带有成见，没有公正的评价，这是可耻的。但那位母亲回复女儿说，她们两个人的生活已经举步维艰了，3个人的日子就更难维持；再说，这样的孩子要了也没用，而且腆着大肚子不做生意是浪费时间。

第二天，有一位助产婆——我们暂且把她当做那位母亲的一个朋友，过来探望路易丝。路易丝已经卧病在床好几天了，后来下床了，但脸色比以往更苍白，身体比以往更虚弱。

3个月过后，一个男人出于同情，设法医治她受伤的身心，但是那次的打击过于沉重，路易丝最终还是因为流产而死。她母亲还活着，生活过得如何？天知道！

当我注视着这些银质用具的时候，这个故事就萦绕在我心头。时间在我陷入回忆时已经悄然流逝，其他人都已经离开，房子里只剩下我和一个看守人，他正站在门口严密地监视着，以防我偷东西。

我走到这位看守人面前，这让他很不安。"先生，"我对他说，"你可以告诉我原来住在这儿的房客的姓名吗？"

"Mademoiselle Marguerite Gautier."

I knew her by name and by sight.

"What!" I said to the attendant; "Marguerite Gautier is dead?"

"Yes, sir."

"When did she die?"

"Three weeks ago, I believe."

"And why are the rooms on view?"

"The creditors believe that it will send up the prices. People can see beforehand the effect of the things; you see that induces them to buy."

"She was in debt, then?"

"To some extent, sir."

"But the sale will cover it?"

"And more too."

"Who will get what remains over?"

"Her family."

"She had a family?"

"It seems so."

"Thanks."

The attendant, reassured as to my intentions, touched his hat, and I went out.

"Poor girl!" I said to myself as I returned home; "she must have had a sad death, for, in her world, one has friends only when one is perfectly well." And in spite of myself I began to feel melancholy over the fate of Marguerite Gautier.

It will seem absurd to many people, but I have an unbounded sympathy for women

"玛格丽特·戈蒂埃小姐。"

我听说过她的名字，也见过她。

"什么！"我对看守人说，"玛格丽特·戈蒂埃已经死了？"

"是的，先生。"

"那是什么时候？"

"3个星期前吧。"

"那为什么她的住宅要供人参观呢？"

"债权人觉得这样做可以抬高价钱。你知道，让人们提前看看这些东西，可以吸引顾客。"

"她还背着债？"

"是的，先生，她欠了很多呢！"

"拍卖所得可以还清吧？"

"还能剩。"

"那剩下来的钱归谁呢？"

"她家人。"

"她还有家？"

"好像有。"

"谢谢你，先生。"

看守人弄清我的意图后放松了警惕，对我行了个礼，我便离开了。

"可怜的姑娘！"我回家时自言自语道，"她死的时候一定很悲惨，因为在她的圈子里，只有身体健康才会有朋友。"我情不自禁地对玛格丽特的命运感到悲伤。

或许很多人会认为这很可笑，但是我对沦落风尘的女子总是感到

of this kind, and I do not think it necessary to apologize for such sympathy.

One day, as I was going to the Prefecture for a passport, I saw in one of the neighbouring streets a poor girl who was being marched along by two policemen. I do not know what was the matter. All I know is that she was weeping bitterly as she kissed an infant only a few months old, from whom her arrest was to separate her. Since that day I have never dared to despise a woman at first sight.

无尽的怜悯，甚至也不想为这种怜悯态度向他人辩解。

一天，在我去警察局领取护照的时候，看见邻街有两个警察正押走一个姑娘。我不知道这个姑娘做错了什么，只见她痛哭流涕地亲吻着怀里才几个月大的孩子，因为她被捕后，母子就要骨肉分离。从那天起，我就再也不敢光凭第一印象就蔑视一个女人了。

CHAPTER 2

第二章

The sale was to take place on the 16th. A day's interval had been left between the visiting days and the sale, in order to give time for taking down the hangings, curtains, etc.

I had just returned from abroad. It was natural that I had not heard of Marguerite's death among the pieces of news which one's friends always tell on returning after an absence. Marguerite was a pretty woman; but though the life of such women makes sensation enough, their death makes very little. They are suns which set as they rose, unobserved. Their death, when they die young, is heard of by all their lovers at the same moment, for in Paris almost all the lovers of a well-known woman are friends. A few recollections are exchanged, and everybody's life goes on as if the incident had never occurred, without so much as a tear.

Nowadays, at twenty-five, tears have become so rare a thing that they are not to be squandered indiscriminately. It is the

拍卖在 16 日举行。在参观和拍卖之间隔有一天，用来拆卸挂饰和帘子。

那时候，我刚从外地回来。当一个人离开一段时间再回到巴黎时，朋友总是要告诉他一些重要新闻的。但是没有人向我提起玛格丽特去世的事，这也是很自然的。玛格丽特是个漂亮的女人，但是，这样的女人生前的生活闹得满城风雨，她们的去世却无人问津。她们就像恒星，陨落时和初升时一样暗无光彩。如果她们年轻时就死了，那她们所有的情人都会在同一时刻得知。因为在巴黎，一位名妓的所有情人几乎都是朋友。大家会相互交流一些有关她的回忆，然后各自继续自己的生活，就像事情从来没有发生过一样，谁也不会为此而流一滴眼泪。

现在，眼泪对于 25 岁的人来讲已变得十分珍贵，绝不能随便乱流，

most that can be expected if the parents who pay for being wept over are wept over in return for the price they pay.

As for me, though my initials did not occur on any of Marguerite's belongings, that instinctive indulgence, that natural pity that I have already confessed, set me thinking over her death, more perhaps than it was worth thinking over. I remembered having often met Marguerite in the Bois, where she went regularly every day in a little blue coupe drawn by two magnificent bays, and I had noticed in her a distinction quite apart from other women of her kind, a distinction which was enhanced by a really exceptional beauty.

These unfortunate creatures whenever they go out are always accompanied by somebody or other. As no man cares to make himself conspicuous by being seen in their company, and as they are afraid of solitude, they take with them either those who are not well enough off to have a carriage, or one or another of those elegant, ancient ladies, whose elegance is a little inexplicable, and to whom one can always go for information in regard to the women whom they accompany.

In Marguerite's case it was quite

最多只对为他们花费过金钱的父母才流几滴眼泪，来报答他们曾经所做的付出。

至于我，虽然我姓名的首字母没有出现在玛格丽特任何一件用品上，可是我刚才坦白过的本能的宽容和天生的怜悯使我对她的死念念不忘，虽然她或许并不值得我如此想念。我记得过去常常在布洛涅树林[1]遇到玛格丽特，她每天都坐着一辆由两匹栗色骏马拉着的蓝色四轮轿式小马车到那儿。她拥有一种有别于她那一类人的气质，而她那超凡脱俗的美貌，则更衬托出了这种气质的与众不同。

不管什么时候出门，这些不幸的人儿身边总是有人陪着。因为没有一个男人愿意由于和这种女人走在一起而成为他人关注的焦点，而她们又害怕孤独，所以总是有贴身女伴。这些女伴要么是因为境况不如她们，自己没有马车，要么是容颜已逝的老妇人。如果有谁想打听她们陪同的女主人的任何事情，那么尽可以毫无顾忌地向她们去请教。

玛格丽特却特立独行，她总是

---

[1] 布洛涅树林，巴黎著名的绿地，曾是王室御用庭园，19 世纪成为巴黎人最喜欢的休憩场所。

different. She was always alone when she drove in the Champs-Elysees, lying back in her carriage as much as possible, dressed in furs in winter, and in summer wearing very simple dresses; and though she often passed people whom she knew, her smile, when she chose to smile, was seen only by them, and a duchess might have smiled in just such a manner. She did not drive to and fro like the others, from the Rond-Point to the end of the Champs-Elysees. She drove straight to the Bois. There she left her carriage, walked for an hour, returned to her carriage, and drove rapidly home.

All these circumstances which I had so often witnessed came back to my memory, and I regretted her death as one might regret the destruction of a beautiful work of art.

It was impossible to see more charm in beauty than in that of Marguerite. Excessively tall and thin, she had in the fullest degree the art of repairing this oversight of Nature by the mere arrangement of the things she wore. Her cashmere reached to the ground, and showed on each side the large flounces of a silk dress, and the heavy muff which she

独自坐车到香榭丽舍大街[1]去，尽量往车内坐以避开人们的视线。她冬天裹着皮衣，夏天穿着素净的长裙。她经常遇到熟人，有时对他们微微一笑，也只有他们才能看到，而这是一种只有公爵夫人才有的微笑。她也不像其他同行那样，喜欢在圆形广场和香榭丽舍大街街口之间散步，她坐车径直来到郊外的布洛涅树林，在那里下车，漫步一个小时，然后重新回到马车上，疾驰回家。

这些我所亲眼目睹的情景到现在还历历在目，我很叹惜她的早逝，就像人们惋惜一件精致的艺术品被毁一样。

玛格丽特真是个绝世佳人，魅力无人可比。她身材也许有些过高过瘦，可她有一种超凡的才能，只要用心打扮，就能掩饰这种造化的疏忽。她披着及地的开司米大披肩，两边露出丝绸长裙的宽阔的镶边，她那紧贴在胸前藏手用的厚厚的暖手笼四周的褶裥都做得十分精巧，因此不管用怎样挑剔的眼光来看，

---

[1] 香榭丽舍大街，巴黎最著名的大街之一，东起协和广场，西至星形广场，东段是林荫道，西段是高级商业区。常是高雅繁华、浪漫流行的代名词。

held pressed against her bosom was surrounded by such cunningly arranged folds that the eye, however exacting, could find no fault with the contour of the lines. Her head, a marvel, was the object of the most coquettish care. It was small, and her mother, as Musset would say, seemed to have made it so in order to make it with care.

Set, in an oval of indescribable grace, two black eyes, surmounted by eyebrows of so pure a curve that it seemed as if painted; veil these eyes with lovely lashes, which, when drooped, cast their shadow on the rosy hue of the cheeks; trace a delicate, straight nose, the nostrils a little open, in an ardent aspiration toward the life of the senses; design a regular mouth, with lips parted graciously over teeth as white as milk; colour the skin with the down of a peach that no hand has touched, and you will have the general aspect of that charming countenance. The hair, black as jet, waving naturally or not, was parted on the forehead in two large folds and draped back over the head, leaving in sight just the tip of the ears, in which there glittered two diamonds, worth four to five thousand francs each. How it was that her ardent life had left on Marguerite's face the virginal,

线条都是完美无缺的。她的头部很美，是一件精妙的珍品，它长得精致小巧，就如同缪塞[1]所说的那样，她母亲似乎是刻意让它长得如此小巧，以便把它精心打扮一番。

在一张流露着难以描绘其秀美的鹅蛋脸上，镶着两只黑亮的大眼睛，上面两道弯弯的眉毛，纯净得好似用画笔画上去的一样，眼睛上盖着浓密的睫毛，当眼帘低垂时，玫瑰色的双颊便投去一抹淡淡的阴影；精致而挺直的鼻子透出一股灵气，鼻翼微鼓，像是强烈渴望情欲生活；一张端正的小嘴线条分明，红唇微张，露出一口洁白如雪的牙齿；皮肤颜色就像未经人手触摸过的鲜桃上的绒衣那样白皙。这些就是这张漂亮的脸蛋给你的大体印象。乌黑亮丽的头发，不知是天生的还是梳理而成的，像波浪般鬈曲着，在额前分梳成两大绺，一直拖到脑后，露出两个耳垂，上面两颗各值 4000~5000 法郎的钻石耳环闪闪发光。玛格丽特过着自由放纵的生活，但是她的脸上却流露出处女般的神情，甚至还带着孩子气的表

---

[1] 缪塞，19 世纪法国浪漫主义作家。

almost childlike expression, which characterized it, is a problem which we can but state, without attempting to solve it.

Marguerite had a marvellous portrait of herself, by Vidal, the only man whose pencil could do her justice. I had this portrait by me for a few days after her death, and the likeness was so astonishing that it has helped to refresh my memory in regard to some points which I might not otherwise have remembered.

Some among the details of this chapter did not reach me until later, but I write them here so as not to be obliged to return to them when the story itself has begun.

Marguerite was always present at every first night, and passed every evening either at the theatre or the ball. Whenever there was a new piece she was certain to be seen, and she invariably had three things with her on the ledge of her ground-floor box: her opera-glass, a bag of sweets, and a bouquet of camellias.

For twenty-five days of the month the camellias were white, and for five they were red; no one ever knew the reason of this change of colour, which I mention though I can not explain it; it was noticed both by her friends and by the habitue's of the theatres to which she most often went.

情，这真使我们感到十分的困惑不解。

玛格丽特有一幅自己的肖像，是维达尔[1]的杰作，也只有他才能把玛格丽特画得如此传神。在她去世以后的几天，我曾持有这幅画像。它和她本人惊人的相似，让我重新记起了一些遗忘的细节。

这章里的一些细节是我后来才知道的，但我先在这里讲明是为了避免开始讲故事的时候还得回到这些情节上去。

玛格丽特每逢首演都会在场。每天晚上，她都在剧场里或舞会上度过。不管什么时候有新剧上演，她都一定会出席。在她位于底层的包间的前栏上总是放着她随身带的3件东西：一副望远镜、一袋蜜饯和一束茶花。

每月有 25 天放的是白茶花，而另外 5 天却是红色的，没有人知道她这样做的原因。我提起此事，但也无法给出原因。她的朋友和她经常光顾的剧院的老观众都注意到了这一点。她自始至终都只带过山茶花。因此，在她常去买花的巴尔戎

---

[1] 维达尔，19 世纪法国著名肖像画家。

She was never seen with any flowers but camellias. At the florist's, Madame Barjon's, she had come to be called "the Lady of the Camellias," and the name stuck to her.

Like all those who move in a certain set in Paris, I knew that Marguerite had lived with some of the most fashionable young men in society, that she spoke of it openly, and that they themselves boasted of it; so that all seemed equally pleased with one another. Nevertheless, for about three years, after a visit to Bagnees, she was said to be living with an old duke, a foreigner, enormously rich, who had tried to remove her as far as possible from her former life, and, as it seemed, entirely to her own satisfaction.

This is what I was told on the subject. In the spring of 1842 Marguerite was so ill that the doctors ordered her to take the waters, and she went to Bagneres. Among the invalids was the daughter of this duke; she was not only suffering from the same complaint, but she was so like Marguerite in appearance that they might have been taken for sisters; the young duchess was in the last stage of consumption, and a few days after Marguerite's arrival she died.

One morning, the duke, who had

夫人的花店里，有人给她取了一个外号，称她为"茶花女"，后来这个称呼就叫开了。

就像所有其他在某个圈子里生活的人一样，我知道玛格丽特曾经和一些上流社会的时尚青年生活在一起，她对此毫不避讳，那些青年也为此在他人面前吹嘘，说明他们双方似乎都很愉快。然而，据说在一次从巴涅尔[1]旅行回来以后，大概有 3 年她都只和一个外国的老公爵住在一起。这位老公爵十分富有，他尽他所能让玛格丽特远离过去的生活。而且，看来这也正合她的意愿。

我是听别人讲述这件事的。1842 年春天，玛格丽特病得十分严重，医生建议她到温泉疗养，于是她去了巴涅尔。来疗养的病人中有位公爵的女儿，她不仅和玛格丽特患有相同的病，而且外貌也极为相似，以至于人们都以为她们是姐妹。不过公爵小姐的肺病已经到了晚期，玛格丽特没到几天公爵小姐便去世了。为了能留在埋葬心爱女儿的地方附近，公爵没有离开巴涅尔。

一天早晨，公爵在一条小路的

---

[1] 巴涅尔，法国著名的温泉疗养地。

remained at Bagneres to be near the soil that had buried a part of his heart, caught sight of Marguerite at a turn of the road. He seemed to see the shadow of his child, and going up to her, he took her hands, embraced and wept over her, and without even asking her who she was, begged her to let him love in her the living image of his dead child. Marguerite, alone at Bagneres with her maid, and not being in any fear of compromising herself, granted the duke's request. Some people who knew her, happening to be at Bagneres, took upon themselves to explain Mademoiselle Gautier's true position to the duke. It was a blow to the old man, for the resemblance with his daughter was ended in one direction, but it was too late. She had become a necessity to his heart, his only pretext, his only excuse, for living. He made no reproaches, he had indeed no right to do so, but he asked her if she felt herself capable of changing her mode of life, offering her in return for the sacrifice every compensation that she could desire. She consented.

It must be said that Marguerite was just then very ill. The past seemed to her sensitive nature as if it were one of the main causes of her illness, and a sort of superstition led her to hope that God would

拐角处瞥见了玛格丽特。他仿佛看到了自己女儿的影子，便走过去拉住了她的手，将她揽入怀里，伤心地哭起来，甚至都不问她究竟是谁，就恳求允许把她当做自己去世女儿的替身来疼爱她。和玛格丽特一起到巴涅尔去的只有她的侍女，再说她也不担心会损害自己的名声，就答应了公爵的请求。碰巧有认识玛格丽特的人在巴涅尔，他们专诚拜访公爵，将戈蒂埃小姐的社会地位如实地告诉了公爵。这对这位老人来说是个沉重的打击，因为这样就再也谈不上玛格丽特和他女儿还有什么相似之处了，但一切都太晚了，这个姑娘已经走进了他的心，成了他生活中难以割舍的一部分，简直成了他活下去的唯一借口和托词。他没有责备她，他也没有权利这样做，只是问她是否可以改变原来的生活方式，并提供她为之做出牺牲所需要的所有补偿。玛格丽特答应了。

必须说明的是，生性热情的玛格丽特当时病得很厉害，她觉得过去的生活似乎是她患病的主要原因之一。出于一种迷信的想法，她希望上帝能恢复她的健康和美丽，作

restore to her both health and beauty in return for her repentance and conversion. By the end of the summer, the waters, sleep, the natural fatigue of long walks, had indeed more or less restored her health. The duke accompanied her to Paris, where he continued to see her as he had done at Bagneres.

This liaison, whose motive and origin were quite unknown, caused a great sensation, for the duke, already known for his immense fortune, now became known for his prodigality. All this was set down to the debauchery of a rich old man, and everything was believed except the truth. The father's sentiment for Marguerite had, in truth, so pure a cause that anything but a communion of heart would have seemed to him a kind of incest, and he had never spoken to her a word which his daughter might not have heard.

Far be it from me to make out our heroine to be anything but what she was. As long as she remained at Bagnères, the promise she had made to the duke had not been hard to keep, and she had kept it; but, once back in Paris, it seemed to her – accustomed to a life of dissipation, of balls, of orgies – as if the solitude, only interrupted by the duke's stated visits, would kill her with boredom, and the hot

为她忏悔和皈依的回报。到夏末的时候，温泉澡、散步、自然的体力消耗和正常的睡眠，确实或多或少地帮助她恢复了健康。公爵陪同她回到了巴黎，他还是和在巴涅尔一样，经常去看望她。

人们既不知道他们这种关系的确切动机，也不知道其真正原因，所以在巴黎引起了巨大轰动。公爵之前就因富有而远近闻名，现在又因挥霍无度而为人所知。人们把老公爵和玛格丽特的亲密关系归因于有钱老头儿好色的毛病，对他们的种种猜测都没有猜到真情。其实这位父亲对玛格丽特的感情是出于很纯洁的动机，除了跟她有心灵交流之外，任何其他不恰当的行为在公爵看来都意味着乱伦。他从来没有对她说过一句不适宜对女儿讲的话。

我对女主人公只是如实地描写，根本没有添油加醋的成分。只要玛格丽特还待在巴涅尔，她还是能够遵守对公爵所作出的承诺，她确实遵守了。但是一旦回到巴黎，这个习惯于喝酒狂欢，跳舞享乐的糜烂生活的姑娘似乎就忍受不住了，这种只有老公爵定期来访才可以解闷的孤寂生活使她无聊到室

breath of her old life came back across her head and heart.

We must add that Marguerite had returned more beautiful than she had ever been; she was but twenty, and her malady, sleeping but not subdued, continued to give her those feverish desires which are almost always the result of diseases of the chest.

It was a great grief to the duke when his friends, always on the lookout for some scandal on the part of the woman with whom, it seemed to them, he was compromising himself, came to tell him, indeed to prove to him, that at times when she was sure of not seeing him she received other visits, and that these visits were often prolonged till the following day. On being questioned, Marguerite admitted everything to the duke, and advised him, without arriere-pensee, to concern himself with her no longer, for she felt incapable of carrying out what she had undertaken, and she did not wish to go on accepting benefits from a man whom she was deceiving. The duke did not return for a week; it was all he could do, and on the eighth day he came to beg Marguerite to let him still visit her, promising that he would take her as she was, so long as he might see her, and swearing that he would never utter a reproach against her, not though he

息，过去生活的火辣气息一下子涌上了她的脑海和心头。

而且，玛格丽特在这次旅行回来后显得前所未有的妩媚动人，她正当 20 岁的大好年华，她的病看起来已经好转，但实际上并未痊愈，因此激起了她狂热的欲望，而这种欲望就是肺病的症状。

公爵的朋友们总是认为公爵和玛格丽特这样的女人在一起是自毁名誉，他们时刻监视她，以期找到她不良行为的证据。他们来告诉公爵，并向他证实，玛格丽特确定公爵不会去看她的时候，接待了其他拜访者，而且这些人会待到第二天。公爵知道后非常伤心。玛格丽特在公爵质询的时候坦白了一切，还坦率地劝告他以后不要再花心思在她身上，因为她觉得自己没有办法再继续履行承诺，她也不想再接受一个被她欺骗的男人的帮助了。公爵有一个星期没去看玛格丽特，这是他所能坚持的极限。到了第八天，他终于忍不住恳求玛格丽特能继续跟他来往，只要能够见到玛格丽特，公爵愿意接受按原来方式生活的她，还向她发誓说，就算要了他的命，他也决不再责备她。

were to die of it.

This, then, was the state of things three months after Marguerite's return; that is to say, in November or December, 1842.

这就是玛格丽特回来 3 个月后，也就是 1842 年 11 月或 12 月的情况。

CHAPTER 3

第三章

At one o'clock on the 16th I went to the Rue d'Antin. The voice of the auctioneer could be heard from the outer door. The rooms were crowded with people. There were all the celebrities of the most elegant impropriety, furtively examined by certain great ladies who had again seized the opportunity of the sales in order to be able to see, close at hand, women whom they might never have another occasion of meeting, and whom they envied perhaps in secret for their easy pleasures. The Duchess of F. elbowed Mlle. A., one of the most melancholy examples of our modern courtesan; the Marquis de T. hesitated over a piece of furniture the price of which was being run high by Mme. D., the most elegant and famous adulteress of our time; the Duke of Y., who in Madrid is supposed to be ruining himself in Paris, and in Paris to be ruining himself in Madrid, and who, as a matter of fact, never even reaches the limit of his income, talked with Mme. M., one of our wittiest story-tellers, who from

16 日下午 1 点钟，我去了昂坦街。拍卖竞标人的喊叫声在大门口就能够听到。房间里挤满了围观的人。所有花街柳巷的名媛都过来了，有几个贵妇人在暗地里打量她们。这一次她们又可以趁着参加拍卖的机会，仔细观察那些她们没有其他适当的时机与之见面的女人，也许她们还暗暗羡慕这些女人放荡的享乐生活。F 公爵夫人的胳膊撞到了 A 小姐，A 小姐是现如今最不幸的妓女之一；T 侯爵夫人正在考虑要不要买下那件被 D 夫人不断抬高价格的家具；D 夫人是时下最优雅最出名的荡妇。那位 Y 公爵，马德里那边谣传他在巴黎快要破产了，而巴黎这边又谣传他在马德里快要破产了，但事实上他从来都没有花完每年的收入。这时候他一面在跟 M 太太聊天，一面却在和 N 夫人眉来眼去。M 太太风趣幽默，讲故事的本领是数一数二的，她时不时把自己讲的东西写下来，并签上自己的名字。N 夫人经常路过香榭丽舍大街，

time to time writes what she says and signs what she writes, while at the same time he exchanged confidential glances with Mme. de N., a fair ornament of the Champs-Elysees, almost always dressed in pink or blue, and driving two big black horses which Tony had sold her for 10,000 francs, and for which she had paid, after her fashion; finally, Mlle. R., who makes by her mere talent twice what the women of the world make by their dot and three times as much as the others make by their amours, had come, in spite of the cold, to make some purchases, and was not the least looked at among the crowd.

We might cite the initials of many more of those who found themselves, not without some mutual surprise, side by side in one room. But we fear to weary the reader. We will only add that everyone was in the highest spirits, and that many of those present had known the dead woman, and seemed quite oblivious of the fact. There was a sound of loud laughter; the auctioneers shouted at the top of their voices; the dealers who had filled the benches in front of the auction table tried in vain to obtain silence, in order to transact their business in peace. Never was there a noisier or a more varied gathering.

为之增添了一份美丽，几乎总是穿着粉红和天蓝两种颜色的衣服，坐在由两匹高大的黑色骏马驾着的车里。这两匹马，托尼[1]开价 1 万法郎……按她一贯的做事风格，她如数照付。最后还有 R 小姐，她完全依靠自己的才能争取的地位使那些靠嫁妆争取到低位的上流社会妇人自愧不如，那些靠爱情的女人更是无法企及。尽管天气寒冷，她还是赶过来买一些东西，自然也吸引了不少人的目光。

我们还可以列举出聚集在这间屋里的很多人的姓氏首字母，在这里相遇他们彼此都感到惊讶，不过为了不使读者感到厌烦，我就不再一一赘述。值得一提的是，大家当时兴致都很高。这些人中有很多人认识死者，但这时候好像完全忘记了这回事。大家高声谈笑，拍卖竞标人大声叫喊。商人们满满地坐在拍卖桌前的长凳上，他们试图让人们安静下来，好让自己能安静地做买卖，但都是徒劳的。像这样鱼龙混杂，嘈杂不堪的集会还真是头一次见到。

---

[1] 托尼，当时著名的马商。

I slipped quietly into the midst of this tumult, sad to think of when one remembered that the poor creature whose goods were being sold to pay her debts had died in the next room. Having come rather to examine than to buy, I watched the faces of the auctioneers, noticing how they beamed with delight whenever anything reached a price beyond their expectations. Honest creatures, who had speculated upon this woman's prostitution, who had gained their hundred per cent out of her, who had plagued with their claims the last moments of her life, and who came now after her death to gather in, at once, the fruits of their dishonourable calculations and the interest on their shameful credit! How wise were the ancients in having only one God for traders and robbers!

Dresses, cashmeres, jewels, were sold with incredible rapidity. There was nothing that I cared for, and I still waited. All at once I heard: "A volume, beautifully bound, gilt-edged, entitled *Manon Lescaut*. There is something written on the first page. Ten francs."

"Twelve," said a voice after a longish silence.

"Fifteen," I said.

我悄悄地混进了杂乱的人群。一想到这个要用拍卖家具来抵偿生前债务的可怜女人就在隔壁房间离世，心里就感到十分伤心。我与其说是来买东西，倒不如说是来瞧热闹的，我看着几个拍卖商的脸，每当一件物品叫到出乎他们意料的高价时，他们便眉开眼笑，心花怒放。那些在这个女人的妓女生涯中搞过投机买卖的人，那些通过她大发横财的人，那些在她弥留之际拿着借据来纠缠她的人，还有那些在她死后就来收取他们冠冕堂皇的账款和卑鄙可耻的高利贷利息的人，所有那些人可都是所谓的正直人啊！难怪古人说，商人和盗贼信仰的是同一个上帝，说得相当正确！

长裙、开司米披肩、首饰，很快就全部卖完了，快得让人难以相信，可是没有一件东西对我有用，我继续等待着。忽然，我听到有人在喊："精装书一册，考究装订，烫金书边，书名《曼侬·莱斯科》[1]，扉页上写有几个字，10 法郎。"

一段相当长的沉默后，有个人叫道："12 法郎。"

"15 法郎。"我说。

---

[1] 《曼侬·莱斯科》，18 世纪著名爱情小说，作者普雷渥。普契尼根据本书改成的同名歌剧至今为人传诵。

Why? I did not know. Doubtless for the something written.

"Fifteen," repeated the auctioneer.

"Thirty," said the first bidder in a tone which seemed to defy further competition.

It had now become a struggle. "Thirty-five," I cried in the same tone.

"Forty."

"Fifty."

"Sixty."

"A hundred."

If I had wished to make a sensation I should certainly have succeeded, for a profound silence had ensued, and people gazed at me as if to see what sort of a person it was who seemed to be so determined to possess the volume.

The accent which I had given to my last word seemed to convince my adversary; he preferred to abandon a conflict which could only have resulted in making me pay ten times its price for the volume, and, bowing, he said very gracefully, though indeed a little late:

"I give way, sir."

Nothing more being offered, the book was assigned to me.

As I was afraid of some new fit of obstinacy, which my amour propre might have sustained somewhat better than my purse, I wrote down my name, had the

为什么出价？我自己也不知道，可能是为了扉页上的那几个字吧。

"15。"拍卖人又喊了一次。

"30。"第一个出价的人喊道，口气听上去似乎对别人抬价感到恼火。

这下拍卖变成了一场较量。

"35！"我以相同的口气喊道。

"40！"

"50！"

"60！"

"100！"

如果我是想引人注意的话，那么肯定已经成功了，因为在这次竞价后，全场一片寂静，大家都盯着我，想知道这位一心要得到这本书的先生到底是什么样的人。

我最后一次喊价的口吻好像把对手给震住了，他最后还是放弃了这场角逐，而我却因此要花10倍的价钱买下这本书。于是，他向我鞠了个躬，虽说迟了点，但非常客气地对我说：

"我让给你了，先生。"

那时也没有其他人再加价，书归了我。

因为我怕自己又犯倔脾气，而身上带的钱也不多，我请他们把我的名字记下，把书先放在一边，然后离开了。那些在场的人肯定对我

book put on one side, and went out. I must have given considerable food for reflection to the witnesses of this scene, who would nodoubt ask themselves what my purpose could have been in paying a hundred francs for a book which I could have had anywhere for ten, or, at the outside, fifteen.

An hour after, I sent for my purchase. On the first page was written in ink, in an elegant hand, an inscription on the part of the giver. It consisted of these words:

Manon to Marguerite. Humility.

It was signed *Armand Duval*.

What was the meaning of the word Humility? Was Manon to recognise in Marguerite, in the opinion of M. Armand Duval, her superior in vice or in affection? The second interpretation seemed the more probable, for the first would have been an impertinent piece of plain speaking which Marguerite, whatever her opinion of herself, would never have accepted.

I went out again, and thought no more of the book until at night, when I was going to bed.

Manon Lescaut is a touching story. I know every detail of it, and yet whenever I come across the volume the same sympathy always draws me to it; I open it,

作了各种猜测，他们一定会暗自揣测，我花 100 法郎的高价买下这本书的目的到底是什么，这本书随处都可以买到，只要花费 10 法郎，最多也不过 15 法郎。

过了一个小时后，我差人取回我买下的那本书。扉页上是赠书人用钢笔写下的一行秀丽的字迹：

曼侬对玛格丽特。惭愧。

署名是阿尔芒·迪瓦尔。

"惭愧"这两个字写在这里有什么用意呢？在阿尔芒·迪瓦尔先生看来，曼侬是不是承认无论是在放荡生活方面，还是在内心的情感方面，自己都输给了玛格丽特？第二种解释似乎更有可能，因为第一种解释是唐突无礼的，不管玛格丽特怎样看待自己，她都不会接受的。

我又出去了，一直到晚上要睡的时候，我才想起那本书。

《曼侬·莱斯科》是一个感人的故事，我虽然对故事的每一个细节都了如指掌，可是不管什么时候，只要看到这本书，我对这本书的感

and for the hundredth time I live over again with the heroine of the Abbe Prevost. Now this heroine is so true to life that I feel as if I had known her; and thus the sort of comparison between her and Marguerite gave me an unusual inclination to read it, and my indulgence passed into pity, almost into a kind of love for the poor girl to whom I owed the volume. Manon died in the desert, it is true, but in the arms of the man who loved her with the whole energy of his soul; who, when she was dead, dug a grave for her, and watered it with his tears, and buried his heart in it; while Marguerite, a sinner like Manon, and perhaps converted like her, had died in a sumptuous bed (it seemed, after what I had seen, the bed of her past), but in that desert of the heart, a more barren, a vaster, a more pitiless desert than that in which Manon had found her last resting-place.

Marguerite, in fact, as I had found from some friends who knew of the last circumstances of her life, had not a single real friend by her bedside during the two months of her long and painful agony.

Then from Manon and Marguerite my mind wandered to those whom I knew, and whom I saw singing along the way which led to just such another death. Poor souls! if it is not right to love them, is it not well

情总是将我拉向它。我翻开书，普雷厄神甫塑造的女主人公似乎就在眼前，这种情况反反复复有 100 多次了。这位女主人公被描绘得如此栩栩如生，以至使我感觉似乎真的见过她。因此这里将曼侬和玛格丽特作比较让我尤其想阅读这本书。出于对这位可怜的姑娘的同情，甚至可以说是喜爱，我更加怜悯她了，我得到的这本书就是她的遗物。曼侬是在荒凉的沙漠中死去的，但是她是在一个真正爱她的情人怀中死去。曼侬去世后，这个情人亲自为她挖了一个墓穴，他的泪水洒落在她身上，并将他的心一起埋葬在里面。而玛格丽特和曼侬一样是个罪人，也可能跟曼侬一样悔过了，但她是死在富贵奢华的床上（在我看到这张床后，我感觉它似乎就代表着玛格丽特的过去），在她的内心却是一片贫瘠的沙漠，比埋葬曼侬的沙漠更荒凉，更广袤，更无情。

我从几个知道她临终情况的朋友那儿了解到，在玛格丽特长达 2 个月特别痛苦的病危期间，没有一个人在她身边给她一点儿安慰。

曼侬和玛格丽特让我想起了我认识的那些女人，我看着她们唱着歌走向那几乎总是没有例外的最后归宿。可怜的女人啊！如果说爱她们是错误的，那难道连同情也不可

to pity them? You pity the blind man who has never seen the daylight, the deaf who has never heard the harmonies of nature, the dumb who has never found a voice for his soul, and, under a false cloak of shame, you will not pity this blindness of heart, this deafness of soul, this dumbness of conscience, which sets the poor afflicted creature beside herself and makes her, in spite of herself, incapable of seeing what is good, of bearing the Lord, and of speaking the pure language of love and faith.

Hugo has written Marion Delorme, Musset has written Bernerette, Alexandre Dumas has written Fernande, the thinkers and poets of all time have brought to the courtesan the offering of their pity, and at times a great man has rehabilitated them with his love and even with his name. If I insist on this point, it is because many among those who have begun to read me will be ready to throw down a book in which they will fear to find an apology for vice and prostitution; and the author's age will do something, no doubt, to increase this fear. Let me undeceive those who think thus, and let them go on reading, if nothing but such a fear hinders them.

I am quite simply convinced of a certain principle, which is: For the woman whose education has not taught her what is right,

以吗？你们同情从来看不到阳光的盲人，听不到大自然和谐之声的聋子，不能用声音来表达自己思想的哑巴；但是，借着一个虚假的所谓廉耻的幌子，你们却不愿意怜悯这些心灵上的盲人，灵魂上的聋子和良心上的哑巴。这些障碍逼得那个可怜的忍受折磨的女人发疯，使她无法看到善良，无法听到天主的声音，也讲不出爱情和信仰的纯洁语言。

雨果刻画了玛丽翁·德·萝尔姆，缪塞塑造了贝尔娜雷特，大仲马创造了费尔南特。各个时期的思想家和诗人都对风尘女子怀有仁慈的怜悯之心。有时候一个伟人会用他的爱情，甚至以他的姓名来为她们恢复名誉。我一再强调这一点的原因是在那些开始阅读我这本书的读者当中，恐怕已经有很多人准备抛开这本书，不再继续看了，害怕这是一本专门为邪恶和淫欲辩解的书，而且作者的年龄势必更容易让人有这种顾虑。希望这些人不要有这样的想法，如果单单只是因为这一点，那就请继续看下去。

我只坚信一个原则：对于没有受过教育、不能明辨是非的女人，上帝总是给她们两条路通向他的面

God almost always opens two ways which lead thither the ways of sorrow and of love. They are hard; those who walk in them walk with bleeding feet and torn hands, but they also leave the trappings of vice upon the thorns of the wayside, and reach the journey's end in a nakedness which is not shameful in the sight of the Lord.

Those who meet these bold travellers ought to succour them, and to tell all that they have met them, for in so doing they point out the way. It is not a question of setting at the outset of life two sign-posts, one bearing the inscription "The Right Way," the other the inscription "The Wrong Way," and of saying to those who come there, "Choose." One must needs, like Christ, point out the ways which lead from the second road to the first, to those who have been easily led astray; and it is needful that the beginning of these ways should not be too painful nor appear too impenetrable.

Here is Christianity with its marvellous parable of the Prodigal Son to teach us indulgence and pardon. Jesus was full·of love for souls wounded by the passions of men; he loved to bind up their wounds and to find in those very wounds the balm which should heal them. Thus he said to

前：痛苦或者爱情。这两条路走起来都异常艰辛。那些女人走得双脚流血，双手破裂，但同时，她们把罪孽的诱惑留在沿途的荆棘上，赤裸裸地抵达旅途尽头，而这样全身赤裸地来到天主跟前是不用感到害羞的。

当人们遇到这些勇敢的女旅客时，都应当伸出援助之手，并且告诉他人说自己曾经遇见过这些女人，因为宣扬这件事情也就是给她们指出了道路。解决问题的方法不是简单地在人生道路的入口处竖起两块告示牌：一块写着"正途"，另一块写着"歧途"，并且对那些走过来的人说"选择吧"。应该像基督那样，给那些容易迷失的人指出从第二条路通往第一条路的途径，尤其不能让这些路途的开始那一段太崎岖，显得太不好走。

基督教有关浪子回头的精彩寓言目的就是教导我们要仁慈，宽厚待人。耶稣深爱着那些饱受情欲折磨的灵魂，他喜欢替他们包扎伤口，并从伤口本身取出治伤口的香膏。因此，他对玛特莱娜说"因你深厚的爱，你的很多罪行被赦免了[1]"，

---

[1] 出自《圣经·路加福音》。

the Magdalen: "Much shall be forgiven thee because thou hast loved much," a sublimity of pardon which can only have called forth a sublime faith.

Why do we make ourselves more strict than Christ? Why, holding obstinately to the opinions of the world, which hardens itself in order that it may be thought strong, do we reject, as it rejects, souls bleeding at wounds by which, like a sick man's bad blood, the evil of their past may be healed, if only a friendly hand is stretched out to lave them and set them in the convalescence of the heart?

It is to my own generation that I speak, to those for whom the theories of M. de Voltaire happily exist no longer, to those who, like myself, realize that humanity, for these last fifteen years, has been in one of its most audacious moments of expansion. The science of good and evil is acquired forever; faith is refashioned, respect for sacred things has returned to us, and if the world has not all at once become good, it has at least become better. The efforts of every intelligent man tend in the same direction, and every strong will is harnessed to the same principle: Be good, be young, be true! Evil is nothing but vanity, let us have the pride of good, and above all let us never despair. Do not let us

只有这种崇高的宽恕行为才能唤起一种崇高的信仰。

我们为什么要比基督严厉呢？这个世界为了让人们认为它很强大而故作严厉，我们也就固执地接受了它的成见。我们为什么要和它一样抛弃那些伤口流血的灵魂呢？从这些伤口里渗出他们过去的罪恶，就像病人流出污血一样。但只要有一只友好的手来包扎这些伤口，那么他们这些灵魂心头的创伤就能够被治愈。

我在此呼吁与我同时代的人们，呼吁那些幸而已经不再信奉伏尔泰先生理论的人，呼吁那些和我一样懂得 15 年来人道主义正在迅猛发展。善恶的学识已经得到公认，信仰又重新建立，我们重新开始尊重神圣的事物。如果这个世界还算不上十全十美，至少比从前大有改善。聪明人全部都致力于一个相同的目标，一切伟大的意志都遵从于一个相同的原则：我们要善良，要有活力，要真实！邪恶只不过是虚荣心在作祟，我们要为行善而感到骄傲，最重要的是，我们一定不要灰心丧气，不要蔑视那些并非母亲、姐妹，又不是女儿、妻子的女人，不要减弱对亲人的尊重和对自私的

despise the woman who is neither mother, sister, maid, nor wife. Do not let us limit esteem to the family nor indulgence to egoism. Since "there is more joy in heaven over one sinner that repenteth than over ninety and nine just persons that need no repentance," let us give joy to heaven. Heaven will render it back to us with usury. Let us leave on our way the alms of pardon for those whom earthly desires have driven astray, whom a divine hope shall perhaps save, and, as old women say when they offer you. some homely remedy of their own, if it does no good it will do no harm.

Doubtless it must seem a bold thing to attempt to deduce these grand results out of the meagre subject that I deal with; but I am one of those who believe that all is in little. The child is small, and he includes the man; the brain is narrow, and it harbours thought; the eye is but a point, and it covers leagues.

宽容。既然和 100 个从未犯过罪的正直人相比上天更加偏爱一个忏悔的罪人，那就让我们尽量博得上天的喜爱吧，上天会赐予我们福音的。在我们前行的道路上，给那些被世俗欲望驱使而误入歧途的人留下我们宽恕的芬芳，也许神圣的希望可以拯救他们，就像那些老婆子在劝人接受她们的偏方时所说的：即使没有多少疗效，也不会有什么害处。

我觉得从细小的话题当中得出伟大的结论似乎过于狂妄草率。我相信一切都存在于渺小之中。孩子虽然年幼，却是未来的成年人；脑袋虽然狭窄，但蕴藏着无限的思想；眼珠很小，却可以看到宽广的天地。

CHAPTER 4

第四章

Two days after, the sale was ended. It had produced 3.50,000 francs. The creditors divided among them two thirds, and the family, a sister and a grand-nephew, received the remainder.

The sister opened her eyes very wide when the lawyer wrote to her that she had inherited 50,000 francs. The girl had not seen her sister for six or seven years, and did not know what had become of her from the moment when she had disappeared from home. She came up to Paris in haste, and great was the astonishment of those who had known Marguerite when they saw as her only heir a fine, fat country girl, who until then had never left her village. She had made the fortune at a single stroke, without even knowing the source of that fortune. She went back, I heard afterward, to her countryside, greatly saddened by her sister's death, but with a sadness which was somewhat lightened by the investment at four and a half per cent which she had been able to make.

两天之后，拍卖会结束了，一共售得 35 万法郎。债主们拿走了 2/3，剩下的由玛格丽特的家人——姐姐和小外甥继承。

当律师写信告知这位姐姐可以继承 5 万法郎的遗产时，她惊讶得目瞪口呆。这个姑娘和她妹妹已经有六七年没有见面了。自从她妹妹离家出走之后就杳无音信，不知道她过得怎样。她姐姐急匆匆地赶到了巴黎。那些认识玛格丽特的人见到了她都感到十分诧异，因为玛格丽特唯一的继承人竟然是一个胖胖的漂亮的乡下姑娘，在此之前她还从来没有离开过家乡。她一下子发了大财，也不知道这笔意外之财是怎么降临到她头上的。后来我听说，她回到村子里以后，为她妹妹的去世感到非常伤心，然而她把这笔钱以 4.5% 的利息存了起来，这样就减轻了她的悲伤。

All these circumstances, often repeated in Paris, the mother city of scandal, had begun to be forgotten, and I was even little by little forgetting the part I had taken in them, when a new incident brought to my knowledge the whole of Marguerite's life, and acquainted me with such pathetic details that I was taken with the idea of writing down the story which I now write.

The rooms, now emptied of all their furniture, had been to let for three or four days when one morning there was a ring at my door.

My servant, or, rather, my porter, who acted as my servant, went to the door and brought me a card, saying that the person who had given it to him wished to see me.

I glanced at the card and there read these two words: *Armand Duval.*

I tried to think where I had seen the name, and remembered the first leaf of the copy of *Manon Lescaut.* What could the person who had given the book to Marguerite want of me? I gave orders to ask him in at once.

I saw a young man, blond, tall, pale, dressed in a travelling suit which looked as if he had not changed it for some days, and had not even taken the trouble to brush it on arriving at Paris, for it was covered with dust.

在巴黎这个谣传纷纷的罪恶之源，这些事情被人到处重复谈论着，随着时间的流逝，逐渐也就被遗忘了。如果不是我忽然又遇上了一件事，我甚至也一点一点地忘记自己在这些事情里充当的角色。通过这件事，我了解到了玛格丽特的身世，而且还知道了一些非常感人的细节。这使我萌发了将这个故事写下来的想法。现在我要写这个故事。

所有家具售完后房子空了下来，后来又被重新租出去了，在那以后三四天的一个早晨，有人按响了我家的门铃。

我的仆人（事实上是我的看门人，但他兼做仆人的事情）去开了门，回来递给我一张名片，说来访的人要求见我。

我看了一下名片，上面印着：阿尔芒·迪瓦尔。

我用力回想自己曾经在哪个地方看见过这个名字，我想起了《曼侬·莱斯科》这本书的扉页。给玛格丽特送这本书的人为什么要见我呢？我吩咐马上请那个拜访的人进来。

我看到了一个年轻人。他头发金黄，身材颀长，脸色苍白，身着一套旅行装，这套好像已经穿了好几天，即便到了巴黎也没抽空刷洗一下，因为上面沾满了尘土。

M. Duval was deeply agitated; he made no attempt to conceal his agitation, and it was with tears in his eyes and a trembling voice that he said to me:

"Sir, I beg you to excuse my visit and my costume; but young people are not very ceremonious with one another, and I was so anxious to see you today that I have not even gone to the hotel to which I have sent my luggage, and have rushed straight here, fearing that, after all, I might miss you, early as it is."

I begged M. Duval to sit down by the fire; he did so, and, taking his handkerchief from his pocket, hid his face in it for a moment.

"You must be at a loss to understand," he went on, sighing sadly, "for what purpose an unknown visitor, at such an hour, in such a costume, and in tears, can have come to see you. I have simply come to ask of you a great service."

"Speak on, sir, I am entirely at your disposal."

"You were present at the sale of Marguerite Gautier?"

At this word the emotion, which he had got the better of for an instant, was too much for him, and he was obliged to cover his eyes with his hand.

"I must seem to you very absurd," he

迪瓦尔先生十分激动，也不想掩饰自己的情绪，就这样含泪用颤抖的声音对我说道：

"先生，请原谅我突然的造访和衣冠不整。不过年轻人不大注意这些形式上的东西，而且我迫不及待地想在今天就和你见面。因此我只是把行李送到了旅店，自己就立马赶到你这儿来。尽管时间还早，我还是担心会碰不上你。"

我请迪瓦尔先生坐到炉火边上。他一边坐下，一边将手帕从口袋里掏出来，把脸捂了一会儿。

"你一定很困惑，"他深深地叹了口气，接着说，"一个素不相识的人，在这个时候，穿着这样的衣服，哭成这样子地来拜访你，到底是出于什么样的原因。先生，我来只是想请你帮我一个忙。"

"请说吧，先生，我愿意为你效劳。"

"你参加了在玛格丽特·戈蒂埃家里举行的拍卖吧？"

一提到玛格丽特的名字，这个年轻人暂时控制住的激动情绪又失控了，他不得不用双手捂住眼睛。

"在你看来，我一定很可笑，"

added, "but pardon me, and believe that I shall never forget the patience with which you have listened to me."

"Sir," I answered, "if the service which I can render you is able to lessen your trouble a little, tell me at once what I can do for you, and you will find me only too happy to oblige you."

M. Duval's sorrow was sympathetic, and in spite of myself I felt the desire of doing him a kindness. Thereupon he said to me:

"You bought something at Marguerite's sale?"

"Yes, a book."

"Manon Lescaut?"

"Precisely."

"Have you the book still?"

"It is in my bedroom."

On hearing this, Armand Duval seemed to be relieved of a great weight, and thanked me as if I had already rendered him a service merely by keeping the book.

I got up and went into my room to fetch the book, which I handed to him.

"That is it indeed," he said, looking at the inscription on the first page and turning over the leaves; "that is it in deed," and two big tears fell on the pages. "Well, sir," said he, lifting his head, and no longer trying to hide from me that he had wept and was even then on the point of weeping,

他又说，"请再一次原谅我的失态。请你相信我决不会忘记你能耐心听我说话的好意。"

"先生，"我对他说，"如果我真的能够帮助你稍微减轻一些痛苦的话，请直言告诉我，我该怎样帮助你。你会知道我非常乐意为你提供便利。"

迪瓦尔先生的悲伤实在令人同情，这让我不由得想尽量能够帮到他。于是他对我说：

"在玛格丽特的财产拍卖会上，你是不是买了什么东西？"

"是的，买了一本书。"

"是《曼侬·莱斯科》吧？"

"是的。"

"你还拿着这本书吗？"

"在我卧室里。"

阿尔芒·迪瓦尔听我这样说，仿佛心里的一块石头终于落地了，立刻向我表示感谢，好像我仍留着这本书就已经是帮了他的忙似的。

于是我起身，走进卧室将书取来，给了他。

"就是它，"他说，同时看了看扉页上的题词就翻看起来，"就是它。"两颗大大的泪水落在书页上。

"那么，先生，"他抬头对我说，这时候他根本不向我掩饰他刚刚哭过，而且几乎又要哭出声来，"你很珍惜这本书吗？"

"do you value this book very greatly?"

"Why?"

"Because I have come to ask you to give it up to me."

"Pardon my curiosity, but was it you, then, who gave it to Marguerite Gautier?"

"It was I."

"The book is yours, sir; take it back. I am happy to be able to hand it over to you."

"But," said M. Duval with some embarrassment, "the least I can do is to give you in return the price which you paid for it."

"Allow me to offer it to you. The price of a single volume in a sale of that kind is a mere nothing, and I do not remember how much I gave for it."

"You gave one hundred francs."

"True," I said, embarrassed in my turn, "how do you know?"

"It is quite simple. I hoped to reach Paris in time for the sale, and I only managed to get here this morning. I was absolutely resolved to have something which had belonged to her, and I hastened to the auctioneer and asked him to allow me to see the list of the things sold and of the buyers' names. I saw that this volume had been bought by you, and I decided to ask you to give it up to me, though the price

"先生，为什么你会这样问？"

"因为我想恳求你把它让给我。"

"请原谅我的好奇，"这时我说，"就是你送给玛格丽特·戈蒂埃这本书的吗？"

"就是我。"

"这本书归你了，先生，你拿去吧，我很高兴能将这本书物归原主。"

"可是，"迪瓦尔先生不好意思地说，"那么至少我也得付你当时买下这本书的钱。"

"请让我把它赠送给你吧。在这样一次拍卖中，一本小书能值多少钱，我自己也记不清到底花多少钱买下它。"

"你花了 100 法郎。"

"哦，对，"我说，这次轮到我觉得尴尬了，"你是如何知道的？"

"这很容易，我本来打算及时赶到巴黎，参加玛格丽特的遗物拍卖会，但是我今天早上才赶到。无论如何我也要得到她一件遗物，我就立马到拍卖人那里，请他给我看一下售出物品的买主的名单。我发现这本书被你买下来了，就决定到这儿来请求你割爱，不过令我担心的是，你出了这么高的价钱，是不是因为它对你有什么特殊纪念意

you had set upon it made me fear that you might yourself have some souvenir in connection with the possession of the book."

As he spoke, it was evident that he was afraid I had known Marguerite as he had known her. I hastened to reassure him.

"I knew Mlle. Gautier only by sight," I said; "her death made on me the impression that the death of a pretty woman must always make on a young man who had liked seeing her. I wished to buy something at her sale, and I bid higher and higher for this book out of mere obstinacy and to annoy some one else, who was equally keen to obtain it, and who seemed to defy me to the contest. I repeat, then, that the book is yours, and once more I beg you to accept it; do not treat me as if I were an auctioneer, and let it be the pledge between us of a longer and more intimate acquaintance."

"Good," said Armand, holding out his hand and pressing mine; "I accept, and I shall be grateful to you all my life."

I was very anxious to question Armand on the subject of Marguerite, for the inscription in the book, the young man's hurried journey, his desire to possess the volume, piqued my curiosity; but I feared if I questioned my visitor that I might seem

义，所以才买下这本书？"

阿尔芒说这话，很明显是担心我和玛格丽特之间的关系也和他与她之间的那样亲密。我连忙解释让他宽心。

"我只不过是见过她，知道她是谁而已，"我对他说，"一个年轻人对一个他喜欢遇见的美丽女人的去世会产生的那种感受，就是我的感受。我想在那次拍卖中买点东西，后来有一位先生一个劲地跟我抬价，好像故意想让我买不到这本书。我也是一时犯了犟脾气，被他惹怒，才拼命地跟他抢这本书。所以，我再重复一遍，先生，这本书是你的了，而且我再一次恳请你接受它，不要把我当做拍卖人，我还希望这本书能帮助我们之间结下更长久深厚的友谊。"

"真是太好了！"阿尔芒伸手紧紧握住我的手说，"我接受了。我将永远铭记你对我的好意。"

我很想向阿尔芒问问有关玛格丽特的事情，因为扉页上的题词，这位年轻人的长途跋涉和他极力想得到这本书的愿望都让我感到十分好奇，但是我怕贸然向客人提出这些问题的话，他会以为我拒绝他的

to have refused his money only in order to have the right to pry into his affairs.

It was as if he guessed my desire, for he said to me:

"Have you read the volume?"

"All through."

"What did you think of the two lines that I wrote in it?"

"I realized at once that the woman to whom you had given the volume must have been quite outside the ordinary category, for I could not take those two lines as a mere empty compliment."

"You were right. That woman was an angel. See, read this letter." And he handed to me a paper which seemed to have been many times reread.

I opened it, and this is what it contained:

"MY DEAR ARMAND: – I have received your letter. You are still good, and I thank God for it. Yes, my friend, I am ill, and with one of those diseases that never relent; but the interest you still take in me makes my suffering less. I shall not live long enough, I expect, to have the happiness of pressing the hand which has written the kind letter I have just received; the words of it would be enough to cure me, if anything could cure me. I shall not see you, for I am quite near

钱只是为了有权干涉他的私事。

他可能看出了我的心思,因为他对我说:

"你看过这本书吗?"

"全看过了。"

"你看过我写的题词后,有没有思考过它是什么意思?"

"我一看这两行题词就知道,在你眼里,那位接受你赠书的可怜姑娘是超凡脱俗的,因为我不想把这两行字看做是空洞的恭维话。"

"你说得很正确,先生,她是一位天使,你看,"他对我说,"看这封信!"他递给我一张信纸,这封信显然已被翻来覆去看过很多遍了。

我打开它,上面写着:

"亲爱的阿尔芒,你的来信我已经收到了,你还是像以前那样心地善良,我真要感谢上帝。是的,我的朋友,我生病了,而且是绝症。但是你还是依旧关心我,这就大大地减轻了我的痛苦。我恐怕剩下的时间不多了。我刚刚收到了你那封写得令人感动不已的信,可是我不能有幸再握一握写信人的手了。如果要说有什么东西可以医治我的病,那么这封信中写的话就可以做到。我再也见不到你

death, and you are hundreds of miles away. My poor friend! your Marguerite of old times is sadly changed. It is better perhaps for you not to see her again than to see her as she is. You ask if I forgive you; oh, with all my heart, friend, for the way you hurt me was only a way of proving the love you had for me. I have been in bed for a month, and I think so much of your esteem that I write every day the journal of my life, from the moment we left each other to the moment when I shall be able to write no longer. If the interest you take in me is real, Armand, when you come back go and see Julie Duprat. She will give you my journal. You will find in it the reason and the excuse for what has passed between us. Julie is very good to me; we often talk of you together. She was there when your letter came, and we both cried over it.

"If you had not sent me any word, I would have told her to give you those papers when you returned to France. Do not thank me for it. This daily looking back on the only happy moments of my life does me an immense amount of good, and if you will find in reading it some excuse for the past. I, for my part, find a continual solace in it. I should like to leave you something which would always remind you of me, but everything

了,你我之间相隔千里,而我又支撑不了多久了。可怜的朋友!你的玛格丽特现在和过去已经完全不一样了。与其让你看到她如今这个样子,还是不见的好。你问我可不可以原谅你,我已经彻底地原谅了你。朋友,因为你以前伤害我正好证明了你是爱我的。我卧病在床已经有一个月了,我非常珍视你对我的尊重,因此我天天坚持写日记,从我们分离那时开始一直写到我不能握笔为止。如果你是真正关心我,阿尔芒,你回来以后,就去朱莉·杜普拉那儿。她会将这些日记转交给你,你将会从中知道发生在我们之间的这些事情的缘由和我对此的解释。朱莉对我很好,我们常常在一起谈到你。收到你的来信时,她也在旁边,看信的时候我们都哭了。

"如果你没有给我回信,我会让朱莉在你回到法国的时候把这些日记交给你。不要谢我写下了这些日记,它们使我每天都能重温我一生当中拥有幸福的短暂几天,这让我获益匪浅。如果你看了这些日记以后,能够谅解过去的事的话,那么我将得到永久的安慰。我想留给你一些让你能够永远记着我的纪念品,可是我家里所有的东西都被查封了,我现在一无

here has been seized, and I have nothing of my own.

"Do you understand, my friend? I am dying, and from my bed I can hear a man walking to and fro in the drawing room; my creditors have put him there to see that nothing is taken away, and that nothing remains to me in case I do not die. I hope they will wait till the end before they begin to sell.

"Oh, men have no pity! or rather, I am wrong, it is God who is just and inflexible!

"And now, dear love, you will come to my sale, and you will buy something, for if I put aside the least thing for you, they might accuse you of embezzling seized goods.

"It is a sad life that I am leaving!

"It would be good of God to let me see you again before I die. According to all probability, goodbye, my friend. Pardon me if I do not write a longer letter, but those who say they are going to cure me wear me out with bloodletting, and my hand refuses to write any more.

"MARGUERITE GAUTIER."

The last two words were scarcely legible.

I returned the letter to Armand, who had, no doubt, read it over again in his mind while I was reading it on paper, for he said

所有。

"你明白吗，我的朋友？我已经奄奄一息了，在卧室就能听到有人在客厅里走来走去。他是我的债主们派来的，以防别人拿走什么东西。就算我不死也已倾家荡产了。希望他们能等到我断气以后再拍卖！

"啊！人是多么冷酷无情！不！更应该说上帝是公正无私的。

"好吧，亲爱的，你要来参加我财产的拍卖会，这样你就可以买到些东西。因为要是我现在为你留一件即使最没有价值的东西，别人也可能会控告你私吞查封的财产。

"我临死前的生活是多么凄惨啊！

"如果我在临死前还能再见上你一面，那么上帝是多么眷顾我！以现在的情况看来，我们再也不能相见了。朋友，请原谅我没办法再写下去了。那些帮我治病的人总是给我放血，弄得我十分的虚弱，我的手已经不听使唤了。

"玛格丽特·戈蒂埃"

最后几个字写得几乎都无法辨认。

我把信还给了阿尔芒。刚才在

to me as he took it:

"Who would think that a kept woman could have written that?" And, overcome by recollections, he gazed for some time at the writing of the letter, which he finally carried to his lips.

"And when I think," he went on, "that she died before I could see her, and that I shall never see her again, when I think that she did for me what no sister would ever have done, I can not forgive myself for having left her to die like that. Dead! Dead and thinking of me, writing and repeating my name, poor dear Marguerite!"

And Armand, giving free outlet to his thoughts and his tears, held out his hand to me, and continued:

"People would think it childish enough if they saw me lament like this over a dead woman such as she; no one will ever know what I made that woman suffer, how cruel I have been to her! how good, how resigned she was! I thought it was I who had to forgive her, and today I feel unworthy of the forgiveness which she grants me. Oh, I would give ten years of my life to weep at her feet for an hour!"

It is always difficult to console a sorrow that is unknown to one, and nevertheless I felt so lively a sympathy for the young man, he made me so frankly the confidant

我看信的时候，他一定又在心里默念了一遍。因为他一边把信拿回去一边对我说：

"谁会相信一个风尘女子会写下这样的信！"旧日的情思一下子涌上心头，他显得很激动。他凝视着信上的字迹，过了一会儿，把信拿到唇边亲吻着。

"我一想到，"他接着又说，"在她临死之前不能和她再见一面，而且永远也看不到她了。又想到她待我比亲姐妹还好，我怎么也不能原谅自己就这样让她离开人世。她死了！临死时还想着我，还写着信，呼喊着我的名字。可怜的，亲爱的玛格丽特！"

阿尔芒尽情释放自己的情绪和泪水，一边将手伸给我，一边继续说道：

"人们看到因为这样一个姑娘的去世，我感到如此伤心，可能会认为我太幼稚，可是他们从来不会清楚过去我是如何折磨这个女人的。那时候我对她是多么的残忍！她又是多么善良，忍受了多少屈辱！我原以为应该是我去宽恕她。而现在，我觉得是我根本不配得到她的原谅。啊！如果可以在她脚下哭上一个小时，我宁愿少活 10 年。"

在不了解一个人的痛苦缘由时去安慰他，总是十分困难的。然而

of his distress, that I believed a word from me would not be indifferent to him, and I said:

"Have you no parents, no friends? Hope. Go and see them; they will console you. As for me, I can only pity you."

"It is true," he said, rising and walking to and fro in the room, "I am wearying you. Pardon me, I did not reflect how little my sorrow must mean to you, and that I am intruding upon you something which can not and ought not to interest you at all."

"You mistake my meaning. I am entirely at your service; only I regret my inability to calm your distress. If my society and that of my friends can give you any distraction, if, in short, you have need of me, no matter in what way, I hope you will realize how much pleasure it will give me to do anything for you."

"Pardon, pardon," said he; "sorrow sharpens the sensations. Let me stay here for a few minutes longer, long enough to dry my eyes, so that the idlers in the street may not look upon it as a curiosity to see a big fellow like me crying. You have made me very happy by giving me this book. I do not know how I can ever express my gratitude to you."

"By giving me a little of your friendship," said I, "and by telling me the

对这位年轻人，我却产生了强烈的同情心。他坦率地向我倾吐自己的痛苦，我不禁相信，我再怎样安慰他也无济于事。于是我对他说：

"你没有亲戚朋友吗？想开点，去看看他们，他们会安慰你，因为我只能同情你。"

"是啊，"他站起来说，并在我的房间里来来回回地走着，"我让你不耐烦了，请原谅我，我没有考虑到你和我的痛苦一点儿关系也没有，我没有考虑到我拿那件事来烦你，你根本不可能也不会感兴趣。"

"你误会我了，我完全听从你的吩咐。只是我遗憾自己不能减轻你的痛苦。如果我，或者我的朋友可以帮你消除烦恼，总之不管哪方面，只要你需要我的帮助，我希望你清楚能够为你效劳我是非常愉快的。"

"请原谅，原谅我，"他对我说，"痛苦容易使人过于敏感，请允许我多留一会儿，好让我擦干眼泪，以免街上的路人把我看做一个傻瓜，这么大的人了还哭哭啼啼。你刚才把这本书送给我，让我很开心。我真不知道该如何表达我对你的谢意。"

"那就给我一点儿友谊，"我对阿尔芒说，"你就告诉我是什么原因

cause of your suffering. One feels better while telling what one suffers."

"You are right. But today I have too much need of tears; I can not very well talk. One day I will tell you the whole story, and you will see if I have reason for regretting the poor girl. And now," he added, rubbing his eyes for the last time, and looking at himself in the glass, "say that you do not think me too absolutely idiotic, and allow me to come back and see you another time."

He cast on me a gentle and amiable look. I was near embracing him. As for him, his eyes again began to fill with tears; he saw that I perceived it and turned away his head.

"Come," I said, "courage."

"Good-bye," he said.

And, making a desperate effort to restrain his tears, he rushed rather than went out of the room.

I lifted the curtain of my window, and saw him get into the cabriolet which awaited him at the door; but scarcely was he seated before he burst into tears and hid his face in his pocket handkerchief.

让你如此伤心，将内心的苦痛都说出来的话，就会感到轻松一些。"

"你说得没错，但是我今天只是想哭。我没法和你说清楚，改天我再告诉你整件事情的来龙去脉，你就会理解我为这个可怜的姑娘感到伤心是有理由的。可是现在，"他最后一次擦了擦眼睛，照着镜子对我说，"希望你不要认为我是一个傻子，并且允许我改日再来拜访你。"

这个年轻人用温柔而又亲切的目光看了我一眼，让我几乎想拥抱他。而他呢，眼眶里噙着泪水。他注意到我已经发觉，便将头转向一边。

"好了，"我对他说，"振作些。"

"再见。"他对我说。

他强忍住泪水，从我家里冲了出去，因为很难说他是走出去的。

我撩起窗帘，看见他登上了一辆在门口停着的轻便双轮马车。一进车厢，他便再也控制不住泉涌的泪水，拿出手帕掩面恸哭起来。

CHAPTER 5
第五章

A good while elapsed before I heard anything more of Armand, but, on the other hand, I was constantly hearing of Marguerite.

I do not know if you have noticed, if once the name of anybody who might in the natural course of things have always remained unknown, or at all events indifferent to you, should he mentioned before you, immediately details begin to group themselves about the name, and you find all your friends talking to you about something which they have never mentioned to you before. You discover that this person was almost touching you and has passed close to you many times in your life without your noticing it; you find coincidences in the events which are told you, a real affinity with certain events of your own existence. I was not absolutely at that point in regard to Marguerite, for I had seen and met her, I knew her by sight and by reputation; nevertheless, since the moment of the sale, her name came to my

在相当长的一段时间里我没有获得关于阿尔芒的任何消息，而玛格丽特却经常被人提及。

我不知道你是否曾经注意过这样的情形：一个看上去与你素不相识或者在任何方面都毫无瓜葛的人，如果他的姓名在你的面前被提起，与之相关的种种琐事就会渐渐地汇集在一起，你的朋友们也都来和你谈论那些以前从来也没有对你说过的事，你就会觉得这个人似乎就能接触到你，你将发现，这个人曾多次地出现在你的生活中，只不过是你不曾注意过罢了。你能在别人说给你听的那些事情里寻找到与你生活中某些经历相互吻合的地方。我与玛格丽特倒不完全属于这种情况，因为我以前曾经见过她，并认识了她。我还能记起她的容貌，了解她的习惯。然而，自那次拍卖会之后，我就不断地听到有人提起她的名字。由于我在前面一章中曾说到过的那种情况，这个名字被拿

ears so frequently, and, owing to the circumstance that I have mentioned in the last chapter, that name was associated with so profound a sorrow, that my curiosity increased in proportion with my astonishment. The consequence was that whenever I met friends to whom I had never breathed the name of Marguerite, I always began by saying:

"Did you ever know a certain Marguerite Gautier?"

"The Lady of the Camellias?"

"Exactly."

"Oh, very well!"

The word was sometimes accompanied by a smile which could leave no doubt as to its meaning.

"Well, what sort of a girl was she?"

"A good sort of girl."

"Is that all?"

"Oh, yes; more intelligence and perhaps a little more heart than most."

"Do you know anything particular about her?"

"She ruined Baron de G."

"No more than that?"

"She was the mistress of the old Duke of ..."

"Was she really his mistress?"

"So they say; at all events, he gave her a great deal of money."

来与极其巨大的悲痛联系在一起。所以我越来越觉得诧异，好奇心也越来越重。此前，我从来没有和朋友们谈论过玛格丽特这个人，如今，我每次碰到他们都会问：

"你以前认识一个叫做玛格丽特·戈蒂埃的人吗？"

"你说的是茶花女吗？"

"就是那个人。"

"啊，我和她太熟悉了！"

当他们说出这句话时，有时候脸上还挂着那种意义明显的微笑。

"那么，她是个怎样的姑娘呢？"我接着问道。

"一个不错的姑娘。"

"这些就完了吗？"

"啊！对啊，比其他人更聪明一些，或许比她们还要善良一些。"

"你是否知道关于她的什么特殊的事情吗？"

"她曾经让 G 男爵破了产。"

"此外还有吗？"

"她以前是老公爵的情妇。"

"她真是老公爵的情妇吗？"

"大家都这样说，无论如何，那个人给过她大量的钱。"

The general outlines were always the same. Nevertheless I was anxious to find out something about the relations between Marguerite and Armand. Meeting one day a man who was constantly about with known women, I asked him: "Did you know Marguerite Gautier?"

The answer was the usual: "Very well."

"What sort of a girl was she?"

"A fine, good girl. I was very sorry to hear of her death."

"Had she not a lover called Armand Duval?"

"Tall and blond?"

"Yes.

"It is quite true."

"Who was this Armand?"

"A fellow who squandered on her the little money he had, and then had to leave her. They say he was quite wild about it."

"And she?"

"They always say she was very much in love with him, but as girls like that are in love. It is no good to ask them for what they can not give."

"What has become of Armand?"

"I don't know. We knew him very little. He was with Marguerite for five or six months in the country. When she came back, he had gone."

"And you have never seen him since?"

都是那套一模一样的泛泛之谈。可是，我非常渴望了解一些有关玛格丽特与阿尔芒之间的故事。某一天我碰上了一个与那些欢场名媛过从甚密的人。我向她打听："你是否认识玛格丽特·戈蒂埃这个人呢？"

回答同样是"非常熟悉"。

"她是个什么样的姑娘啊？"

"非常的美丽善良。我对她的死深表遗憾。"

"她是否有过一个名叫阿尔芒·迪瓦尔的情人呢？"

"个子高高的、金黄色头发？"

"对！"

"确实有过这么个人。"

"这个阿尔芒又是什么人？"

"一个在玛格丽特身上花光了自己仅有的一点儿积蓄的年轻人，然后就不得不离开她。听说他简直为此发了疯。"

"那玛格丽特又怎么样呢？"

"大家都说她也非常爱他，然而这种爱就跟其他姑娘的爱一样，向她们要求那些无法给予的东西是没什么好处的。"

"然后阿尔芒怎么样了呢？"

"我也不知道。我对他的了解有限。他与玛格丽特在乡村一同度过了五六个月的时光。等到她回到巴黎，他就离开了。"

"Never."

I, too, had not seen Armand again. I was beginning to ask myself if, when he had come to see me, the recent news of Marguerite's death had not exaggerated his former love, and consequently his sorrow, and I said to myself that perhaps he had already forgotten the dead woman, and along with her his promise to come and see me again. This supposition would have seemed probable enough in most instances, but in Armand's despair there had been an accent of real sincerity, and, going from one extreme to another, I imagined that distress had brought on an illness, and that my not seeing him was explained by the fact that he was ill, perhaps dead.

I was interested in the young man in spite of myself. Perhaps there was some selfishness in this interest; perhaps I guessed at some pathetic love story under all this sorrow; perhaps my desire to know all about it had much to do with the anxiety which Armand's silence caused me.

Since M. Duval did not return to see me, I decided to go and see him. A pretext was not difficult to find; unluckily I did not know his address, and no one among those whom I questioned could give it to me.

I went to the Rue d'Antin; perhaps Marguerite's porter would know where

"后来你就不曾见过他了？"

"再也没见过。"

我也一样，后来就没见过阿尔芒了。我甚至开始自问，他来看我，是不是由于他知道了玛格丽特前些日子过世的消息而引发了旧情，所以才感到悲伤。我告诉自己，或许他早就把那个死去的女人连同再来看我的诺言一起忘得干干净净了。这种疑虑在大多数情况下都很可能，但阿尔芒不会。那时他灰心失望的语调是源于真正的悲伤。因此我又从一个极端走向了另一个极端，猜测阿尔芒是忧伤成疾，我没有见到他，实际情况是他生病了，也可能已经死了。

我不由自主地对这个年轻人产生了兴趣。这种兴趣或许掺杂了某些私心，或许我已经揣测到在他的痛苦之下掩藏的一个缠绵悱恻的爱情故事。也可能正是我急于想获知这个故事的强烈欲望才令我因阿尔芒的销声匿迹而感到如此焦虑。

既然迪瓦尔先生后来就不曾再来看我，我就决心去他的家里。想找一个借口去拜访他并不困难，只是不巧我不知晓他的住址。我四处打听，可谁都无法告诉我。

我去了昂坦街，想着玛格丽特的看门人或许知道阿尔芒住在什么

Armand lived. There was a new porter; he knew as little about it as I. I then asked in what cemetery Mlle. Gautier had been buried. It was the Montmartre Cemetery. It was now the month of April; the weather was fine, the graves were not likely to look as sad and desolate as they do in winter; in short, it was warm enough for the living to think a little of the dead, and pay them a visit. I went to the cemetery, saying to myself: "One glance at Marguerite's grave, and I shall know if Armand's sorrow still exists, and perhaps I may find out what has become of him."

I entered the keeper's lodge, and asked him if on the 22nd of February a woman named Marguerite Gautier had not been buried in the Montmartre Cemetery. He turned over the pages of a big book in which those who enter this last resting-place are inscribed and numbered, and replied that on the 22nd of February, at 12 o'clock, a woman of that name had been buried.

I asked him to show me the grave, for there is no finding one's way without a guide in this city of the dead, which has its streets like a city of the living. The keeper called over a gardener, to whom he gave the necessary instructions; the gardener interrupted him, saying: "I know, I know. –

地方。可那里换了一个新的看门人，他对阿尔芒的了解简直和我一样少。我就向他打听戈蒂埃小姐葬在哪里。他回答说在蒙马特公墓。当时已经是四月，天朗气清，阳光明媚，坟墓看上去并不像冬天时那样阴森凄凉。简而言之，天气已经相当暖和，足以令活着的人追忆起死者，并动身前去进行一次探望。我在去往公墓的路上想，只需看一眼玛格丽特的坟，就能够知道阿尔芒是不是还沉浸在悲痛之中，或许还能发现一些他现在的情况。

我走进公墓看守的屋子，问他在2月22日当天，是否有一个叫玛格丽特·戈蒂埃的女人葬入了蒙马特公墓。看守在一本厚厚的簿子里翻找，那上面按号码顺序记录着每一个来到这处最后归宿地的人的姓名。随后答复我说，2月22日那天中午，确实曾有一位叫这个名字的女人被葬在了这里。

我请他带着我去那座坟墓看看，因为在这个容纳死亡的城市里，就和在活人生活的城市一样有着纵横交错的街道，如果没有向导，是很难找到正确的道路的。看守找来一个园丁，向他交代一些必要的事情。园丁打断他，说道："我知道，

It is not difficult to find that grave," he added, turning to me.

"Why?"

"Because it has very different flowers from the others."

"Is it you who look after it?"

"Yes, sir; and I wish all relations took as much trouble about the dead as the young man who gave me my orders."

After several turnings, the gardener stopped and said to me: "Here we are."

I saw before me a square of flowers which one would never have taken for a grave, if it had not been for a white marble slab bearing a name.

The marble slab stood upright, an iron railing marked the limits of the ground purchased, and the earth was covered with white camellias.

"What do you say to that?" said the gardener.

"It is beautiful."

"And whenever a camellia fades, I have orders to replace it."

"Who gave you the order?"

"A young gentleman who cried the first time he came here; an old pal of hers, I suppose, for they say she was a gay one. Very pretty, too, I believe. Did you know her, sir?"

"Yes."

我知道……"随即转身朝着我说，"那个坟墓一点儿也不难找！"

"为什么这么说呢？"我问道。

"因为那座坟上的花与别的坟上的很不一样。"

"是你照看那座坟墓的吗？"

"是的，先生，是一位年轻人吩咐的。我真希望所有死者的亲人对死者都能像他一样尽心就好了。"

我们拐了几个弯，园丁停下脚步，对我说："这里就是了。"

一片方形的花丛出现在我面前，倘若不是一块刻着名字的白色大理石矗立在那儿的话，谁也不会认为这竟然是一座坟墓。

那块大理石笔直地立在那里，一圈铁栅栏将这片被买下的坟地圈了起来，土地上满满地覆盖着白色的茶花。

"你看这里怎么样？"园丁问。

"真是太美了。"

"每次有朵茶花枯萎了，我就按照吩咐用新的替换上去。"

"是谁吩咐你这么做的呢？"

"是个年轻人，他头一回来的时候哭得特别伤心，可能是死者的老相好吧，因为那个女的过去似乎生活不太检点呢。我想她长得一定很漂亮。先生，你也知道她？"

"是的。"

"Like the other?" said the gardener, with a knowing smile.

"No, I never spoke to her."

"And you come here, too! It is very good of you, for those that come to see the poor girl don't exactly cumber the cemetery."

"Doesn't anybody come?"

"Nobody, except that young gentleman who came once."

"Only once?"

"Yes, sir."

"He never came back again?"

"No, but he will when he gets home."

"He is away somewhere?"

"Yes."

"Do you know where he is?"

"I believe he has gone to see Mlle. Gautier's sister."

"What does he want there?"

"He has gone to get her authority to have the corpse dug up again and put somewhere else."

"Why won't he let it remain here?"

"You know, sir, people have queer notions about dead folk. We see something of that every day. The ground here was only bought for five years, and this young gentleman wants a perpetual lease and a bigger plot of ground; it will be better in the new part."

"和那位先生一样？"园丁露出一副了解的样子，微笑着说。

"不，我都没有和她说过话。"

"可你却到这里看她，你真是个好心肠的人！因为到这里来探望这个可怜姑娘的人真是太少了！"

"难道没有什么人到这儿来？"

"除了那位年轻先生曾经来过一次之外，就再没有其他的人了。"

"他就来过一次吗？"

"没错，先生。"

"后来他再也没来过吗？"

"是的，不过他回来之后一定还会来的。"

"那么他是去什么地方了？"

"对的。"

"你知道他去哪儿了吗？"

"我猜他是去找戈蒂埃小姐的姐姐了。"

"他去找她要干什么呢？"

"他是去取得玛格丽特姐姐的授权把遗体挖掘出来，迁葬到其他地方。"

"为什么他不让她待在这儿呢？"

"你知道的，先生，有些人对死者抱持着许多看法。这样的事，我们天天都能见到。这块墓地只有5年的租用期，那个年轻人想找一块能永久出让、面积也更大一些的

"What do you call the new part?"

"The new plots of ground that are for sale, there to the left. If the cemetery had always been kept like it is now, there wouldn't be the like of it in the world; but there is still plenty to do before it will be quite all it should be. And then people are so queer!"

"What do you mean?"

"I mean that there are people who carry their pride even here. Now, this Mademoiselle Gautier, it appears she lived a bit free, if you'll excuse my saying so. Poor lady, she's dead now; there's no more of her left than of them that no one has a word to say against. We water them every day. Well, when the relatives of the folk that are buried beside her found out the sort of person she was, what do you think they said? That they would try to keep her out from here, and that there ought to be a piece of ground somewhere apart for these sort of women, like there is for the poor. Did you ever hear of such a thing? I gave it to them straight, I did: well to do folk who come to see their dead four times a year, and bring their flowers themselves, and what flowers! and look twice at the keep of them they pretend to cry over, and write on their tombstones all about the tears they haven't shed, and come and make

墓地, 最好能在新区里。"

"你说的新区是怎么回事? "

"就是这会儿正在出售的新墓地, 在这片地的左边。倘若这个公墓从以前就能像现在这样来管理, 很可能它已经是世界上独一无二的了。可是要让一切都达到尽善尽美, 还差得远呢。况且人们又那么可笑。"

"你的话是什么意思呢? "

"我是想说, 有的人就算到了这里还是神气活现的。拿这位戈蒂埃小姐来说吧, 听说她生活不太检点, 请原谅我这么说。如今, 这位可怜的女士已经死了, 她留下的东西一点儿也不比那些不曾给人落下过什么话柄的女人多。我们也会天天给她们坟上的花浇水。然而, 当那些葬在她旁边的死者的亲戚们得知她是个怎样的人之后, 你猜他们都说了些什么? 他们起劲地想要把她从这儿弄出去, 还说这种女人应该有一个专门的地方埋葬, 就像穷人一样。谁见过这样的事? 我干脆地拒绝了他们: 那些正派的人每年只来 4 次看望自己死去的亲人, 还自己带着花束, 天哪, 那都是些什么花啊! 看看他们说要为之痛哭的人埋葬的地方吧。他们在死者的墓碑上写上悲恸欲绝的词句, 自己却一滴眼泪也没有流过, 如今还要来

difficulties about their neighbours. You may believe me or not, sir, I never knew the young lady; I don't know what she did. Well, I'm quite in love with the poor thing; I look after her well, and I let her have her camellias at an honest price. She is the dead body that I like the best. You see, sir, we are obliged to love the dead, for we are kept so busy, we have hardly time to love anything else."

I looked at the man, and some of my readers will understand, without my needing to explain it to them, the emotion which I felt on hearing him. He observed it, no doubt, for he went on:

"They tell me there were people who ruined themselves over that girl, and lovers that worshipped her; well, when I think there isn't one of them that so much as buys her a flower now, that's queer, sir, and sad. And, after all, she isn't so badly off for she has her grave to herself, and if there is only one who remembers her, he makes up for the others. But we have other poor girls here, just like her and just her age, and they are just thrown into a pauper's grave, and it breaks my heart when I hear their poor bodies drop into the earth. And not a soul thinks about them any more, once they are dead! 'T isn't a merry trade, ours, especially when we have a little heart left.

找他们邻居的麻烦。无论你信不信，先生，我从没见过这位年轻的小姐，也不知道她都干过些什么事，可是我非常喜欢这个可怜的姑娘，我非常用心地照顾她，给她拿来的茶花价格都十分公道。她是我最喜爱的死者了。你知道的，先生，我们这些人只有死人可以去爱了，因为我们实在太忙，几乎没有时间去爱其他的什么东西了。"

我看着这个人，无须我多作解释，一些读者也能体会到，在我听到他说的这些话时，心里的感情是多么激动。毫无疑问，他同样看了出来，因为他接下去又说道：

"他们说有人为了这个姑娘而破产，还说她的情人特别迷恋她，那么，当我想起居然都没有一个人来买一朵花给她，不由得感到既奇怪又悲哀。可是，她毕竟也没什么可抱怨的了，因为她至少还有自己的坟墓，虽说怀念她的只有一个，就这一个足以弥补别人的份了。我们这儿还有几个和她身世一样年龄相近的可怜女孩，她们只能埋在公共墓地里面。每次当我听到有她们可怜的尸体丢进墓地的消息都会心碎不已。当她们死去之后就没有一个人会惦念她们了。我们这个职业啊，特别是对于那些还有点良心的人来说，可不是一个开心快活的买

What do you expect? I can't help it. I have a fine, strapping girl myself; she's just twenty, and when a girl of that age comes here I think of her, and I don't care if it's a great lady or a vagabond, I can't help feeling it a bit. But I am taking up your time, sir, with my tales, and it wasn't to hear them you came here. I was told to show you Mlle. Gautier's grave; here you have it. Is there anything else I can do for you?"

"Do you know M. Armand Duval's address?" I asked.

"Yes; he lives at Rue de –; at least, that's where I always go to get my money for the flowers you see there."

"Thanks, my good man."

I gave one more look at the grave covered with flowers half longing to penetrate the depths of the earth and see what the earth had made of the fair creature that had been cast to it; then I walked sadly away.

"Do you want to see M. Duval, sir?" said the gardener, who was walking beside me.

"Yes."

"Well, I am pretty sure he is not back yet, or he would have been here already."

"You don't think he has forgotten Marguerite?"

卖哟。你说还能怎么样呢？我也是帮不上忙的啊！我自己也有一个20岁的美丽的女儿，每当有和她年纪相仿的女尸被送来时，我都会想起她来，无论那具尸体是阔小姐还是流浪女，我都免不了会动感情。我这是在用自己的啰唆事浪费你的时间吧，再说你来这儿也不是为了听这些故事的。我被吩咐领你去戈蒂埃小姐的坟，现在已经到了，你还有什么事需要我去办吗？"

"你是否知道阿尔芒·迪瓦尔先生的住址呢？"我问道。

"是的，他就住在××街，你看到这些花了吧，至少我一直是去那里收这些花的费用的。"

"谢谢了，我的朋友。"

我又望了一眼那个布满鲜花的坟墓，心中不由得生出一个念头，想探测一下这墓穴究竟有多深，看看泥土下掩埋的那个美丽女人变成什么样了，随后，我心怀伤感地离去了。

"先生是否要去拜会迪瓦尔先生？"在我身边走着的园丁问道。

"没错。"

"好吧，我能断定他还没回来呢，否则他早就会到这儿来了。"

"那么你不会认为他已经把玛格丽特忘记了，对吗？"

"I am not only sure he hasn't, but I would wager that he wants to change her grave simply in order to have one more look at her."

"Why do you think that?"

"The first word he said to me when he came to the cemetery was: 'How can I see her again?' That can't be done unless there is a change of grave, and I told him all about the formalities that have to be attended to in getting it done; for, you see, if you want to move a body from one grave to another you must have it identified, and only the family can give leave for it under the direction of a police inspector. That is why M. Duval has gone to see Mlle. Gautier's sister, and you may be sure his first visit will be for me."

We had come to the cemetery gate. I thanked the gardener again, putting a few coins into his hand, and made my way to the address he had given me.

Armand had not yet returned. I left word for him, begging him to come and see me as soon as he arrived, or to send me word where I could find him.

Next day, in the morning, I received a letter from Duval, telling me of his return, and asking me to call on him, as he was so worn out with fatigue that it was impossible for him to go out.

"我不仅可以断言他没有，而且我还敢打赌，他要为玛格丽特迁葬就是为了能够再见她一面。"

"你为什么会这么想呢？"

"他来到这片公墓时和我说的第一句话就是'我怎样才能再见到她呢？'这样的事情除了迁葬是不可能办得到的，于是我就把迁葬所需的手续全都告诉了他，原因嘛，你知道的，想把一具尸体从一块墓地迁葬到另一块，就必须先验明正身，而且一定要得到死者家属的许可，还要在警长的主持之下才能完成。这就是迪瓦尔先生去拜访戈蒂埃小姐的姐姐的原因了。这样你就能肯定，他一回来肯定会第一个来找我们的。"

我们一同走到公墓门口，我再一次向园丁表示感谢，在他手里塞了几枚硬币，然后就去了他告诉我的那个住址。

阿尔芒还没有回家。我给他留了话，请他一回来就去找我，或是告诉我到什么地方能够找到他。

第二天上午的时候，我收到迪瓦尔先生写来的一封信，信中说他已经回来了，但由于疲劳过度无法外出，因此邀请我去他家里做客。

CHAPTER 6

第六章

I found Armand in bed. On seeing me he held out a burning hand.

"You are feverish," I said to him.

"It is nothing, the fatigue of a rapid journey; that is all."

"You have been to see Marguerite's sister?"

"Yes; who told you?"

"I knew it. Did you get what you wanted?"

"Yes; but who told you of my journey, and of my reason for taking it?"

"The gardener of the cemetery."

"You have seen the tomb?"

I scarcely dared reply, for the tone in which the words were spoken proved to me that the speaker was still possessed by the emotion which I had witnessed before, and that every time his thoughts or speech travelled back to that mournful subject emotion would still, for a long time to come, prove stronger than his will. I contented myself with a nod of the head.

"He has looked after it well?" continued

阿尔芒是躺在床上接见我的。他一见面就把滚烫的手朝我伸来。

"你正在发烧。"我说道。

"没什么大不了的,只是因为路上赶得太急了而已。"

"你见到玛格丽特的姐姐了?"

"是的,是谁和你说的?"

"我知道了这个消息。那么你要办的事谈妥了没有?"

"谈妥了,不过是谁告诉你我的出行,以及这次出行的目的呢?"

"是那片公墓的园丁。"

"你去那座坟墓看过了吗?"

我几乎不敢答话,因为他在讲话时的语调告诉我他的心情依然十分痛苦,就和我上一次见到他时的情绪一样。每当他自己想到或是旁人的话语触及这个令他感伤的话题时,他都会有相当长一段时间心情激动,无法自持。所以我仅是点点头,表示了肯定的答复。

"他是不是把坟墓照管得很

Armand. Two big tears rolled down the cheeks of the sick man, and he turned away his head to hide them from me. I pretended not to see them, and tried to change the conversation.

"You have been away three weeks," I said.

Armand passed his hand across his eyes and replied, "Exactly three weeks."

"You had a long journey."

"Oh, I was not travelling all the time. I was ill for a fortnight, or I should have returned long ago; but I had scarcely got there when I took this fever, and I was obliged to keep my room."

"And you started to come back before you were really well?"

"If I had remained in the place for another week, I should have died there."

"Well, now you are back again, you must take care of yourself; your friends will come and look after you; myself, first of all, if you will allow me."

"I shall get up in a couple of hours."

"It would be very unwise."

"I must."

"What have you to do in such a great hurry?"

"I must go to the inspector of police."

"Why do you not get one of your friends to see after the matter? It is likely to make

好？"阿尔芒又说。两颗大大的泪珠沿着这位病人的脸颊滚落，他转过头去想在我面前掩饰。我装作没看见，试图岔开话题。

"你这次出门花了 3 个星期左右吧。"我说道。

阿尔芒用手抹了抹眼睛，答道："正好是 3 个星期。"

"真是一次长时间的旅行哪。"

"哦，我并没有一直不停地走。有两个星期我都在生病，要不然早就回来了。但是我一回来就开始发烧，不得不待在自己的房间里。"

"那么你身体还没有完全康复就动身回来了吗？"

"如果让我再在那儿一动不动地待一个星期，没准就会死在那个地方了。"

"呃，好在现在你又回来了，你应该多保重自己的身体，你的朋友们会来探望和照顾你的。倘若你能同意，就把我算作第一个吧。"

"我 2 小时之后就要起床了。"

"这是非常不明智的举动。"

"我必须要起来。"

"有什么事情一定要这样急着去办呢？"

"我必须去警长那里。"

"你为什么不委托一位朋友去

you worse than you are now."

"It is my only chance of getting better. I must see her. Ever since I heard of her death, especially since I saw her grave, I have not been able to sleep. I can not realize that this woman, so young and so beautiful when I left her, is really dead. I must convince myself of it. I must see what God has done with a being that I have loved so much, and perhaps the horror of the sight will cure me of my despair. Will you accompany me, if it won't be troubling you too much?"

"What did her sister say about it?"

"Nothing. She seemed greatly surprised that a stranger wanted to buy a plot of ground and give Marguerite a new grave, and she immediately signed the authorization that I asked her for."

"Believe me, it would be better to wait until you are quite well."

"Have no fear; I shall be quite composed. Besides, I should simply go out of my mind if I were not to carry out a resolution which I have set myself to carry out. I swear to you that I shall never be myself again until I have seen Marguerite. It is perhaps the thirst of the fever, a sleepless night's dream, a moment's delirium; but though I were to become a Trappist, like M. de Rance', after having

处理这件事呢？你亲自前去很可能会使病情加重的。"

"只有办成这件事我才有康复的希望，我一定要见她一面。自从我得知她的死讯之后，特别是看过她的坟墓之后就再也没睡过了。我无法想象，当我们分离的时候那个姑娘还那么年轻漂亮，可如今竟然已经不在人世了。我必须亲眼见到才能相信。我必须去看看上帝把我那深爱的人变成了什么样子，而且这个令人恐惧的景象或许能治愈我的悲伤和失望。如果不是太过麻烦你的话，你可以陪我一起去吗？"

"她姐姐都和你说什么了？"

"什么都没说。她听说有个陌生人想买一块地为玛格丽特修一座新的坟墓，似乎感到极为吃惊，马上就签了名，授权给我去做这件事。"

"请相信我，等你完全康复之后再去办迁葬这件事比较好。"

"唉，不用担心，我肯定能好起来的。再说，我好不容易才下定决心，倘若不趁现在赶快把这件事情办了，我一定会发疯的。我可以向你发誓，如果我不能再看一眼玛格丽特，我是无法平静下来的。它或许是高烧中的渴念，无眠之夜里的幻梦，或者一时的谵妄发作。至于我是否会如朗塞先生一般变成苦

seen, I will see."

"I understand," I said to Armand, "and I am at your service. Have you seen Julie Duprat?"

"Yes, I saw her the day I returned, for the first time."

"Did she give you the papers that Marguerite had left for you?"

Armand drew a roll of papers from under his pillow, and immediately put them back.

"I know all that is in these papers by heart," he said. "For three weeks I have read them ten times over every day. You shall read them, too, but later on, when I am calmer, and can make you understand all the love and tenderness hidden away in this confession. For the moment I want you to do me a service."

"What is it?"

"Your cab is below?"

"Yes.

"Well, will you take my passport and ask if there are any letters for me at the poste restante? My father and sister must have written to me at Paris, and I went away in such haste that I did not go and see before leaving. When you come back we will go together to the inspector of police, and arrange for tomorrow's ceremony."

Armand handed me his passport, and I

修士，则要等到我见到她之后再说了。"

"我能理解，"我对阿尔芒说，"也乐意为你效劳，你见过朱莉·杜普拉了吗？"

"是的。我是在回来的那一天第一次见到她的。"

"那么她是否已经把玛格丽特留给你的日记拿给你了？"

阿尔芒从他的枕头底下抽出一卷纸，又将它马上放了回去。

"这些纸上所写的东西我已经全都记在心里了，"他说道，"这3个星期里，我每天都会把它们读上十来遍。你日后也可以读一读，不过还得再等几天，让我更加平静一些，等到我可以把这份日记里面隐含的所有爱恋和温柔的表白逐一解释给你听的时候吧。这会儿我想请你帮我一个忙。"

"是什么呢？"

"你的马车停在外面吧？"

"对的。"

"那好，你能不能拿着我的护照去一次邮局，看一下是否有寄给我的留局待领的来信？我父亲跟妹妹在巴黎肯定给我写过信，上次我动身离开时实在太过仓促，抽不出时间去打听这个事。等你从邮局回来之后，我们再一块儿去找警长，安排明天迁葬的事宜。"

went to Rue Jean Jacques Rousseau. There were two letters addressed to Duval. I took them and returned. When I re-entered the room Armand was dressed and ready to go out.

"Thanks," he said, taking the letters. "Yes," he added, after glancing at the addresses, "they are from my father and sister. They must have been quite at a loss to understand my silence."

He opened the letters, guessed at rather than read them, for each was of four pages; and a moment after folded them up. "Come," he said, "I will answer tomorrow."

We went to the police station, and Armand handed in the permission signed by Marguerite's sister. He received in return a letter to the keeper of the cemetery, and it was settled that the disinterment was to take place next day, at ten o'clock, that I should call for him an hour before, and that we should go to the cemetery together.

I confess that I was curious to be present, and I did not sleep all night. judging from the thoughts which filled my brain, it must have been a long night for Armand. When I entered his room at nine on the following morning he was frightfully pale, but seemed calm. He smiled and held out his hand. His candles

阿尔芒把他的护照给了我，然后我去了让－雅克－卢梭大街。那儿有两封写给迪瓦尔先生的来信，我取到之后立刻返回。当我踏进他家门时，阿尔芒已然穿戴整齐，准备出发了。

"多谢了，"他接过信说道，"没错，"他看了一眼来信的地址，又说，"是我父亲和妹妹写来的。我一直没回信，他们一定觉得特别奇怪。"

他拆开信件，每封信都有4页，他只是匆匆瞄了一眼，几乎都没看，很快就把它们重新折了起来。"走吧，"他说道，"我明天会给他们写回信的。"

我们去了警察局，阿尔芒递交了玛格丽特姐姐给他的委托书。作为回复，他收到了一张写给公墓看守人的通知书，并且约好迁葬事宜将在次日上午10点进行。我会在此前一小时去阿尔芒那里，随后与他一块儿到公墓去。

我承认自己对参加这样一次迁葬也是非常感兴趣的，整个晚上都没睡好。想到充斥在我的脑子里的那些乱糟糟的念头，就能知道这一夜对阿尔芒来说一定是十分漫长的。次日早上9点钟，我来到阿尔芒家里，他脸色苍白得可怕，不过看上去还算神态平稳。他朝我笑了

were burned out; and before leaving he took a very heavy letter addressed to his father, and no doubt containing an account of that night's impressions.

Half an hour later we were at Montmartre. The police inspector was there already. We walked slowly in the direction of Marguerite's grave. The inspector went in front; Armand and I followed a few steps behind.

From time to time I felt my companion's arm tremble convulsively, as if he shivered from head to feet. I looked at him. He understood the look, and smiled at me; we had not exchanged a word since leaving the house.

Just before we reached the grave, Armand stopped to wipe his face, which was covered with great drops of sweat. I took advantage of the pause to draw in a long breath, for I, too, felt as if I had a weight on my chest.

What is the origin of that mournful pleasure which we find in sights of this kind? When we reached the grave the gardener had removed all the flower pots, the iron railing had been taken away, and two men were turning up the soil.

Armand leaned against a tree and watched. All his life seemed to pass before his eyes. Suddenly one of the two pickaxes

笑，把手递过来。他的蜡烛都烧尽了，在出门以前，他拿了一封地址是他父亲的厚厚的信，毫无疑问，里面一定充满了他昨夜里的感想。

过了半个小时，我们就来到了蒙马特公墓。警长已经等在那里了。我们一起慢慢地走向玛格丽特的坟墓，最前面是警长，阿尔芒与我落下了几步，在后面跟着。

我能感到我同伴的胳膊在时不时地抽搐，好像不停地有股寒流从头到脚透过他的全身。我看了看他，他也明白我目光的含义，露出一个微笑。事实上，从他家里出来之后，我们就再也没有说过一句话了。

快要走到坟墓所在位置的时候，阿尔芒站住了，擦了擦他那布满豆大汗珠的脸。我也趁此机会赶紧长出了一口气，因为我感到自己的心也变得格外沉重了似的。

在这样痛苦的场合之中，怎么会有任何快乐的事情呢！当我们来到坟前时，园丁已经移走了所有的花盆，也搬走了铁栅栏，还有两名工人正在翻土。

阿尔芒靠着一棵树，一直看着这边。他的全部生命似乎都集中在那两只眼睛里面了。忽然间，有把

struck against a stone. At the sound Armand recoiled, as at an electric shock, and seized my hand with such force as to give me pain.

One of the grave-diggers took a shovel and began emptying out the earth; then, when only the stones covering the coffin were left, he threw them out one by one.

I scrutinized Armand, for every moment I was afraid lest the emotions which he was visibly repressing should prove too much for him; but he still watched, his eyes fixed and wide open, like the eyes of a madman, and a slight trembling of the cheeks and lips were the only signs of the violent nervous crisis under which he was suffering.

As for me, all I can say is that I regretted having come.

When the coffin was uncovered the inspector said to the grave-digger: "Open it." They obeyed, as if it were the most natural thing in the world.

The coffin was of oak, and they began to unscrew the lid. The humidity of the earth had rusted the screws, and it was not without some difficulty that the coffin was opened. A painful odour arose in spite of the aromatic plants with which it was covered.

"O my God, my God!" murmured

鹤嘴锄碰到了石头，发出刺耳的响声。那个声音令阿尔芒好像被电击一样地往后缩去，并用力捏住我的手，力道大得甚至让我感到了疼痛。

其中一个掘墓人挥着一把巨大的铁铲，开始慢慢清除墓穴内的积土；当墓穴中只留有盖在棺材上的石块时，他就一块一块地把它们扔到外面。

我一直在看着阿尔芒，始终担心那明显压抑着的情感会将他击垮。然而他一直大大地瞪着双眼，直直地看着，简直和疯子一样，只有从他略微抖动的脸颊与嘴唇上才能看出，实际上他的神经已经处于一种非常紧张的状态之中了。

而我呢，我所能说的就只有一句话，那就是非常后悔来到这里。

等棺木被全部挖掘出来之后，警长向掘墓的工人们说道："把它打开！"那些人依言照办，就像这是世界上最顺理成章的一件事。

棺材是橡木做成的，工人们开始拆卸那上面的螺丝钉，由于地下的潮湿，这些螺丝都已经朽坏了，因此没费多少工夫就打开了棺材。尽管棺材四周被芬芳的花草所覆盖，但还是感到一股恶臭扑鼻而来。

"啊，天哪！我的天哪！"阿尔

Armand, and turned paler than before.

Even the grave-digger drew back.

A great white shroud covered the corpse, closely outlining some of its contours. This shroud was almost completely eaten away at one end, and left one of the feet visible.

I was nearly fainting, and at the moment of writing these lines I see the whole scene over again in all its imposing reality.

"Quick," said the inspector. Thereupon one of the men put out his hand, began to unsew the shroud, and taking hold of it by one end suddenly laid bare the face of Marguerite.

It was terrible to see, it is horrible to relate. The eyes were nothing but two holes, the lips had disappeared, vanished, and the white teeth were tightly set. The black hair, long and dry, was pressed tightly about the forehead, and half veiled the green hollows of the cheeks; and yet I recognised in this face the joyous white and rose face that I had seen so often.

Armand, unable to turn away his eyes, had put the handkerchief to his mouth and bit it.

For my part, it was as if a circle of iron tightened about my head, a veil covered my eyes, a rumbling filled my ears, and all I could do was to unstop a smelling bottle which I happened to have with me, and to

芒口中喃喃地说，脸变得更白了。

甚至就连掘墓人也朝后退去。

一块大大的白色裹尸布包在尸体外面，只能依稀看出尸体的轮廓。尸布从一端开始几乎已经完全烂掉，只能看到一只脚露在外面。

我几乎要晕过去，就是现在我写这几行字的时候，那幕景象还仿佛就在眼前。

"行动快点吧。"警长说道。于是两个工人中的一个就解开了尸布，抓着一边把它掀开，玛格丽特的脸一下子就暴露了出来。

她的样子实在不忍卒睹，就是说起来也令人不寒而栗。原来是眼睛的地方只剩下两个窟窿，嘴唇已经烂掉，白森森的牙齿紧紧咬着，黑色的头发既长又干，贴在太阳穴上，稀稀拉拉地垂下来盖住深深凹陷下去的青灰色脸庞。然而，我依旧能从这张脸上辨认出以前常常见到的她白里透红、充满欢乐的面容。

阿尔芒盯着这张脸无法转开目光，把手帕放在嘴里紧紧咬着。

而我就像有一只铁环箍在头上，眼前模糊不清，耳朵里轰轰地响，我所能做的只有把以前带在身上以防万一的嗅盐瓶拧开，使劲地嗅着。

draw in long breaths of it.

Through this bewilderment I heard the inspector say to Duval, "Do you identify?"

"Yes," replied the young man in a dull voice.

"Then fasten it up and take it away," said the inspector.

The grave-diggers put back the shroud over the face of the corpse, fastened up the coffin, took hold of each end of it, and began to carry it toward the place where they had been told to take it.

Armand did not move. His eyes were fixed upon the empty grave; he was as white as the corpse which we had just seen. He looked as if he had been turned to stone.

I saw what was coming as soon as the pain caused by the spectacle should have abated and thus ceased to sustain him. I went up to the inspector. "Is this gentleman's presence still necessary?" I said, pointing to Armand.

"No," he replied, "and I should advise you to take him away. He looks ill."

"Come," I said to Armand, taking him by the arm.

"What?" he said, looking at me as if he did not recognise me.

"It is all over," I added. "You must come, my friend; you are quite white; you

在一片晕眩之中，我听见警长对迪瓦尔先生说："你确认了吗？"

"是的。"年轻人用低沉的声音答道。

"那就把棺材重新钉上搬走。"警长下令道。

掘墓工人们将裹尸布重新盖在死人的脸上，合上棺盖钉牢，一人一头地抬着棺材，朝着事先告诉他们的地方走了过去。

阿尔芒却一动未动，双眼凝视着那个空空的墓穴，脸色简直和我们刚刚看见的死尸一样惨白。看起来他似乎变成了一座石像。

我清楚是这一幕惨象带来的痛苦在支持着他，也知道等这种痛苦缓解之后将会发生什么样的事情。我走上前去，指了指阿尔芒问警长说："请问是否还需要这位先生留在这里呢？"

"不，不需要，"他回答说，"而且我还要劝你带他离开，他看上去似乎不大舒服。"

我上前挽住阿尔芒的手臂，说道："我们走吧！"

"你说什么？"他开口道，看着我的目光好像不认识我似的。

"都已经结束了，"我补充说，

are cold. These emotions will be too much for you."

"You are right. Let us go," he answered mechanically, but without moving a step.

I took him by the arm and led him along. He let himself be guided like a child, only from time to time murmuring, "Did you see her eyes?" and he turned as if the vision had recalled her.

Nevertheless, his steps became more irregular; he seemed to walk by a series of jerks; his teeth chattered; his hands were cold; a violent agitation ran through his body. I spoke to him; he did not answer. He was just able to let himself be led along. A cab was waiting at the gate. It was only just in time. Scarcely had he seated himself, when the shivering became more violent, and he had an actual attack of nerves, in the midst of which his fear of frightening me made me press my hand and whisper: "It is nothing, nothing. I want to weep."

His chest laboured, his eyes were injected with blood, but no tears came. I made him smell the salts which I had with me, and when we reached his house only the shivering remained.

With the help of his servant I put him to bed, lit a big fire in his room, and hurried off to my doctor, to whom I told all that had happened. He hastened with me.

"你必须要走了，我的朋友，你脸色苍白，浑身发冷，这样的激动是会让你送命的。"

"你说得没错，我们走吧。"他机械地回答着，可脚下一步都没有挪动。

我抓着他的胳膊引着他走。他就像个孩子似的跟在后面，只是嘴里不时喃喃自语："你看见她的眼睛了吗？"一边说一边回过头去看，如同那个幻觉在召唤他一般。

不仅如此，他的脚步比来时更加不稳了，几乎是跟跟跄跄地向前走着。他的牙齿上下相击，双手冰冷，身体整个都在剧烈地颤抖。我试着和他讲话，但没有得到一句回答。他唯一能做的就是跟着我往前走。好在我们碰巧遇到一辆马车等在门口，他刚刚上车坐下，就开始更剧烈地抽搐，是真正的全身痉挛。他怕我害怕，还紧握住我的手，小声地安慰说："这没什么，没什么的，我只是想哭罢了。"

他大声地喘粗气，双眼充血，却流不出一滴眼泪。我给他闻了闻自己方才用过的嗅盐瓶。等到我们返回他的家里，他还在不停地颤抖。

我在仆人的帮助下将他扶到床上躺好，又把房里的炉火拨旺，然后连忙去叫我的医生，和他讲了刚才的情况。他马上就跟着我来了。

Armand was flushed and delirious; he stammered out disconnected words, in which only the name of Marguerite could be distinctly heard.

"Well?" I said to the doctor when he had examined the patient.

"Well, he has neither more nor less than brain fever, and very lucky it is for him, for I firmly believe (God forgive me!) that he would have gone out of his mind. Fortunately, the physical malady will kill the mental one, and in a month's time he will be free from the one and perhaps from the other."

阿尔芒脸颊通红，神志不清，结结巴巴地吐出一些胡话，其中能够听清楚的就只有玛格丽特的名字。

等医生给他做过检查以后，我就问医生说："他怎么样？"

"嗯，他得了脑膜炎，并不是什么别的病，这已经是他的幸运了。天主饶恕我，本来我很确定他是得了失心疯。好在他肉体上的病把精神上的病给压倒了。再过上一个月，或许他这两种病就全都痊愈了。"

CHAPTER 7

第七章

Illnesses like Armand's have one fortunate thing about them: they either kill outright or are very soon overcome. A fortnight after the events which I have just related Armand was convalescent, and we had already become great friends. During the whole course of his illness I had hardly left his side.

Spring was profuse in its flowers, its leaves, its birds, its songs; and my friend's window opened gaily upon his garden, from which a reviving breath of health seemed to come to him. The doctor had allowed him to get up, and we often sat talking at the open window, at the hour when the sun is at its height, from twelve to two. I was careful not to refer to Marguerite, fearing lest the name should awaken sad recollections hidden under the apparent calm of the invalid; but Armand, on the contrary, seemed to delight in speaking of her, not as formerly, with tears in his eyes, but with a sweet smile which reassured me as to the state of his mind.

幸运的是，阿尔芒所得的病属于那种干脆爽快的，要么一下子就要了人的命，否则便用不了几天就会痊愈了。在我前文所述的情况之后半个月，阿尔芒就已全然康复，我们两个也成为了好友。在他患病的时间里，我几乎一步也没有离开过他的身边。

春天到了，带来了绿叶繁花，百鸟歌唱，我朋友房间里的窗户正向着他的花园，此时欢乐地打开了，花园里清新健康的空气一阵阵吹过他的身边。医生已经允许他下床，当每天中午12点到下午2点太阳升得最高的时候，我们经常坐在敞开的窗户旁边聊天。我始终留意着不要谈及玛格丽特，唯恐一提起这个名字就会让情绪好不容易安定下来的病人再次想起那些过去的伤心事。可阿尔芒却正相反，他好像很喜欢谈起她，也不再似以前那样一说到她就眼含泪水，而是挂着一种甜蜜的微笑，这笑容使我安下了心，相信他的心灵已经平复了。

I had noticed that ever since his last visit to the cemetery, and the sight which had brought on so violent a crisis, sorrow seemed to have been overcome by sickness, and Marguerite's death no longer appeared to him under its former aspect. A kind of consolation had sprung from the certainty of which he was now fully persuaded, and in order to banish the sombre picture which often presented itself to him, he returned upon the happy recollections of his liaison with Marguerite, and seemed resolved to think of nothing else.

The body was too much weakened by the attack of fever, and even by the process of its cure, to permit him any violent emotions, and the universal joy of spring which wrapped him round carried his thoughts instinctively to images of joy. He had always obstinately refused to tell his family of the danger which he had been in, and when he was well again his father did not even know that he had been ill.

One evening we had sat at the window later than usual; the weather had been superb, and the sun sank to sleep in a twilight dazzling with gold and azure. Though we were in Paris, the verdure which surrounded us seemed to shut us off from the world, and our conversation was

我留意到，自从他上次到公墓去，目睹了那个令他突然发病的情景以来，他的悲伤痛苦似乎已被疾病所压倒，对于玛格丽特的去世，他的想法较过去发生了改变。他对她的死亡已然确信无疑，心中反倒变得轻松了，为了把那些经常在他眼前浮现的阴暗形象驱散，他总是在追忆那些与玛格丽特交往中最幸福的时刻，而且他看起来除了这些，也不愿意去回忆别的事情。

阿尔芒的身体还没有完全从高烧带来的极度虚弱中恢复过来，精神上也不宜过分激动。随着春天的到来，大自然欣欣向荣的景象围绕在他的身边，令他情不自禁地回想起过去那些快乐的时光。他始终固执地不肯将病危的事情告知家人，直到他已经脱离了险境，他的父亲对此事还一无所知。

有一天晚上，我们在窗边坐着，时间比平时晚了一些，那天天气很好，太阳在闪耀着蔚蓝与金黄光芒的暮色中沉入睡眠。虽然我们身处巴黎，可是周围环绕的翠色仿佛将我们与世界隔离开来，除了街上偶尔传来路过车辆的辚辚声，再没有

only now and again disturbed by the sound of a passing vehicle.

"It was about this time of the year, on the evening of a day like this, that I first met Marguerite," said Armand to me, as if he were listening to his own thoughts rather than to what I was saying. I did not answer. Then turning toward me, he said:

"I must tell you the whole story; you will make a book out of it; no one will believe it, but it will perhaps be interesting to do."

"You will tell me all about it later on, my friend," I said to him; "you are not strong enough yet."

"It is a warm evening, I have eaten my ration of chicken," he said to me, smiling; "I have no fever, we have nothing to do, I will tell it to you now."

"Since you really wish it, I will listen."

This is what he told me, and I have scarcely changed a word of the touching story.

Yes (Armand went on, letting his head sink back on the chair), yes, it was just such an evening as this. I had spent the day in the country with one of my friends, Gaston R –. We returned to Paris in the evening, and not knowing what to do we went to the Varietes. We went out during one of the entr'actes, and a tall woman

其他声响来干扰我们两人的谈话。

"大约就在一年中的这个季节，这样一个晚上，我认识了玛格丽特。"阿尔芒开口说。他沉浸在遐想中，我知道他并不期待我的回答。因此我什么也没说。随后，他转过身来对我说道：

"我一定要把整个故事讲给你听，你可以据此写出一本书，或许没有人会相信，不过这本书写出来或许会非常有趣。"

"你可以过几天再讲给我，我的朋友。"我回答说，"现在你的身体还没有完全康复呢。"

"今天晚上天气暖和，我还吃了一点儿鸡脯肉，"他带着微笑对我说，"我的烧已经退了，我们也没有别的事要干，就让我现在把这个故事讲给你听吧。"

"既然这是你的愿望，我会洗耳恭听的。"

下文便是他讲述的内容，这个故事生动感人，我几乎不曾改动一词。

是的（阿尔芒将头靠到椅背上，继续说道），是的，那就是这样的一个傍晚！我和一个叫 R·加斯顿的朋友在乡下玩了一天，晚上时回到巴黎，由于无聊，我们决定去杂耍剧院看戏。其中一次幕间休息的时

passed us in the corridor, to whom my friend bowed.

"Whom are you bowing to?" I asked.

"Marguerite Gautier," he said.

"She seems much changed, for I did not recognise her," I said, with an emotion that you will soon understand.

"She has been ill; the poor girl won't last long."

I remember the words as if they had been spoken to me yesterday.

I must tell you, my friend, that for two years the sight of this girl had made a strange impression on me whenever I came across her. Without knowing why, I turned pale and my heart beat violently. I have a friend who studies the occult sciences, and he would call what I experienced "the affinity of fluids"; as for me, I only know that I was fated to fall in love with Marguerite, and that I foresaw it.

It is certainly the fact that she made a very definite impression upon me, that many of my friends had noticed it and that they had been much amused when they saw who it was that made this impression upon me.

The first time I ever saw her was in the Place de la Bourse, outside Susse's; an open carriage was stationed there, and a

候，我们来到走廊里，遇到了一个身材修长的女人经过，我的朋友向她躬身以示致意。

"你在向谁鞠躬啊？"我问他。

"玛格丽特·戈蒂埃。"他回答。

"她看上去变了好多，我差一点儿就认不出她了。"我心情激动地说。至于原因等会儿你就知道了。

"她病了，那个可怜的姑娘活不了多久了。"

至今这些话我还记得清清楚楚，就像昨天刚刚听到的一样。

我要和你说，我的朋友，这两年来，我每次见到这个姑娘的时候，都会油然而生一种无法言说的感觉。我会原因不明地脸色发白，心扑通扑通跳。我有一个研究秘术的友人，他把我这种情况叫做"流体的亲和力"。对我来说，我只知道一点，那就是我命中注定会爱上玛格丽特，而当时我也预感到了这一点。

毫无疑问，她给我留下了极其深刻的印象，我的朋友们都亲眼目睹了我的情况，当他们得知我这种印象是从何而来的时候，都会大笑不止。

我第一次遇到她的地点是交易所广场的絮斯商店[1]门口。当时那里停着一辆敞篷四轮马车，车上走下

---

[1] 絮斯商店，当时巴黎著名的时装店。

woman dressed in white got down from it. A murmur of admiration greeted her as she entered the shop. As for me, I was rivetted to the spot from the moment she went in till the moment when she came out again. I could see her through the shop windows selecting what she had come to buy. I might have gone in, but I dared not. I did not know who she was, and I was afraid lest she should guess why I had come in and be offended. Nevertheless, I did not think I should ever see her again.

She was elegantly dressed; she wore a muslin dress with many flounces, an Indian shawl embroidered at the corners with gold and silk flowers, a straw hat, a single bracelet, and a heavy gold chain, such as was just then beginning to be the fashion.

She returned to her carriage and drove away. One of the shopmen stood at the door looking after his elegant customer's carriage. I went up to him and asked him what was the lady's name.

"Mademoiselle Marguerite Gautier," he replied. I dared not ask him for her address, and went on my way.

The recollection of this vision, for it was really a vision, would not leave my mind like so many visions I had seen, and I looked everywhere for this royally beautiful woman in white.

来一位穿着一身白衣的女士。当她走进商店时，一片低低的赞叹声随之响起。而我就像被钉在了地上一样，从她进门一直到出门，完全没有动过。我隔着橱窗看她在店铺里挑选东西。我原本也能进去的，可是我不敢。我不了解那位女士是什么人，我怕她知道了我走进店铺的用意而感到生气。但是那个时候，我并没有想过以后还能再见到她。

她穿着高雅，身上是一条镶满花边的细纱长裙，一块印度方巾披在肩上，四角都镶着金边和丝绣的花朵，头戴一顶意大利草帽，手上还有一只手镯，是那个时候刚刚开始流行的一种粗金链子。

她回到她的敞篷马车上离开了。一个店里的小伙计站在门前，目送这位服饰高雅、容貌美丽的女客的车子远去。我走上前去，请他告诉我那位女士的名字。

"那是玛格丽特·戈蒂埃小姐。"伙计回答说。我没敢打听她的地址，就那样走了。

这一幕情景就像是幻觉，但它没有像以前那些幻影一样不久后便被我忘掉，它总是出现在我的脑海里。于是我四处去寻找那位身穿白衣的绝色佳人。

A few days later there was a great performance at the Opera Comique. The first person I saw in one of the boxes was Marguerite Gautier.

The young man whom I was with recognised her immediately, for he said to me, mentioning her name: "Look at that pretty girl."

At that moment Marguerite turned her opera-glass in our direction and, seeing my friend, smiled and beckoned to him to come to her.

"I will go and say 'How do you do?' to her," he said, "and will be back in a moment."

"I could not help saying "Happy man!"

"Why?"

"To go and see that woman."

"Are you in love with her?"

"No," I said, flushing, for I really did not know what to say; "but I should very much like to know her."

"Come with me. I will introduce you."

"Ask her if you may."

"Really, there is no need to be particular with her; come."

What he said troubled me. I feared to discover that Marguerite was not worthy of the sentiment which I felt for her.

In a book of Alphonse Karr entitles *Am*

几天之后，我到喜剧歌剧院去观赏一场盛大的演出。玛格丽特·戈蒂埃就在台前旁侧的包厢里，我第一眼就看到了她。

我的年轻同伴也立即认出了她，他叫着她的名字和我说着："看哪！这个姑娘真漂亮！"

就在这时候，玛格丽特举起望远镜看了看我们这边，她认出了我的朋友，就朝着他莞尔一笑，用手势示意让他到她那边去。

"我去跟她打个招呼，"朋友对我说，"很快我就会回来。"

我不由自主地说："真幸福啊！"

"这是怎么说？"

"因为你就要去拜访她了。"

"你难道是爱上她了？"

"不。"我说着，脸变得通红，是真的有些不知所措了，"不过我还是很想和她相识。"

"那和我一起来吧，我来介绍。"

"你得先去征得她的同意吧。"

"真是的，和她真的是不用那么讲究，过来吧。"

他的话令我非常难过，我害怕由此发现玛格丽特并不值得我付出这么多感情。

Rauchen, there is a man who one evening follows a very elegant woman, with whom he had fallen in love with at first sight on account of her beauty. Only to kiss her hand he felt that he had the strength to undertake anything, the will to conquer anything, the courage to achieve anything. He scarcely dares glance at the trim ankle which she shows as she holds her dress out of the mud. While he is dreaming of all that he would do to possess this woman, she stops at the corner of the street and asks if he will come home with her. He turns his head, crosses the street, and goes sadly back to his own house.

I recalled the story, and, having longed to suffer for this woman, I was afraid that she would accept me too promptly and give me at once what I fain would have purchased by long waiting or some great sacrifice. We men are built like that, and it is very fortunate that the imagination lends so much poetry to the senses, and that the desires of the body make thus such concession to the dreams of the soul. If any one had said to me, You shall have this woman tonight and be killed tomorrow, I would have accepted. If any one had said to me, you can be her lover for ten pounds,

阿尔封斯·卡尔[1]曾在一本叫做《烟雾》的小说里写道：某天晚上，有个男人跟在一个非常漂亮的女人身后。她体态窈窕，姿容艳丽，令他一见倾心。他觉得只要吻一吻这个女人的手，就能得到无穷的力量，可以去夺得一切、征服一切。那个女人因为怕衣服沾上泥，就掀了一下裙子，露出了迷人的脚踝，他几乎看都不敢看一眼。正当他梦想着所有可能得到这个女人的办法时，女人却在街角处叫住了他，问他是否愿意和她一起回家里去。他转头就走，穿过街道，垂头丧气地回到了自己的住处。

我想起了这个故事。我原本渴望着为这个女人而吃苦头，我担心她过快地接纳我，害怕她匆忙地爱上我。我宁可要那种经过漫长的等待、历尽艰辛之后才能获得的爱情。我们男人就是这样的脾气，假如头脑中的想象能更加地富有诗意，在幻想中灵魂能够高于肉欲就会感到非常幸福。简而言之，倘若有人和我说："今天晚上你能够拥有这个女人，不过明天你就会被杀死。"我会欣然接受的。倘若有人和我说："只需 10 个路易[2]，你就能够成为她的情夫。"我会断然拒绝，还会痛哭一

---

[1] 阿尔封斯·卡尔，19 世纪教授、记者，曾是《费加罗报》主编。
[2] 1 路易约 20 法郎。

I would have refused. I would have cried like a child who sees the castle he has been dreaming about vanish away as he awakens from sleep.

All the same, I wished to know her; it was my only means of making up my mind about her. I therefore said to my friend that I insisted on having her permission to be introduced to her, and I wandered to and fro in the corridors, saying to myself that in a moment's time she was going to see me, and that I should not know which way to look. I tried (sublime childishness of love!) to string together the words I should say to her.

A moment after my friend returned. "She is expecting us," he said.

"Is she alone?" I asked.

"With another woman."

"There are no men?"

"No."

"Come, then."

My friend went toward the door of the theatre.

"That is not the way," I said.

"We must go and get some sweets. She asked me for some."

We went into a confectioner's in the passage de l'Opera. I would have bought the whole shop, and I was looking about to see what sweets to choose, when my friend

场，如同一个孩子在醒来之后发现夜里梦到的宫殿和城堡都已经化为乌有一般。

然而，我还是想认识她，这是了解她是怎样一个人的唯一办法。因此我对朋友说，他必须事先征得玛格丽特的同意，之后才能把我介绍给她。我一个人在走廊踱来踱去，脑子里一直想着，她马上就要看到我了，可我却不知道在她的注视之下要采取什么样的态度才好。我尽力考虑着自己要对她说的话。哦，这是多么纯真、多么无邪的爱情啊！

没过多长时间，我的朋友就回来了，对我说道："她在等我们呢。"

"就她一个人吗？"我问他。

"是和另一个女的在一块儿。"

"那里没有男人吗？"

"是的，没有。"

"那么我们过去吧。"

于是我的朋友走向了剧院的大门口。

"是不是走错路了？"我说道。

"我们得去买点蜜饯，刚才玛格丽特让我给她带一些的。"

我们去的是一间开在剧场过道上的糖果铺。我想要把整间铺子都为她买下来。正当我打量着想选择一些什么东西的时候，我朋友已经

asked for a pound of raisins glaces.

"Do you know if she likes them?"

"She eats no other kind of sweets; everybody knows it.

"Ah," he went on when we had left the shop, "do you know what kind of woman it is that I am going to introduce you to? Don't imagine it is a duchess. It is simply a kept woman, very much kept, my dear fellow; don't be shy, say anything that comes into your head."

"Yes, yes," I stammered, and I followed him, saying to myself that I should soon cure myself of my passion.

When I entered the box Marguerite was in fits of laughter. I would rather that she had been sad. My friend introduced me; Marguerite gave me a little nod, and said, "And my sweets?"

"Here they are."

She looked at me as she took them. I dropped my eyes and blushed.

She leaned across to her neighbour and said something in her ear, at which both laughed. Evidently I was the cause of their mirth, and my embarrassment increased. At that time I had as mistress, a very affectionate and sentimental little person, whose sentiment and whose melancholy letters amused me greatly. I realized the pain I must have given her by what I now

开口要了一斤糖渍葡萄。

"你知道她喜欢吃这种吗？"

"她从来不吃其他种类的蜜饯，人人都知道的。"

"哦！"离开店铺的时候，我的朋友接着说，"你知道我准备把你介绍给一个怎样的女人吗？不要以为那是一位公爵夫人，那只不过是一个妓女而已，是个地地道道的妓女。我亲爱的朋友，不用觉得不好意思，想说什么就说什么吧。"

"好的，好的，"我喃喃地说，跟在朋友后面往回走，对自己说，看来我的热情很快就要冷下去了。

我走进包厢时，玛格丽特正放声大笑。我倒是宁愿看她愁眉苦脸的样子。我的朋友介绍了我，她就对我微微点了一下头，随后便问道："我的蜜饯在哪儿呢？"

"这就是了。"

她在拿蜜饯的时候看了我一眼，我眼睛看着下方，脸涨得通红。

她向邻座的女伴身边靠过去，在她耳畔低声地说了几句话，接着两个人全都开始大笑。十分明显，我变成了她们的笑柄，这使得我越发的窘迫。当时我已经有了一个情妇，非常温柔纤细、多愁善感。她敏感的情绪和忧伤的情书总是令我发笑。而由于此刻的感受，我终于了解到自己从前对她的态度一定

experienced, and for five minutes I loved her as no woman was ever loved.

Marguerite ate her raisins glaces without taking any more notice of me. The friend who had introduced me did not wish to let me remain in so ridiculous a position.

"Marguerite," he said, "you must not be surprised if M. Duval says nothing, you overwhelm him to such a degree that he can not find a word to say."

"I should say, on the contrary, that he has only come with you because it would have bored you to come here by yourself."

"If that were true," I said, "I should not have begged Ernest to ask your permission to introduce me."

"Perhaps that was only in order to put off the fatal moment."

However little one may have known women like Marguerite, one can not but know the delight they take in pretending to be witty and in teasing the people whom they meet for the first time. It is no doubt a return for the humiliations which they often have to submit to on the part of those whom they see every day.

To answer them properly, one requires a certain knack, and I had not had the opportunity of acquiring it; besides, the idea that I had formed of Marguerite accentuated the effects of her mockery.

令她十分痛苦，因此有 5 分钟的时间我以一种从未在任何女人身上产生过的感情深爱着她。

玛格丽特开始吃她的糖渍葡萄，不再分给我多一点的注意力。引见我的朋友却不愿令我陷入这样困窘可笑的境地。

"玛格丽特，"他说道，"倘若迪瓦尔先生什么也没说，你也不必觉得奇怪。他已经为你倾倒，以至于连一个字也说不出来了。"

"我要说，正相反，你是因为一个人过来无聊才让他一起来的。"

"倘若当真如此，"我开口道，"那么我就不会先拜托欧内斯特来，请求你同意将我引见给你了。"

"这或许是为了拖延这个倒霉时刻而采取的办法。"

只要有人稍微了解一点儿像玛格丽特这样的姑娘，他就会知道她们总是以装疯卖傻为乐，喜欢戏弄初次见面的人。因为她们不得不忍受那些天天都能见面的人的侮辱，这种恶作剧毫无疑问是对所受侮辱的某种报复。

所以想要恰当地回复她们，也要用到她们圈内人的某种方式，而这种方式是我此前一直没有机会学到的。此外，由于我对玛格丽特原有的观感，让我看待她玩笑的方式

Nothing that dame from her was indifferent to me. I rose to my feet, saying in an altered voice, which I could not entirely control:

"If that is what you think of me, madame, I have only to ask your pardon for my indiscretion, and to take leave of you with the assurance that it shall not occur again."

Thereupon I bowed and quitted the box. I had scarcely closed the door when I heard a third peal of laughter. It would not have been well for anybody who had elbowed me at that moment.

I returned to my seat. The signal for raising the curtain was given. Ernest came back to his place beside me.

"What a way you behaved!" he said, as he sat down. "They will think you are mad."

"What did Marguerite say after I had gone?"

"She laughed, and said she had never seen any one so funny. But don't look upon it as a lost chance; only do not do these women the honour of taking them seriously. They do not know what politeness and ceremony are. It is as if you were to offer perfumes to dogs – they would think it smelled bad, and go and roll in the gutter."

过分认真，对于这个女人的任何事情，我都做不到无动于衷。我站起身来，用一种难以控制的沮丧语调对她说：

"倘若你觉得我是这样一个人的话，夫人，那么我只有请你宽宥我的冒失，我必须要告辞了，我向你保证，这样的事以后决不会再发生。"

然后我躬了躬身就走出了包厢。我刚关上包厢的门，里面就传来了第三次哄笑声。那时候我真希望能有人来给我一拳。

我回到了自己的座位上。开幕的钟声响起时，欧内斯特出现在我旁边的座位上。

"你都干了些什么啊！"他一边坐下来一边说着，"她们都觉得你疯了。"

"我走之后，玛格丽特说过什么吗？"

"她放声大笑，还说她从来都没见过像你这么滑稽的人。不过你千万不要以为你失去了一次难得机会，对这些女人用不着那么认真。她们根本不懂得风度和礼貌究竟是什么，这就和往狗身上洒香水一样，它们会觉得味道难闻，然后就跑到水沟里去打个滚去掉香气。"

"After all, what does it matter to me?" I said, affecting to speak in a nonchalant way. "I shall never see this woman again, and if I liked her before meeting her, it is quite different now that I know her."

"Bah! I don't despair of seeing you one day at the back of her box, and of hearing that you are ruining yourself for her. However, you are right, she hasn't been well brought up; but she would be a charming mistress to have."

Happily, the curtain rose and my friend was silent. I could not possibly tell you what they were acting. All that I remember is that from time to time I raised my eyes to the box I had quitted so abruptly, and that the faces of fresh visitors succeeded one another all the time.

I was far from having given up thinking about Marguerite. Another feeling had taken possession of me. It seemed to me that I had her insult and my absurdity to wipe out; I said to myself that if I spent every penny I had, I would win her and win my right to the place I had abandoned so quickly.

Before the performance was over Marguerite and her friend left their box. I rose from my seat.

"Are you going?" said Ernest.

"Yes."

"总之，这和我有什么关系？"我尽可能做出毫不介意的样子说，"我再也不想见这个女人了，倘若说在我认识她之前还对她抱有好感，可现在情况已经完全不同了。"

"得了吧！假如有一天我看见你和她一起坐在包厢里，或是听到你为她倾家荡产的消息也不会觉得奇怪的。可是，即便如此也不能怪你，她的确没有教养，不过却是一个值得弄到手的迷人的情妇啊！"

万幸的是启幕了，我的朋友恢复了沉默。如果要我告诉你那天上演的是什么剧目，那是不可能的。我唯一能记起来的，就是我总是抬起眼睛望向我方才匆匆走出的包厢，那儿一直有新的来访者进进出出。

然而，我根本就无法忘记玛格丽特，另外的情绪控制了我。我想自己不应该始终不忘她对我的侮辱与我自己的愚蠢可笑。我对自己说，哪怕花掉我所有的钱财，也要得到这个姑娘，把那个我方才一下子就放弃了的位置据为己有。

玛格丽特和她的朋友没有等到演出结束就走出了包厢。我不由自主地跟着离开了我的座位。

"你要走了？"欧内斯特问道。

"没错。"

"Why?"

At that moment he saw that the box was empty.

"Go, go," he said, "and good luck, or rather better luck."

I went out.

I heard the rustle of dresses, the sound of voices, on the staircase. I stood aside, and, without being seen, saw the two women pass me, accompanied by two young men. At the entrance to the theatre they were met by a footman.

"Tell the coachman to wait at the door of the Cafe' Anglais," said Marguerite. "We will walk there."

A few minutes afterward I saw Marguerite from the street at a window of one of the large rooms of the restaurant, pulling the camellias of her bouquet to pieces, one by one. One of the two men was leaning over her shoulder and whispering in her ear.

I took up my position at the Maison d'Or, in one of the first-floor rooms, and did not lose sight of the window for an instant. At one in the morning Marguerite got into her carriage with her three friends. I took a cab and followed them. The carriage stopped at No. 9, Rue d'Antin. Marguerite got out and went in alone. It was no doubt a mere chance, but the

"怎么了？"

与此同时，他看到那个包厢已经空了。

"去吧，去吧，"他说，"祝你好运，或者说愿你万事顺利。"

我走了出去。

我听到一阵窸窸窣窣的衣裙声与谈话声从楼梯上传来。我闪到一边不让人看见，发现是两个青年陪在两个女人身边走了过来。在剧场的门口有一个小厮迎上了她们。

"告诉车夫，让他去英国咖啡馆门口等着，"玛格丽特吩咐，"我们会走着到那儿去。"

几分钟之后，我看到玛格丽特靠在那个咖啡馆某间大包间的窗栏上，一片一片地揪她那束茶花的花瓣。两个青年中的一个低着头靠在她肩上，在她的耳边窃窃私语。

我在附近金屋咖啡馆二楼的楼厅找了个位置，坐下来目不转睛地盯着那个窗口。直到深夜1点钟，玛格丽特和那3个朋友一块儿上了她的四轮马车。我也叫了一辆轻便的马车跟在她们后面。她的车子在昂坦街9号的门前停了下来。玛格丽特走下马车，一个人进了屋子。毫无疑问，她独自回家只是一个偶

chance filled me with delight.

From that time forward, I often met Marguerite at the theatre or in the Champs-Élysées. Always there was the same gaiety in her, the same emotion in me.

At last a fortnight passed without my meeting her. I met Gaston and asked after her.

"Poor girl, she is very ill," he answered.

"What is the matter?"

"She is consumptive, and the sort of life she leads isn't exactly the thing to cure her. She has taken to her bed; she is dying."

The heart is a strange thing; I was almost glad at hearing it.

Every day I went to ask after her, without leaving my name or my card. I heard she was convalescent and had gone to Bagnères.

Time went by, the impression, if not the memory, faded gradually from my mind. I travelled; love affairs, habits, work, took the place of other thoughts, and when I recalled this adventure I looked upon it as one of those passions which one has when one is very young, and laughs at soon afterward.

For the rest, it was no credit to me to have got the better of this recollection, for I had completely lost sight of Marguerite,

然，可这偶然却令我感到非常幸福。

从那以后，我频繁地在剧院里或是香榭丽舍大街上见到玛格丽特，她总是那么快活，而我激动的心情也是始终如一。

后来，一连两个星期我都没有碰见她。于是在见到加斯顿时，我就问他关于玛格丽特的消息。

"那可怜的姑娘生了重病。"他回答道。

"是什么病呢？"

"她得了肺病，而且她过的那种生活对她身体的康复是毫无好处的，这会儿她正躺在床上就快死了。"

人心真是奇怪的东西，我听到她生病的消息几乎觉得很高兴。

我每天都去问候她的病况，不过我没有留下自己的名字，也没有给她我的名片。就这样，我得知她的病已经痊愈，然后又去了巴涅尔。

日子一天天过去，假如不能说我已经忘记了她，那就是给我留下的印象渐渐淡薄了。我出门旅游，与亲友往来，日常琐事和繁忙的工作占据了我的思维。就算我回想起那次邂逅，也不过认为它是一时的激情冲动，这样的情绪一个人年轻时总会有的，过后很快一笑了之。

话说回来，我可以忘却前情也

and, as I told you, when she passed me in the corridor of the Varietes, I did not recognise her. She was veiled, it is true; but, veiled though she might have been two years earlier, I should not have needed to see her in order to recognise her: I should have known her intuitively. All the same, my heart began to beat when I knew that it was she; and the two years that had passed since I saw her, and what had seemed to be the results of that separation, vanished in smoke at the mere touch of her dress.

说明不了什么的，因为我已经有很久的时间完全见不到玛格丽特了，所以，就像我方才和你说的那样，当她出现在杂耍剧院的走廊里，还走过了我的身边时，我都认不出她了。虽说当时她戴着面纱，可是如果在两年之前，就算不看她的脸，我也能一眼认出她来，我的直觉能告诉我是她。即便如此，当我得知她就是玛格丽特时，心又开始怦怦乱跳。因为两年未见而逐渐淡漠的对她的感情，一遇到她的衣裙，转瞬间便又再次燃烧起来了。

CHAPTER 8

第八章

However (continued Armand after a pause), while I knew myself to be still in love with her, I felt more sure of myself, and part of my desire to speak to Marguerite again was a wish to make her see that I was stronger than she.

How many ways does the heart take, how many reasons does it invent for itself, in order to arrive at what it wants!

I could not remain in the corridor, and I returned to my place in the stalls, looking hastily around to see what box she was in. She was in a ground-floor box, quite alone. She had changed, as I have told you, and no longer wore an indifferent smile on her lips. She had suffered; she was still suffering. Though it was April, she was still wearing a winter costume, all wrapped up in furs.

I gazed at her so fixedly that my eyes attracted hers. She looked at me for a few seconds, put up her opera-glass to see me better, and seemed to think she recognised me, without being quite sure who I was, for

然而，（阿尔芒停顿了一下又接着说）一方面我清楚自己依然爱着玛格丽特，一方面又认为我较之以前变得更坚强了，我盼望着能与玛格丽特再会，还要让她看看如今我比她优越得多。

为了达成心中的这个愿望，我该耗费多少心力，想出多少理由啊！

于是，我再也无法在走廊里待下去了，就返回正厅坐下，往大厅里很快地瞄了一眼，想找出她所在的那个包厢。她坐在底层台前的包厢里，只有一个人。刚才我也和你说过，她变了不少，嘴上那种满不在乎的微笑消失了。她大病了一场，而且现在还没有完全康复。虽然已经 4 月份了，她还穿着冬天里的衣服，全身都裹在天鹅绒里面。

我目不转睛地盯着她看，终于引来了她的目光。她打量了我一会儿，接着又举起望远镜想瞧得更仔细些，她肯定感觉有点面熟，可是一下子又记不起我是谁。我的依据

when she put down her glasses, a smile, that charming, feminine salutation, flitted across her lips, as if to answer the bow which she seemed to expect; but I did not respond, so as to have an advantage over her, as if I had forgotten, while she remembered. Supposing herself mistaken,, she looked away.

The curtain went up. I have often seen Marguerite at the theatre. I never saw her pay the slightest attention to what was being acted. As for me, the performance interested me equally little, and I paid no attention to anything but her, though doing my utmost to keep her from noticing it.

Presently I saw her glancing across at the person who was in the opposite box; on looking, I saw a woman with whom I was quite familiar. She had once been a kept woman, and had tried to go on the stage, had failed, and, relying on her acquaintance with fashionable people in Paris, had gone into business and taken a milliner's shop. I saw in her a means of meeting with Marguerite, and profited by a moment in which she looked my way to wave my hand to her. As I expected, she beckoned to me to come to her box.

Prudence Duvernoy (that was the milliner's auspicious name) was one of those fat women of forty with whom one

是当她放下望远镜以后，嘴角处露出了一丝微笑，那是女人用来致意的笑容，十分妩媚，显然她正准备对我即将向她表示的敬意做出回应。然而我却毫无如此做的意思，似乎有意想显得比她更高贵，做出一副她已经想起了我，我却忘掉了她的样子。她想自己认错了人，就移开了视线。

舞台的幕拉开了。剧中我朝玛格丽特那里望了好几次，但哪一次未见她在认真地看演出。就我而言，对剧目同样也是心不在焉的，始终忙着关心她，却又尽量不让她觉察出来。

我见到她在与对面包厢里的人交换眼色，就往那边望去，发现那里面坐着的是一个我非常熟悉的女人。她以前也做过妓女，还有过进戏班子的打算，可是没有成功。后来她倚仗自己与巴黎那些时髦女子的关系，开始做生意，经营一家妇女时装店铺。从她身上我看到了一个与玛格丽特见面的方法，就趁她朝我这边看过来的时候，用手势跟眼神和她打招呼。正如我所预料的那样，她示意我到她的包厢里去。

那位妇女时装店店主的芳名叫普鲁登斯·迪韦尔诺瓦，40岁上下，身材发福，想从她们这种女人那里

requires very little diplomacy to make them understand what one wants to know, especially when what one wants to know is as simple as what I had to ask of her.

I took advantage of a moment when she was smiling across at Marguerite to ask her, "Whom are you looking at?"

"Marguerite Gautier."

"You know her?"

"Yes, I am her milliner, and she is a neighbour of mine."

"Do you live in the Rue d'Antin?"

"No. 7. The window of her dressing-room looks on to the window of mine."

"They say she is a charming girl."

"Don't you know her?"

"No, but I should like to."

"Shall I ask her to come over to our box?"

"No, I would rather for you to introduce me to her."

"At her own house?"

"Yes.

"That is more difficult."

"Why?"

"Because she is under the protection of a jealous old duke."

"'Protection' is charming."

"Yes, protection," replied Prudence. "Poor old man, he would be greatly

打听出什么消息是用不着多费力气的，况且我准备向她打听的事情又特别平常。

我找到一个她再次朝玛格丽特微笑致意的机会问她说："你看的人是谁啊？"

"她叫玛格丽特·戈蒂埃。"

"你和她相识？"

"是的，她会来光顾我的铺子，而且我们还是邻居。"

"你也是住在昂坦街的吗？"

"我住7号，我们两个人梳妆间的窗子正好对着。"

"人们都说她是一个非常迷人的姑娘。"

"你难道不认识她吗？"

"我不认识她，不过我很乐意认识她。"

"那我叫她来我们包厢里？"

"还是不了，我更希望你能把我介绍给她。"

"去她的家里吗？"

"没错。"

"这就困难多啦。"

"为什么呢？"

"因为她正处在一个嫉妒心很重的老公爵的监护之下。"

"监护，这个词真是太妙了！"

"没错，是监护，"普鲁登斯重复道，"那老头儿也真可怜，要是他

embarrassed to offer her anything else."

Prudence then told me how Marguerite had made the acquaintance of the duke at Bagneres.

"That, then," I continued, "is why she is alone here?"

"Precisely."

"But who will see her home?"

"He will."

"He will come for her?"

"In a moment."

"And you, who is seeing you home?"

"No one."

"May I offer myself?"

"But you are with a friend, are you not?"

"May we offer, then?"

"Who is your friend?"

"A charming fellow, very amusing. He will be delighted to make your acquaintance."

"Well, all right; we will go after this piece is over, for I know the last piece."

"With pleasure; I will go and tell my friend."

"Go, then. Ah," added Prudence, as I was going, "there is the duke just coming into Marguerite's box."

I looked at him. A man of about seventy had sat down behind her, and was giving her a bag of sweets, into which she dipped at once, smiling. Then she held it out

还能给她别的什么东西简直就是羞耻了。"

接着普鲁登斯就和我说了玛格丽特在巴涅尔结识公爵的过程。

"那么,"我又说,"她会一个人来这儿,也是这个原因吗?"

"非常准确。"

"可是谁来接她回家呢?"

"他会接的。"

"那么他会来找她啰?"

"马上他就会来的。"

"那么你呢,谁来送你回家?"

"没人和我一起。"

"我能推荐自己吗?"

"但你是和朋友一起来的吧。"

"那么能让我们两个一块儿陪你回去吗?"

"你的朋友是个怎样的人?"

"一个非常迷人的小伙子,为人风趣,他一定会很高兴认识你的。"

"好吧,那就这样吧,等这幕戏结束之后我们 3 个一起走,最后一幕我以前看过了。"

"非常荣幸。我去叫朋友来。"

"那你去吧。啊!"我正准备出去时普鲁登斯又说道,"那个公爵刚刚走进玛格丽特的包厢里。"

我朝他看过去。一个大约 70 岁的老头儿坐在了她的身后,把一袋蜜饯递给她,她马上笑眯眯地从纸

toward Prudence, with a gesture which seemed to say, "Will you have some?"

"No," signalled Prudence.

Marguerite drew back the bag, and, turning, began to talk with the duke.

It may sound childish to tell you all these details, but everything relating to Marguerite is so fresh in my memory that I can not help recalling them now.

I went back to Gaston and told him of the arrangement I had made for him and for me. He agreed, and we left our stalls to go round to Mme. Duvernoy's box. We had scarcely opened the door leading into the stalls when we had to stand aside to allow Marguerite and the duke to pass. I would have given ten years of my life to have been in the old man's place.

When they were on the street he handed her into a phaeton, which he drove himself, and they were whirled away by two superb horses.

We returned to Prudence's box, and when the play was over we took a cab and drove to 7, Rue d'Antin. At the door, Prudence asked us to come up and see her showrooms, which we had never seen, and of which she seemed very proud. You can imagine how eagerly I accepted. It seemed to me as if I was coming nearer and nearer to Marguerite. I soon turned the

袋里掏蜜饯吃，接着又把袋子递到包厢的前头，朝普鲁登斯扬了扬，好像是在问："你要吃一点儿吗？"

"不了。"普鲁登斯比画着说。

玛格丽特收回那袋蜜饯，转回身去开始和公爵说话。

把这些琐事都讲给你听似乎有点幼稚了，可是和玛格丽特有关的每件事情都记得十分清楚，所以还是不由自主地一一回忆起来了。

我回到加斯顿那里告诉他我方才为我们两人作出的安排。他也同意了。我们就动身想去楼上迪韦尔诺瓦夫人的包厢。我们才打开正厅的门就不得不停下，让玛格丽特跟公爵走出去。如果能和那个老头儿换个位置，我宁愿少活 10 年。

他们来到街上后，公爵扶玛格丽特登上一辆四轮的敞篷马车，自己赶着车，驾着两匹骏马远去了。

我们回到普鲁登斯的包厢，等演出结束就下楼离开，叫了一辆普通的出租马车，一同来到昂坦街 7 号。到普鲁登斯家门口以后，她请我们到楼上参观一下那些她引以为傲的商品，说是我们不曾见过的。你一定能想到我接受她邀请时的心情是多么急切。我仿佛看到自己正一步步地接近玛格丽特，没过多久，

conversation in her direction.

"The old duke is at your neighbours," I said to Prudence.

"Oh, no; she is probably alone."

"But she must be dreadfully bored," said Gaston.

"We spend most of our evenings together, or she calls to me when she comes in. She never goes to bed before two in the morning. She can't sleep before that."

"Why?"

"Because she suffers in the chest, and is almost always feverish."

"Hasn't she any lovers?" I asked.

"I never see any one remain after I leave; I don't say no one ever comes when I am gone. Often in the evening I meet there a certain Comte de N., who thinks he is making some headway by calling on her at eleven in the evening, and by sending her jewels to any extent; but she can't stand him. She makes a mistake; he is very rich. It is in vain that I say to her from time to time, 'My dear child, there's the man for you.' She, who generally listens to me, turns her back and replies that he is too stupid. Stupid, indeed, he is; but it would be a position for her, while this old duke might die any day. Old men are egoists; his family are always reproaching him for his

我便把话题引到了她的身上。

"那个老公爵现在你邻居的家里吗?"我问普鲁登斯道。

"啊,不会,她可能一人在家。"

"那她肯定会觉得十分寂寞。"加斯顿说道。

"我们晚上经常在一块儿消磨时间,或者等她从外面回来之后再叫我过去。她半夜 2 点之前是不会睡觉的,早于那个时间她睡不着。"

"为什么呢?"

"因为她得了肺病,几乎总是在发烧。"

"她难道没有情人吗?"我说。

"每次我从她家出来时,从没见过有人留下来,不过我不能保证我走后没有人返回去。晚上我在她家里经常碰见一位 N 伯爵,这位伯爵自以为只要经常在晚上 11 点去拜访她,不管她要多少首饰都买给她,就能逐渐地博得她的欢心。可是她一见他就觉得讨厌。她是错的,那可是个阔少爷。我总是和她说:'亲爱的孩子,你正需要这样的男人!'可是无济于事。她平时都很听我的话,但一听我说这个就把脸转过去,回答说他实在太蠢了。说他蠢,这是实话,不过对她来说,总能算是个着落吧,那位老公爵说不定哪一天就一命归西了。老公爵什

affection for Marguerite; there are two reasons why he is likely to leave her nothing. I give her good advice, and she only says it will be plenty of time to take on the count when the duke is dead.

"It isn't all fun," continued Prudence, "to live like that. I know very well it wouldn't suit me, and I should soon send the old man about his business. He is so dull; he calls her his daughter; looks after her like a child; and is always in the way. I am sure at this very moment one of his servants is prowling about in the street to see who comes out, and especially who goes in."

"Ah, poor Marguerite!" said Gaston, sitting down to the piano and playing a waltz. "I hadn't a notion of it, but I did notice she hasn't been looking so gay lately."

"Hush," said Prudence, listening. Gaston stopped.

"She is calling me, I think."

We listened. A voice was calling, "Prudence!"

"Come, now, you must go," said Mme. Duvernoy.

"Ah, that is your idea of hospitality," said Gaston, laughing; "we won't go till we please."

"Why should we go?"

么都不会留给她的，一方面是因为老头子个个都是自私的，一方面他家里人对他钟爱玛格丽特一直持反对态度。我跟她讲道理，希望能说服她，她老是回答说，公爵死了以后再和伯爵好也完全来得及。

"这并不总是很有趣的，"普鲁登斯接着说，"我是说像她这么过日子，我也清楚这一点。换了我就受不了，很快我就会把这个老家伙赶跑的。那个老头儿真是让人腻烦死了，他用女儿来称呼玛格丽特，像照顾孩子一样照顾她，老是监视着她，我敢肯定现在就有他的一个仆人在街上来回走，盯着有谁从她房子里出来，尤其要看着有谁走进了她的屋里。"

"哦，玛格丽特真是可怜！"加斯顿说，他坐在钢琴前开始弹一首圆舞曲，"这些事我都不了解，不过我也发现这一阵她不像过去那么快乐了。"

"嘘！"普鲁登斯说着竖起耳朵。加斯顿也停止了弹奏。

"我想是她在叫我。"

我们一起静静听着。果然，有一个声音在喊着"普鲁登斯！"

"来吧，先生们，现在你们得走啦。"迪韦尔诺瓦夫人说道。

"噢！你就是这么招待客人的吗？"加斯顿笑着说，"在我们满意

"I am going over to Marguerite's."

"We will wait here."

"You can't."

"Then we will go with you."

"That still less."

"I know Marguerite," said Gaston; "I can very well pay her a call."

"But Armand doesn't know her."

"I will introduce him."

"Impossible."

We again heard Marguerite's voice calling to Prudence, who rushed to her dressing-room window. I followed with Gaston as she opened the window. We hid ourselves so as not to be seen from outside.

"I have been calling you for ten minutes," said Marguerite from her window, in almost an imperious tone of voice.

"What do you want?"

"I want you to come over at once."

"Why?"

"Because the Comte de N. is still here, and he is boring me to death."

"I can't now."

"What is hindering you?"

"There are two young fellows here who won't go."

"Tell them that you must go out."

"I have told them."

"Well, then, leave them in the house.

之前是不会走的。"

"为什么我们必须走呢？"

"我要去玛格丽特家里啦。"

"那我们可以在这儿等。"

"不行的。"

"那么我们和你一块儿去。"

"那样更不行。"

"我和玛格丽特认识，"加斯顿说，"我去拜访她一下是很自然的。"

"可是阿尔芒跟她不认识呀！"

"我会为他介绍的。"

"这不可能。"

我们又听见了玛格丽特叫普鲁登斯的声音。普鲁登斯跑到梳妆间里，我和加斯顿随后跟了进去。她推开窗户，我们两人藏起身形，以免让外面的人瞧见。

"我都叫了你 10 分钟了。"玛格丽特用几乎生硬的口吻靠在她的窗边说。

"你有什么事吗？"

"我希望你马上过来。"

"怎么了？"

"因为 N 伯爵这会儿还在，我真的快被他烦死了。"

"我没办法马上过去。"

"是谁不让你来啦？"

"我这儿有两个年轻人，他们不愿离开。"

"告诉他们你非出门不可。"

"我已经说过了。"

They will soon go when they see you have gone."

"They will turn everything upside down."

"But what do they want?"

"They want to see you."

"What are they called?"

"You know one, M. Gaston R."

"Ah, yes, I know him. And the other?"

"M. Armand Duval; and you don't know him."

"No, but bring them along. Anything is better than the count. I expect you. Come at once."

Marguerite closed her window and Prudence hers. Marguerite, who had remembered my face for a moment, did not remember my name. I would rather have been remembered to my disadvantage than thus forgotten.

"I knew," said Gaston, "that she would be delighted to see us."

"Delighted isn't the word," replied Prudence, as she put on her hat and shawl. "She will see you in order to get rid of the count. Try to be more agreeable than he is, or (I know Marguerite) she will put it all down to me."

We followed Prudence downstairs. I trembled; it seemed to me that this visit was to have a great influence on my life. I

"好吧，那就让他们在你家里等着好啦，他们见你出了门，马上就会走了。"

"他们会把我家全翻一遍的！"

"他们究竟想干什么？"

"他们想要见你。"

"他们都是谁啊？"

"你认识其中一个，R·加斯顿先生。"

"啊！没错，我是认识他，另外一个呢？"

"是阿尔芒·迪瓦尔先生。而你没见过他的。"

"的确不认识。但让他们一起来吧，什么人都比伯爵好些。我等着你，马上过来吧。"

两位女士都关上了窗户。玛格丽特方才曾一度忆起了我的样子，可这会儿又忘记了我的名字。我宁愿她还记着我，即便印象不好也无所谓，但不希望她就这样把我忘了。

"我就知道，"加斯顿说，"她会很乐意见到我们的。"

"乐意这个词用得不准。"普鲁登斯披上披肩，戴好帽子，重复着说，"她接待你们是为了让伯爵走，你们可要尽力表现得比伯爵知趣一些，要不然，我了解玛格丽特这个人，她一定会都怪在我身上的。"

我们随着普鲁登斯走下了楼。我浑身战栗，仿佛预见了这次访问

was still more agitated than on the evening when I was introduced in the box at the Opera Comique. As we reached the door that you know, my heart beat so violently that I was hardly able to think.

We heard the sound of a piano. Prudence rang. The piano was silent. A woman who looked more like a companion than a servant opened the door. We went into the drawing-room, and from that to the boudoir, which was then just as you have seen it since. A young man was leaning against the mantel-piece. Marguerite, seated at the piano, let her fingers wander over the notes, beginning scraps of music without finishing them. The whole scene breathed boredom, the man embarrassed by the consciousness of his nullity, the woman tired of her dismal visitor. At the voice of Prudence, Marguerite rose, and coming toward us with a look of gratitude to Mme. Duvernoy, said:

"Come in, and welcome."

将对我的人生产生巨大的影响。我激动极了，比上次在喜剧歌剧院包厢里被介绍给玛格丽特时更加激动。当我们来到你已认得的那座房子门口的时候，我的心怦怦乱跳，几乎已经丧失思考的能力了。

我们听到了钢琴的声音。普鲁登斯拉响了门铃，琴声随之消失了。一个女人过来开门，她看上去更像一个雇来的女伴而不是用人。我们走过大客厅，来到小客厅，你已经看见过那间小客厅了。一个年轻人靠在壁炉旁边。玛格丽特坐在钢琴前，手指在琴键上漫不经心地跳跃着，反复地弹奏她弹不下去的曲子。房间里的气氛非常沉闷，男士因为自己一筹莫展而手足无措，女士因为自己厌烦的家伙的来访而心浮气躁。一听见普鲁登斯的声音，玛格丽特立即起身向我们迎了过来，她投给普鲁登斯一个感激的眼神，说道：

"快请进来，欢迎光临。"

CHAPTER 9

第九章

"Good-evening, my dear Gaston," said Marguerite to my companion. "I am very glad to see you. Why didn't you come to see me in my box at the Varietes?"

"I was afraid it would be indiscreet."

"Friends," and Marguerite lingered over the word, as if to intimate to those who were present that in spite of the familiar way in which she greeted him, Gaston was not and never had been anything more than a friend, "friends are always welcome."

"Then, will you permit me to introduce M. Armand Duval?"

"I had already authorized Prudence to do so."

"As far as that goes, madame," I said, bowing, and succeeding in getting more or less intelligible sounds out of my throat, "I have already had the honour of being introduced to you."

Marguerite's beautiful eyes seemed to be looking back in memory, but she could not, or seemed not to, remember.

"Madame," I continued, "I am grateful

"晚上好，我亲爱的加斯顿，"玛格丽特对我的伙伴说道，"非常高兴见到你。那时在杂耍剧院，你怎么没有到我的包厢去呢？"

"我怕那样会显得冒昧。"

"作为朋友，"——玛格丽特特别咬重了"朋友"这个词，就像她要让在场的人知道，虽然她非常亲热地接待了加斯顿，可是无论过去还是现在他都只不过是个朋友罢了，"朋友永远都是受欢迎的。"

"那么，你是否允许我向你引见阿尔芒·迪瓦尔先生？"

"这件事我已经答应过普鲁登斯了。"

"尽管如此，夫人，"我鞠了一躬，喉咙终于能发出几个勉强听得清的音节，"经人引见，我早已有幸被介绍给你了。"

从玛格丽特美丽的眼睛中看得出她正在记忆中搜索，可是却一无所获，或者说，看上去似乎是这样的。

to you for having forgotten the occasion of my first introduction, for I was very absurd and must have seemed to you very tiresome. It was at the Opera Comique, two years ago; I was with Ernest de – ."

"Ah, I remember," said Marguerite, with a smile. "It was not you who were absurd; it was I who was mischievous, as I still am, but somewhat less. You have forgiven me?"

And she held out her hand, which I kissed.

"It is true," she went on; "you know I have the bad habit of trying to embarrass people the first time I meet them. It is very stupid. My doctor says it is because I am nervous and always ill; believe my doctor."

"But you seem quite well."

"Oh! I have been very ill."

"I know."

"Who told you?"

"Every one knew it; I often came to inquire after you, and I was happy to hear of your convalescence."

"They never gave me your card."

"I did not leave it."

"Was it you, then, who called every day while I was ill, and would never leave your name?"

"Yes, it was I."

"Then you are more than indulgent, you

"夫人，"我继续说道，"我很感激你已然忘记了我第一次被介绍给你时的情景，因为当时我非常愚蠢可笑，一定让你厌烦了。那是两年之前，在喜剧歌剧院，我与欧内斯特·德在一起……"

"啊！我想起来了！"玛格丽特噙着微笑说道，"那时你并非愚蠢可笑，而是我爱恶作剧，虽然现在也是一样，不过比起过去还是要好一些了。你是否原谅我了呢？"

她说着把手递了过来，我吻了一下。

"这是真的，"她接着说，"你知道我有这样的坏脾气，喜欢在第一次见面时给人难堪，这是非常愚蠢的做法。我的医生说那是由于我有点神经质，而且身体一直不太好的缘故，请你相信他说的话吧。"

"可是现在你看上去很健康。"

"啊！我刚刚才大病过一场。"

"我知道的。"

"是谁告诉你的？"

"每个人都知道你生病的消息，我也常来打听。听到你康复了我感到非常高兴。"

"可是他们没给我你的名片。"

"是我没有留下名片。"

"听说在我生病期间，有位年轻人每天都来拜访，可始终未曾留下姓名，难道那个人就是你吗？"

are generous. You, count, wouldn't have done that," said she, turning toward M. de N., after giving me one of those looks in which women sum up their opinion of a man.

"I have only known you for two months," replied the count.

"And this gentleman only for five minutes. You always say something ridiculous."

Women are pitiless toward those whom they do not care for. The count reddened and bit his lips.

I was sorry for him, for he seemed, like myself, to be in love, and the bitter frankness of Marguerite must have made him very unhappy, especially in the presence of two strangers.

"You were playing the piano when we came in," I said, in order to change the conversation. "Won't you be so good as to treat me as an old acquaintance and go on?"

"Oh," said she, flinging herself on the sofa and motioning us to sit down, "Gaston knows what my music is like. It is all very well when I am alone with the count, but I won't inflict such a punishment on you."

"You show me that preference?" said M. de N., with a smile which he tried to render

"是的，是我。"

"如此说来，你不仅为人宽厚，而且心地善良。"她看了我一眼。女人们认为仅仅靠语言难以评价一个男人的时候，往往会用这种眼光作补充。然后她转身对 N 伯爵说："伯爵，如果是你就不会做这些了吧。"

"可我不过两个月前才刚刚认识你呀。"伯爵分辩道。

"而这位先生认识我才刚刚 5 分钟。你总是讲那些蠢话。"

女人们对自己不在乎的人都是不留情面的。伯爵的脸红了，咬着嘴唇。

我为他感到难过，因为他看上去似乎像我一样坠入了爱河，可是玛格丽特坦率得近乎生硬的态度一定令他很难堪，特别是还有两个陌生人在场呢。

"我们进屋时你正在弹钢琴吧，"我想换一个话题，于是开口道，"你能否把我当做一个老朋友，再接着弹下去呢？"

"啊！"她做了个手势让我们坐下，自己倒在长沙发上道，"加斯顿知道我弹琴的水平。倘若只有我和伯爵两个人，弹弹倒还可以，我可不想让你们两位也遭受这种折磨。"

"你竟然对我如此偏爱？" N 伯爵说着，自嘲地笑了笑。

delicately ironical.

"Don't reproach me for it. It is the only one." It was fated that the poor man was not to say a single word. He cast a really supplicating glance at Marguerite.

"Well, Prudence," she went on, "have you done what I asked you to do?"

"Yes.

"All right. You will tell me about it later. We must talk over it; don't go before I can speak with you."

"We are doubtless intruders," I said, "and now that we, or rather I, have had a second introduction, to blot out the first, it is time for Gaston and me to be going."

"Not in the least. I didn't mean that for you. I want you to stay."

The count took a very elegant watch out of his pocket and looked at the time. "I must be going to my club," he said. Marguerite did not answer. The count thereupon left his position by the fireplace and going up to her, said: "Adieu, madame."

Marguerite rose. "Adieu, my dear count. Are you going already?"

"Yes, I fear I am boring you."

"You are not boring me today more than any other day. When shall I be seeing you?"

"When you permit me."

"不要因为这个就责怪我啊，我指的只是这一件事而已。"这个可怜的青年只有保持沉默一条路可走了，他看向玛格丽特的目光简直带有哀求的意味了。

"那么，普鲁登斯，"她又说道，"我拜托你的事是否已经办好了？"

"已经办好了。"

"好极了。过一会儿你再和我说吧。我们必须要谈谈那件事，在我们谈话之前，你可别先走了。"

"我们这些不速之客显然来得不是时候，"我说，"如今我们，更确切点说是我，已经第二次介绍过自己，这样就能忘掉第一次的情形了。加斯顿和我也该告辞了。"

"完全不是这样。我不是说给你们听的，我希望你们能留下。"

伯爵从口袋里掏出一块极其漂亮雅致的表，看了一眼时间。"我要去俱乐部了。"他说。玛格丽特没有说话。于是伯爵从壁炉旁起身，来到她面前说道："再会，夫人。"

玛格丽特站起身来。"再会，我亲爱的伯爵，你就准备走了吗？"

"不错，我怕自己已经令你厌烦了。"

"今天你没有比以前更令我厌烦。什么时候我才能再见到你呢？"

"你允许的时候。"

"Good-bye, then."

It was cruel, you will admit. Fortunately, the count had excellent manners and was very good-tempered. He merely kissed Marguerite's hand, which she held out to him carelessly enough, and, bowing to us, went out.

As he crossed the threshold, he cast a glance at Prudence. She shrugged her shoulders, as much as to say:

"What do you expect? I have done all I could."

"Nanine!" cried Marguerite. "Light M. le Comte to the door."

We heard the door open and shut.

"At last," cried Marguerite, coming back, "he has gone! That man gets frightfully on my nerves!"

"My dear child," said Prudence, "you really treat him too badly, and he is so good and kind to you. Look at this watch on the mantelpiece, that he gave you: it must have cost him at least three thousand francs, I am sure."

And Mme. Duvernoy began to turn it over, as it lay on the mantelpiece, looking at it with covetous eyes.

"My dear," said Marguerite, sitting down to the piano, "when I put on one side what he gives me and on the other what he says to me, it seems to me that he buys his

"那么，再见吧！"

你必须承认，她的态度是残忍的。好在伯爵有着极佳的风度，脾气也很好。他只是吻了吻玛格丽特的手，那只是她漫不经心地递过去的，接着向我们躬了躬身就出去了。

当他正要跨出房门的时候，朝普鲁登斯望了一眼。后者耸了耸肩，那副神情就像在说：

"你还要怎么样呢，能做的事情我都已经做了。"

"纳尼娜！"玛格丽特高声喊着，"帮伯爵照个亮，送他出门。"

我们听到门打开和关上的声音。

"他终于走了！"玛格丽特走回来，大声说，"这人真是让我难受。"

"我亲爱的孩子，"普鲁登斯说，"你对他真是太过分了，他对你那么好，温柔体贴。你看壁炉架上的这块表还是他送给你的，我敢肯定这至少花了他3000法郎呢。"

于是迪韦尔诺瓦夫人走了过去，拿起壁炉架上的那块表把玩着，眼中流露出贪婪的光芒。

"亲爱的，"玛格丽特说着，来到钢琴前坐下，"如果把他送我的东西放在天平的这边，再把他和我说的话放在那边来衡量的话，我感觉

visits very cheap."

"The poor fellow is in love with you."

"If I had to listen to everybody who was in love with me, I shouldn't have time for my dinner."

And she began to run her fingers over the piano, and then, turning to us, she said:

"What will you take? I think I should like a little punch."

"And I could eat a little chicken," said Prudence. "Suppose we have supper?"

"That's it, let's go and have supper," said Gaston.

"No, we will have supper here."

She rang, and Nanine appeared.

"Send for some supper."

"What must I get?"

"Whatever you like, but at once, at once."

Nanine went out.

"That's it," said Marguerite, jumping like a child, "we'll have supper. How tiresome that idiot of a count is!"

The more I saw her, the more she enchanted me. She was exquisitely beautiful. Her slenderness was a charm. I was lost in contemplation.

What was passing in my mind I should have some difficulty in explaining. I was full of indulgence for her life, full of

容忍他的来访还是太便宜他了。"

"那个可怜的人爱你。"

"如果谁爱我我就要听他说话，那我连吃饭的时间都不会有。"

她的手指在琴键上随意跳跃着，弹了一会儿后，她转身面向我们，说道："你们有什么想吃的吗？我想我需要喝一点儿潘趣酒[1]。"

"我想吃一点儿鸡肉，"普鲁登斯说，"我们去吃夜宵怎么样？"

"就是这个。我们去吃夜宵吧。"加斯顿说。

"不，我们要在这里吃饭。"

她拉了拉铃，纳尼娜出现了。

"吩咐下去，准备一些夜宵。"

"你们想吃点什么呢？"

"你随便拿点来吧，不过要快，立刻就要。"

纳尼娜转身出了门。

"好啦，"玛格丽特跳着说，就像一个孩子，"我们这就吃夜宵。那个笨蛋伯爵多让人讨厌啊！"

我注视这个女人的时间越长，就越发为她着迷。她真是美得令人心醉。甚至连她的瘦削也散发出一种魅力。我不禁失了神。

我脑子里究竟在想些什么，连自己也搞不明白。我对她的生活充满着同情，为她的美貌倾倒不已。

---

[1] 潘趣酒，一种酒精度较低的饮料酒。

admiration for her beauty. The proof of disinterestedness that she gave in not accepting a rich and fashionable young man, ready to waste all his money upon her, excused her in my eyes for all her faults in the past.

There was a kind of candour in this woman. You could see she was still in the virginity of vice. Her firm walk, her supple figure, her rosy, open nostrils, her large eyes, slightly tinged with blue, indicated one of those ardent natures which sbed around them a sort of voluptuous perfume, like Eastern vials, which, close them as tightly as you will, still let some of their perfume escape. Finally, whether it was simple nature or a breath of fever, there passed from time to time in the eyes of this woman a glimmer of desire, giving promise of a very heaven for one whom she should love. But those who had loved Marguerite were not to be counted, nor those whom she had loved.

In this girl there was at once the virgin whom a mere nothing had turned into a courtesan, and the courtesan whom a mere nothing would have turned into the most loving and the purest of virgins. Marguerite had still pride and independence, two sentiments which, if they are wounded, can be the equivalent of a sense of shame. I did

她不愿接受一个英俊富有，可以为她倾家荡产的青年，在我眼中，这种不为功利所动的态度足以令我原谅她以往的所有过失。

这个女人身上有某种坦率而纯粹的东西。你可以看到，她的生活虽然放荡，但内心还保持着纯洁。她那稳重的举止，婀娜的体态，微张着的玫瑰色的鼻翼，大大的眼睛周围一圈淡淡的蓝色晕迹都在诉说着她那种热情的天性。在这样的人身边总是散发着一股性感诱人的香气，就像来自东方的香水瓶一样，无论盖子关得多严，里面的香味儿依然会泄漏出来。最后，不知是因为她的气质，还是她疾病的一种症状，她的眼中不时会划过一道希冀的光辉，这似乎等于一种天启，是她已倾心于你的暗示。然而，那些爱过玛格丽特的人多如过江之鲫，不计其数，而他们之中却没有一个人能赢得她的芳心呢。

这个姑娘的内在似乎还是一个纯洁的处子，只是失足堕落成为娼妓；又仿佛是一个妓女，只是很容易变成最为纯真多情的贞节女子。在玛格丽特身上还保留着一份骄傲和独立性，当这两种感情受到伤害后，就会转化成某种与廉耻心相类

not speak a word; my soul seemed to have passed into my heart and my heart into my eyes.

"So," said she all at once, "it was you who came to inquire after me when I was ill?"

"Yes."

"Do you know, it was quite splendid of you! How can I thank you for it?"

"By allowing me to come and see you from time to time."

"As often as you like, from five to six, and from eleven to twelve. Now, Gaston, play the Invitation *A la Valse*."

"Why?"

"To please me, first of all, and then because I never can manage to play it myself."

"What part do you find difficult?"

"The third part, the part in sharps."

Gaston rose and went to the piano, and began to play the wonderful melody of Weber, the music of which stood open before him.

Marguerite, resting one hand on the piano, followed every note on the music, accompanying it in a low voice, and when Gaston had come to the passage which she had mentioned to him, she sang out, running her fingers along the top of the

似的感情。我一个字也没说,我的灵魂似乎驻进了我的心坎,我的心灵似乎进入了我的眼睛。

"如此说来,"她突然开口道,"那个在我生病期间经常来访,询问我病况的人就是你喽?"

"是我。"

"你知道吗,你真是太善良了,我该怎么感谢你才好呢?"

"只要你能允许我经常来探望就好了。"

"你想来多少次都可以,5点到6点,11点到12点都行。好了,加斯顿,请弹那首《邀舞》[1]吧。"

"怎么想起它来了?"

"首先,是为了让我高兴;其次,是因为我自己从来都弹不好这首曲子。"

"你觉得哪一段比较难弹?"

"第三部分有高半音的地方。"

加斯顿站起来坐到钢琴前,弹起了这首韦伯创作的动人旋律,乐谱立在他面前的谱架上。

玛格丽特一边一手放在琴上,随着琴谱中的每一个音符移动着,一边低声吟唱。当加斯顿弹到她提及的那一节时,她唱出了声来,手指也在钢琴盖上有节奏地敲打着:

1　《邀舞》,又称《华丽回旋曲》,德国作曲家卡尔·马力亚·冯·韦伯作于1819年。

piano:

"Do, re, mi, do, re, fa, mi, re; that is what I can not do. Over again."

Gaston began over again, after which Marguerite said:

"Now, let me try."

She took her place and began to play; but her rebellious fingers always came to grief over one of the notes.

"Isn't it incredible," she said, exactly like a child, "that I can not succeed in playing that passage? Would you believe that I sometimes spend two hours of the morning over it? And when I think that that idiot of a count plays it without his music, and beautifully, I really believe it is that that makes me so furious with him." And she began again, always with the same result.

"The devil take Weber, music, and pianos!" she cried, throwing the music to the other end of the room. "How can I play eight sharps one after another?" She folded her arms and looked at us, stamping her foot. The blood flew to her cheeks, and her lips half opened in a slight cough.

"Come, come," said Prudence, who had taken off her hat and was smoothing her hair before the glass, "you will work yourself into a rage and do yourself harm. Better come and have supper; for my part,

"Do, re, mi, do, re, fa, mi, re, 就是这里我总也弹不好, 你再重弹一遍。"

于是加斯顿又开始重弹, 弹完之后, 玛格丽特开口说:

"现在我来试一试吧。"

她坐到位子上开始弹奏, 可是当她那不怎么听话的手指在弹那几个音符时, 又弹错了一个。

"真令人难以置信," 她用几乎是孩子气的口吻说着, "难道我就弹不好这一段了吗! 你们能相信吗, 我早上经常就这样反复练习, 一直弹2个多钟头! 每次我一想起那个蠢伯爵居然不用乐谱就可以弹得那么好, 简直就恨透他了, 我真的认为我就是因为这一点才那么恨他的。" 随后她又开始弹, 可结果还是一样的。

"什么韦伯、音乐还有钢琴, 通通见鬼去吧!" 她说着, 把乐谱远远扔到房间的那一头, "我为什么就弹不了8个连续的高半音呢?" 她抱着胳膊望着我们, 跺着脚说着, 脸颊泛起嫣红, 一阵轻微的咳嗽让她的嘴微微地张开了。

"看哪, 看哪," 普鲁登斯摘下了帽子, 在镜子前一边梳理两鬓的头发一边说, "你又生气了, 又会让你感觉不舒服, 我们还是出去吃夜

I am dying of hunger."

Marguerite rang the bell, sat down to the piano again, and began to hum over a very bawdy song, which she accompanied without difficulty. Gaston knew the song, and they gave a sort of duet.

"Don't sing those beastly things," I said to Marguerite, imploringly.

"Oh, how proper you are!" she said, smiling and giving me her hand. "It is not for myself, but for you."

Marguerite made a gesture as if to say, "Oh, it is long since that I have done with propriety!"

At that moment Nanine appeared.

"Is supper ready?" asked Marguerite.

"Yes, madame, in one moment."

"Apropos," said Prudence to me, "you have not looked round; come, and I will show you."

As you know, the drawing-room was a marvel.

Marguerite went with us for a moment; then she called Gaston and went into the dining-room with him to see if supper was ready.

"Ah," said Prudence, catching sight of a little Saxe figure on a side-table, "I never knew you had this little gentleman."

"Which?"

"A little shepherd holding a bird-cage."

宵好了，我都要饿死了。"

玛格丽特又拉了一次铃，随后再次坐到钢琴前弹了起来，口中曼声哼唱着一首有些轻佻的歌。在弹唱这歌曲的时候，她一点儿错误都没有出。加斯顿也知道这首歌，于是他们就开始了二重唱。

"别唱这些令人不快的东西了。"我用恳求的口吻对玛格丽特说道。

"啊，你真是正经人啊！"她一边带着笑说话，一边把手递给我，"这可不是为我，是为你啊。"

玛格丽特做了个手势，仿佛在说：啊，礼节规矩早就跟我绝缘了。

正在这时纳尼娜出现了。

"可以吃夜宵了吗？"玛格丽特问她。

"可以，夫人，马上就好了。"

"鉴于，"普鲁登斯对我说，"你还不曾在这屋子里转过呢，这下正好，来，我带你去看看。"

正如你所知，客厅非常漂亮。

玛格丽特又陪我们待了一会儿，就叫加斯顿和她一同去餐室瞅瞅夜宵是不是弄好了。

"哈，"普鲁登斯朝一只多层的架子瞥了一眼，从上面取下一个萨克森小塑像，说，"我都不知道你这儿还有这么一个小绅士呢。"

"哪个啊？"

"Take it, if you like it."

"I won't deprive you of it."

"I was going to give it to my maid. I think it hideous; but if you like it, take it."

Prudence only saw the present, not the way in which it was given. She put the little figure on one side, and took me into the dressing-room, where she showed me two miniatures hanging side by side, and said:

"That is the Comte de G., who was very much in love with Marguerite; it was he who brought her out. Do you know him?"

"No. And this one?" I inquired, pointing to the other miniature.

"That is the little Vicomte de L. He was obliged to disappear."

"Why?"

"Because he was all but ruined. That's one, if you like, who loved Marguerite."

"And she loved him, too, no doubt?"

"She is such a queer girl, one never knows. The night he went away she went to the theatre as usual, and yet she had cried when he said good-bye to her."

Just then Nanine appeared, to tell us that supper was served.

When we entered the dining-room, Marguerite was leaning against the wall, and Gaston, holding her hands, was speaking to her in a low voice.

"一个手里拎着鸟笼的牧童。"

"倘若你喜欢，就送给你吧。"

"我不能把它从你这儿夺走啊。"

"我觉得这个塑像非常丑，本来想把它送给我的女仆的，不过如果你喜欢，就把它拿去吧。"

普鲁登斯看重的只是礼物本身，并不计较礼物送出的方式。她将塑像放到一旁，将我带到梳妆间，指着在那儿挂着的两张微型肖像画说道：

"那个是 G 伯爵，他曾经爱玛格丽特爱得要死，她算是他捧出来的。你认识伯爵吗？"

"不认识。这一位又是谁呢？"我指着另外一幅肖像询问。

"那位是小 L 子爵，他不得已和她分开了。"

"什么原因呢？"

"因为他差点就破产了。可以说，是又一个爱上玛格丽特的人！"

"那么她无疑也非常爱他吧。"

"她是个非常古怪的姑娘，别人永远也不能看透她。小 L 子爵动身的那晚，她跟平常一样去剧院看戏，可是在他对她说再见的时候，她却哭出来了。"

就在这时纳尼娜过来了，告诉我们夜宵已然准备完毕。

当我们进入餐厅时，玛格丽特

"You are mad," replied Marguerite. "You know quite well that I don't want you. It is no good at the end of two years to make love to a woman like me. With us, it is at once, or never. Come, gentlemen, supper!"

And, slipping away from Gaston, Marguerite made him sit on her right at table, me on her left, then called to Nanine:

"Before you sit down, tell them in the kitchen not to open to anybody if there is a ring."

This order was given at one o'clock in the morning.

We laughed, drank, and ate freely at this supper. In a short while mirth had reached its last limit, and the words that seem funny to a certain class of people, words that degrade the mouth that utters them, were heard from time to time, amidst the applause of Nanine, of Prudence, and of Marguerite. Gaston was thoroughly amused; he was a very good sort of fellow, but somewhat spoiled by the habits of his youth. For a moment I tried to forget myself, to force my heart and my thoughts to become indifferent to the sight before me, and to take my share of that gaiety which seemed like one of the courses of the meal. But little by little I withdrew from the noise; my glass remained full, and

靠在墙上，加斯顿正拉着她的手，与她轻声交谈。

"你简直疯了，"玛格丽特回复，"你非常清楚我不会想要你的，都认识两年了，现在才来向一个如我这般的女人求爱，这可不怎么好呢。我们这种人，要么当时便委身于人，否则就永远都不会。来，先生们，就坐吧。"

玛格丽特将手从加斯顿手中抽出，让他坐在她右手边，而我坐在左手边。随后她叫过纳尼娜说：

"你入座之前先去一下厨房，关照那里的人，就算有人拉铃也别开门。"

她交代这件事的时候已是凌晨1点钟。

我们纵情地笑着、喝着酒，大吃特吃。没过多久，欢乐就已达到顶点，时不能够听到几句不堪入耳的脏话，类似的话在这圈子里却被认为是非常有趣的，纳尼娜，普鲁登斯与玛格丽特听后都鼓掌欢呼。加斯顿完全放纵了自己，这个年轻人心地很不错，不过头脑有些糊涂。我一时间真的试图不再强迫自己的心灵和思想保持清醒，而是干脆投入到他们这场如同晚餐正常节目一样的欢乐中去。然而慢慢地我就同这场喧闹疏远了，我不再喝酒，在边上看着这个20岁的美丽女

I felt almost sad as I saw this beautiful creature of twenty drinking, talking like a porter, and laughing the more loudly the more scandalous was the joke.

Nevertheless, this hilarity, this way of talking and drinking, which seemed to me in the others the mere results of bad company or of bad habits, seemed in Marguerite a necessity of forgetting, a fever, a nervous irritability. At every glass of champagne her cheeks would flush with a feverish colour, and a cough, hardly perceptible at the beginning of supper, became at last so violent that she was obliged to lean her head on the back of her chair and hold her chest in her hands every time that she coughed.

I suffered at the thought of the injury to so frail a constitution which must come from daily excesses like this. At length, something which I had feared and foreseen happened. Toward the end of supper Marguerite was seized by a more violent fit of coughing than any she had had while I was there. It seemed as if her chest were being torn in two. The poor girl turned crimson, closed her eyes under the pain, and put her napkin to her lips. It was stained with a drop of blood. She rose and ran into her dressing-room.

"What is the matter with Marguerite?"

性喝酒，她的谈笑像是一个脚夫那样粗鲁，别人的话越是下流，她就越发笑得起劲，我心里也越来越感到忧郁。

不过，这样的放纵欢乐，这种说话跟喝酒的样子，对在座的客人们来说，似乎可算是放荡、坏习气或是精力旺盛造成的。可是在玛格丽特身上，我却感到是由于她忘却现实的需要，是一种冲动或神经质的激动。每喝下一杯香槟，她脸上就会泛起一阵发烧般的红色。刚开始吃饭时，她还只是很轻微地咳，渐渐却越咳越厉害，必须把头仰靠在椅背上才行，每次咳嗽发作，她的双手都会用力按住胸口。

我为她感到心痛，她身体虚弱，每天却还要过如此放荡的生活来折磨自己。过了一会儿，我担心且有所预感的事情发生了。欢宴快结束时，玛格丽特突然猛烈地咳嗽起来，这是我到她家里直至此刻她咳得最为厉害的一次，我感觉似乎她的肺都在胸膛里面撕碎了。这个可怜的姑娘脸色通红，痛苦得双眼紧闭。她拿起餐巾擦过嘴唇，餐巾上竟出现了一滴鲜血。她马上站了起来，跑进了化妆间。

"玛格丽特发生什么事了？"

asked Gaston.

"She has been laughing too much, and she is spitting blood. Oh, it is nothing; it happens to her every day. She will be back in a minute. Leave her alone. She prefers it."

I could not stay still; and, to the consternation of Prudence and Nanine, who called to me to come back, I followed Marguerite."

加斯顿问。

"她笑得太猛，造成了咳血，"普鲁登斯说，"哦，没关系，她天天都是如此。她很快就回来。让她自己待在那儿就好，她喜欢那样。"

我却再也忍不住了，不顾普鲁登斯和纳尼娜的惊讶——她们还想叫住我，我依旧站起身来径自随着玛格丽特去了。

CHAPTER 10

第十章

The room to which she had fled was lit only by a single candle. She lay back on a great sofa, her dress undone, holding one hand on her heart, and letting the other hang by her side. On the table was a basin half full of water, and the water was stained with streaks of blood.

Very pale, her mouth half open, Marguerite tried to recover breath. Now and again her bosom was raised by a long sigh, which seemed to relieve her a little, and for a few seconds she would seem to be quite comfortable.

I went up to her; she made no movement, and I sat down and took the hand which was lying on the sofa.

"Ah! it is you," she said, with a smile.

I must have looked greatly agitated, for she added:

"Are you unwell, too?"

"No, but you: do you still suffer?"

"Very little;" and she wiped off with her handkerchief the tears which the coughing had brought to her eyes; "I am used to it

她躲着的那个房间里只有一支蜡烛发出光亮。她斜倚在一张很大的沙发上，裙衣敞开，一只手在心口处按着，另一只手垂在沙发外侧，桌上放着一只银脸盆，里面是半盆清水。水中可以看见一缕缕大理石花纹般的血丝漂浮着。

她的脸色惨白如死，嘴唇半开，竭力想要喘过气来。她不住地深深吸气，接着长吁一声，好像如此这般就会感觉轻松一些，获得几秒钟的舒畅。

我来到她的跟前，她依然没有动。我随即坐了下来，将她搁在沙发上的那只手握在手里。

"啊！是你啊！"她微笑着说道。

我脸上的表情一定非常紧张，因为她又接下去问道：

"难道你也不舒服吗？"

"不，不是，是你，你还觉得难受吗？"

"还是有一点儿，"她拿手绢将咳出来的眼泪拭去，说，"如今我已

now."

"You are killing yourself, madame," I said to her in a moved voice. "I wish I were a friend, a relation of yours, that I might keep you from doing yourself harm like this."

"Ah! it is really not worth your while to alarm yourself," she replied in a somewhat bitter tone; "see how much notice the others take of me! They know too well that there is nothing to be done."

Thereupon she got up, and, taking the candle, put it on the mantel piece and looked at herself in the glass.

"How pale I am!" she said, as she fastened her dress and passed her fingers over her loosened hair. "Come, let us go back to supper. Are you coming?"

I sat still and did not move.

She saw how deeply I had been affected by the whole scene, and, coming up to me, held out her hand, saying:

"Come now, let us go."

I took her hand, raised it to my lips, and in spite of myself two tears fell upon it.

"Why, what a child you are!" she said, sitting down by my side again. "You are crying! What is the matter?"

"I must seem very silly to you, but I am frightfully troubled by what I have just seen."

经习惯这种情况了。"

"你这样就等于自杀，夫人，"我用异常激动的语调对她说，"我希望能做你的朋友，你的亲人，我想帮助你不再这么糟蹋自己。"

"啊！你真的不必这样大惊小怪的，"她用有点儿辛酸的语气回答说，"你看看别人的人是不是还在关心我！因为他们都清楚得很，这种病是没有办法治的。"

说完以后她就站起身来，将蜡烛拿去放在壁炉上，看着镜子里面的自己。

"看我的脸色有多苍白啊！"她一边系着裙衣一边说，手指在散乱的头发上掠过，"啊！好了！来吧，我们回到桌边去。你不过来吗？"

可是我依旧坐着没有动。

她看到我被眼前的这幕景象震慑得如此之深，便来到我的身边，把手递过来说：

"来吧，我们一起去。"

我握住她的手，放在唇边轻吻，两滴泪水却不由自主地流了出来，滴在她的手上。

"哦，你真是个孩子！"她一边说一边再次在我身旁坐下，"啊，你哭了！发生什么事啦？"

"你一定觉得我很愚蠢吧，但我看到方才的情景感觉非常难过。"

"You are very good! What would you have of me? I can not sleep. I must amuse myself a little. And then, girls like me, what does it matter, one more or less? The doctors tell me that the blood I spit up comes from my throat; I pretend to believe them it is all I can do for them."

"Listen, Marguerite," I said, unable to contain myself any longer; "I do not know what influence you are going to have over my life, but at this present moment there is no one, not even my sister, in whom I feel the interest which I feel in you. It has been just the same ever since I saw you. Well, for Heaven's sake, take care of yourself, and do not live as you are living now."

"If I took care of myself I should die. All that supports me is the feverish life I lead. Then, as for taking care of oneself, that is all very well for women with families and friends; as for us, from the moment we can no longer serve the vanity or the pleasure of our lovers, they leave us, and long nights follow long days. I know it. I was in bed for two months, and after three weeks no one came to see me."

"It is true I am nothing to you," I went on, "but if you will let me, I will look after you like a brother, I will never leave your side, and I will cure you. Then, when you are strong again, you can go back to the

"你真是个善良的人！你让我怎么办才好呢？我无法入睡，必须找点什么事来消遣消遣。再说，像我这般的女人，多一个少一个又有什么要紧呢？医生说我咳出来的血是喉咙里的，我就假装相信了，这是我唯一能为他们做的了。"

"听着，玛格丽特，"我再也无法抑制自己的感情，开口道，"我不清楚你会对我的生命造成怎样的影响，可是我非常清楚，此时此刻我心中再没有别人，甚至是我的妹妹，能够让我如此关心。这份心情自从第一次见到你就有了。啊，请看在上帝的分上，保重你的身体吧，不要再过你现在这样的生活了！"

"如果我真的保重身体反而会死去。现在的我完全靠这种充满狂热的生活支撑着。而且，保重身体都只是对那些有家庭、朋友的女士而言的。对我们这种人，一旦情人的虚荣心得不到满足，不能再和他们寻欢作乐，他们马上就把我们扔在一边，我们就只能慢慢挨过一个个漫长的黑夜白天。这些事我清楚得很！我躺了整整 2 个月，过了第三个星期就再也没有人来看我了。"

"的确，我对你来说根本不算什么，"我说，"可是，倘若你不嫌弃，我会如一个兄弟那样照顾你，我不会离开你的身边，会治好你的

life you are leading, if you choose; but I am sure you will come to prefer a quiet life, which will make you happier and keep your beauty unspoiled."

"You think like that tonight because the wine has made you sad, but you would never have the patience that you pretend to."

"Permit me to say, Marguerite, that you were ill for two months, and that for two months I came to ask after you every day."

"It is true, but why did you not come up?"

"Because I did not know you then."

"Need you have been so particular with a girl like me?"

"One must always be particular with a woman; it is what I feel, at least."

"So you would look after me?"

"Yes."

"You would stay by me all day?"

"Yes.

"And even all night?"

"As long as I did not weary you."

"And what do you call that?"

"Devotion."

"And what does this devotion come from?"

"The irresistible sympathy which I have for you."

"So you are in love with me? Say it

病。然后，等你的身体好了，如果你喜欢，可以重新恢复现在这种生活。不过我能肯定，你会喜欢清静的生活，那会令你感觉更加幸福，使你的美丽永不消退。"

"今天晚上你只是由于酒后伤感而这么想，不过，你是不会拥有你所说的那份耐心的。"

"请允许我说，玛格丽特，你曾有两个月生病在床，在这两个月里，我是每天都来问候你的。"

"的确如此，可你为什么不到楼上来呢？"

"因为当时我还不认识你。"

"跟我这样的女人还有什么好讲究的呢？"

"与一位女士在一起人都会讲究一些的，至少我是这么想的。"

"如此说来，你当真会照顾我？"

"没错。"

"你会每天陪在我身边吗？"

"没错。"

"甚至还有整个晚上吗？"

"只要你不讨厌我，都会。"

"你认为这种感情是什么？"

"是忠诚。"

"这种忠诚又从何而来呢？"

"来自我对你无可克制的同情。"

"这么说你是爱上我了？你可

straight out, it is much more simple."

"It is possible; but if I am to say it to you one day, it is not today."

"You will do better never to say it."

"Why?"

"Because only one of two things can come of it."

"What?"

"Either I shall not accept: then you will have a grudge against me; or I shall accept: then you will have a sorry mistress; a woman who is nervous, ill, sad, or gay with a gaiety sadder than grief, a woman who spits blood and spends a hundred thousand francs a year. That is all very well for a rich old man like the duke, but it is very bad for a young man like you, and the proof of it is that all the young lovers I have had have very soon left me."

I did not answer; I listened. This frankness, which was almost a kind of confession, the sad life, of which I caught some glimpse through the golden veil which covered it, and whose reality the poor girl sought to escape in dissipation, drink, and wakefulness, impressed me so deeply that I could not utter a single word.

"O me," continued Marguerite, "we are talking mere childishness. Give me your arm and let us go back to the dining-room. They won't know what we mean by our

以直接这样说，这会简单得多。"

"可能如此，不过，就算我有一天会对你说，也一定不是今天。"

"你最好永远也不要对我说。"

"什么原因呢？"

"因为在那之后只会有两种结果。"

"都是什么？"

"一种是我拒绝了你，而你会记恨我；一种是我答应你，而你就会有一个多愁善感的情人。这个女人神经质，重病缠身，心情忧郁，快乐的时候甚至比痛苦时更加悲伤，咳得吐血，一年要花掉难以计数的金钱。这些对公爵那样的有钱老头儿来说没什么关系，可是对你这样的年轻人来说就非常麻烦了。以前我也有过年轻的情夫，但他们全部很快地弃我而去，就是证据了。"

我并没有答话，我听着她几乎是忏悔的剖白，仿佛见到了她在纸醉金迷的生活表象掩盖下那无尽的痛苦。这个现实中可怜的姑娘用放荡、酗酒和失眠来逃避生活。我对这一切感慨万千，以至于无法成言。

"哦，算了，"玛格丽特接着说，"我们两个的谈话简直太幼稚了。挽上我的手，让我们一块儿回餐室去吧，不要让他们知道我们在离席

absence."

"Go in, if you like, but allow me to stay here."

"Why?"

"Because your mirth hurts me."

"Well, I will be sad."

"Marguerite, let me say to you something which you have no doubt often heard, so often that the habit of hearing it has made you believe it no longer, but which is none the less real, and which I will never repeat."

"And that is …?" she said, with the smile of a young mother listening to some foolish notion of her child.

"It is this, that ever since I have seen you, I know not why, you have taken a place in my life; that, if I drive the thought of you out of my mind, it always comes back; that when I met you today, after not having seen you for two years, you made a deeper impression on my heart and mind than ever; that, now that you have let me come to see you, now that I know you, now that I know all that is strange in you, you have become a necessity of my life, and you will drive me mad, not only if you will not love me, but if you will not let me love you."

"But, foolish creature that you are, I

的这段时间里都干了些什么。"

"如果你喜欢去就回去吧，可是请你允许我待在这里。"

"为什么呢？"

"由于你的欢乐令我十分痛苦。"

"好吧，那我会显得愁苦些。"

"玛格丽特，请允许我对你说一件事，你一定也经常听别人这么说，因为听得惯了，也不会怎样认真。可是这确实是我的真心话，我此后也永远不会再和你重复了。"

"那么是什么事？"她对我说，脸上挂着年轻母亲倾听她们的孩子说傻话时经常露出的那种微笑。

"我想说，自从我和你见面以后，不明白是怎么回事，你就在我的生命中占据了一席之地，我也曾想过把你忘掉，却做不到，你始终萦绕在我的心里。我上一次见你已经是两年前的事了，可是今天，当我再次遇到你，你在我心中的分量反倒愈加重了。然后，你允许我来见你，让我更了解你，我知道了你的一切奇特遭遇，这使你成了我生命中不可或缺的一份子，不用说你不爱我，就算你不允许我爱你，我也会失去理智的。"

"可你这样实在太可怜了，我

shall say to you, like Mme. D., 'You must be very rich, then!' Why, you don't know that I spend six or seven thousand francs a month, and that I could not live without it; you don't know, my poor friend, that I should ruin you in no time, and that your family would cast you off if you were to live with a woman like me. Let us be friends, good friends, but no more. Come and see me, we will laugh and talk, but don't exaggerate what I am worth, for I am worth very little. You have a good heart, you want some one to love you, you are too young and too sensitive to live in a world like mine. Take a married woman. You see, I speak to you frankly, like a friend."

"But what the devil are you doing there?" cried Prudence, who had come in without our hearing her, and who now stood just inside the door, with her hair half coming down and her dress undone. I recognised the hand of Gaston.

"We are talking sense," said Marguerite; "leave us alone; we will be back soon."

"Good, good! Talk, my children," said Prudence, going out and closing the door behind her, as if to further empbasize the tone in which she had said these words.

"Well, it is agreed," continued

拿 D 太太[1]讲过的话来对你说了，'那你一定很有钱了！'你难道不清楚我每月都要花费六七千法郎。这种支出已经变成了我的生活需要，你不清楚吗，可怜的朋友，用不了多长时间我就会让你破产。如果你要和一个我这样的女人一道生活，你的家庭便不会再支付给你任何费用。请像一位好友那样爱我吧，不能超出这个限度。你经常来探望我，我们一起说说笑笑，不用觉得我很重要，我真的一点儿也不重要。你有一颗善良的心，你需要有人来爱你。但在我们这个圈子中，你实在太年轻，太多愁善感了。一个有夫之妇更适合做你的情人。你看，我对你说话有多坦白，就像朋友一样。"

"你们俩在这里都干了些什么啊？"普鲁登斯在我们都没发觉的时候走了进来，叫着说道。她头发松散，衣衫不整，我能看出是加斯顿的手搞出来的。

"我们正说正经事呢，"玛格丽特回答，"让我们接着聊几句，马上就会回去的。"

"好吧，好吧，孩子们，你们聊。"普鲁登斯说着走了出去，还帮忙关上了门，就像是为加重她方才那几句话的语气一样。

---

[1] D 太太，即普鲁登斯·迪韦尔诺瓦太太。

Marguerite, when we were alone, "you won't fall in love with me?"

"I will go away."

"So much as that?"

I had gone too far to draw back; and I was really carried away. This mingling of gaiety, sadness, candour, prostitution, her very malady, which no doubt developed in her a sensitiveness to impressions, as well as an irritability of nerves, all this made it clear to me that if from the very beginning I did not completely dominate her light and forgetful nature, she was lost to me.

"Come, now, do you seriously mean what you say?" she said.

"Seriously."

"But why didn't you say it to me sooner?"

"When could I have said it?"

"The day after you had been introduced to me at the Opera Comique."

"I thought you would have received me very badly if I had come to see you."

"Why?"

"Because I had behaved so stupidly."

"That's true. And yet you were already in love with me."

"Yes."

"And that didn't hinder you from going to bed and sleeping quite comfortably. One knows what that sort of love means."

"那么我们就达成一致了，"玛格丽特在屋里只有我们两人时继续说道，"你不会爱上我了吧？"

"我会立刻离开。"

"居然到这步田地了吗？"

我真是进退两难，而且这个姑娘已经令我神魂颠倒了。这种感觉是既有欢乐，也有悲伤，既有纯真，又有放荡的混合体，还有那令她神经亢奋，易于激动的病情，这一切都让我知道，假如在一开始我无法控制这个女人轻浮而健忘的个性，我一定会失去她的。

"好吧，那么，你说的话是真的吗？"她问。

"完全发自肺腑。"

"那你为何早先不和我说？"

"我应当何时向你说起它们呢？"

"在喜剧歌剧院，你被引见给我的第二天就完全可以说了。"

"我觉得倘若我来探望你的话，你大概会很冷淡地对待我。"

"什么原因呢？"

"因为我的表现实在有点蠢。"

"这倒是没错，不过，那个时候你不是已经爱上了我吗？"

"的确。"

"而这份爱情并没有阻止你散戏后回家就寝，睡得安稳。人们都

"There you are mistaken. Do you know what I did that evening, after the Opera Comique?"

"No."

"I waited for you at the door of the Cafe Anglais. I followed the carriage in which you and your three friends were, and when I saw you were the only one to get down, and that you went in alone, I was very happy."

Marguerite began to laugh.

"What are you laughing at?"

"Nothing."

"Tell me, I beg of you, or I shall think you are still laughing at me."

"You won't be cross?"

"What right have I to be cross?"

"Well, there was a sufficient reason why I went in alone."

"What?"

"Some one was waiting for me here."

If she had thrust a knife into me she would not have hurt me more. I rose, and holding out my hand, "Goodbye," said I.

"I knew you would be cross," she said; "men are frantic to know what is certain to give them pain."

"But I assure you," I added coldly, as if wishing to prove how completely I was cured of my passion, "I assure you that I am not cross. It was quite natural that some

知道此类所谓的爱情是怎么回事。"

"这你就说错了。你知道那天晚上我离开喜剧歌剧院之后又去做什么了吗？"

"我不清楚。"

"我就等在英国咖啡馆的门口，接着尾随你和你三位朋友所坐的马车，直到你的家门口。我看着你自己下了车，一个人回到家中，当时心里特别高兴。"

玛格丽特笑出声来。

"有什么可笑的吗？"

"不，没什么。"

"请告诉我，我求你了，否则我会认为你在嘲笑我。"

"你不会感觉被冒犯吗？"

"我有什么权利这样认为？"

"好的，我独自回家是因为一个很美妙的理由。"

"什么理由？"

"已经有人在这儿等着我了。"

就算她捅我一刀也不会比现在更加痛苦了，我站起身来，把手递给她。"再会了。"我说道。

"我就知道你肯定会生气，"玛格丽特说，"男人都是这样，急不可待地想听那些让他们难受的事情。"

"可是，我可以保证，"我冷淡地说道，好像这样就能证明我已完全控制住自己激动的情绪，"我可以保证我并没生气。有人在这儿等你，

one should be waiting for you, just as it is quite natural that I should go from here at three in the morning."

"Have you, too, some one waiting for you?"

"No, but I must go."

"Good-bye, then."

"You send me away?"

"Not the least in the world."

"Why are you so unkind to me?"

"How have I been unkind to you?"

"In telling me that some one was waiting for you."

"I could not help laughing at the idea that you had been so happy to see me come in alone when there was such a good reason for it."

"One finds pleasure in childish enough things, and it is too bad to destroy such a pleasure when, by simply leaving it alone, one can make somebody so happy."

"But what do you think I am? I am neither maid nor duchess. I didn't know you till today, and I am not responsible to you for my actions. Supposing one day I should become your mistress, you are bound to know that I have had other lovers besides you. If you make scenes of jealousy like this before, what will it be after, if that after should ever exist? I never met any one like you."

这是非常自然的事，好比我希望在凌晨 3 点钟告辞一样，都非常自然。"

"是否也会有人为了你等在家里呢？"

"不是的，但我一定要走。"

"既然如此，再见啦。"

"你在赶我走吗？"

"绝不是这回事。"

"为什么要这样伤害我？"

"我怎样伤害你啦？"

"你告诉我那个时候有人在这里等你。"

"可是我一想到你见我独自回家就感到那么开心，而当时却是因为这么一个绝妙的理由时，就实在忍不住想笑了。"

"人们经常会因一些孩子气的东西而感到快乐，如果令这种快乐持续下去，就能使人感到幸福的话，那去摧毁他的快乐实在太残忍了。"

"但是你究竟把我当成什么人了？我既不是纯洁少女，也不是公爵夫人。我在今天以前甚至不认识你，我的行为和你毫不相干，即便将来有一天我可能做了你的情妇，你也该明白，除了你我还会有其他情人，倘若你现在还不曾成为我的情人却开始吃起醋来，那等将来，假定有这个'将来'，你该怎么办呢？我还从没遇见过你这样的人。"

"That is because no one has ever loved you as I love you."

"Frankly, then, you really love me?"

"As much as it is possible to love, I think."

"And that has lasted since – ?"

"Since the day I saw you go into Susse's, three years ago.

"Do you know, that is tremendously fine? Well, what am to do in return?"

"Love me a little," I said, my heart beating so that I could hardly speak; for, in spite of the half-mocking smiles with which she had accompanied the whole conversation, it seemed to me that Marguerite began to share my agitation, and that the hour so long awaited was drawing near.

"Well, but the duke?"

"What duke?"

"My jealous old duke."

"He will know nothing."

"And if he should?"

"He would forgive you."

"Ah, no, he would leave me, and what would become of me?"

"You risk that for some one else."

"How do you know?"

"By the order you gave not to admit any one tonight."

"It is true; but that is a serious friend."

"那是因为以前从来也没有一个人爱你像我这样深。"

"坦率地说，你真的爱我吗？"

"我想我可以为这份爱献出一切。"

"而这感情是从……"

"从我见到你走进絮斯商店的那天开始的，在3年之前。"

"这实在太美了，你知道吗？我要怎样才能报答你呢？"

"有那么一点儿爱上我。"我回答，心脏猛烈地跳动，几乎说不出话来，因为尽管玛格丽特在交谈中始终挂着一抹含讥带讽的微笑，我依然能感觉到，她好像也同我一样心慌意乱，我长久以来一直等待的时刻正在渐渐临近。

"那么，公爵要怎么办？"

"什么公爵？"

"我爱嫉妒的老公爵。"

"他不会知道任何事情。"

"如果被他知道了呢？"

"他一定会原谅你。"

"啊，不可能！他就会抛弃我，我会变成什么样呢？"

"你现在就在为别人冒这个险。"

"你怎么会知道？"

"因为你刚才吩咐说，今晚不要放人进来。"

"For whom you care nothing, as you have shut your door against him at such an hour."

"It is not for you to reproach me, since it was in order to receive you, you and your friend."

Little by little I had drawn nearer to Marguerite. I had put my arms about her waist, and I felt her supple body weigh lightly on my clasped hands.

"If you knew how much I love you!" I said in a low voice.

"Really true?"

"I swear it."

"Well, if you will promise to do everything I tell you, without a word, without an opinion, without a question, perhaps I will say yes."

"I will do everything that you wish!"

"But I forewarn you I must be free to do as I please, without giving you the slightest details what I do. I have long wished for a young lover, who should be young and not self-willed, loving without distrust, loved without claiming the right to it. I have never found one. Men, instead of being satisfied in obtaining for a long time what they scarcely hoped to obtain once, exact from their mistresses a full account of the present, the past, and even the future. As they get accustomed to her, they want to

"这倒没错，不过那是一位很正经的朋友。"

"既然在那个时候你还可以把他拒之门外，说明他对你来说也不算什么。"

"这也轮不到你来责备我呀，我是为了招待你们，你跟你朋友。"

我慢慢地拉近与玛格丽特的距离，我轻轻地环上她的腰，她纤细的身躯在我掌中显得不盈一握。

"如果你能知道我有多么爱你！"我低声对她说。

"你说的是真的吗？"

"我可以发誓。"

"那么，如果你能承诺什么事都听我的，不反驳，不提出异议，不盘问我，或许我会答应你的。"

"只要是你的话我全都听！"

"我要事先警告你，我必须有自由去做任何我喜欢的事，我不会向你一一交代我生活的细节。长期以来我一直想找个年轻又听话的情人，对我多情却不怀疑，能接受我的爱但又不会据此提出要求。可我一直没有找到。男人都是一样的，原来求而不得的东西一旦到手，时间一长，就会不满足，进而要求知晓自己情人现在、过去，甚至未来的事情。当他们和情人逐渐熟悉之后，就会想要控制她，对方越是迁

rule her, and the more one gives them the more exacting they become. If I decide now on taking a new lover, he must have three very rare qualities: he must be confiding, submissive, and discreet."

"Well, I will be all that you wish."

"We shall see."

"When shall we see?"

"Later on."

"Why?"

"Because," said Marguerite, releasing herself from my arms, and, taking from a great bunch of red camellias a single camellia, she placed it in my buttonhole, "because one can not always carry out agreements the day they are signed."

"And when shall I see you again?" I said, clasping her in my arms.

"When this camellia changes colour."

"When will it change colour?"

"Tomorrow night between eleven and twelve. Are you satisfied?"

"Need you ask me?"

"Not a word of this either to your friend or to Prudence, or to anybody whatever."

"I promise."

"Now, kiss me, and we will go back to the dining-room."

She held up her lips to me, smoothed her hair again, and we went out of the room, she singing, and I almost beside myself.

就，他们就越发得寸进尺。如果我这会打定主意想再找一个情人，我愿他能拥有这 3 种罕见的美德：信任，顺从，言行谨慎。"

"嗯，只要你想要我做到。"

"让我们以后走着瞧吧！"

"那么是什么时候呢？"

"再过段时间。"

"什么原因呢？"

"因为，"玛格丽特从我的臂弯里挣脱出去，从一大束早晨送来的红色茶花中掐下一朵插到我衣扣的纽孔里，说，"条约是永远不会在签字当天就付诸执行的。"

"那么我何时才能再次和你见面呢？"我说着，用手将她紧紧地搂在怀中。

"当这朵茶花颜色变了以后。"

"什么时候才会变色呢？"

"明晚，11 点到 12 点之间，你是否满意？"

"这你还需要问吗？"

"这件事你不要对任何人说，无论是你朋友、普鲁登斯，或者是另外的什么人。"

"我可以保证。"

"那么，给我一个吻，我们一块儿去餐厅吧。"

她的唇向我挨了过来，接着她

In the next room she stopped for a moment and said to me in a low voice:

"It must seem strange to you that I am ready to take you at a moment's notice. Shall I tell you why? It is," she continued, taking my hand and placing it against her heart so that I could feel how rapidly and violently it palpitated; "it is because I shall not live as long as others, and I have promised myself to live more quickly."

"Don't speak to me like that, I entreat you."

"Oh, make yourself easy," she continued, laughing; "however short a time I have to live, I shall live longer than you will love me!"

And she went singing into the dining-room.

"Where is Nanine?" she said, seeing Gaston and Prudence alone.

"She is asleep in your room, waiting till you are ready to go to bed," replied Prudence.

"Poor thing, I am killing her! And now gentlemen, it is time to go."

Ten minutes after, Gaston and I left the house. Marguerite shook hands with me and said good-bye. Prudence remained behind.

"Well," said Gaston, when we were in the street, "what do you think of

又再次梳了两下头发，我们出门的时候她哼着歌，而我几乎是疯了。

她在客厅里站了一会儿，压低声音和我说：

"我这种好像立刻就接受你的模样一定会让你觉得奇怪吧，要我告诉你这是为什么吗？原因就是，"她将我的手压在了她的胸口上，这样我就能感觉到她的心跳动得有多么快、多么剧烈，然后说，"原因就是很显然我的寿命比其他人都短，我的生活也要比别人节奏更快。"

"求你了，不要再对我说这样的话。"

"啊！放轻松点，"她笑了，接了下去，"就算我活不了多久，那时间总也会比你爱我的时候更长些。"

随后她走进了餐厅。

"纳尼娜去哪儿了？"她一见只剩下加斯顿和普鲁登斯，就发问。

"她正在你的房间打盹，等着一会儿服侍你上床。"普鲁登斯说道。

"可怜的人！我会累死她的！好吧，先生们，是时候告辞了。"

过了10分钟，加斯顿同我两人离开了房间，玛格丽特与我握手道别，普鲁登斯则留了下来。

"好了，"等我们来到街上，加斯顿问道，"你对玛格丽特的看法如

Marguerite?"

"She is an angel, and I am madly in love with her." "So I guessed; did you tell her so?"

"Yes."

"And did she promise to believe you?"

"No."

"She is not like Prudence."

"Did she promise to?"

"Better still, my dear fellow. You wouldn't think it; but she is still not half bad, poor old Duvernoy!"

何？"

"她简直是个天使，我疯狂地爱上了她。""我猜就会这样，这话你告诉过她了吗？"

"是的。"

"那么她是否表示相信你？"

"她没有。"

"普鲁登斯就完全不同。"

"那她答应你了？"

"比这还要多，我亲爱的伙计！你绝对想不到的，不过她仍相当不错，可怜的老迪韦尔诺瓦！"

CHAPTER 11

第十一章

At this point Armand stopped.

"Would you close the window for me?" he said. "I am beginning to feel cold. Meanwhile, I will get into bed."

I closed the window. Armand, who was still very weak, took off his dressing-gown and lay down in bed, resting his head for a few moments on the pillow, like a man who is tired by much talking or disturbed by painful memories.

"Perhaps you have been talking too much," I said to him. "Would you rather for me to go and leave you to sleep? You can tell me the rest of the story another day."

"Are you tired of listening to it?"

"Quite the contrary."

"Then I will go on. If you left me alone, I should not sleep."

When I returned home (he continued, without needing to pause and recollect himself, so fresh were all the details in his mind), I did not go to bed, but began to reflect over the day's adventure. The

讲到此处，阿尔芒停了下来。

"请你帮我关上窗子好吗？"他说，"我开始觉得冷了，而且，我该去睡觉了。"

我关上了窗户。阿尔芒的身体依然非常虚弱，他把晨衣脱下，躺到床上，将头靠在枕头上休息了一会儿，就像是一个走过漫长旅途而精疲力竭的游子，或者一个被过去的苦痛纠缠得心烦意乱的失意人。

"可能你是话讲得多了，"我对他说，"是不是我先告辞，让你睡觉比较好？你可以改天再为我讲故事余下的部分。"

"你听着觉得无聊了？"

"完全相反。"

"那么我还是接着讲，假如你让我自己独处，我也无法入睡的。"

当我回到家里（他继续讲了下去，完全无须多加回忆，因为所有的细节在他的脑海里就像刚刚发生一样清晰），并没有睡觉，而是开始回忆这一天中的奇遇：与玛格丽特

meeting, the introduction, the promise of Marguerite, had followed one another so rapidly, and so unexpectedly, that there were moments when it seemed to me I had been dreaming. Nevertheless, it was not the first time that a girl like Marguerite had promised herself to a man on the morrow of the day on which he had asked for the promise.

Though, indeed, I made this reflection, the first impression produced on me by my future mistress was so strong that it still persisted. I refused obstinately to see in her a woman like other women, and, with the vanity so common to all men, I was ready to believe that she could not but share the attraction which drew me to her.

Yet, I had before me plenty of instances to the contrary, and I had often heard that the affection of Marguerite was a thing to be had more or less dear, according to the season.

But, on the other hand, how was I to reconcile this reputation with her constant refusal of the young count whom we had found at her house? You may say that he was unattractive to her, and that, as she was splendidly kept by the duke, she would be more likely to choose a man who was attractive to her, if she were to take another lover. If so, why did she not choose

的见面、相识，获得了她的诺言。一件接一件的事情来得这么快，这么出人意料，有几次我觉得自己好像是在做梦。可是，当一个男人向玛格丽特那样的姑娘争取承诺，而她竟答应在一天之后就满足他，也肯定不是第一次了。

尽管我确实想到了这些，可是这位未来情妇给我留下的第一印象实在太过深刻，我始终无法忘怀。我还是一门心思地觉得她与其他姑娘是不同的。我和普通男人一样有自己的虚荣心，坚信她对我的感情就像我对她的那样深切。

但是，我以前也看到过不少互相矛盾的例子，而且我经常听到传闻说玛格丽特的爱情像是商品，价格依据季节的不同而有涨有落。

不过另一方面，我们却又在她家里看到，她坚决地拒绝了那位年轻的伯爵，这件事与她的传闻怎么能联系得起来呢？或许你要说那是由于他对她没什么吸引力，况且她现在被一位公爵供养着，生活奢靡，如果她想多找一个情人，自然会找一个自己喜欢的男人。如果是这样，那她为什么没有选择富有聪明，又

Gaston, who was rich, witty, and charming, and why did she care for me, whom she had thought so ridiculous the first time she had seen me?

It is true that there are events of a moment which tell more than the courtship of a year. Of those who were at the supper, I was the only one who had been concerned at her leaving the table. I had followed her, I had been so affected as to be unable to hide it from her, I had wept as I kissed her hand. This circumstance, added to my daily visits during the two months of her illness, might have shown her that I was somewhat different from the other men she knew, and perhaps she had said to herself that for a love which could thus manifest itself she might well do what she had done so often that it had no more consequence for her.

All these suppositions, as you may see, were improbable enough; but whatever might have been the reason of her consent, one thing was certain, she had consented.

Now, I was in love with Marguerite. I had nothing more to ask of her. Nevertheless, though she was only a kept woman, I had so anticipated for myself, perhaps to poetize it a little, a hopeless love, that the nearer the moment approached when I should have nothing

俊俏的加斯顿，而是对第一次与她见面就令她感到愚蠢可笑的我如此上心呢？

确实，有的时候一分钟之内发生的事会比整整一年的艰苦追求来得更加有效。在那晚一起用餐的人中，只有我对她的离席表示关心。我跟着她进屋，激动得根本无法在她面前掩饰。我亲吻着她的手泪流满面。此情此景，再加上在她生病卧床的两个月里，我每天去询问她的病情，因此让她感觉我的确与众不同，或许她还在心里琢磨，对一个用这种方式来诉说爱情的对象，她完全能够照常生活，她在过去都做过那么多次，以至于这种事对她已经完全无所谓了。

上述所有的设想，你也能看出都有可能会成真，可是，无论她同意的原因到底是什么，有一件事情可以肯定：她的确已经同意了。

现在，我已经和玛格丽特两情相悦了，我不可能再对她有任何奢求了。不过，尽管玛格丽特是一个妓女，但以前我总是期望太高——或许我有点把她诗意化了——这是一份绝望的爱情，以至于随着那个希望获得满足的时刻离我越来越

more to hope, the more I doubted. I did not close my eyes all night.

I scarcely knew myself. I was half demented. Now, I seemed to myself not handsome or rich or elegant enough to possess such a woman, now I was filled with vanity at the thought of it; then I began to fear lest Marguerite had no more than a few days' caprice for me, and I said to myself that since we should soon have to part, it would be better not to keep her appointment, but to write and tell her my fears and leave her. From that I went on to unlimited hope, unbounded confidence. I dreamed incredible dreams of the future; I said to myself that she should owe to me her moral and physical recovery, that I should spend my whole life with her, and that her love should make me happier than all the maidenly loves in the world.

But I can not repeat to you the thousand thoughts that rose from my heart to my head, and that only faded away with the sleep that came to me at daybreak.

When I awoke it was two o'clock. The weather was superb. I don't think life ever seemed to me so beautiful and so full of possibilities. The memories of the night before came to me without shadow or hindrance, escorted gaily by the hopes of the night to come. From time to time my

近，我心中的疑虑就越发深重起来，最后睁着眼睛直到天亮。

我如痴似醉，半癫半狂。一会儿我感到自己还不够英俊，不够富有，不够优雅，没有资格拥有那样的一个女人；一会儿，我又为可以拥有她而得意洋洋，虚荣心膨胀。随后我又开始担忧玛格丽特只是逢场作戏，对我的感情只能维持几天，预感我们这段关系会很快结束，不会有好的结局。我心里想着，晚上最好还是不去她家里为好，而且还应把我的疑虑写封信和她说，然后再离开她。过一会儿，我又生出了无限希望跟无与伦比的信心。我梦想着几乎不可思议的美好未来。我想着要医治好这位姑娘肉体上和精神上的伤痛，与她一同白头偕老，她的爱比世界上最纯洁无瑕的爱情更令我感到幸福。

但是，其实我根本无法向你描述当时我脑中、心中涌动的万千思绪。黎明时分我终于迷迷糊糊地睡着了，那些念头才在蒙眬中渐渐消逝。

当我清醒过来时已经下午2点了。天气特别好，我感觉我的生活从来不曾这样美好，充满了无限可能。我的脑海中清楚地浮现出昨夜的情景，毫无阴影和滞涩，随后又快活地憧憬着今晚美好时光的到

heart leaped with love and joy in my breast. A sweet fever thrilled me. I thought no more of the reasons which had filled my mind before I slept. I saw only the result, I thought only of the hour when I was to see Marguerite again.

It was impossible to stay indoors. My room seemed too small to contain my happiness. I needed the whole of nature to unbosom myself.

I went out. Passing by the Rue d'Antin, I saw Marguerite's coupe' waiting for her at the door. I went toward the Champs-Elysees. I loved all the people whom I met. Love gives one a kind of goodness.

After I had been walking for an hour from the Marly horses to the Rond-Point, I saw Marguerite's carriage in the distance; I divined rather than recognised it. As it was turning the corner of the Champs-Elysees it stopped, and a tall young man left a group of people with whom he was talking and came up to her. They talked for a few moments; the young man returned to his friends, the horses set out again, and as I came near the group I recognised the one who had spoken to Marguerite as the

来。我穿戴整齐,感到心满意足。我的心因为快乐与爱情剧烈跳动,一种甜蜜的激情使我战栗不已。昨夜那让我为之辗转反侧的念头不见踪影。我眼前只看到了成功,脑中只想着与玛格丽特相会的那一刻。

我再也无法待在家里了,我觉得自己的房间太小,根本容纳不下满满的幸福,我需要向整个大自然吐露衷肠。

我出了家门,经过昂坦街。我看见玛格丽特的马车停在她家门口等着,我朝香榭丽舍大街走过去。我对所遇到的每一个人心怀亲切!爱情使人变得多么善良美好啊!

当我在玛利石马像[1]跟圆形广场[2]之间徘徊了一个小时之后,远远看见了玛格丽特的马车,其实不能算认出来,只能说是猜出来的。她在香榭丽舍大街的拐角上让马车停下,一个个子很高的青年与一起谈话的人群分开,迎上去同她谈话。他们聊了一会儿,那个青年就回到他的朋友之中去了。马车再次向前行进,我朝那群人走过去,认出刚才跟玛格丽特说话的人正是 G 伯爵,我以前见到过他的肖像画,普

---

1 玛利石马像,著名雕刻家古斯图的作品,当时位于香榭丽舍大街入口处协和广场上,现真品收藏于卢浮宫博物馆。

2 圆形广场,香榭丽舍大街东西两段的分界处,以东是林荫大道,以西是高级商业区。

Comte de G., whose portrait I had seen and whom Prudence had indicated to me as the man to whom Marguerite owed her position. It was to him that she had closed her doors the night before; I imagined that she had stopped her carriage in order to explain to him why she had done so, and I hoped that at the same time she had found some new pretext for not receiving him on the following night.

How I spent the rest of the day I do not know; I walked, smoked, talked, but what I said, whom I met, I had utterly forgotten by ten o'clock in the evening.

All I remember is that when I returned home, I spent three hours over my toilet, and I looked at my watch and my clock a hundred times, which unfortunately both pointed to the same hour.

When it struck half past ten, I said to myself that it was time to go.

I lived at that time in the Rue de Provence; I followed the Rue du Mont-Blanc, crossed the Boulevard, went up the Rue Louis-le-Grand, the Rue de Port-Mahon, and the Rue d'Antin. I looked up at Marguerite's windows. There was a light. I rang. I asked the porter if Mlle. Gautier was at home. He replied that she never came in before eleven or a quarter past eleven. I looked at my watch. I

鲁登斯和我说过玛格丽特能有今天的地位全靠了他。他也正是昨晚被玛格丽特吩咐拒之门外的那个人，我猜想她方才停车下来就是为了和他解释昨晚没有让他进屋的原因，我希望她能找到一个新的借口让他即将到来的这个晚上也不要出现。

这一天剩下的时间我究竟是怎么过的，我根本毫无印象，只是散步、吸烟、聊天，可是，等晚上 10 点钟的时候，我就把这一天里的这些事情全都忘得一干二净。

我所能记起的事情只有这个：我返回家中，在盥洗室打扮了 3 个钟头，几百次地看挂钟和手表，不幸的是它们显示的时间都是一样的。

当钟敲响 10 点半的时候，我对自己说：是时候出发啦！

当时我在普罗旺斯街住，我选择沿着勃朗峰街前行，经过林荫大道，再走过路易大帝街跟马洪港街，最后到达昂坦街。我抬头望着玛格丽特的窗户，里面透出了灯光。我拉响门铃，向看门人询问戈蒂埃小姐是否在家。得到回复说戈蒂埃小姐从来不曾在 11 点或是 11 点 15 分之前回家。我看了一下表。我本来

intended to come quite slowly, and I had come in five minutes from the Rue de Provence to the Rue d'Antin.

I walked to and fro in the street; there are no shops, and at that hour it is quite deserted. In half an hour's time, Marguerite arrived. She looked around her as she got down from her coupe', as if she were looking for some one. The carriage drove off; the stables were not at the house. Just as Marguerite was going to ring, I went up to her and said, "Good-evening."

"Ah, it is you," she said, in a tone that by no means reassured me as to her pleasure in seeing me.

"Did you not promise me that I might come and see you today?"

"Quite right. I had forgotten."

This word upset all the reflections I had made in the morning, and all the hopes I had had during the day. Nevertheless, I was beginning to get used to her ways, and I did not leave her, as I should certainly have done once. We entered. Nanine had already opened the door.

"Has Prudence come?" said Marguerite.

"No, madame."

"Say that she is to be admitted as soon as she comes. But first put out the lamp in the drawing-room, and if any one comes, say that I have not come back and shall not

觉得自己走得非常慢，可实际上我只用了 5 分钟就从普罗旺斯街走到昂坦街了！

我在这条街上来回走着。这里没有商店，这个时间已经颇为冷清。过了半小时，玛格丽特回来了。她跳下马车，朝四周看了一圈，就像在找什么人似的。因为马厩并不在这座房子里，马车缓缓离开了。当玛格丽特刚想去拉门铃的时候，我走了过去，问候道："晚安！"

"啊！是你啊。"她开口说，听语气好像她不太高兴在这儿见到我。

"你不是同意我今天来这儿探望你的吗？"

"的确是这样，我给忘记了。"

一句话将我早晨的想法与白天的憧憬一扫而光。然而，我已经开始习惯了她的处事方式，所以我没有拂袖而去，倘若是从前，我一定会当即离开的。我们走进屋子。纳尼娜已经把门打开了。

"普鲁登斯有没有来？"玛格丽特问。

"她没来，夫人。"

"去和她说一声，让她一回来就来这儿。不过你先去把客厅里的灯关了，倘使有人来，就说我还没

be coming back."

She was like a woman who is preoccupied with something, and perhaps annoyed by an unwelcome guest. I did not know what to do or say. Marguerite went toward her bedroom; I remained where I was.

"Come," she said.

She took off her hat and her velvet cloak and threw them on the bed, then let herself drop into a great armchair beside the fire, which she kept till the very beginning of summer, and said to me as she fingered her watch-chain:

"Well, what news have you got for me?"

"None, except that I ought not to have come tonight."

"Why?"

"Because you seem vexed, and no doubt I am boring you."

"You are not boring me; only I am not well; I have been suffering all day. I could not sleep, and I have a frightful headache."

"Shall I go away and let you go to bed?"

"Oh, you can stay. If I want to go to bed I don't mind your being here."

At that moment there was a ring.

"Who is coming now?" she said, with an impatient movement.

A few minutes after there was another ring.

回来呢，而且今天都不会回来了。"

她表现得就像一个明显有心事的女人，或者也可能是对某位不知趣的不速之客心存反感。我完全不知道该做些什么，或是说些什么才好。玛格丽特朝着她的卧室走过去，我却呆呆地站在原地木然不动。

"过来吧。"她开口说。

她摘下帽子，把天鹅绒外衣脱掉，将它们一股脑扔到床上，然后往火炉边的一张大扶手椅里一躺，炉火依她的吩咐总会生到春末夏初。她一边用手指玩弄着表链一边对我说：

"嗳，有什么新鲜事说给我听听？"

"没什么新鲜的，除了我今晚不该来这里。"

"什么原因呢？"

"因为你看上去很烦恼，毫无疑问，我让你厌烦了。"

"你没有惹我讨厌，只是我觉得不大舒服，已经难受整整一天了。昨晚没法入睡，今天头疼得厉害。"

"那我先告辞让你休息？"

"噢！你可以留下来，假如我想睡觉，你在这儿也一样可以。"

正在这时有人拉响了门铃。

"这个时候谁还会来呀？"她露出不耐烦的样子说道。

过了一会儿，铃又响了。

"Isn't there any one to go to the door? I shall have to go."

She got up and said to me, "Wait here."

She went through the rooms, and I heard her open the outer door. I listened.

The person whom she had admitted did not come farther than the dining-room. At the first word I recognised the voice of the young Comte de N.

"How are you this evening?" he said.

"Not well," replied Marguerite drily.

"Am I disturbing you?"

"Perhaps."

"How you receive me! What have I done, my dear Marguerite?"

"My dear friend, you have done nothing. I am ill; I must go to bed, so you will be good enough to go. It is sickening not to be able to return at night without your making your appearance five minutes afterward. What is it you want? For me to be your mistress? Well, I have already told you a hundred times, No; you simply worry me, and you might as well go somewhere else. I repeat to you today, for the last time, I don't want to have anything to do with you; that's settled. Good-bye. Here's Nanine coming in; she can light you to the door. Good-night."

Without adding another word, or listening to what the young man

"难道没人去应门了吗，我还得自己过去开。"

她站起身来，对我说道："你在这里等一下。"

她走过房间来到外边，我听见了门打开的声音。我竖起耳朵听着。

玛格丽特让进来的人到了餐厅就没有再走了。对方刚一开口，我就听出那声音是年轻的 N 伯爵。

"你今晚身体怎么样？"他问。

"不太舒服。"玛格丽特硬邦邦地回答说。

"我是不是打扰到你了？"

"或许吧。"

"你怎么能这样对我！我做了什么冒犯的事，亲爱的玛格丽特？"

"我亲爱的朋友，你什么坏事也没做，可我病了，我必须去睡觉，所以你如果能离开这里的话，我将非常感激。每晚我回来不到 5 分钟就能见到阁下光临，这简直要我的命。你究竟想怎么样？想让我做你的情人吗？我都已经说过 100 遍了，答案是不！你只是在惹我讨厌，还是另打主意为好。今天我再和你说一遍，这是最后一遍了：我不想和你扯上任何关系！这总行了吧，再见。哦，是纳尼娜回来了，她会拿灯送你的，晚安。"

玛格丽特再也没说一句话，或是留在那儿听那个年轻人含含糊糊

stammered out, Marguerite returned to the room and slammed the door. Nanine entered a moment after.

"Now understand," said Marguerite, "you are always to say to that idiot that I am not in, or that I will not see him. I am tired out with seeing people who always want the same thing; who pay me for it, and then think they are quit of me. If those who are going to go in for our hateful business only knew what it really was they would sooner be chambermaids. But no, vanity, the desire of having dresses and carriages and diamonds carries us away; one believes what one hears, for here, as elsewhere, there is such a thing as belief, and one uses up one's heart, one's body, one's beauty, little by little; one is feared like a beast of prey, scorned like a pariah, surrounded by people who always take more than they give; and one fine day one dies like a dog in a ditch, after having ruined others and ruined one's self."

"Come, come, madame, be calm," said Nanine; "your nerves are a bit upset tonight."

"This dress worries me," continued Marguerite, unhooking her bodice; "give me a dressing-gown. Well, and Prudence?"

"She has not come yet, but I will send her to you, madame, the moment she

的唠叨，她走回卧室，重重地摔上门。过了一会儿，纳尼娜走了进来。

"现在你听着，"玛格丽特说道，"以后如果那个笨蛋再来，你就对他说我不在，或者说我不想见他。这些人一个劲地来向我提同样的要求，我已经受够了。他们给了我钱，就认为跟我算是两讫了。倘若那些准备投身这行下流营生的女人能弄清楚里头究竟是怎么一回事，她们一定宁愿去做女用人的。可是不行，我们爱慕虚荣，对衣裙、马车和钻石的渴望让我们不得不去做。人们相信了耳朵所听到的，以为这一行也有它的原则，而我们就一点点地出卖自己的心灵、身体跟姿色；人们像看猛兽一样提防我们，像看贱民一样蔑视我们。我们总是被那些贪得无厌想占便宜的人所包围，总有一天，等到我们毁灭了别人也毁灭了自己，就会像条狗那样地死去。"

"好了，好了，夫人，冷静下来，"纳尼娜劝道，"今晚你的神经有点太紧张了。"

"这衣服让我觉得不舒服，"玛格丽特一边说，一边拉开了胸衣的搭扣，"给我拿件浴衣过来，还有，普鲁登斯来了吗？"

"她还没回来呢，不过等她回

comes."

"There's one, now," Marguerite went on, as she took off her dress and put on a white dressing-gown, "there's one who knows very well how to find me when she is in want of me, and yet she can't do me a service decently. She knows I am waiting for an answer. She knows how anxious I am, and I am sure she is going about on her own account, without giving a thought to me."

"Perhaps she had to wait."

"Let us have some punch."

"It will do you no good, madame," said Nanine.

"So much the better. Bring some fruit, too, and a pate or a wing of chicken; something or other, at once. I am hungry."

Need I tell you the impression which this scene made upon me, or can you not imagine it?

"You are going to have supper with me," she said to me; "meanwhile, take a book. I am going into my dressing-room for a moment."

She lit the candles of a candelabra, opened a door at the foot of the bed, and disappeared.

I began to think over this poor girl's life, and my love for her was mingled with a great pity. I walked to and fro in the room,

来我会让她到你这儿来的。"

"看哪,这儿还有一位,"玛格丽特说着脱下了长裙,拿一件白色浴衣披着,"有个人在用得着我的时候非常清楚怎样才能找到我,可连一次忙都不愿意帮。她明白我今晚等着她的回音呢,而且是一直在盼着,等得非常心急,可是我能够肯定她绝对把我的事抛诸脑后,只顾着自己玩去了。"

"或许她是被谁留住了呢。"

"帮我们拿点潘趣酒过来。"

"夫人,这对你的身体不好。"纳尼娜说。

"那更好了。再拿点水果和馅饼,或者拿只鸡翅什么的,随便什么别的也行,马上拿来,我非常饿。"

这样的场景给我留下了什么样印象,还需要多说吗?难道你会想象不出来?

"你一会儿和我一块儿吃夜宵吧,"她说,"在那之前,你先拿本书看着好了,我得去下梳妆间。"

她拿过一只枝形烛台,把上面的几支蜡烛点燃,打开床脚那边的一扇门,消失了。

我则开始思考这位可怜姑娘的生活,对她的爱恋中混合了极大的怜悯。我一边想着,一边迈着大步

thinking over things, when Prudence entered.

"Ah, you here?" she said, "where is Marguerite?"

"In her dressing-room."

"I will wait. By the way, do you know she thinks you charming?"

"No."

"She hasn't told you?"

"Not at all."

"How are you here?"

"I have come to pay her a visit."

"At midnight?"

"Why not?"

"Joker!"

"She has received me, as a matter of fact, very badly."

"She will receive you better by and by."

"Do you think so?"

"I have some good news for her."

"No harm in that. So she has spoken to you about me?"

"Last night, or rather tonight, when you and your friend went. By the way, what is your friend called? Gaston R., his name is, isn't it?"

"Yes," said I, not without smiling, as I thought of what Gaston had confided to me, and saw that Prudence scarcely even knew his name.

"He is quite nice, that fellow; what does

在房间里来回踱步，这时普鲁登斯过来了。

"哦，你在这儿？"她说道，"玛格丽特去哪里了？"

"在她的梳妆间里。"

"那我等会儿，话说回来，你知道她觉得你很有魅力吗？"

"我不知道。"

"她从未和你说起过吗？"

"一次也没有。"

"你怎么会出现在这儿呢？"

"我过来看望一下她。"

"在半夜里来看她？"

"为什么不行呢？"

"简直是个笑话！"

"事实上，她接待我的时候情绪很坏。"

"她马上就会客气地对你了。"

"你真的这么想吗？"

"我带了一个好消息给她。"

"这倒不错。那么她曾经和你提起过我吗？"

"那是昨晚，更确切地说是今天早上，等你和你的朋友走后。问一下，你的朋友叫什么来着？是叫R·加斯顿没错吧？"

"对。"我说，一想到加斯顿和我说的那些知心话，再看看普鲁登斯几乎都不知道他的名字，真让我忍不住要笑出来。

"那个小伙子非常不错，他是

he do?"

"He has twenty-five thousand francs a year."

"Ah, indeed! Well, to return to you. Marguerite asked me all about you: who you were, what you did, what mistresses you had had; in short, everything that one could ask about a man of your age. I told her all I knew, and added that you were a charming young man. That's all."

"Thanks. Now tell me what it was she wanted to say to you last night."

"Nothing at all. It was only to get rid of the count; but I have really something to see her about today, and I am bringing her an answer now."

At this moment Marguerite reappeared from her dressing-room, wearing a coquettish little night-cap with bunches of yellow ribbons, technically known as "cabbages." She looked ravishing. She had satin slippers on her bare feet, and was in the act of polishing her nails.

"Well," she said, seeing Prudence, "have you seen the duke?"

"Yes, indeed."

"And what did he say to you?"

"He gave me –"

"How much?"

"Six thousand."

"Have you got it?"

做什么的？"

"他有 2.5 万法郎年金。"

"啊！天哪！好吧，还是回来谈谈你的事吧，玛格丽特跟我打听你的一切，你是什么人，干什么的，你从前有过什么样的情妇。总而言之，像你这种年纪的人应当打听的事情她全都问到了。我把自己知道的都和她说了，还补充说，你是个非常迷人的小伙子。这就是全部了。"

"非常感谢。现在请你和我说说她昨天托你办的事是什么吧。"

"什么事情都没有。她只说要把伯爵给赶走，不过今天她倒是让我办了一件事，今晚我就是过来给她回音的。"

正在这时，玛格丽特走出了梳妆间，她戴着一顶婀娜多姿的睡帽，上面缀着黄色缎带，这种装饰在技术上的学名叫甘蓝式缎结。她的样子动人极了。她光着脚跟着缎子拖鞋，一边走一边擦着指甲。

"哦，"一见普鲁登斯她就问道，"你看见公爵了？"

"是的，的确见到了。"

"他都和你说了些什么？"

"他给了我……"

"多少呢？"

"6000。"

"Yes.

"Did he seem put out?"

"No."

"Poor man!"

This "Poor man!" was said in a tone impossible to render. Marguerite took the six notes of a thousand francs.

"It was quite time," she said. "My dear Prudence, are you in want of any money?"

"You know, my child, it is the 15th in a couple of days, so if you could lend me three or four hundred francs, you would do me a real service."

"Send over tomorrow; it is too late to get change now."

"Don't forget."

"No fear. Will you have supper with us?"

"No, Charles is waiting for me."

"You are still devoted to him?"

"Crazy, my dear! I will see you tomorrow. Good-bye, Armand."

Mme. Duvernoy went out.

Marguerite opened the drawer of a side-table and threw the bank-notes into it.

"Will you permit me to get into bed?" she said with a smile, as she moved toward the bed.

"Not only permit, but I beg of you."

She turned back the covering and got into bed.

"你拿过来了吗？"

"是的。"

"他看上去有点不高兴？"

"不像。"

"真是可怜的人！"

她说"真是可怜的人"这句话时，语气简直难以形容。玛格丽特接过 6 张 1000 法郎面值的钞票。

"来得非常及时呢，"她说，"我亲爱的普鲁登斯，需要些钱用吗？"

"你知道的，我的孩子，离 15 号没有几天了，假如你可以借我三四百法郎，就真是帮我的大忙了。"

"等明天再派人来取吧，这个时候去兑钱未免太晚了。"

"你可不要忘了呀。"

"尽管放心。你和我们一块儿吃夜宵吗？"

"不吃了，夏尔在家等我呢。"

"你还喜欢着他吗？"

"我为他疯狂，亲爱的！我明天再来。再见，阿尔芒。"

迪韦尔诺瓦夫人离开了。

玛格丽特打开边桌的抽屉，将钞票扔进去。

"你允许我去床上躺着吗？"她微笑着，一边说一边朝床边走去。

"不仅允许，我请求你这么做。"

她将床上铺着的镶有镂空花边的床罩拉下去，随后躺下了。

"Now," said she, "come and sit down by me, and let's have a talk."

Prudence was right: the answer that she had brought to Marguerite had put her into a good humour.

"Will you forgive me for my bad temper tonight?" she said, taking my hand.

"I am ready to forgive you as often as you like."

"And you love me?"

"Madly."

"In spite of my bad disposition?"

"In spite of all."

"You swear it?"

"Yes," I said in a whisper.

Nanine entered, carrying plates, a cold chicken, a bottle of claret, and some strawberries.

"I haven't had any punch made," said Nanine; "claret is better for you. Isn't it, sir?"

"Certainly," I replied, still under the excitement of Marguerite's last words, my eyes fixed ardently upon her.

"Good," said she; "put it all on the little table, and draw it up to the bed; we will help ourselves. This is the third night you have sat up, and you must be in want of sleep. Go to bed. I don't want anything more."

"Shall I lock the door?"

"这会儿，"她说，"来吧，坐到我身边来，我们聊聊天吧。"

普鲁登斯是对的，她带回的答复让玛格丽特变得高兴起来了。

"今晚我的脾气不好，你可以原谅我吗？"她握着我的手问道。

"我无论何时都会原谅你的。"

"那么你爱我吗？"

"我疯狂地爱着你。"

"即使我的脾气很坏？"

"不管怎样我都爱你。"

"你能向我发誓吗？"

"当然能。"我轻声地对她说。

纳尼娜端着几个盘子走了进来，一只冷的熟鸡，一瓶波尔多红葡萄酒，还有一些草莓与两副刀叉。

"我不曾让人给你调潘趣酒，"纳尼娜说，"葡萄酒对你的身体好一些。对不对，先生？"

"当然。"我回答，还沉浸在玛格丽特方才那几句话带来的激动和亢奋中，用火辣辣的目光凝视着她。

"也好，"她说道，"把它们都放到小桌子上吧，把小桌子挪到床前面来，我们可以自己吃。你已经连着3个晚上熬夜啦，一定很困了吧，去睡觉吧，我不会需要什么了。"

"需要我把门锁上吗？"

"I should think so! And above all, tell them not to admit anybody before midday."

"我想是的！重要的是告诉他们，明天中午之前不要让任何人进来。"

CHAPTER 12
第十二章

At five o'clock in the morning, as the light began to appear through the curtains, Marguerite said to me: "Forgive me if I send you away; but I must. The duke comes every morning; they will tell him, when he comes, that I am asleep, and perhaps he will wait until I wake."

I took Marguerite's head in my hands; her loosened hair streamed about her; I gave her a last kiss, saying:

"When shall I see you again?"

"Listen," she said; "take the little gilt key on the mantelpiece, open that door; bring me back the key and go. In the course of the day you shall have a letter, and my orders, for you know you are to obey blindly."

"Yes; but if I should already ask for something?"

"What?"

"Let me have that key."

"What you ask is a thing I have never done for any one."

"Well, do it for me, for I swear to you

清早 5 点钟，微亮的晨光穿过窗帘照了进来，玛格丽特和我说道："非常抱歉，请原谅我得让你走了，我必须这么做，公爵每天早上都会来。如果他来了，而我还在睡，很可能他会一直等到我醒过来。"

我将玛格丽特的脸捧在手中，她蓬松的头发散乱地披落下来，我最后吻了她一下，说道：

"我什么时候能再见到你？"

"听好，"她开口说，"你去壁炉上拿那把金色的钥匙，去打开这扇门再回来把钥匙还我，你就离开吧。在今天之内你会收到我的一封信，告诉你我的命令，你知道的，你应该无条件地服从我。"

"是这样，可是我现在能否向你要求一件东西呢？"

"你想要什么？"

"让我把这把钥匙拿走。"

"你在问我要求一件我从来不曾给过别人的东西。"

"那么，请为我破例吧，因为

that I don't love you as the others have loved you."

"Well, keep it; but it only depends on me to make it useless to you, after all."

"How?"

"There are bolts on the door."

"Wretch!"

"I will have them taken off."

"You love, then, a little?"

"I don't know how it is, but it seems to me as if I do! Now, go; I can't keep my eyes open."

I held her in my arms for a few seconds and then went.

The streets were empty, the great city was still asleep, a sweet freshness circulated in the streets that a few hours later would be filled with the noise of men. It seemed to me as if this sleeping city belonged to me; I searched my memory for the names of those whose happiness I had once envied; and I could not recall one without finding myself the happier.

To be loved by a pure young girl, to be the first to reveal to her the strange mystery of love, is indeed a great happiness, but it is the simplest thing in the world. To take captive a heart which has had no experience of attack, is to enter an unfortified and ungarrisoned city. Education, family feeling, the sense of

我曾向你发过誓,我对你的爱和别人的并不一样。"

"好吧,那你就拿着它吧,不过它是否对你有用依旧取决于我。"

"你能怎么做呢?"

"门的里侧装了插销。"

"你这个坏蛋!"

"我会叫人把插销给拆了。"

"这么说,你真的爱我吗,哪怕就一点点?"

"我也不清楚是怎么回事,可是我似乎真的爱上你。这会儿你就走吧,我非常困了。"

我又把她抱在怀里紧紧拥了一会儿,就离开了。

街上空无一人,这个大城市还在酣睡,四处吹着一缕缕柔和的风,几个小时之后,此处就会熙来攘往,喧哗不已了。此刻这沉睡的城市就像是只属于我一个人。以前我总是羡慕别人运气好,我逐一回想着那些人的名字,然而我无论如何也想不出有谁比我现在更加幸福了。

得到一个纯洁少女的爱,第一个为她揭开神秘之爱的奥秘,这的确是莫大的幸福,然而这也是世上最最简单的事情了。征服一颗不曾获得过爱情的心,就等同于进驻一个没有设防的城市。所受的教育、责任感与家庭是强有力的哨兵,不过对一个16岁少女的天性来说,无

duty, the family, are strong sentinels, but there are no sentinels so vigilant as not to be deceived by a girl of sixteen to whom nature, by the voice of the man she loves, gives the first counsels of love, all the more ardent because they seem so pure.

The more a girl believes in goodness, the more easily will she give way, if not to her lover, at least to love, for being without mistrust she is without force, and to win her love is a triumph that can be gained by any young man of five-and-twenty. See how young girls are watched and guarded! The walls of convents are not high enough, mothers have no locks strong enough, religion has no duties constant enough, to shut these charming birds in their cages, cages not even strewn with flowers. Then how surely must they desire the world which is hidden from them, how surely must they find it tempting, how surely must they listen to the first voice which comes to tell its secrets through their bars, and bless the hand which is the first to raise a corner of the mysterious veil!

But to be really loved by a courtesan: that is a victory of infinitely greater difficulty. With them the body has worn out the soul, the senses have burned up the heart, dissipation has blunted the feelings. They have long known the words that we

论多么机警的哨兵都免不了会被骗过，通过她所爱男子的声音，为她作出第一次的爱情谕示，这一切来得如此猛烈，正因为它是如此的纯洁。

越是相信爱情美好的少女就越容易失身，即使不是失身于情人，至少也会失身于爱情。一个人一旦丧失警惕就相当于失去了力量，从一个这样的少女那里赢得爱情虽说是一场胜利，可这样的胜利任何一个 25 岁的男子什么时候想要就能弄到手。虽然在这些少女周围的确守卫森严，不过想把这些可爱的小鸟全都关在笼子里，而这笼子甚至连鲜花的点缀也没有，那么修道院的围墙远不会够高，母亲的看管远不能够严，宗教戒条的威慑力远不能持久。那些姑娘们对那别人不许她们了解的外部世界该有多么地向往啊！她们该会多么坚信那个世界绝对极为引人入胜，当有人第一次来隔着栅栏向她们倾诉爱恋的奥秘，她们又会多么高兴，对头一回掀开神奇帘幕一角的那只手，她们又该给予怎样的感激和祝福！

然而若能真正得到一个妓女的爱，那将是一场极为难得的胜利，她们的灵魂已被肉体腐蚀，心灵遭到情欲的灼伤，心肠早因放纵的生

say to them, the means we use; they have sold the love that they inspire. They love by profession, and not by instinct. They are guarded better by their calculations than a virgin by her mother and her convent; and they have invented the word caprice for that unbartered love which they allow themselves from time to time, for a rest, for an excuse, for a consolation, like usurers, who cheat a thousand, and think they have bought their own redemption by once lending a sovereign to a poor devil who is dying of hunger without asking for interest or a receipt.

Then, when God allows love to a courtesan, that love, which at first seems like a pardon, becomes for her almost without penitence. When a creature who has all her past to reproach herself with is taken all at once by a profound, sincere, irresistible love, of which she had never felt herself capable; when she has confessed her love, how absolutely the man whom she loves dominates her! How strong he feels with his cruel right to say: You do no more for love than you have done for money. They know not what proof to give. A child, says the fable, having often amused himself by crying "Help! a wolf!" in order to disturb the labourers in the field, was one day devoured by a Wolf,

活而硬如铁石。她们早已听腻了他人的表白，惯用的手腕也都早已烂熟于心，她们就算有过爱情也早就被卖掉了。她们的爱恋并非出自感情，而是为了金钱。她们精于算计，防范远比一个被母亲和修道院守卫的处女要周密得多。她们将不在生意范畴以内的爱情称为逢场作戏，这种爱情经常会有，被她们当成消遣、借口也是安慰，就好比放高利贷的人，他们剥削过成千的人，可某天竟借了 20 法郎给一个就快饿死的穷人，没有朝他要利息，不曾逼他立借据，就觉得罪都被赎清了。

那么，当上帝将爱情降临到一个妓女身上的时候，这份感情开始时就像宽恕，但后来却几乎都会变成对她的惩罚。不曾忏悔就说不上宽恕。倘若某个女人有过一段理应受到谴责的生活，忽然感觉自己萌生了一种深切、真挚、无法自抑的爱情，那种她从来认为不可能会有的爱情，在她承认的那一刻，她所爱的男子就能够统治她了！这个男子该有多得意，他会得到权利对她说"你的爱情和买卖差不多"。可是，这种权利太过残酷。此时她们真不知道如何才能表明自己的真心。有个寓言里讲道：一个孩子想戏弄农民们，就老是在田野里喊"救命啊，狼来啦！"可当狼真的来了时，那些

because those whom he had so often deceived no longer believed in his cries for help. It is the same with these unhappy women when they love seriously. They have lied so often that no one will believe them, and in the midst of their remorse they are devoured by their love.

Hence those great devotions, those austere retreats from the world, of which some of them have given an example.

But when the man who inspires this redeeming love is great enough in soul to receive it without remembering the past, when he gives himself up to it, when, in short, he loves as he is loved, this man drains at one draught all earthly emotions, and after such a love his heart will be closed to every other.

I did not make these reflections on the morning when I returned home. They could but have been the presentiment of what was to happen to me, and, despite my love for Marguerite, I did not foresee such consequences. I make these reflections today. Now that all is irrevocably ended, they a rise naturally out of what has taken place.

But to return to the first day of my liaison.

When I reached home I was in a state of mad gaiety. As I thought of how the

上过当的人却不再相信他的求救声，最后他被狼吃掉了。那些产生真正爱情的可怜姑娘也是一样。她们撒谎的次数已经太多，没人会相信她们的话，最终她们将满怀悔恨地被自己的爱情所毁灭。

从此而后，那些伟大的献身，那些从喧嚣红尘中一丝不苟的退避，便获得了一个极好的典范。

然而，当一个男子被这种超脱的爱情所感染，愿意忘记这个女人的过去而接纳她，当他投身于这份情感。简言之，当他如被她所爱那般地爱上她时，这个男子一时间便享尽了人间一切美好的感情，在这样的爱情经历之后，他再也不会爱上别的什么人了。

当我那天早上回家的时候是没有这些想法的。或许我会想到，但不会预感到那些会发生在我身上的事，因此尽管我爱玛格丽特，却不曾产生过类似的念头，直到今天我才想到了这些。现在一切都已过去了，对于曾经发生的事，产生这样的想法是非常自然的。

还是先来看看我们这段感情的第一天吧。

当我回到住处，不禁感到欣喜若狂。每当想起我想象中那些存在

barriers which my imagination had placed between Marguerite and myself had disappeared, of how she was now mine; of the place I now had in her thoughts, of the key to her room which I had in my pocket, and of my right to use this key, I was satisfied with life, proud of myself, and I loved God because he had let such things be.

One day a young man is passing in the street, he brushes against a woman, looks at her, turns, goes on his way. He does not know the woman, and she has pleasures, griefs, loves, in which he has no part. He does not exist for her, and perhaps, if he spoke to her, she would only laugh at him, as Marguerite had laughed at me. Weeks, months, years pass, and all at once, when they have each followed their fate along a different path, the logic of chance brings them face to face. The woman becomes the man's mistress and loves him. How? why? Their two existences are henceforth one; they have scarcely begun to know one another when it seems as if they had known one another always, and all that had gone before is wiped out from the memory of the two lovers. It is curious, one must admit.

As for me, I no longer remembered how I had lived before that night. My whole

于玛格丽特与我之间的障碍都已消失，我已拥有了她，而我在她的心中已经获得了一定的地位，再想到我口袋里就装着她房间的钥匙，而且我还有权使用它，我就感到生活异常美好，我为自己而骄傲，我感谢上帝，是他赐予了我这一切。

有一天，当一个年轻人在街上走过，看见一个女人，他看了她一眼，回头就走了。他并不认识她。那个女人有自己的快乐、悲哀与爱情，但和那个男人毫不相干。她的心里也没有他的位置，倘若他想和她搭话，她或许会和玛格丽特嘲笑我一样去嘲笑他。接着过了几个星期，几个月，甚至几年。忽然，在他们在各自原本命运的道路上行走的时候，一份偶然的机缘让他们再次相会。这个女人坠入爱河，变成了男人的情人。怎么会这样呢，原因又是什么呢？从此以后这两个年轻人就难舍难离，虽然他们刚刚相遇，却仿佛爱情由来已久，一切往事都在这两个有情人的心目中消失了。我们必须承认，这是非常奇怪的现象。

而对我来说，这天晚上之前我的生活是怎样的，已经是毫无印象

being was exalted into joy at the memory of the words we had exchanged during that first night. Either Marguerite was very clever in deception, or she had conceived for me one of those sudden passions which are revealed in the first kiss, and which die, often enough, as suddenly as they were born.

The more I reflected the more I said to myself that Marguerite had no reason for feigning a love which she did not feel, and I said to myself also that women have two ways of loving, one of which may arise from the other: they love with the heart or with the senses. Often a woman takes a lover in obedience to the mere will of the senses, and learns without expecting it the mystery of immaterial love, and lives henceforth only through her heart; often a girl who has sought in marriage only the union of two pure affections receives the sudden revelation of physical love, that energetic conclusion of the purest impressions of the soul.

In the midst of these thoughts I fell asleep; I was awakened by a letter from Marguerite containing these words:

Here are my orders: Tonight at the Vaudeville.

Come during the third entr'acte.

了。一想到第一个夜晚我俩说过的话，就全身舒畅。或者是玛格丽特善于欺骗，或者是她对我突然产生了一股热情，这种热情在第一次接吻的时候就有所显露了，可是后来那几次，这种激情又同它迸发时一般骤然熄灭了。

我越想就越肯定玛格丽特完全没有理由假装爱上我。我还对自己说，女人的恋爱方式可以分为互为因果的两种表现：要么是从心底里去爱一个人，要么是因为感官的需要去爱一个人。女人选择一个情人往往只是为了满足自己感官上的需求，然而她在不自觉的情况下了解了超越肉欲爱情的奥秘，并且在后来的日子里过着仅有精神爱情的生活。一位年轻的姑娘往往最初只是觉得婚姻是两人纯洁感情的结合，而后才突然认识到肉体的爱情，这也是灵魂中最为纯洁的感情产生的有力后果。

我就这样在沉思中慢慢睡着了。是玛格丽特的来信唤醒了我，信中这样写道：

这是我的命令：今晚在歌舞剧院见面。

在第三次幕间休息时过来找我。

M.G.

玛·戈

I put the letter into a drawer, so that I might always have it at band in case I doubted its reality, as I did from time to time.

She did not tell me to come to see her during the day, and I dared not go; but I had so great a desire to see her before the evening that I went to the Champs-Elysees, where I again saw her pass and repass, as I had on the previous day.

At seven o'clock I was at the Vaudeville. Never had I gone to a theatre so early. The boxes filled one after another. Only one remained empty, the stage box. At the beginning of the third act I heard the door of the box, on which my eyes had been almost constantly fixed, open, and Marguerite appeared. She came to the front at once, looked around the stalls, saw me, and thanked me with a look.

That night she was marvellously beautiful. Was I the cause of this coquetry? Did she love me enough to believe that the more beautiful she looked the happier I should be? I did not know, but if that had been her intention she certainly succeeded, for when she appeared all heads turned, and the actor who was then on the stage looked to see who had produced such an

我将信收进一个抽屉里。这样一来，在我时不时怀疑此事的真实性时，就能有个实实在在的凭据。

她并没有告诉我在白天去找她，我也不敢贸然前去。然而我实在太想在傍晚之前就见到她了，所以我就去了香榭丽舍大街。与昨天一样，我又在那儿眼见着她经过，还走下了马车。

晚上 7 点钟我就来到了歌舞剧院，以前从未这么早就去剧院。那些包厢里渐渐坐满了人，可还有一个包厢空无一人：底层台前包厢。当第三幕开始，我听到那个包厢门开启的声音，此前我几乎是目不转睛地盯着那个包厢。玛格丽特出现了。她很快来到包厢前面，朝正厅前座那里寻找，看见我之后就向我投以感谢的目光。

这天晚上她真是美得惊人！她是为了我才如此盛装打扮的吗？难道她对我的爱已经到了如此的地步，觉得她打扮得越是漂亮，我就会感到更加幸福吗？这我还不清楚，但倘若她真的是这么想的，那么她的确成功了，因为她的身影刚一出现，观众的头就像一片波涛一般纷纷朝她转去，甚至舞台上的演

effect on the audience by her mere presence there.

And I had the key of this woman's room, and in three or four hours she would again be mine!

People blame those who let themselves be ruined by actresses and kept women; what astonishes me is that twenty times greater follies are not committed for them. One must have lived that life, as I have, to know how much the little vanities which they afford their lovers every day help to fasten deeper into the heart, since we have no other word for it, the love which he has for them.

Prudence next took her place in the box, and a man, whom I recognised as the Comte de G., seated himself at the back. As I saw him, a cold shiver went through my heart.

Doubtless Marguerite perceived the impression made on me by the presence of this man, for she smiled to me again, and, turning her back to the count, appeared to be very attentive to the play. At the third entr'acte she turned and said two words: the count left the box, and Marguerite beckoned to me to come to her.

"Good-evening," she said as I entered, holding out her hand.

"Good-evening," I replied to both

员都对着她看，因为她才刚露面就已经令观众为之倾倒。

而我却保有着这个女人房间的钥匙，而且三四个小时之后，她又会是我的了！

人们总是谴责那些为了女演员和妓女而散尽家财的人，而让我感到奇怪的却是，他们为什么没有为这些女人干出更为荒唐的事情呢。一定要过上如我这般的生活，一个人才会了解到，她们在日常生活之中是如何地满足了情人们的各种微小的虚荣心，因此才能巩固那些情人对她们的爱情——只有"爱情"可以表达，我们找不到别的字眼了。

随后是普鲁登斯出现在她的包厢里，还有一个男人同样在包厢的后座坐了下来，他就是我所认识的G伯爵。见到了他，我一下子感觉浑身冰冷。

玛格丽特肯定察觉到她包厢里的男人对我的情绪造成了影响，因为她又朝我笑了笑，随后便背对着伯爵，看上去像一门心思在看戏。等第三次幕间休息的时候，她回过身去，讲了几句话，然后伯爵走出了包厢，接着玛格丽特便做手势让我过去找她。

"晚上好。"她在我进门的时候说道，同时将手朝我伸了过来。

"晚上好。"我同样问候了玛格

Marguerite and Prudence.

"Sit down."

"But I am taking some one's place. Isn't the Comte de G. coming back?"

"Yes; I sent him to fetch some sweets, so that we could talk by ourselves for a moment. Mme. Duvernoy is in the secret."

"Yes, my children," said she; "have no fear. I shall say nothing."

"What is the matter with you tonight?" said Marguerite, rising and coming to the back of the box and kissing me on the forehead.

"I am not very well."

"You should go to bed," she replied, with that ironical air which went so well with her delicate and witty face.

"Where?"

"At home."

"You know that I shouldn't be able to sleep there."

"Well, then, it won't do for you to come and be pettish here because you have seen a man in my box."

"It is not for that reason."

"Yes, it is. I know; and you are wrong, so let us say no more about it. You will go back with Prudence after the theatre, and you will stay there till I call. Do you understand?"

"Yes."

丽特和普鲁登斯。

"你请坐。"

"那我岂不是把别人的位子占啦，G伯爵不会回来了吗？"

"他要回来，我让他去买点蜜饯来，这样我们就能单独聊一会儿，迪韦尔诺瓦夫人会为我们保密的。"

"不错，我的孩子们，"迪韦尔诺瓦夫人开口道，"不必担心，我什么都不会说的。"

"你今天晚上是怎么了？"玛格丽特站了起来，来到包厢后面搂住我，在我的额头轻轻吻着。

"我感觉不太舒服。"

"你应该去床上休息一会儿。"她接着说，那俏皮的神色与精致娇小的面容极为相配。

"去哪里休息呢？"

"当然是你家里！"

"你明白的，我在自己家里无法入睡。"

"那么，好吧，你就不该因为见到有个男人出现在我包厢里，就来这儿小题大做地发脾气呀。"

"原因其实并不是这个。"

"没错，是这个原因，我知道的。而且是你错了，我们不要再说这些事了。散场之后你去普鲁登斯家里吧，等到我找你为止，明白了吗？"

"是的。"

How could I disobey?

"You still love me?"

"Can you ask?"

"You have thought of me?"

"All day long."

"Do you know that I am really afraid that I shall get very fond of you? Ask Prudence."

"Ah," said she, "it is amazing!"

"Now, you must go back to your seat. The count will be coming back, and there is nothing to be gained by his finding you here."

"Because you don't like seeing him."

"No; only if you had told me that you wanted to come to the Vaudeville tonight I could have got this box for you as well as he."

"Unfortunately, he got it for me without my asking him, and he asked me to go with him; you know well enough that I couldn't refuse. All I could do was to write and tell you where I was going, so that you could see me, and because I wanted to see you myself; but since this is the way you thank me, I shall profit by the lesson."

"I was wrong; forgive me."

"Well and good; and now go back nicely to your place, and, above all, no more jealousy."

She kissed me again, and I left the box.

我怎么能提出抗议呢？

"你依旧爱着我吗？"

"你怎么能问我这个问题？"

"你想念我吗？"

"一天到晚都在想。"

"你知道吗，我是真的害怕自己变得非常喜欢你了。你可以问问普鲁登斯。"

"啊！"普鲁登斯回答道，"那可真是太让人吃惊了。"

"现在，你必须回到自己的座位上去了，伯爵很快就会回来，让他在这里看见你可没有什么好处。"

"因为你并不喜欢看到他。"

"不，不是，不过假如你提前告诉我你今天晚上想来歌舞剧院，我也会如他一般为你送上这个包厢的票的。"

"非常不幸，我并没有和他说什么，他就给我送过来了，邀请我和他一起来。你一定非常清楚，我是不能够拒绝的。我唯一能做的就是写信通知你我会去哪里，这样一来你就能够见到我，因为我自己也非常希望能早一点儿看见你。既然这就是你感谢我的方式，那么我会记住这次教训的。"

"是我错了，请你原谅我吧。"

"太好了，现在乖乖回到你的座位上去吧，不要再吃醋了。"

她又吻了我一下，我就离开了

In the passage I met the count coming back. I returned to my seat.

After all, the presence of M. de G. in Marguerite's box was the most natural thing in the world. He had been her lover, he sent her a box, he accompanied her to the theatre; it was all quite natural, and if I was to have a mistress like Marguerite I should have to get used to her ways.

Nonetheless, I was very unhappy all the rest of the evening, and went away very sadly after having seen Prudence, the count, and Marguerite get into the carriage, which was waiting for them at the door.

However, a quarter of an hour later I was at Prudence's. She had only just got in.

包厢。在走廊里我碰上了返回的伯爵。我回到自己的位子上坐下。

归根结底，G 伯爵出现在玛格丽特的包厢里是件再平常不过的事了。他曾经是她的情人，送了她一张包厢的票，陪她一同来到剧院，这一切都十分自然。既然我要一个玛格丽特这样的姑娘做自己的情人，自然就应该习惯她的生活方式。

尽管如此，这天晚上后来的时间我也没有觉得更好受一些，看到普鲁登斯、伯爵与玛格丽特一块儿坐上在剧院门口等着的四轮马车之后，我也心情郁郁地走了。

然而 15 分钟之后我就到了普鲁登斯家里，她也刚刚回去。

CHAPTER 13

第十三章

"You have come almost as quickly as we," said Prudence.

"Yes," I answered mechanically. "Where is Marguerite?"

"At home."

"Alone?"

"With M. de G."

I walked to and fro in the room.

"Well, what is the matter?"

"Do you think it amuses me to wait here till M. de G. leaves Marguerite's?"

"How unreasonable you are! Don't you see that Marguerite can't turn the count out of doors? M. de G. has been with her for a long time; he has always given her a lot of money; he still does. Marguerite spends more than a hundred thousand francs a year; she has heaps of debts. The duke gives her all that she asks for, but she does not always venture to ask him for all that she is in want of. It would never do for her to quarrel with the count, who is worth to her at least ten thousand francs a year. Marguerite is very fond of you, my dear

"你几乎来得和我们一样迅速！"普鲁登斯说。

"是啊，"我机械地回答，"玛格丽特呢？"

"在家呢。"

"她一个人吗？"

"和 G 伯爵在一起。"

我在屋里来来回回踱着步。

"哎，怎么了？"

"难道你以为在这儿等 G 伯爵从玛格丽特那儿离开我很开心吗？"

"你太不可理喻了。你不是不知道，玛格丽特可不能把伯爵拒之门外。G 伯爵和她交往已久，一直以来，他大把大把地给她钱，现在还在给。玛格丽特一年的花销多达 10 多万法郎，她负债累累。她要多少，公爵就给多少，但她也不敢向公爵索要她需要的所有费用。她绝不会和这个每年在她身上扔万把法郎的伯爵闹翻的。我亲爱的朋友，玛格丽特深深爱着你，但是为了你们两个人的利益着想，你不应该过

fellow, but your liaison with her, in her interests and in yours, ought not to be serious. You with your seven or eight thousand francs a year, what could you do toward supplying all the luxuries which a girl like that is in need of? It would not be enough to keep her carriage. Take Marguerite for what she is, for a good, bright, pretty girl; be her lover for a month, two months; give her flowers, sweets, boxes at the theatre; but don't get any other ideas into your head, and don't make absurd scenes of jealousy. You know whom you have to do with; Marguerite isn't a saint. She likes you, you are very fond of her; let the rest alone. You amaze me when I see you so touchy; you have the most charming mistress in Paris. She receives you in the greatest style, she is covered with diamonds, she needn't cost you a penny, unless you like, and you are not satisfied. My dear fellow, you ask too much!"

"You are right, but I can't help it; the idea that that man is her lover hurts me horribly."

"In the first place," replied Prudence; "is he still her lover? He is a man who is useful to her, nothing more. She has closed her doors to him for two days; he came this morning – she could not but accept the box

于在意你们的关系。你一年七八千法郎的收入怎么够这个姑娘挥霍？连她的车钱都不够啊。你就只管把玛格丽特当做一个美好、聪明、漂亮的女子,做她一两个月的情人，送她一点儿鲜花、糖果和包厢票就行啦，别再有其他的什么想法啦！也别再争风吃醋啦。你应该知道你在和谁打交道，玛格丽特可不是什么贞洁圣女，她喜欢着你，你也爱着她，这就够了。你居然这么感情用事，太不可思议了。你拥有全巴黎最有魅力的情妇！她用最华丽的方式接待你，浑身上下装饰着钻石，只要你喜欢，她又不会花你一个子儿，你居然还不满足。我亲爱的朋友！你也太贪得无厌了。"

"你说得对，但是我情难自禁，一想到那个人是她的情人，我就心痛万分。"

"不过，"普鲁登斯回答说，"现在他还是不是她的情人就难说了。他只是她的一个棋子罢了。已经有两天了，玛格丽特一直拒绝他，今天早上他来了，没办法，她只能接

and let him accompany her. He saw her home; he has gone in for a moment, he is not staying, because you are waiting here. All that, it seems to me, is quite natural. Besides, you don't mind the duke."

"Yes; but he is an old man, and I am sure that Marguerite is not his mistress. Then, it is all very well to accept one liaison, but not two. Such easiness in the matter is very like calculation, and puts the man who consents to it, even out of love, very much in the category of those who, in a lower stage of society, make a trade of their connivance, and a profit of their trade."

"Ah, my dear fellow, how old-fashioned you are! How many of the richest and most fashionable men of the best families I have seen quite ready to do what I advise you to do, and without an effort, without shame, without remorse, Why, one sees it every day. How do you suppose the kept women in Paris could live in the style they do, if they had not three or four lovers at once? No single fortune, however large, could suffice for the expenses of a woman like Marguerite. A fortune of five hundred thousand francs a year is, in France, an enormous fortune; well, my dear friend, five hundred thousand francs a year would still be too little, and for this reason: a man with such an income has a large house,

受他的包厢票，由他陪着去看戏，然后送她回家，到她家待一会儿。既然你在这儿等着，他也待不久的。在我看来，这一切再平常不过了。再说，你也不是很在意公爵吧？"

"是啊，可那公爵是个老头子啊，我相信玛格丽特绝不会是他的情妇。通常，人们只能接受和一个人有这种关系，怎么还会脚踏两只船呢。这种事情还要行这种方便，岂不是算计别人。接受这种做法的男人，即便是以爱情的名义，也像极了下层社会里那些用投机取巧的方式赚钱的人。"

"啊！我亲爱的伙伴，你也太落伍了！我不知道见过多少大富大贵、引领时尚、门第显赫的人，巴不得做我劝你做的事。而且这又不需要费什么心，用不着害臊羞愧。这种事是再平凡不过的了。而且一个巴黎的妓女，身边要没那么三四个情人围着的话，你要她们如何维持那种排场呢？单单一笔钱——不管多大一笔，都是不够玛格丽特那种女人的开销的。在法国，每年50万法郎的收入，也算是一笔很大的财富了。可是，我亲爱的朋友，一年50万法郎的收入还是不够养一个情妇，因为：有这样一笔收入的男人，总会有豪宅，马匹、仆役、马车，时不时要打打猎，还要应酬

horses, servants, carriages; he shoots, has friends, often he is married, he has children, he races, gambles, travels, and what not. All these habits are so much a part of his position that he can not forego them without appearing to have lost all his money, and without causing scandal. Taking it all around, with five hundred thousand francs a year he can not give a woman more than forty or fifty thousand francs in the year, and that is already a good deal. Well, other lovers make up for the rest of her expenses. With Marguerite, it is still more convenient; she has chanced by a miracle on an old man worth ten millions, whose wife and daughter are dead; who has only some nephews, themselves rich, and who gives her all she wants without asking anything in return. But she can not ask him for more than seventy thousand francs a year; and I am sure that if she did ask for more, despite his health and the affection he has for her he would not give it to her.

"All the young men of twenty or thirty thousand francs a year at Paris, that is to say, men who have only just enough to live on in the society in which they mix, know perfectly well, when they are the lovers of a woman like Marguerite, that she could not so much as pay for the rooms she lives

交际。通常来说，这样的人基本上已经结了婚，有了孩子。他要赛马，要赌博，要旅行，天知道他还会干些什么！所有这些都是象征他身份和地位所不可缺少的部分，一旦改变，就会有人认为他破产了，流言蜚语也会就此传开。所有这些算下来，一年50万法郎的收入，花在一个女人身上的钱不会超过四五万法郎，这已经算是不少了。如此，这个女人就需要有其他的情人来弥补她开支的不足。玛格丽特算是幸运的，奇迹般撞上这样一个百万富翁，那老头儿的妻子和女儿都过世了，只有一些侄子外甥，也都是有钱的主儿。所以他对玛格丽特可谓有求必应，而且不求回报。然而，即便如此，玛格丽特每年从他那儿得到的钱也不过才7万法郎。而且我敢断定，如果玛格丽特再要求得多一些，尽管他很富有，而且很疼爱她，他也不会答应的。

"在巴黎，所有年收入只有两三万法郎，刚够维持自己那个圈子里的生活的年轻人，心里都很清楚，如果他们有一个玛格丽特那样的情妇，他们所付的钱还不够她支付房租和仆役的工资。他们不会告诉她他们知道这些，他们会装聋作哑，

in and the servants who wait upon her with what they give her. They do not say to her that they know it; they pretend not to see anything, and when they have had enough of it they go their way. If they have the vanity to wish to pay for everything they get ruined, like the fools they are, and go and get killed in Africa, after leaving a hundred thousand francs of debt in Paris. Do you think a woman is grateful to them for it? Far from it. She declares that she has sacrificed her position for them, and that while she was with them she was losing money. These details seem to you shocking? Well, they are true. You are a very nice fellow; I like you very much. I have lived with these women for twenty years; I know what they are worth, and I don't want to see you take the caprice that a pretty girl has for you too seriously.

"Then, besides that," continued Prudence; "admit that Marguerite loves you enough to give up the count or the duke, in case one of them were to discover your liaison and to tell her to choose between him and you, the sacrifice that she would make for you would be enormous, you can not deny it. What equal sacrifice could you make for her, on your part, and when you had got tired of her, what could you do to make up for what you had taken

等玩够了就一走了之。如果他们爱慕虚荣，异想天开地想负担一切，那么就会像个傻子一样走上万劫不复的深渊，在巴黎欠下 10 万法郎的债后，落魄到非洲枉送性命。你以为那个女人会因此而心存感激吗？绝对不会，相反，她们会宣称自己为那些人屈尊，和他们相好的时候，自己还倒贴了钱。你觉得这些很不可思议是吗？然而，这些都是事实。你是一个不错的小伙子。我打心眼里喜欢你，我和这些女人打了 20 几年的交道，她们是什么货色我再清楚不过了。我不想看到你把一个漂亮姑娘的逢场作戏当了真。

"那么，除此之外，"普鲁登斯继续说，"如果玛格丽特的其中一个情人发现了你们的私情，让她在你和他之间做出选择，而玛格丽特因为非常爱你而放弃了伯爵或公爵，如此一来，她就为你作出了巨大的牺牲，这一点你不否认吧？你能为她作出同样的牺牲吗？发自内心地说，当你厌倦了她的时候，你拿什么来补偿她的恩情呢？补偿不了！你会与她，以及她的那个世界，那

from her? Nothing. You would have cut her off from the world in which her fortune and her future were to be found; she would have given you her best years, and she would be forgotten. Either you would be an ordinary man, and, casting her past in her teeth, you would leave her, telling her that you were only doing like her other lovers, and you would abandon her to certain misery; or you would be an honest man, and, feeling bound to keep her by you, you would bring inevitable trouble upon yourself, for a liaison which is excusable in a young man, is no longer excusable in a man of middle age. It becomes an obstacle to every thing; it allows neither family nor ambition, man's second and last loves. Believe me, then, my friend, take things for what they are worth, and do not give a kept woman the right to call herself your creditor, no matter in what."

It was well argued, with a logic of which I should have thought Prudence incapable. I had nothing to reply, except that she was right; I took her hand and thanked her for her counsels.

"Come, come," said she, "put these foolish theories to flight, and laugh over them. Life is pleasant, my dear fellow; it all depends on the colour of the glass through which one sees it. Ask your friend

个她的财富和命运所在的世界断绝来往。她把她最美好的年华给了你，最后被你忘得一干二净。你或许是一个普通的男人，在她面前细数着她的过去，告诉她你只不过和其他的情人一样离开了她。最后把她丢弃在悲惨的角落。再或者你是一个有良心的人，觉得有责任养着她，你将无可避免地陷入麻烦中。因为，对于一个青年人来说，这种关系是很好理解的，但对一个成年人来说情况就不一样了。这是男人的第二次，也是最后一次爱情，它将成为事业的绊脚石。它不容于家庭，也使你的雄心壮志丧失殆尽。所以，相信我吧，我的朋友，凡事掂量着来做。不管在哪一方面，也不要欠下妓女的情分。"

普鲁登斯的一番话不容辩驳，而且很有逻辑，这倒是出乎我的意料。我无话可说，只是觉得她说得很对。我握着她的手，感谢她给我的忠告。

"行啦，行啦，"她说，"让这些无聊的客套话见鬼去吧。生活是美好的，亲爱的朋友，就看你抱着什么样的心态去看待它了。去问问你的朋友加斯顿吧，我和他对爱情

Gaston; there's a man who seems to me to understand love as I understand it. All that you need think of, unless you are quite a fool, is that close by there is a beautiful girl who is waiting impatiently for the man who is with her to go, thinking of you, keeping the whole night for you, and who loves you, I am certain. Now, come to the window with me, and let us watch for the count to go; he won't be long in leaving the coast clear."

Prudence opened the window, and we leaned side by side over the balcony. She watched the few passers, I reflected. All that she had said buzzed in my head, and I could not help feeling that she was right; but the genuine love which I had for Marguerite had some difficulty in accommodating itself to such a belief. I sighed from time to time, at which Prudence turned, and shrugged her shoulders like a physician who has given up his patient.

"How one realizes the shortness of life," I said to myself, "by the rapidity of sensations! I have only known Marguerite for two days, she has only been my mistress since yesterday, and she has already so completely absorbed my thoughts, my heart, and my life that the visit of the Comte de G. is a misfortune for

持有同样的观点。别再犯傻啦！你只要想着隔壁那个美丽的女子就好啦！她正急不可耐地等她家里的客人离开，她一心只想着你，一整晚都将和你一起过。她爱着你，这一点我确定。现在，和我一起去窗口等着伯爵离开吧，他很快就会让位给我们的。"

普鲁登斯打开窗户，我们并肩倚在阳台上。普鲁登斯望着路上稀少的行人，而我则思绪万千。她刚刚的一番话让我心乱如麻，不得不承认，她说的是对的。可是我真心爱着玛格丽特，我实在没办法遵循她讲的这些道理。我一直唉声叹气，普鲁登斯回过头来望着我，耸耸肩膀，好像在说我无药可救了。

"人生苦短，"我告诉自己，"是因为人们的感觉很灵敏。我认识玛格丽特也不过两天，她昨天才成为我的情妇，但是我的心思，我的心灵，甚至是我的生命都已经完完全全被她吸引住了，以至于这位G伯爵的来访使我心痛如绞。"

me."

At last the count came out, got into his carriage and disappeared. Prudence closed the window. At the same instant Marguerite called to us:

"Come at once," she said; "they are laying the table, and we'll have supper."

When I entered, Marguerite ran to me, threw her arms around my neck and kissed me with all her might.

"Are we still sulky?" she said to me.

"No, it is all over," replied Prudence. "I have given him a talking to, and he has promised to be reasonable."

"Well and good."

In spite of myself I glanced at the bed; it was not unmade. As for Marguerite, she was already in her white dressing-gown. We sat down to table.

Charm, sweetness, spontaneity, Marguerite had them all, and I was forced from time to time to admit that I had no right to ask of her anything else; that many people would be very happy to be in my place; and that, like Virgil's shepherd, I had only to enjoy the pleasures that a god, or rather a goddess, set before me.

I tried to put in practice the theories of Prudence, and to be as gay as my two

终于，伯爵出来了，坐上马车走了。普鲁登斯刚关上窗子，玛格丽特就叫我们了。

"快来，刀叉已经摆好，"她说，"我们来吃夜宵。"

我一进门，玛格丽特就向我飞奔而来，双手搂住我的脖子，热烈地吻我。

"我们还要继续闹别扭吗？"她对我说。

"不，以后都不会了，"普鲁登斯回答说，"我跟他好好谈过了，他答应要听话了。"

"太好了。"

我情不自禁地向床上望去，床上也并不凌乱，而玛格丽特也已经换上了白色的睡衣。我们围着桌子坐了下来。

玛格丽特集妩媚、温柔、多情于一身。我不得不时时提醒自己，我没有权利再要求她什么了。所有处在我的位置的人都会觉得很幸福。我就像维吉尔笔下的牧羊人[1]一样，坐享神，确切地说是一位女神赐给我的欢乐。

我尽力照普鲁登斯说的去做，尽量使自己看上去和两个女伴一样

---

[1] 维吉尔是古罗马最伟大的诗人，牧羊人形象来自于其成名作《牧歌》，维吉尔以牧羊人对歌或独歌的形式抒发个人的喜怒哀乐和美好的理想。

companions; but what was natural in them was on my part an effort, and the nervous laughter, whose source they did not detect, was nearer to tears than to mirth.

At last the supper was over and I was alone with Marguerite. She sat down as usual on the hearth-rug before the fire and gazed sadly into the flames. What was she thinking of? I know not. As for me, I looked at her with a mingling of love and terror, as I thought of all that I was ready to suffer for her sake.

"Do you know what I am thinking of?"

"No."

"Of a plan that has come into my head."

"And what is this plan?"

"I can't tell you yet, but I can tell you what the result would be. The result would be that in a month I should be free, I should have no more debts, and we could go and spend the summer in the country."

"And you can't tell me by what means?"

"No, only love me as I love you, and all will succeed."

"And have you made this plan all by yourself?"

"Yes."

"And you will carry it out all by yourself?"

"I alone shall have the trouble of it," said Marguerite, with a smile which I shall

快乐。她们是感情的自然流露，而我是强颜欢笑。我那神经质的笑声几乎像哭一样，而她们却并未察觉。

终于吃完饭了，我可以和玛格丽特单独待在一起了。她和往常一样坐在炉火前的地毯上，忧郁地盯着炉子里的火焰。我不知道她在想什么。我怀着一种又爱又怕的复杂心情望着她，想着即将为她忍受的痛苦。

"你知道我在想什么？"

"不知道。"

"我在考虑我想出的一个计划。"

"什么计划？"

"现在还不能告诉你，但是我可以告诉你这个计划的结果，那就是一个月内我可以恢复自由了，我将没有任何欠债，我俩可以去乡下避暑了。"

"不告诉我用什么办法吗？"

"不告诉你，像我爱你一样爱我吧，我们会成功的。"

"那么这个办法也是你一个人想出来的吗？"

"是的。"

"而且你要一个人去办吗？"

"所有的麻烦我一个人就足够能对付了，"玛格丽特带着一种令我

never forget, "but we shall both partake its benefits."

I could not help flushing at the words benefits; I thought of Manon Lescaut squandering with Desgrieux the money of M. de B.

I replied in a hard voice, rising from my seat:

"You must permit me, my dear Marguerite, to share only the benefits of those enterprises which I have conceived and carried out myself."

"What does that mean?"

"It means that I have a strong suspicion that M. de G. is to be your associate in this pretty plan, of which I can accept neither the cost nor the benefits."

"What a child you are! I thought you loved me. I was mistaken; all right."

She rose, opened the piano and began to play the Invitation *a la Valse*, as far as the famous passage in the major which always stopped her. Was it through force of habit, or was it to remind me of the day when we first met? All I know is that the melody brought back that recollection, and, coming up to her, I took her head between my hands and kissed her.

"You forgive me?" I said.

永生难忘的笑容对我说，"剩下的就是一起享受好处。"

听到"好处"两个字我的脸颊不禁绯红。我想起了曼侬·莱斯科和德·格里欧联合起来鱼肉 B 先生的事[1]。

我站起身来，用生硬的语气回答说：

"亲爱的玛格丽特，请原谅，我只享受我自己想出并由我自己完成的果实。"

"什么意思？"

"我的意思是，我很怀疑在这个绝妙的计划里，G 伯爵是不是你的同谋呢。这个计划我没有尽任何责任，也就不会接受它的好处。"

"你太孩子气了。我原以为你是爱我的，看来我错了，好吧。"

说着她起身打开钢琴，开始弹奏那首《邀舞》，一直弹到她总是弹不下去的那段停了下来。也不知道她是习惯性地弹起了这支乐曲呢，还是为了唤醒我对初识那天的记忆。我明白，这首曲子勾起了我对往事的回忆，于是，我走过去捧起她的头吻了吻。

"原谅我，好吗？"我说。

---

[1] 小说《曼侬·莱斯科》里的情节。曼侬瞒着情人与 B 先生来往，诈骗 B 先生的钱财。

"You see I do," she answered; "but observe that we are only at our second day, and already I have had to forgive you something. Is this how you keep your promise of blind obedience?"

"What can I do, Marguerite? I love you too much and I am jealous of the least of your thoughts. What you proposed to me just now made me frantic with delight, but the mystery in its carrying out hurts me dreadfully."

"Come, let us reason it out," she said, taking both my hands and looking at me with a charming smile which it was impossible to resist, "You love me, do you not? and you would gladly spend two or three months alone with me in the country? I too should be glad of this solitude a deux, and not only glad of it, but my health requires it. I can not leave Paris for such a length of time without putting my affairs in order, and the affairs of a woman like me are always in great confusion; well, I have found a way to reconcile everything, my money affairs and my love for you; yes, for you, don't laugh; I am silly enough to love you! And here you are taking lordly airs and talking big words. Child, thrice child, only remember that I love you, and don't let anything disturb you. Now, is it agreed?"

"你瞧，"她说，"我们相识不过两天，你就有事需要我原谅了，难道你就是这样遵守你盲目服从我的诺言的？"

"我该怎么办呢，玛格丽特？我太爱你了，哪怕你的任何一个想法我都要揣测一番。你刚才的提议让我欣喜若狂，但是这个计划执行得如此神秘，我觉得很难受。"

"哎呀，你看开一点儿吧，"她说着握着我的双手，带着一种让我无法抗拒的媚笑望着我，"你是爱我的，对吗？那么倘若就只有你和我两个人在乡下一起过三四个月，你会很开心吧？我也一样，能在乡下过几天只属于我们两个人的清静生活是很幸福的，而且也有利于我的健康。要离开巴黎这么长时间，总会有很多事情需要安排一下吧？尤其像我这样一个女人。还好，总算找到办法安排一切，安排我的生意，还有对你的爱，是的，对你的爱，你别笑，我真够愚蠢，疯狂地爱你。可你却趾高气扬地说着大话。真是幼稚，太幼稚了。你只要记得我爱你，其他的什么也别管，好吗？"

"I agree to all you wish, as you know."

"Then, in less than a month's time we shall be in some village, walking by the river side, and drinking milk. Does it seem strange that Marguerite Gautier should speak to you like that? The fact is, my friend, that when this Paris life, which seems to make me so happy, doesn't burn me, it wearies me, and then I have sudden aspirations toward a calmer existence which might recall my childhood. One has always had a childhood, whatever one becomes. Don't be alarmed; I am not going to tell you that I am the daughter of a colonel on half-pay, and that I was brought up at Saint-Denis. I am a poor country girl, and six years ago I could not write my own name. You are relieved, aren't you? Why is it you are the first whom I have ever asked to share the joy of this desire of mine? I suppose because I feel that you love me for myself and not for yourself, while all the others have only loved me for themselves.

"I have often been in the country, but never as I should like to go there. I count on you for this easy happiness; do not be unkind, let me have it. Say this to yourself: 'She will never live to be old, and I should some day be sorry for not having done for her the first thing she asked of me, such an

"你知道,你的所有想法我都支持。"

"那么,不出一个月,我们就可以去某个乡村,漫步在河边,喝着鲜奶。这样的话从我玛格丽特·戈蒂埃嘴里说出来,你可能觉得不可思议吧?实际上,我的朋友,巴黎这种看似幸福的生活没办法点燃我的激情了,我已经厌倦了。因此我突然很向往那种让我回想起童年时光的安静生活。不管是谁都有自己的童年哦!不要紧张,我不会对你说我是一个退役上校的女儿,也不会说我在圣德尼[1]长大。我是一个穷苦的乡下姑娘,6年前我甚至还不会写自己的名字。这样你就好受多了,是吗?我有生以来第一次对一个人说要和他分享我所拥有的快乐,为什么这个人是你呢?我想是因为我感觉到你是为我,而不是为自己而爱我的。而其他所有的人爱我,都是为了他们自己。

"我以前经常去乡下,但从来没有像这次这样渴望去。这个简简单单的幸福就全指望你啦。发发善心,让我得到这份幸福吧!你就告诉自己:她活不长了,她第一次要我做一件事,一件轻而易举的事,我却没答应她,总有一天我会后悔

---

[1] 圣德尼,据巴黎市中心9公里的城市。圣德尼大教堂是法国第一座哥特式建筑。

easy thing to do!'"

What could I reply to such words, especially with the memory of a first night of love, and in the expectation of a second?

An hour later I held Marguerite in my arms, and, if she had asked me to commit a crime, I would have obeyed her.

At six in the morning I left her, and before leaving her I said: "Till tonight!"

She kissed me more warmly than ever, but said nothing.

During the day I received a note containing these words:

DEAR CHILD: I am not very well, and the doctor has ordered quiet. I shall go to bed early tonight and shall not see you. But, to make up, I shall expect you tomorrow at twelve. I love you.

My first thought was: She is deceiving me!

A cold sweat broke out on my forehead, for I already loved this woman too much not to be overwhelmed by the suspicion. And yet, I was bound to expect such a thing almost any day with Marguerite, and it had happened to me often enough with my other mistresses, without my taking much notice of it. What was the meaning of the hold which this woman had taken

的。"

她都这样说了，我还能说什么呢？尤其是当我回味着第一夜的恩爱，期待着第二夜到来的时候。

一个小时后，我搂着玛格丽特，此刻，就算她要我去犯罪，我也义无反顾。

早晨6点钟，我该走了，走之前我问她："今晚见吗？"

她异常热烈地吻着我，但是什么也没有说。

白天，我收到一封信，上面写着：

亲爱的孩子：我身体不适，医生嘱咐我休息，今晚我得早些睡，就不见你了。但是作为补偿，明天中午12点我等你。我爱你。

我第一个感觉就是：她在骗我！

一阵冷汗爬上我的额头，我已经无可救药地爱上了这个女人，没办法不去胡思乱想。然而，我早该想到，跟玛格丽特在一起，这种事差不多每天都会发生。和别的情妇在一起时这种事也时常遇到，但是我没太在意。为什么这个女人就能左右我的生活呢？

upon my life?

Then it occurred to me, since I had the key, to go and see her as usual. In this way I should soon know the truth, and if I found a man there I would strike him in the face.

Meanwhile I went to the Champs-Elysees. I waited there four hours. She did not appear. At night I went into all the theatres where she was accustomed to go. She was in none of them.

At eleven o'clock I went to the Rue d'Antin. There was no light in Marguerite's windows. All the same, I rang. The porter asked me where I was going.

"To Mlle. Gautier's," I said.

"She has not come in."

"I will go up and wait for her."

"There is no one there."

Evidently I could get in, since I had the key, but, fearing foolish scandal, I went away. Only I did not return home; I could not leave the street, and I never took my eyes off Marguerite's house. It seemed to me that there was still something to be found out, or at least that my suspicions were about to be confirmed.

About midnight a carriage that I knew well stopped before No. 9. The Comte de G. got down and entered the house, after sending away the carriage. For a moment I hoped that the same answer would be

突然间我想到，既然我有她家里的钥匙，我何不像往常一样去看她呢！这样我很快就能知道真相，如果让我撞到一个男人的话，我会扇他的耳光。

这时，我来到了香榭丽舍大街，在那里足足等了 4 个小时，她没有出现。晚上，我去了所有她常去的剧院，但是都没有找到她的影子。

11 点钟的时候，我来到昂坦街。玛格丽特的窗户没有透出任何灯光，我还是按了按门铃。守卫人问我找谁。

"找戈蒂埃小姐。"我回答。

"她还没回来。"

"那我上去等她。"

"她家没人。"

既然我有钥匙，我当然可以进去，但是我怕传出可笑的绯闻，所以我走开了。但是，我没回家，我没办法离开这条街，我的眼睛也没办法离开玛格丽特的房间。我似乎还想打探一些蛛丝马迹，或者至少证实自己的猜疑。

快到午夜的时候，一辆我再熟悉不过的马车停在 9 号门前。G 伯爵走下车，打发走车子后，就进了房子。一时间，我希望他得到像我一样的答复说玛格丽特不在家，希

given to him as to me, and that I should see him come out; but at four o'clock in the morning I was still awaiting him.

I have suffered deeply during these last three weeks, but that is nothing, I think, in comparison with what I suffered that night.

望看到他走出来，但是直到凌晨 4 点，我还在等待。

接下来的 3 个星期，我饱受折磨，但是，和那一晚我所受的痛苦比起来，这都不算什么。

CHAPTER 14

第十四章

When I reached home I began to cry like a child. There is no man to whom a woman has not been unfaithful, once at least, who will not know what I suffered.

I said to myself, under the weight of these feverish resolutions which one always feels as if one had the force to carry out, that I must break with my amour at once, and I waited impatiently for daylight in order to set out forthwith to rejoin my father and my sister, of whose love at least I was certain, and certain that that love would never be betrayed.

However, I did not wish to go away without letting Marguerite know why I went. Only a man who really cares no more for his mistress leaves her without writing to her. I made and remade twenty letters in my head. I had had to do with a woman like all other women of the kind. I had been poetizing too much. She had treated me like a school-boy, she had used in deceiving me a trick which was insultingly simple. My self-esteem got the

回到家，我像个孩子一样哭了起来。一个男人，哪怕只遭遇过一次女人的不忠，就不会不知道我有多么痛苦。

我怒火中烧，暗暗痛下决心：必须马上和这种爱情一刀两断。我几乎等不及天亮，就想要回到我父亲和妹妹那里去。至少我能确定他俩是真的爱着我，而且这种爱永远不会背叛我。

然而，在玛格丽特还没弄清楚我离开的原因之前，我不想就这样一走了之。一个人，只有和情妇恩断情绝的时候才会不辞而别。我反复思量着该如何来写这封信，与我打交道的这个女人和其他所有的妓女没什么两样，她把我骗得云里雾里，把我当小学生一样愚弄。为了欺骗我，她使了一个简单的伎俩侮辱我。这时，我的自尊心占了上风。我必须离开这个女人，我不会让她

upper hand. I must leave this woman without giving her the satisfaction of knowing that she had made me suffer, and this is what I wrote to her in my most elegant handwriting and with tears of rage and sorrow in my eyes:

"MY DEAR MARGUERITE: I hope that your indisposition yesterday was not serious. I came at eleven at night, to ask after you, and was told that you had not come in. M. de G. was more fortunate, for he presented himself shortly afterward, and at four in the morning he had not left.

"Forgive me for the few tedious hours that I have given you, and be assured that I shall never forget the happy moments which I owe to you.

"I should have called today to ask after you, but I intend going back to my father's.

"Good-bye, my dear Marguerite. I am not rich enough to love you as I would, nor poor enough to love you as you would. Let us then forget, you a name which must be indifferent enough to you, I a happiness which has become impossible.

"I send back your key, which I have never used, and which might be useful to you, if you are often ill as you were yesterday."

知道我为她所受的苦楚，让她得意。眼里噙着愤怒和哀伤的泪水，我用最优雅的笔迹给她写了以下这封信：

亲爱的玛格丽特：希望你昨天的不适没那么严重才好。昨晚 11 点，我来探望你，被告知你还没有回来。G 伯爵比我幸运多了，在我之后不久他也来看你，直到清晨 4 点钟还没有离开。

原谅我带给你的不快。我保证，你赐给我的那些幸福时光，我永远都不会忘记。

今天我本应该去看望你，但是我打算回到我父亲那里去了。

再见，亲爱的玛格丽特，我不够富有，不能像我想象的那样爱你。可我也不是一无所有，想难按照你希望的方式爱你。那么让我们忘了彼此吧。对你来说，只是一个无关紧要的名字从此消失；可是对我而言，是一段刻骨铭心的幸福，此生难忘。

钥匙我奉还，还从未使用过，它对你会有用的，假如你会经常像昨天那样身体不适的话。

As you will see, I was unable to end my letter without a touch of impertinent irony, which proved how much in love I still was.

I read and reread this letter ten times over; then the thought of the pain it would give to Marguerite calmed me a little. I tried to persuade myself of the feelings which it professed; and when my servant came to my room at eight o'clock, I gave it to him and told him to take it at once.

"Shall I wait for an answer?" asked Joseph (my servant, like all servants, was called Joseph).

"If they ask whether there is a reply, you will say that you don't know, and wait."

I buoyed myself up with the hope that she would reply. Poor, feeble creatures that we are! All the time that my servant was away I was in a state of extreme agitation. At one moment I would recall how Marguerite had given herself to me, and ask myself by what right I wrote her an impertinent letter, when she could reply that it was not M. de G. who supplanted me, but I who had supplanted M. de G.: a mode of reasoning which permits many women to have many lovers. At another moment I would recall her promises, and endeavour to convince myself that my letter was only too gentle, and that there were not expressions forcible enough to

正如你所看到的，在信的结尾，我狠狠讽刺挖苦了她一番，这说明我心里还是深深爱着她啊。

这封信我反反复复看了 10 来遍，想着它将带给玛格丽特痛苦，我心里有了些许平静。我竭力使自己伪装成信里所写的那样。8 点钟当我的仆人来到我的房间时，我把信交给他，要他马上送去。

"要我等回信吗？"约瑟夫（我的仆人，像所有的仆人一样都叫约瑟夫）问我。

"如果有人问你要不要回信，就说你不知道，然后等着。"

她或许会回信的希望支撑着我。多么可怜，悲哀的傀儡！约瑟夫走了之后，我忐忑不安。一时间，我想起玛格丽特当初如何委身于我。我自问有何权利写这样一封荒唐的信给她，如果她回复我，哪里是 G 先生欺骗了我，分明是我欺骗了 G 先生——那些有很多裙下臣的女人通常这样为自己辩解。一会儿，这个姑娘的誓言又回响在我的耳边。我尽力说服自己，我的信写得还是太客气，措辞还不够尖刻，还不足以惩罚一个玩弄我感情的女人。随后，我又对自己说，我真不该写信给她，当时应该直接去她家，那样我就能看到她落泪而感到痛

punish a woman who laughed at a love like mine. Then I said to myself that I should have done better not to have written to her, but to have gone to see her, and that then I should have had the pleasure of seeing the tears that she would shed. Finally, I asked myself what she would reply to me; already prepared to believe whatever excuse she made.

Joseph returned.

"Well?" I said to him.

"Sir," said he, "madame was not up, and still asleep, but as soon as she rings the letter will be taken to her, and if there is any reply it will be sent."

She was asleep!

Twenty times I was on the point of sending to get the letter back, but every time I said to myself: "Perhaps she will have got it already, and it would look as if I have repented of sending it."

As the hour at which it seemed likely that she would reply came nearer, I regretted more and more that I had written. The clock struck, ten, eleven, twelve. At twelve I was on the point of keeping the appointment as if nothing had happened. In the end I could see no way out of the circle of fire which closed upon me. Then I began to believe, with the superstition which people have when they are waiting, that if I

快。最后，我琢磨着她会怎样答复我，我已经做好准备，相信她为此找的一切借口。

约瑟夫回来了。

"怎么样？"我问他。

"先生，"他回答，"夫人还没睡醒，但是只要她醒来按铃，信就会送到她手里，如果有回信，就会有人送来。"

她还在睡着！

好几次，我几乎要派人把信取回来，但是每一次我都告诉自己："或许信已经在她手上了，如果派人去取，就显得我后悔了。"

该收到她回信的时刻一点点接近，我内心的悔恨也一点点加重。10点，11点，12点的钟声陆续敲过。到了12点的时候，我真想像什么事也没有发生一样去赴约。最后，在我实在没办法摆脱这种焦灼的等待后，我开始相信——像所有等待中的人们所迷信的那样，只要我出去一小会儿，回来时很可能就会看到回信了。我为自己找了个吃午饭

went out for a little while, I should find an answer when I got back. I went out under the pretext of going to lunch.

Instead of lunching at the Cafe Foy, at the corner of the Boulevard, as I usually did, I preferred to go to the Palais Royal and so pass through the Rue d'Antin. Every time that I saw a woman at a distance, I fancied it was Nanine bringing me an answer. I passed through the Rue d'Antin without even coming across a commissionaire. I went to Very's in the Palais Royal. The waiter gave me something to eat, or rather served up to me whatever he liked, for I ate nothing. In spite of myself, my eyes were constantly fixed on the clock. I returned home, certain that I should find a letter from Marguerite.

The porter had received nothing, but I still hoped in my servant. He had seen no one since I went out.

If Marguerite had been going to answer me she would have answered long before.

Then I began to regret the terms of my letter; I should have said absolutely nothing, and that would undoubtedly have aroused her suspicions, for, finding that I did not keep my appointment, she would have inquired the reason of my absence, and only then I should have given it to her. Thus, she would have had to exculpate

的借口上街去了。

我没有像平常那样在富瓦街角的咖啡馆吃午餐，而宁愿到王宫大街去吃，因为那样就可以穿过昂坦街。每当我远远看到一个女人，我就以为那是纳尼娜来给我送回信。我穿过昂坦街，却连一个送信的人也没碰到。我走进王宫大街的韦利饭店。侍者服侍我用餐，可以说把他所能想到的菜全给我端来了，因为我什么也没有吃。我的眼睛始终离不开时钟。回到家，我深信能看到玛格丽特的回信。

守卫那里没有收到任何东西。我还抱着信已经交给仆人的希望，可是他说我走后没有谁来过。

如果玛格丽特打算给我回信，她早该回了。

这时，我开始后悔用那样的方式写信给她。我本应该什么都不说的。这样她发现我没有赴约就会觉得不对劲，就会询问我原因。只有那时，我才应该告诉她我的一切委屈和不平，而那时她就会为自己辩解。而我想要的也不过是她的一个解释而已。我已经觉得，不管她用

herself, and what I wanted was for her to exculpate herself. I already realized that I should have believed whatever reasons she had given me, and anything was better than not to see her again.

At last I began to believe that she would come to see me herself; but hour followed hour, and she did not come.

Decidedly Marguerite was not like other women, for there are few who would have received such a letter as I had just written without answering it at all.

At five, I hastened to the Champs-Elysees. "If I meet her," I thought, "I will put on an indifferent air, and she will be convinced that I no longer think about her."

As I turned the corner of the Rue Royale, I saw her pass in her carriage. The meeting was so sudden that I turned pale. I do not know if she saw my emotion; as for me, I was so agitated that I saw nothing but the carriage.

I did not go any farther in the direction of the Champs-Elysees. I looked at the advertisements of the theatres, for I had still a chance of seeing her. There was a first night at the Palais Royal. Marguerite was sure to be there. I was at the theatre by seven. The boxes filled one after another, but Marguerite was not there. I left the

什么样的理由来为自己辩解，我都会相信。只要能再见到她，我什么都愿意。

最后，我开始相信她会亲自来看我。但是时间一小时又一小时地过去了，她没有来。

玛格丽特的确与众不同，因为很少有女人在收到我刚才写的那样一封信后会无动于衷。

5 点钟，我奔向香榭丽舍大街。"如果遇到她，"我想，"我要装出一副冷漠的样子，这样她就会相信我已经不再想她了。"

在王宫大街拐角处，我看见她乘着马车经过。这次的相遇是如此的突然，我紧张得脸色苍白。我不知道她有没有看出我的紧张。我过于激动，除了她的车子什么也没看到。

我不再逗留在香榭丽舍大街，而是去浏览那些剧院的海报，因为我还有一次见她的机会。在王宫剧院会有一次首映演出，玛格丽特肯定会去那里。7 点钟我到了剧院，包厢已然是满座，但就是没有玛格丽特的影子。我从王宫剧院走出来，所有她常去的剧院我挨个儿跑遍

Palais Royal and went to all the theatres where she was most often to be seen: to the Vaudeville, the Varietes, the Opera Comique. She was nowhere.

Either my letter had troubled her too much for her to care to go to the theatre, or she feared to come across me, and so wished to avoid an explanation. So my vanity was whispering to me on the boulevards, when I met Gaston, who asked me where I had been.

"At the Palais Royal."

"And I at the Opera," said he; "I expected to see you there."

"Why?"

"Because Marguerite was there."

"Ah, she was there?"

"Yes.

"Alone?"

"No; with another woman."

"That's all?"

"The Comte de G. came to her box for an instant; but she went off with the duke. I expected to see you every moment, for there was a stall at my side which remained empty the whole evening, and I was sure you had taken it."

"But why should I go where Marguerite goes?"

"Because you are her lover, surely!"

"Who told you that?"

了：歌舞剧院、杂耍剧院、喜剧歌剧院。可是都没有她的影子。

要么我的信让她过于难过，没心思看戏；要么她在逃避我，逃避解释。走在大街上时，我的虚荣心滋生出这些想法。突然我碰到了加斯顿，他问我去哪儿了。

"王宫剧院。"

"我也从剧院来，"他对我说，"我还以为能在那儿见到你呢。"

"为什么？"

"因为玛格丽特在那儿。"

"啊！她在那儿吗？"

"是的。"

"一个人吗？"

"不，跟另一个女人在一起。"

"没有别人吗？"

"G 伯爵去了她包厢一会儿，但是后来她和公爵一块儿走了。我一直以为你也会在那里的。我旁边那个位子今晚一直空着，我以为是你订下的呢。"

"但是为什么玛格丽特到哪儿，我也得到哪儿呢？"

"因为你是她的情人嘛，对吧？"

"谁告诉你的？"

"Prudence, whom I met yesterday. I give you my congratulations, my dear fellow; she is a charming mistress, and it isn't everybody who has the chance. Stick to her; she will do you credit."

These simple reflections of Gaston showed me how absurd had been my susceptibilities. If I had only met him the night before and he had spoken to me like that, I should certainly not have written the foolish letter which I had written.

I was on the point of calling on Prudence, and of sending her to tell Marguerite that I wanted to speak to her; but I feared that she would revenge herself on me by saying that she could not see me, and I returned home, after passing through the Rue d'Antin. Again I asked my porter if there was a letter for me. Nothing! She is waiting to see if I shall take some fresh step, and if I retract my letter of today, I said to myself as I went to bed; but, seeing that I do not write, she will write to me tomorrow.

That night, more than ever, I reproached myself for what I had done. I was alone, unable to sleep, devoured by restlessness and jealousy, when by simply letting things take their natural course I should have been with Marguerite, hearing the delicious words which I had heard only twice, and

"普鲁登斯，我昨天碰到她了。祝贺你啊，我亲爱的伙伴。这可是一个风情万种的情妇啊，不是每个人都有这样的机会。跟紧她，她会替你争面子的。"

加斯顿这个简单的提示说明我的敏感是多么的荒唐。如果昨天我就遇到他，听他对我讲这些，我是无论如何也不会写早上那封愚蠢的信的。

我迫不及待地想去普鲁登斯家里，请她给玛格丽特传话，说我有话要说。可是我又害怕她记恨我拒绝见我。于是，我又从昂坦街走过，回到了家里。再一次，我问我的守卫，有没有我的信。还是没有！我躺在床上想："她是要看看我还要耍什么新花招，看我是否想收回我今天早上写的信吧。但是她看到我没有再写信给她，明天或许她会写信给我吧。"

那天晚上，思来想去，我对自己的所作所为追悔莫及。如今我寂寞难耐，辗转难眠，任凭烦躁和忌妒折磨着我。想当初我只要简简单单地让一切自由发展，此刻大概正和玛格丽特在一起，听着她的悦耳缠绵的情话，这些曼妙的话语我也

which made my ears burn in my solitude.

The most frightful part of the situation was that my judgment was against me; as a matter of fact, everything went to prove that Marguerite loved me. First, her proposal to spend the summer with me in the country, then the certainty that there was no reason why she should be my mistress, since my income was insufficient for her needs and even for her caprices. There could not then have been on her part anything but the hope of finding in me a sincere affection, able to give her rest from the mercenary loves in whose midst she lived; and on the very second day I had destroyed this hope, and paid by impertinent irony for the love which I had accepted during two nights. What I had done was therefore not merely ridiculous, it was indelicate. I had not even paid the woman, that I might have some right to find fault with her; withdrawing after two days, was I not like a parasite of love, afraid of having to pay the bill of the banquet? What! I had only known Marguerite for thirty-six hours; I had been her lover for only twenty-four; and instead of being too happy that she should grant me all that she did, I wanted to have her all to myself, and to make her sever at one stroke all her past relations which were the

只听过两次，一个人的时候，每当回味起这些话，我都两耳发热。

现在最可怕的就是：我的判断是错的，事实上，所有的一切都证明玛格丽特是爱我的。第一，她提议和我去乡下避暑；第二，她成为我的情妇，是没有任何原因的。我的收入情况是满足不了她的需要的，哪怕是她一次偶然兴起的开支。这样看来，她希望从我身上得到的，仅仅是一种真正的爱，仅此而已。这种真正的爱能让她偶尔从那些商业性的爱中脱出身来，得到些许休息。可就在第二天，我让她的希望幻灭，她两夜的恩情换来我无情的讽刺。因此我的所作所为不但荒谬，而且无耻。我甚至没给过她一个子儿，有什么权利来对她的生活指指点点？如果在第二天，我就溜之大吉，那不就成了情场上的寄生虫，生怕要偿还风流债吗？怎么！我认识玛格丽特不过 36 个小时，做她的情人也不过 24 个小时，我就在跟她怄气了！她竭尽所能来爱我，我非但不感到幸福，还想一人独占她，要她一下子和她以前的所有关系一刀两断，而她今后还要靠这些生活。我凭什么责备她？我什么都没有。她大可以像那些大胆泼辣的女人一样，直截了当地告诉我她要接待别的情人，但是她含蓄地写信告诉我

revenue of her future. What had I to reproach in her? Nothing. She had written to say she was unwell, when she might have said to me quite crudely, with the hideous frankness of certain women, that she had to see a lover; and, instead of believing her letter, instead of going to any street in Paris except the Rue d'Antin, instead of spending the evening with my friends, and presenting myself next day at the appointed hour, I was acting the Othello, spying upon her, and thinking to punish her by seeing her no more. But, on the contrary, she ought to be enchanted at this separation. She ought to find me supremely foolish, and her silence was not even that of rancour; it was contempt.

I might have made Marguerite a present which would leave no doubt as to my generosity and permit me to feel properly quits of her, as of a kept woman, but I should have felt that I was offending by the least appearance of trafficking, if not the love which she had for me, at all events the love which I had for her, and since this love was so pure that it could admit no division, it could not pay by a present, however generous, the happiness that it had received, however short that happiness

她身体不适。我没相信她信里的话，除了昂坦街，我没有去巴黎别的街道去溜达，我没有和朋友一起消磨这个夜晚，等待第二天在她指定的时间赴约，却扮演着奥赛罗[1]的角色，监视她，却想着不再见她，惩罚她。实际上恰恰相反，她应该为这种离开感到高兴，她可能觉得我蠢得无可救药，她的沉默所表达的连怨恨也算不上，是一种蔑视。

或许我该像对待妓女一样送玛格丽特一件礼物，这样她就不会对我的慷慨置疑了，我们之间也就算互不相欠了。但是我应该知道，这样做即使不算在玷污她对我的爱，至少是在玷污我对她的所有感情。既然这份感情纯洁无瑕，容不得其他杂物，那么更不能用一件礼物——不管多么贵重的礼物——来偿还它赐予的幸福——无论这种幸福是多么的稍纵即逝。

---

[1] 奥赛罗，莎士比亚著名悲剧《奥赛罗》中的男主人公，性格矛盾，宽容大度又狐疑猜忌，急躁冒进，捕风捉影。

had been.

That is what I said to myself all night long, and what I was every moment prepared to go and say to Marguerite. When the day dawned I was still sleepless. I was in a fever. I could think of nothing but Marguerite.

As you can imagine, it was time to take a decided step, and finish either with the woman or with one's scruples, if that is, she would still be willing to see me. But you know well, one is always slow in taking a decided step; so, unable to remain within doors and not daring to call on Marguerite, I made one attempt in her direction, an attempt that I could always look upon as a mere chance if it succeeded.

It was nine o'clock, and I went at once to call upon Prudence, who asked to what she owed this early visit. I dared not tell her frankly what brought me. I replied that I had gone out early in order to reserve a place in the coach for C., where my father lived.

"You are fortunate," she said, "in being able to get away from Paris in this fine weather."

I looked at Prudence, asking myself whether she was laughing at me, but her face was quite serious.

"Shall you go and say good-bye to

一整晚，我都这样告诫自己。这也是我随时准备要对玛格丽特说的。一直到天亮，我仍然没有睡意。我发烧了，我满脑子想的只有玛格丽特。

你或许能想象得到，是该做个了断了：要么从此和这个女人分道扬镳，要么从此不再猜忌——如果她还肯见我的话。但是你也知道，人们在下决心以前总是犹豫不决。我在家坐立不安，又不敢去看玛格丽特，于是我就想法子接近她，一旦有幸遇见她，可以说是偶然碰见，这样也能保住面子。

9 点钟一到，我立刻赶往普鲁登斯家里，她问我大清早来找她有什么事。我不敢坦诚地告诉她我的来因，我只说一大早出门是为了在去往 C 城的公共马车上订座：我父亲住在 C 城。

"你真幸运，"她对我说，"在这样的好天气离开巴黎。"

我打量着普鲁登斯，寻思她是不是在嘲笑我。但是她的表情一本正经。

"你要去玛格丽特那儿告别

Marguerite?" she continued, as seriously as before.

"No."

"You are quite right."

"You think so?"

"Naturally. Since you have broken with her, why should you see her again?"

"You know it is broken off?"

"She showed me your letter."

"What did she say about it?"

"She said: 'My dear Prudence, your protege is not polite; one thinks such letters, one does not write them.'"

"In what tone did she say that?"

"Laughingly, and she added: 'He has had supper with me twice, and hasn't even called.'"

That, then, was the effect produced by my letter and my jealousy. I was cruelly humiliated in the vanity of my affection.

"What did she do last night?"

"She went to the opera."

"I know. And afterward?"

"She had supper at home."

"Alone?"

"With the Comte de G., I believe."

So my breaking with her had not changed one of her habits. It is for such reasons as this that certain people say to you: Don't have anything more to do with the woman; she cares nothing about you.

吗？"她又接着说，脸上还是那么严肃。

"不了。"

"很好。"

"你觉得这样好吗？"

"当然，既然你已经和她分手了，又何必再去看她呢？"

"你知道我们分手了？"

"她把你写的信给我看了。"

"那她怎么说的呢？"

"她说：'亲爱的普鲁登斯，你那宝贝不礼貌，这种信，心里想想就好，哪能写出来呢。'"

"这话她用什么语气说的？"

"笑着说的，她还说：'他和我一起吃了两次夜宵，都还没上门道谢呢。'"

这就是我那封信和我的嫉妒所产生的结果。我为自己在爱情方面的虚荣而感到羞愧。

"昨晚她干什么了？"

"她去大歌剧院了。"

"这我知道，后来呢？"

"她在家吃夜宵。"

"一个人？"

"我想，是和 G 伯爵吧。"

看来我和她的分手丝毫没有改变她的习惯。在这样的情形下，有些人就会告诉你："决不要再和这个女人有任何瓜葛了，她根本不在乎你。"

"Well, I am very glad to find that Marguerite does not put herself out for me," I said with a forced smile.

"She has very good reason not to. You have done what you were bound to do. You have been more reasonable than she, for she was really in love with you; she did nothing but talk of you. I don't know what she would not have been capable of doing."

"Why hasn't she answered me, if she was in love with me?"

"Because she realizes she was mistaken in letting herself love you. Women sometimes allow you to be unfaithful to their love; they never allow you to wound their self-esteem; and one always wounds the self-esteem of a woman when, two days after one has become her lover, one leaves her, no matter for what reason. I know Marguerite; she would die sooner than reply."

"What can I do, then?"

"Nothing. She will forget you, you will forget her, and neither will have any reproach to make against the other."

"But if I write and ask her forgiveness?"

"Don't do that, for she would forgive you."

I could have flung my arms round Prudence's neck.

"很好，看到玛格丽特没有因为我而受到影响，我很高兴。"我带着勉强的笑容说。

"她这样做合情合理。你该做的都已经做了，你比她理智多了。她真心爱着你，张口闭口谈的都是你，我知道她什么蠢事都做得出来。"

"既然她爱我，为什么不给我写回信呢？"

"因为她已经意识到爱上你是一种错误。女人们有时候能容忍感情上的不忠，但决不允许自尊心受到伤害，尤其是当一个人只做了她两天情人后就离开她，不管是出于什么原因，都是对女人自尊心的伤害。我了解玛格丽特，她宁死也不会给你写回信的。"

"那我该怎么办呢？"

"就此拉倒吧，你们会彼此相忘，今后谁也别埋怨谁。"

"但是如果我写信求她原谅呢？"

"千万别那样做，她很有可能会原谅你。"

我几乎要搂住普鲁登斯的脖子了。

A quarter of an hour later I was once more in my own quarters, and I wrote to Marguerite:

Some one, who repents of a letter that he wrote yesterday and who will leave Paris tomorrow if you do not forgive him, wishes to know at what hour he might lay his repentance at your feet.

When can he find you alone? for, you know, confessions must be made without witnesses.

I folded this kind of madrigal in prose, and sent it by Joseph, who handed it to Marguerite herself; she replied that she would send the answer later.

I only went out to have a hasty dinner, and at eleven in the evening no reply had come. I made up my mind to endure it no longer, and to set out next day. In consequence of this resolution, and convinced that I should not sleep if I went to bed, I began to pack up my things.

一刻钟以后，我又回到家里，赶紧给玛格丽特写信。

有一个人对他昨天写的信万分后悔，如果你不原谅他，明天他就离开巴黎，他想知道什么时候能拜倒在你的脚下忏悔。

什么时候你可以单独约见他？因为你知道，忏悔的时候是不能有旁人在场的。

我把这封散文式的情书折了起来，让约瑟夫送去。他把信交给了玛格丽特本人，她回话说一会儿就回信。

我一直在家里等着，其间出去吃了一顿匆匆忙忙的饭。到了晚上11 点的时候还没有收到她的回信。这种痛苦我再也忍受不了了。我决定明天就动身。做了这个决定，我便开始收拾行李，因为我很清楚，就算躺在床上，我也是睡不着的。

CHAPTER 15

第十五章

It was hardly an hour after Joseph and I had begun preparing for my departure, when there was a violent ring at the door.

"Shall I go to the door?" said Joseph.

"Go," I said, asking myself who it could be at such an hour, and not daring to believe that it was Marguerite.

"Sir," said Joseph coming back to me, "it is two ladies."

"It is we, Armand," cried a voice that I recognised as that of Prudence.

I came out of my room. Prudence was standing looking around the place; Marguerite, seated on the sofa, was meditating. I went to her, knelt down, took her two hands, and, deeply moved, said to her, "Pardon."

She kissed me on the forehead, and said:

"This is the third time that I have forgiven you."

"I should have gone away tomorrow."

"How can my visit change your plans? I have not come to hinder you from leaving Paris. I have come because I had no time to

约瑟夫和我为我的行程做着准备，忙了快一个小时，突然有人猛按我家的门铃。

"要开门吗？"约瑟夫问我。

"快去开。"我对他说，心里寻思着这个时候会有谁上我家来，因为我不敢相信这会是玛格丽特。

"先生，"约瑟夫回来说，"是两位夫人。"

"是我们，阿尔芒。"一个声音嚷道，我听出是普鲁登斯的声音。

我走出卧室。普鲁登斯站着环视着我的客厅，玛格丽特坐在沙发上沉思。我走近她，跪下去托着她的双手，深情地对她说："原谅我。"

她吻着我的前额对我说：

"这已经是我第三次原谅你了。"

"我本打算明天要走的。"

"我的来访怎么能改变你的计划呢？我来不是要阻止你离开巴黎的。我来，是因为白天我抽不出空

answer you during the day, and I did not wish to let you think that I was angry with you. Prudence didn't want me to come; she said that I might be in the way."

"You in the way, Marguerite! But how?"

"Well, you might have had a woman here," said Prudence, "and it would hardly have been amusing for her to see two more arrive."

During this remark Marguerite looked at me attentively.

"My dear Prudence," I answered, "you do not know what you are saying."

"What a nice place you've got!" Prudence went on. "May we see the bedroom?"

"Yes."

Prudence went into the bedroom, not so much to see it as to make up for the foolish thing which she had just said, and to leave Marguerite and me alone.

"Why did you bring Prudence?" I asked her.

"Because she was at the theatre with me, and because when I leave here I want to have some one to see me home."

"Could not I do?"

"Yes, but, besides not wishing to put you out, I was sure that if you came as far as my door you would want to come up, and as I could not let you, I did not wish to let

回信，又不想让你误以为我在生你的气。普鲁登斯还不让我来呢，她说或许我这时来不合适呢。"

"不合适？玛格丽特！怎么会呢？"

"当然咯！或许你家里有一个女人呢，"普鲁登斯回答说，"她看到又来了两个可不是闹着玩的。"

在普鲁登斯喋喋不休时，玛格丽特眼神专注地望着我。

"我亲爱的普鲁登斯，"我回答说，"你简直是胡说八道。"

"你这套房子可真漂亮啊，"普鲁登斯接着说，"我们看看你的卧室好吗？"

"可以。"

普鲁登斯进了我的卧室，她也不是真想参观我的卧室，只是想弥补一下她刚才的蠢话，让我和玛格丽特单独相处罢了。

"为什么带着普鲁登斯来？"我问道。

"因为看戏时我们就在一起，而且一会儿走的时候也要有人陪我。"

"那不是有我吗？"

"是，可是我不想麻烦你，而且我敢肯定到了我家门口你就会要求进去。可是我不能让你进去，我不希望你因为遭拒绝而埋怨我。"

you go away blaming me for saying 'No.'"

"And why could you not let me come up?"

"Because I am watched, and the least suspicion might do me the greatest harm."

"Is that really the only reason?"

"If there were any other, I would tell you; for we are not to have any secrets from one another now."

"Come, Marguerite, I am not going to take a roundabout way of saying what I really want to say. Honestly, do you care for me a little?"

"A great deal."

"Then why did you deceive me?"

"My friend, if I were the Duchess So and So, if I had two hundred thousand francs a year, and if I were your mistress and had another lover, you would have the right to ask me; but I am Mlle. Marguerite Gautier, I am forty thousand francs in debt, I have not a penny of my own, and I spend a hundred thousand francs a year. Your question becomes unnecessary and my answer useless."

"You are right," I said, letting my head sink on her knees; "but I love you madly."

"Well, my friend, you must either love me a little less or understand me a little better. Your letter gave me a great deal of pain. If I had been free, first of all I would

"那么为什么不能让我进去呢？"

"因为我被监视了，稍不留神就会铸成大错。"

"真的只有这一个原因吗？"

"如果还有别的原因，我会告诉你的，我们彼此之间不再有秘密了。"

"哎，玛格丽特，我不想再兜圈子了，你和我说句实话，你爱我吗？哪怕一点点？"

"爱极了。"

"那么，为什么要骗我？"

"我的朋友，如果我是什么公爵夫人，或者我每年有 20 万法郎的收入，那么我在除你之外还有别的情人的话，或许你有权利质问我。但是我是玛格丽特·戈蒂埃小姐，我身负 4 万法郎的债，没有一个子儿是我自己的，而且我一年要花去10 万法郎。你的问题是多余的，我也不需要回答。"

"你说得对，"我的头贴着玛格丽特的膝盖，"但是我疯狂地爱着你。"

"那么，我的朋友，你要么少爱我一些，要么多理解我一些。你的信让我很心痛。如果我是自由身，

not have seen the count the day before yesterday, or, if I had, I should have come and asked your forgiveness as you ask me now, and in future I should have had no other lover but you. I fancied for a moment that I might give myself that happiness for six months; you would not have it; you insisted on knowing the means. Well, good heavens, the means were easy enough to guess! In employing them I was making a greater sacrifice for you than you imagine. I might have said to you, 'I want twenty thousand francs'; you were in love with me and you would have found them, at the risk of reproaching me for it later on. I preferred to owe you nothing; you did not understand the scruple, for such it was. Those of us who are like me, when we have any heart at all, we give a meaning and a development to words and things unknown to other women; I repeat, then, that on the part of Marguerite Gautier the means which she used to pay her debts without asking you for the money necessary for it, was a scruple by which you ought to profit, without saying anything. If you had only met me today, you would be too delighted with what I promised you, and you would not question me as to what I did the day before yesterday. We are sometimes obliged to

首先前天我就不会接待伯爵的，如果接待了他，我就应该像现在你求我原谅一样，来请求你的原谅，而且以后我不会再有除你之外的情人了。有一阵子我幻想着或许我能拥有 6 个月的幸福生活，可你不愿意给，你非要刨根究底不可。哦，上帝啊！办法再明白不过了。为了那 6 个月的幸福我所作的牺牲比你想象的要大得多，我本来可以告诉你：我需要 2 万法郎，你热恋着我，兴许这会儿能想方设法筹划到，可是以后可能就会埋怨我了。我不想欠你什么，可你却不懂得我的一番苦心。像我们这种女人，当我们还有一点儿良知的时候，我们说的话、做的事都另有含义，别的女人可能无法理解。因此我再说一遍，对玛格丽特·戈蒂埃来说，她惯用的还债方式是对你的体贴，这种还债方式不需要你花钱。你什么都不用说，享受就行了。如果你今天才遇到我，那么我答应你的事你会觉得非常快活，你也就不会再盘问我前天干了什么。有时候我们迫于无奈牺牲肉体来换取精神上的满足，如果以此换来的精神满足也失去了的话，那我们就更加觉得苦不堪言。"

buy the satisfaction of our souls at the expense of our bodies, and we suffer still more, when, afterward, that satisfaction is denied us."

I listened, and I gazed at Marguerite with admiration. When I thought that this marvellous creature, whose feet I had once longed to kiss, was willing to let me take my place in her thoughts, my part in her life, and that I was not yet content with what she gave me, I asked if man's desire has indeed limits when, satisfied as promptly as mine had been, it reached after something further.

"Truly," she continued, "we poor creatures of chance have fantastic desires and inconceivable loves. We give ourselves now for one thing, now for another. There are men who ruin themselves without obtaining the least thing from us; there are others who obtain us for a bouquet of flowers. Our hearts have their caprices; it is their one distraction and their one excuse. I gave myself to you sooner than I ever did to any man, I swear to you; and do you know why? Because when you saw me spitting blood you took my hand; because you wept; because you are the only human being who has ever pitied me. I am going to say a mad thing to you: I once had a little dog who looked at me with a sad look

我赞许地听着她，望着她。一想到这个我曾渴望吻她的脚的尤物，现在愿意让我进入她的思想深处，让我进入她的生活，而我对她给予的一切还不满意，我不禁自问，人类的欲望到底还有没有尽头，一个愿望很快实现后，又想得寸进尺。

"真的是，"她接着说，"我们这些受命运摆布的女人，有着不切实际的欲望和不可思议的爱情。我们为了这样或那样的事委身于人。有些人一辈子毁在我们身上，什么也没有得到，也有些人只用一束鲜花就得到了我们。我们随心所欲，这是我们的消遣方式，我们的借口。我从来没有这么快地把自己交给一个人，我向你发誓，你知道为什么吗？因为你看到我吐血后握着我的手，还流泪了，因为这么久以来你是唯一一个同情我的人。我告诉你一个很不可思议的故事：我曾经养过一只小狗，每当我咳嗽的时候，它总是忧郁地望着我，它是我唯一喜爱过的生物。它死的时候，我哭

when I coughed; that is the only creature I ever loved. When he died I cried more than when my mother died. It is true that for twelve years of her life she used to beat me. Well, I loved you all at once, as much as my dog. If men knew what they can have for a tear, they would be better loved and we should be less ruinous to them.

"Your letter undeceived me; it showed me that you lacked the intelligence of the heart; it did you more harm with me than anything you could possibly have done. It was jealousy certainly, but ironical and impertinent jealousy. I was already feeling sad when I received your letter. I was looking forward to seeing you at twelve, to having lunch with you, and wiping out, by seeing you, a thought which was with me incessantly, and which, before I knew you, I had no difficulty in tolerating.

"Then," continued Marguerite, "you were the only person before whom it seemed to me, from the first, that I could think and speak freely. All those who come about women like me have an interest in calculating their slightest words, in thinking of the consequences of their most insignificant actions. Naturally we have no friends. We have selfish lovers who spend their fortunes, riot on us, as they say, but on their own vanity. For these people we

得很伤心，比死了亲娘还要伤心，确实是这样的，我挨了我母亲12年的打骂。就这样，我在一瞬间爱上了你，就像爱我的狗一样。如果所有男人知道他们的眼泪可以换来什么，他们就会更加讨人欢心，我们也不会肆意糟蹋他们了。

"你的来信骗不了我，这封信告诉我你没有领会我的用心，不管你做了什么事，都比不上这封信伤人。当然这也可以说是忌妒，但这是一种可笑、无礼的忌妒。收到你的信时，我已经够难受的了，本指望你12点能来赴约，我们共进午餐。见到你，才能扫去不断萦绕在我内心的阴霾。而认识你以前，这些事我是根本不当一回事的。

"而且，"玛格丽特继续说，"似乎你是第一个能让我推心置腹，畅所欲言的人。那些围着我这种女人转的人喜欢琢磨她们的一言一语，随便一个无意识的行动，他们也要妄加揣测。当然，我们没有什么朋友，有的只是一些自私的情人，他们在我们身上挥霍钱财，就像他们宣称的那样，但实际上是为了他们自己的虚荣心。在这些人眼里，他们开心的时候，我们必须快乐；当

have to be merry when they are merry, well when they want to sup, sceptics like themselves. We are not allowed to have hearts, under penalty of being hooted down and of ruining our credit.

"We no longer belong to ourselves. We are no longer beings, but things. We stand first in their self-esteem, last in their esteem. We have women who call themselves our friends, but they are friends like Prudence, women who were once kept and who have still the costly tastes that their age does not allow them to gratify. Then they become our friends, or rather our guests at table. Their friendship is carried to the point of servility, never to that of disinterestedness. Never do they give you advice which is not lucrative. It means little enough to them that we should have ten lovers extra, as long as they get dresses or a bracelet out of them, and that they can drive in our carriage from time to time or come to our box at the theatre. They have our last night's bouquets, and they borrow our shawls. They never render us a service, however slight, without seeing that they are paid twice its value. You yourself saw when Prudence brought me the six thousand francs that I had asked her to get from the duke, how she borrowed five hundred francs, which she will never

他们要进餐的时候，我们必须兴致勃勃；当他们疑心重重的时候，我们也要跟着好奇。我们这种人是不能有什么良知的，否则就要被谩骂，被诋毁。

"我们早就不属于自己了，早就不是活生生的人了，只是东西而已。满足自尊心，他们最先想到的是我们；保住自尊心，他们最先丢弃的也是我们。但是我们也有像普鲁登斯那样的女朋友——她们自称为我们的朋友。她们曾经也是妓女，挥霍惯了，但现在她们的年龄不允许她们干这行了。所以，她们成了我们的朋友，或者说是食客。她们的友情几近卑微，但也还不至于毫无私心。她们总是给我们出些捞钱的点子。只要她们能从我们这里借机捞到一些衣物和首饰，能够时常坐着我们的车子逛逛，或者来我们的包厢看看戏，就算我们有 10 多个情人也不关她们的事。她们带走我们隔夜的花束，借用我们的披肩。即使是一件微乎其微的小恩惠，我们也得加倍地感谢才能得到她们的扶持。那天晚上你也亲眼看见了，我让普鲁登斯从公爵那里拿来了6000 法郎，她当场就借去了 500 法郎，这笔钱她是不可能还我的，要么还我几顶绝不是花了钱买来的帽子。

pay me back, or which she will pay me in hats, which will never be taken out of their boxes.

"We can not, then, have, or rather I can not have more than one possible kind of happiness, and this is, sad as I sometimes am, suffering as I always am, to find a man superior enough not to ask questions about my life, and to be the lover of my impressions rather than of my body. Such a man I found in the duke; but the duke is old, and old age neither protects nor consoles. I thought I could accept the life which he offered me; but what would you have? I was dying of ennui, and if one is bound to be consumed, it is as well to throw oneself into the flames as to be asphyxiated with charcoal.

"Then I met you, young, ardent, happy, and I tried to make you the man I had longed for in my noisy solitude. What I loved in you was not the man who was, but the man who was going to be. You do not accept the position, you reject it as unworthy of you; you are an ordinary lover. Do like the others; pay me, and say no more about it."

Marguerite, tired out with this long confession, threw herself back on the sofa, and to stifle a slight cough put up her handkerchief to her lips, and from that to

"这样一来，我们，或者说我，只能有一种可能的幸福，对我这样一个多愁善感，疾病缠身的女人来说，就是找一个修养很高，不追究我们的生活的男人。让他成为一个重感情轻肉欲的情人。公爵就是这样一个人，但他年事已高，保护不了我，也安慰不了我。我原以为我能安于他给我安排的生活，但是你怎么办呢？我真是万分苦恼。如果一个人注定要受煎熬，那么把自己扔到火里烧死和被煤气窒息而死又有什么不同呢！

"这时，我遇到了你，青春、热情、快乐，我想希望你就是那个我苦苦寻找的人，喧嚣背后我总是孤单的。我爱的不是现在这个你，而是以后那个为我而改变的人。你不接受这个身份，认为这个身份不可取而拒绝，那么你也不过是一个很普通的情人，像别人一样付钱给我吧，不用多费口舌了。"

一段长长的倾诉之后，玛格丽特很疲乏了，她靠在沙发椅上，为了忍住轻轻的一阵咳，她用手绢按着嘴，甚至连眼睛都蒙上了。

her eyes.

"Pardon, pardon," I murmured. "I understood it all, but I wanted to have it from your own lips, my beloved Marguerite. Forget the rest and remember only one thing: that we belong to one another, that we are young, and that we love. Marguerite, do with me as you will; I am your slave, your dog, but in the name of heaven tear up the letter which I wrote to you and do not make me leave you tomorrow; it would kill me."

Marguerite drew the letter from her bosom, and handing it to me with a smile of infinite sweetness, said:

"Here it is. I have brought it back."

I tore the letter into fragments and kissed with tears the hand that gave it to me.

At this moment Prudence reappeared.

"Look here, Prudence; do you know what he wants?" said Marguerite.

"He wants you to forgive him."

"Precisely."

"And you do?"

"One has to; but he wants more than that."

"What, then?"

"He wants to have supper with us."

"And do you consent?"

"What do you think?"

"I think that you are two children who

"原谅我，原谅我，"我喃喃地说，"我现在什么都明白了，但是我愿意听你亲口告诉我这些。我最最心爱的玛格丽特，我们暂且把其他的都抛在脑后，只记得一点，那就是我们属于彼此，我们青春年少，我们相亲相爱。"玛格丽特，你对我做什么都行，我是你的奴隶，你的狗。但是看在上帝的分上，把我写给你的那封信撕了吧，明天别让我离开你，否则我宁愿死了。"

玛格丽特从怀里取出信，还给了我，无限甜美地对我笑着说：

"给你，我把信给你带来了。"

我把信撕成了碎片，含着泪吻着那双给我递信的手。

这时候普鲁登斯又来了。

"快看看，普鲁登斯，你知道他想要我干什么吗？"玛格丽特说。

"他要求你原谅。"

"正是。"

"你原谅了吧？"

"那是当然，但是他还有一个要求。"

"什么要求？"

"他想和我们共享夜宵。"

"你同意了吗？"

"你说呢？"

"要我说啊你俩都是孩子，都

haven't an atom of sense between you; but I also think that I am very hungry, and that the sooner you consent the sooner we shall have supper."

"Come," said Marguerite, "there is room for the three of us in my carriage."

"By the way," she added, turning to me, "Nanine will be gone to bed. You must open the door; take my key, and try not to lose it again."

I embraced Marguerite until she was almost stifled.

Thereupon Joseph entered.

"Sir," he said, with the air of a man who is very well satisfied with himself, "the luggage is packed."

"All of it?"

"Yes, sir."

"Well, then, unpack it again; I am not going."

很幼稚。但是现在我也觉得肚子很饿，你俩早一点儿讲和，我们就可以早一点儿吃夜宵。"

"走吧，"玛格丽特说，"我的车子坐得下 3 个人。"

"还有，"她转过来说道，"纳尼娜就要睡觉了，你去开门吧，拿着我的钥匙，可别再弄丢了。"

我紧紧拥抱着玛格丽特，她都快要窒息了。

这时候约瑟夫进来了。

"先生，"他沾沾自喜地说，"行李捆好了。"

"都捆好了吗？"

"是的，先生。"

"那么，再把它打开吧，我不走了。"

CHAPTER 16

第十六章

I might have told you of the beginning of this liaison in a few lines, but I wanted you to see every step by which we came, I to agree to whatever Marguerite wished, Marguerite to be unable to live apart from me.

It was the day after the evening when she came to see me that I sent her *Manon Lescaut*.

From that time, seeing that I could not change my mistress's life, I changed my own. I wished above all not to leave myself time to think over the position I had accepted, for, in spite of myself, it was a great distress to me. Thus my life, generally so calm, assumed all at once an appearance of noise and disorder. Never believe, however disinterested the love of a kept woman may be, that it will cost one nothing. Nothing is so expensive as their caprices, flowers, boxes at the theatre, suppers, days in the country, which one can never refuse to one's mistress.

As I have told you, I had little money.

我本可以把我们这种关系的起因三言两语告诉你，但是我想让你知道我们经历了哪些曲折后，我会对玛格丽特言听计从，玛格丽特的生活从此不能没有我。

就在她找过我的第二天，我把《曼侬·莱斯科》送给了她。

从那以后，眼看改变不了我情妇的生活，我就只有改变我自己的生活。首先我不让自己有时间来思考我所接受的身份。因为一想到这事，我还是忍不住难过。因此我原本还算平静的生活，突然变得杂乱无章了。千万不要认为和一个不贪图钱财的妓女恋爱花不了几个钱。没有什么比她们的嗜好更费钱：花束、包厢、夜宵、郊游，情妇的这些要求是没办法拒绝的。

正如我和你说过的，我几乎没

My father was, and still is, treasurer of C. He has a great reputation there for loyalty, thanks to which he was able to find the security which he needed in order to attain this position.It is worth forty thousand francs a year, and during the ten years that he has had it, he has paid off the security and put aside a dowry for my sister. My father is the most honourable man in the world. When my mother died, she left six thousand francs a year, which he divided between my sister and myself on the very day when he received his appointment; then, when I was twenty-one, he added to this little income an annual allowance of five thousand francs, assuring me that with eight thousand francs a year I might live very happily at Paris, if, in addition to this, I would make a position for myself either in law or medicine. I came to Paris, studied law, was called to the bar, and, like many other young men, put my diploma in my pocket, and let myself drift, as one so easily does in Paris.

My expenses were very moderate; only I used up my year's income in eight months, and spent the four summer months with my father, which practically gave me twelve thousand francs a year, and, in addition, the reputation of a good son. For the rest, not a penny of debt.

什么财产。我父亲一直是 C 城的总税务官，他为人正直，声誉极佳，因此他借到了获得这个职位所必需的保证金。有了这个职务，他每年就有 4 万法郎的收入，10 年下来他已还清了保证金，并为我妹妹置办好了嫁妆。我父亲是这个世界上最可敬的人。我母亲去世的时候留下一笔每年有 6000 法郎收入的财产，我父亲在他得到职位的那天就把这笔财产平分给我和我妹妹了。后来，到了我 21 岁那年，父亲又在我那笔小小的收入上增加了一笔每年 5000 法郎的津贴，这样我每年就有了 8 千法郎。除此之外，如果我还愿意在司法界或者医务界谋得一职的话，那么我在巴黎的日子会过得很惬意。因此我来到巴黎，攻读法律，获得了律师资格证。和其他年轻人一样，我把文凭揣在兜儿里，让自己在巴黎潇洒几天。

我非常节俭，可是不到 8 个月我全年的收入就花光了。夏天有 4 个月我会和父亲一起度过，这样我每年实际上有 12000 法郎收入而且还赢得了孝名。最终，我没有一个铜子儿的债。

This, then, was my position when I made the acquaintance of Marguerite. You can well understand that, in spite of myself, my expenses soon increased. Marguerite's nature was very capricious, and, like so many women, she never regarded as a serious expense those thousand and one distractions which made up her life. So, wishing to spend as much time with me as possible, she would write to me in the morning that she would dine with me, not at home, but at some restaurant in Paris or in the country. I would call for her, and we would dine and go on to the theatre, often having supper as well; and by the end of the evening I had spent four or five louis, which came to two or three thousand francs a month, which reduced my year to three months and a half, and made it necessary for me either to go into debt or to leave Marguerite. I would have consented to anything except the latter.

Forgive me if I give you all these details, but you will see that they were the cause of what was to follow. What I tell you is a true and simple story, and I leave to it all the naivete of its details and all the simplicity of its developments.

I realized then that as nothing in the world would make me forget my mistress,

这就是我在认识玛格丽特时候的情况。你应该能理解，除了养活我自己，我的开销很快就增加了，玛格丽特天性花钱大手大脚。和其他所有女人一样，她根本不把这种生活小插曲式的消费看得有多么了不起。因此，为了尽可能多地跟我在一起，她会在上午写信约我一起吃晚饭，但不是在她家里，而是在巴黎或者郊外的饭店里。我会去接她，然后我们一起吃饭，一起去看戏，有时还会一起吃夜宵，每天晚上我都要花去四五个路易，这样一个月就要花去 2500 到 3000 法郎，一年的收入在 3 个半月内就花得精光，我要么借款，要么离开玛格丽特。可是除了离开玛格丽特，我什么都可以接受。

请原谅我讲了这么多琐碎的细节给你听，不过你会发现这些是以后将要发生的事情的起因。我给你讲的是一个真实而简单的故事，那么我就保持这个故事朴实无华的细节和简单明了的发展过程。

这会儿，我意识到世界上没有任何东西可以让我忘掉我的情妇，

it was needful for me to find some way of meeting the expenses into which she drew me. Then, too, my love for her had so disturbing an influence upon me that every moment I spent away from Marguerite was like a year, and that I felt the need of consuming these moments in the fire of some sort of passion, and of living them so swiftly as not to know that I was living them.

I began by borrowing five or six thousand francs on my little capital, and with this I took to gambling. Since gambling houses were destroyed gambling goes on everywhere. Formerly, when one went to Frascati, one had the chance of making a fortune; one played against money, and if one lost, there was always the consolation of saying that one might have gained; whereas now, except in the clubs, where there is still a certain rigour in regard to payments, one is almost certain, the moment one gains a considerable sum, not to receive it. You will readily understand why. Gambling is only likely to be carried on by young people very much in need of money and not possessing the fortune necessary for supporting the life they lead; they gamble, then, and with this result; or else they gain, and then those who lose serve to pay for their horses and

我必须想个法子来应付因为她而增加的花费。而且，我对她的爱狂热痴迷，不在玛格丽特身边的日子度日如年，我感觉要用情欲的火焰焚毁这些熬人的时光。希望时光飞逝，好让这种倍受煎熬的日子快点过去。

我开始从我这笔小小的财产中挪出五六千法郎，用来赌钱。自从赌场被取缔以后，赌博随处可见。以前，只要走进弗拉斯卡第赌场的人就能得到发财的机会。人们玩着金钱游戏，如果赌钱输了，人们总是安慰自己说还能赢回来。而现在，除了在俱乐部里，人们对于输赢还比较认真外，而在其他地方，赢得的钱几乎是拿不到的。原因很不言自明。那些赌博的人差不多都是些急需要钱来维持他们所过的生活的年轻人。所以他们赌钱的结果大多是这样的：如果他们赢了，那么输的一方就为他们的马车和情妇埋单。这是很丢人的。于是债台高筑，赌桌上的朋友在争吵中结束，名誉和生命也会因此而受到损伤。或许你是一个诚实的人，但是还会有更加诚实的人让你不名一文，这些年轻人唯一的缺陷就是没有每年 20

mistresses, which is very disagreeable. Debts are contracted, acquaintances begun about a green table end by quarrels in which life or honour comes to grief; and though one may be an honest man, one finds oneself ruined by very honest men, whose only defect is that they have not two hundred thousand francs a year.

I need not tell you of those who cheat at play, and of how one hears one fine day of their hasty disappearance and tardy condemnation.

I flung myself into this rapid, noisy, and volcanic life, which had formerly terrified me when I thought of it, and which. had become for me the necessary complement of my love for Marguerite. What else could I have done?

The nights that I did not spend in the Rue d'Antin, if I had spent them alone in my own room, I could not have slept. Jealousy would have kept me awake, and inflamed my blood and my thoughts; while gambling gave a new turn to the fever which would otherwise have preyed upon my heart, and fixed it upon a passion which laid hold on me in spite of myself, until the hour struck when I might go to my mistress. Then, and by this I knew the violence of my love, I left the table without a moment's hesitation, whether I was

万法郎的收入。

当然也有在赌博中作弊的人，这我就不多说了，他们混不了多久，也就不会有好下场的。

我陷入一种杂乱无章，水深火热的生活。这种以前我想都不敢想的生活，现在成了我对玛格丽特的爱情所不可或缺的补充，我还能怎么办呢？

那些没有在昂坦街度过，独自在家里的夜晚，我总是孤枕难眠。忌妒的火焰总是引燃我的思想和血液，让我辗转难眠。而赌博则可以暂时缓解我的相思之苦，转向另一种热情，让我沉浸其中，直到可以会我的情妇时为止。至此，我看到了我的爱是多么的热烈，不管是赢是输，我总是带着对那些还在激战的赌徒们的怜悯，毫不留恋地离开赌桌，他们可没我好运，能带着幸福感离开赌桌。对大多数赌徒来说，赌博是一种需要，而对我来说

winning or losing, pitying those whom I left behind because they would not, like me, find their real happiness in leaving it. For the most of them, gambling was a necessity; for me, it was a remedy. Free of Marguerite, I should have been free of gambling.

Thus, in the midst of all that, I preserved a considerable amount of self-possession; I lost only what I was able to pay, and gained only what I should have been able to lose.

For the rest, chance was on my side. I made no debts, and I spent three times as much money as when I did not gamble. It was impossible to resist an existence which gave me an easy means of satisfying the thousand caprices of Marguerite. As for her, she continued to love me as much, or even more than ever.

As I told you, I began by being allowed to stay only from midnight to six o'clock, then I was asked sometimes to a box in the theatre, then she sometimes came to dine with me. One morning I did not go till eight, and there came a day when I did not go till twelve.

But, sooner than the moral metamorphosis, a physical metamorphosis came about in Marguerite. I had taken her cure in hand, and the poor girl, seeing my

只是暂时的麻醉。如果我不爱玛格丽特，我也不会去赌博。

因此，赌钱的时候我相当淡定，我只输我付得起的钱，只赢我输得起的钱。

至于其他，赌运是在我这边的。我非但没有负债，而且收入比我没有赌钱以前多了 3 倍。尽管这终究不是长久之计，但我可以很轻易地满足玛格丽特上千种异想天开的要求。玛格丽特和以前一样地爱我，甚至比以前更爱我了。

我已经讲过，开始的时候我只能从半夜 12 点待到第二天早晨 6 点，后来她允许我偶尔去她的包厢，再后来，她能偶尔和我一起吃晚饭。有一天早晨我一直待到了 8 点，还有一天我一直待到了中午。

但是，在玛格丽特的精神还没好转的时候，她的身体却先发生了病变。我精心地呵护她，想治好她。这个可怜的姑娘体会到我的用心，

aim, obeyed me in order to prove her gratitude. I had succeeded without effort or trouble in almost isolating her from her former habits. My doctor, whom I had made her meet, had told me that only rest and calm could preserve her health, so that in place of supper and sleepless nights, I succeeded in substituting a hygienic regime and regular sleep. In spite of herself, Marguerite got accustomed to this new existence, whose salutary effects she already realized. She began to spend some of her evenings at home, or, if the weather was fine, she wrapped herself in a shawl, put on a veil, and we went on foot, like two children, in the dim alleys of the Champs-Elysees. She would come in tired, take a light supper, and go to bed after a little music or reading, which she had never been used to do. The cough, which every time that I heard it seemed to go through my chest, had almost completely disappeared.

At the end of six weeks the count was entirely given up, and only the duke obliged me to conceal my liaison with Marguerite, and even he was sent away when I was there, under the pretext that she was asleep and had given orders that she was not to be awakened.

The habit or the need of seeing me

服从我对她的安排以示感谢。我没费什么周折就让她基本上远离了以前的生活习惯。我让她会诊的医生告诉我,只有静养才能保持健康。于是我制定出了合理的饮食和睡眠制度,成功地取缔了她以前吃夜宵,少睡眠的习惯。不知不觉间,玛格丽特习惯了这种新的生活方式,自己也感觉到这种生活方式的好处。她开始偶尔在家过夜,或者遇上天气好的时候,就裹上一条开司米披肩,戴上面纱,和我漫步在香榭丽舍那昏黄的街道上,就像两个孩子。累了的时候她就回家,少吃一点儿东西,听会儿轻音乐,或者看会儿书便睡觉了。这在以前是从没有过的事。从前那种让我心痛的咳嗽几乎完全消失了。

第六个星期快结束的时候,伯爵已经完全被我们抛在脑后了,只是我还得继续对公爵隐瞒我们的私情。不过当我在玛格丽特那里的时候,她经常借口在睡觉,不准打扰把公爵打发走。

现在,玛格丽特已经习惯了我

which Marguerite had now contracted had this good result: that it forced me to leave the gaming-table just at the moment when an adroit gambler would have left it. Settling one thing against another, I found myself in possession of some ten thousand francs, which seemed to me an inexhaustible capital.

The time of the year when I was accustomed to join my father and sister had now arrived, and I did not go; both of them wrote to me frequently, begging me to come. To these letters I replied as best I could, always repeating that I was quite well and that I was not in need of money, two things which, I thought, would console my father for my delay in paying him my annual visit.

Just then, one fine day in summer, Marguerite was awakened by the sunlight pouring into her room, and, jumping out of bed, asked me if I would take her into the country for the whole day.

We sent for Prudence, and all three set off, after Marguerite had given Nanine orders to tell the duke that she had taken advantage of the fine day to go into the country with Mme. Duvernoy.

Besides the presence of Mme. Duvernoy being needful on account of the old duke, Prudence was one of those women who

的陪伴，或者说需要我的陪伴，这种习惯产生了一种美妙的效果：我恰如其分地离开赌台。有失必有得，我发现手里已有万把法郎，对我而言，这似乎是一笔取之不尽的财产。

每年这个时候我都会如期回家探望父亲和妹妹，但是今年我没去。他俩经常写信请我回去，我总是尽可能婉转得体地回复他们，我告诉他们我身体很好，也不缺钱花。我想这两点或许能稍稍抚慰父亲由于我没回家而产生的失落。

一个明媚的夏天，太阳光射进屋内，唤醒了玛格丽特。她从床上跳下来问我可否带她去乡下玩一天。

我们派人请来普鲁登斯，玛格丽特叮嘱纳尼娜，要她告诉公爵，她要趁着天气好，和迪韦尔诺瓦太太一起去乡下玩。随后我们三人就出发了。

普鲁登斯似乎就是为郊游而生的。有她同行，除了老公爵会放心之外，我们的旅途也不会有片刻烦

seem made on purpose for days in the country. With her unchanging good-humour and her eternal appetite, she never left a dull moment to those whom she was with, and was perfectly happy in ordering eggs, cherries, milk, stewed rabbit, and all the rest of the traditional lunch in the country.

We had now only to decide where we should go. It was once more Prudence who settled the difficulty.

"Do you want to go to the real country?" she asked.

"Yes."

"Well, let us go to Bougival, at the Point du Jour, at Widow Arnould's. Armand, order an open carriage."

An hour and a half later we were at Widow Arnould's.

Perhaps you know the inn, which is a hotel on week days and a tea garden on Sundays. There is a magnificent view from the garden, which is at the height of an ordinary first floor. On the left the Aqueduct of Marly closes in the horizon, on the right one looks across bill after hill; the river, almost without current at that spot, unrolls itself like a large white watered ribbon between the plain of the Gabillons and the island of Croissy, lulled

闷。她诙谐幽默，永远那么的精力旺盛，而且很善于订购鸡蛋、樱桃、牛奶、炸兔肉以及其他所有郊游野餐必不可少的传统食物。

现在，我们只要定好去哪儿就行了。这个难题又是普鲁登斯替我们解决的。

"你们想不想去一个地地道道的乡村呢？"她问。

"想。"

"那好，我们去布吉瓦尔[1]，到阿尔努寡妇的曙光饭店去。阿尔芒，去租一辆敞篷四轮马车。"

一个半小时后，我们到了阿尔努寡妇的饭店。

或许你知道这个饭店，这是一个平常是旅馆，星期天是咖啡馆的饭店。从这儿的一个两层楼高的花园里往远处眺望，风景优美极了。左边是马尔利引水渠，右边是连绵不断的小山丘。在加比隆平原和克罗西岛之间有一条银白色的河，像一条宽阔的缎带一样向两面伸展开去，人们几乎看不出它在流动。两岸高大的杨树被风吹得呼呼响，柳树也在喃喃细语，它们一起为小河

---

[1] 布吉瓦尔，巴黎西部的小村镇。

eternally by the trembling of its high poplars and the murmur of its willows. Beyond, distinct in the sunlight, rise little white houses, with red roofs, and manufactories, which, at that distance, put an admirable finish to the landscape. Beyond that, Paris in the mist! As Prudence had told us, it was the real country, and, I must add, it was a real lunch.

It is not only out of gratitude for the happiness I owe it, but Bougival, in spite of its horrible name, is one of the prettiest places that it is possible to imagine. I have travelled a good deal, and seen much grander things, but none more charming than this little village gaily seated at the foot of the hill which protects it.

Mme. Arnould asked us if we would take a boat, and Marguerite and Prudence accepted joyously.

People have always associated the country with love, and they have done well; nothing affords so fine a frame for the woman whom one loves as the blue sky, the odours, the flowers, the breeze, the shining solitude of fields, or woods. However much one loves a woman, whatever confidence one may have in her, whatever certainty her past may offer us as to her future, one is always more or less jealous. If you have been in love, you must

演奏着一曲永不停歇的催眠曲。远处矗立着一片红瓦白墙的屋舍和一些工厂，它们在阳光的笼罩下为这幅田园画添上了美妙的一笔。再远处，是云雾笼罩下的巴黎。就像普鲁登斯对我们讲的那样，这是一个真正的乡村，而且，我还要补充一点，这是一场视觉盛宴。

我这样说，并不完全是出于感谢——我从这里得到了幸福。可是布吉瓦尔，尽管它的名字很难听，却是人们所能想象到的最美妙的风景区之一。我到过很多地方，也见过不少壮丽的景色，但是没有一个能比得上这个小乡村，它实在是太迷人了。

阿尔努夫人问我们是否要划船。玛格丽特和普鲁登斯兴然应允。

人们总是把乡村和爱情联系起来，这不无道理。没有什么能比旷野或森林里的蓝天、芳草、鲜花和微风更能和你心爱的女人相映成趣了。不管你多么爱一个女人，不管你对她有多少信心，也不管她的过往能在多大程度上保证她的将来，你多多少少总会有些妒意的。如果你曾经恋爱过，你一定有过这种把深爱的女人和世界隔绝开来的欲望。不管你心爱的女人对周围的人

have felt the need of isolating from this world the being in whom you would live wholly. It seems as if, however indifferent she may be to her surroundings, the woman whom one loves loses something of her perfume and of her unity at the contact of men and things. As for me, I experienced that more than most. Mine was not an ordinary love; I was as much in love as an ordinary creature could be, but with Marguerite Gautier; that is to say, that at Paris, at every step, I might elbow the man who had already been her lover or who was about to, while in the country, surrounded by people whom we had never seen and who had no concern with us, alone with nature in the spring-time of the year, that annual pardon, and shut off from the noise of the city, I could hide my love, and love without shame or fear.

The courtesan disappeared little by little. I had by me a young and beautiful woman, whom I loved, and who loved me, and who was called Marguerite; the past had no more reality and the future no more clouds. The sun shone upon my mistress as it might have shone upon the purest bride. We walked together in those charming spots which seemed to have been made on

如何的冷漠，只要她和别的男人或事物接触，似乎她的香味就要打折扣，似乎就变得不完整。这一点上，我的体会比其他所有人都深刻。我的爱情不是普通的爱情，像一个普通人一样，我全身心地恋爱着。可是我爱上的是玛格丽特·戈蒂埃，这就是说在巴黎，我要步步为营，因为随时有可能碰到她曾经的情人，或者是她未来的情人。而在乡下，我们完全置身于一个陌生的圈子，这里没有人会在意我们。在这一年一度的春天，我们投身于大自然的怀抱。在这远离喧嚣的地方，我可以敞开心扉，无所顾忌地去爱。

妓女的身份渐渐被稀释。我拥有的是一个青春貌美的女子，叫做玛格丽特。我爱着她，她也爱着我，过去的一切变得不再真实，未来的天空再也没有阴云遮挡。太阳照在我的情妇身上，就像照耀着一个最纯洁的新娘。我们在这美妙的地方散步，这些地方巧夺天工，似乎就是为了回味拉马丁[1]的诗句和斯居

---

[1] 拉马丁，法国19世纪浪漫派抒情诗人，浪漫主义文学的前驱和巨擘。

purpose to recall the verses of Lamartine or to sing the melodies of Scudo. Marguerite was dressed in white, she leaned on my arm, saying over to me again under the starry sky the words she had said to me the day before, and far off the world went on its way, without darkening with its shadow the radiant picture of our youth and love.

That was the dream that the hot sun brought to me that day through the leaves of the trees, as, lying on the grass of the island on which we had landed, I let my thought wander, free from the human links that had bound it, gathering to itself every hope that came in its way.

Add to this that from the place where I was I could see on the shore a charming little house of two stories, with a semicircular railing; through the railing, in front of the house, a green lawn, smooth as velvet, and behind the house a little wood full of mysterious retreats, where the moss must efface each morning the pathway that had been made the day before. Climbing flowers clung about the doorway of this uninhabited house, mounting as high as the first story.

I looked at the house so long that I began by thinking of it as mine, so perfectly did it embody the dream that I

杜[1]的歌曲而生成。玛格丽特身着一袭白色长裙，斜依在我的胳臂上。夜晚，在繁星点点的苍穹下，她反复诉说着她前一天对我说的话。远处的城市一如既往地喧闹，但是它现在玷污不了我们用青春和爱情编织的曼妙图画。

那天，船驶到一个岛上停了下来，我们躺在那里的草地上，割断一切人情关系，任凭思绪像脱缰的马儿一样自由驰骋。炙热的太阳光穿过树叶的空隙给我捎来了上面的美梦。

从我的视线方向望去，岸边有一座玲珑可爱的3层小楼，外面围着半圈栅栏，栅栏与房屋之间是一块像天鹅绒一样平整的翠绿草坪，房子后面有一片幽深的小树林。这里头天被踏出的小径，第二天就被新生的苔藓掩盖。这座空房子的台阶爬满了花藤，一直延伸到二楼。

我长时间凝视着这座房子，开始幻想着这座房子属于我了，它就是我梦想的类型。似乎看到我和玛

---

[1] 斯居杜，法国 19 世纪作曲家。

was dreaming; I saw Marguerite and myself there, by day in the little wood that covered the hillside, in the evening seated on the grass, and I asked myself if earthly creatures had ever been so happy as we should be.

"What a pretty house!" Marguerite said to me, as she followed the direction of my gaze and perhaps of my thought.

"Where?" asked Prudence.

"Yonder," and Marguerite pointed to the house in question.

"Ah, delicious!" replied Prudence. "Do you like it?"

"Very much."

"Well, tell the duke to take it for you; he would do so, I am sure. I'll see about it if you like."

Marguerite looked at me, as if to ask me what I thought. My dream vanished at the last words of Prudence, and brought me back to reality so brutally that I was still stunned with the fall.

"Yes, yes, an excellent idea," I stammered, not knowing what I was saying.

"Well, I will arrange that," said Marguerite, freeing my hand, and interpreting my words according to her own desire. "Let us go and see if it is to let."

格丽特就住在那里，白天在山冈上的树林之中嬉戏，晚上一起坐在绿草地上。我心里在想，这个世界上还有谁能像我们这样幸福呢！

"多么漂亮的房子啊！"玛格丽特对我说。随着我的视线她看到了这座房子，或许还读懂了我的想法。

"在哪儿？"普鲁登斯问。

"那边。"玛格丽特指着那所房子。

"啊！真美，"普鲁登斯接着说，"你喜欢它吗？"

"非常喜欢。"

"那么，请公爵为你租这个房子，我敢肯定，他会同意的。如果你喜欢，这事儿就交给我去办。"

玛格丽特望着我，似乎在征求我对这个意见的看法。我的美梦随着普鲁登斯最后几句话幻灭了，残酷的现实一下子回到眼前，我都还没回过神来。

"是，是，这个主意妙极了。"我结结巴巴地说，也不知道自己在说些什么。

"很好，一切由我来安排，"玛格丽特松开我的手说，她顺着自己的愿望来理解我的话的，"走，我们去看看这座房子是不是出租。"

The house was empty, and to let for two thousand francs.

"Would you be happy here?" she said to me.

"Am I sure of coming here?"

"And for whom else should I bury myself here, if not for you?"

"Well, then, Marguerite, let me take it myself."

"You are mad; not only is it unnecessary, but it would be dangerous. You know perfectly well that I have no right to accept it save from one man. Let me alone, big baby, and say nothing."

"That means," said Prudence, "that when I have two days free I will come and spend them with you."

We left the house, and started on our return to Paris, talking over the new plan. I held Marguerite in my arms, and as I got down from the carriage, I had already begun to look upon her arrangement with less critical eyes.

房子空着，2000法郎可以租到。

"在这里你会快活吗？"她问我说。

"我肯定能来这儿吗？"

"我躲到这儿来不是为了你，又是为谁呢？"

"好吧，那么，玛格丽特，这座房子我来租吧。"

"你疯了。非但没有必要，而且还有危险，你明知道我只能接受一个人的安排，我一个人处理就好，傻小子，别再多说了。"

"这样一来，"普鲁登斯说，"如果我连着有两天空闲，就来陪你们。"

我们离开这座房子，踏上了回巴黎的旅程，一路上还在谈论着这个新计划。我搂着玛格丽特，从马车里下来的时候，已经能不那么抵触地审视我情妇的计划了。

CHAPTER 17

第十七章

Next day Marguerite sent me away very early, saying that the duke was coming at an early hour, and promising to write to me the moment he went, and to make an appointment for the evening. In the course of the day I received this note:

"I am going to Bougival with the duke; be at Prudence's tonight at eight."

At the appointed hour Marguerite came to me at Mme. Duvernoy's. "Well, it is all settled," she said, as she entered.

"The house is taken?" asked Prudence.

"Yes; he agreed at once."

I did not know the duke, but I felt ashamed of deceiving him.

"But that is not all," continued Marguerite.

"What else is there?"

"I have been seeing about a place for Armand to stay."

"In the same house?" asked Prudence, laughing.

"No, at Point du Jour, where we had dinner, the duke and I. While he was

第二天，玛格丽特很早就打发我走了，她告诉我公爵很早就会过来，并答应我公爵一走就写信约我晚上见面。果然，白天我收到了她的信。

"我要和公爵一起去布吉瓦尔，晚上 8 点在普鲁登斯家里见。"

玛格丽特在约定的时间来迪韦尔诺瓦太太家会我。"行啦，都办妥了。"她进来的时候说。

"房子租下来了？"普鲁登斯问道。

"是的，他立马同意了。"

我不认识公爵，但是这样欺辱他，我羞愧难当。

"但是还没有完呢！"玛格丽特继续说。

"还有什么事？"

"我在想把阿尔芒安置在哪里。"

"你们不住一起吗？"普鲁登斯笑着问道。

"不，让他住在我们，我是指我和公爵吃过午饭的曙光饭店里。

admiring the view, I asked Mme. Arnould (she is called Mme. Arnould, isn't she?) if there were any suitable rooms, and she showed me just the very thing: salon, anteroom, and bedroom, at sixty francs a month; the whole place furnished in a way to divert a hypochondriac. I took it. Was I right?"

I flung my arms around her neck and kissed her.

"It will be charming," she continued. "You have the key of the little door, and I have promised the duke the key of the front door, which he will not take, because he will come during the day when he comes. I think, between ourselves, that he is enchanted with a caprice which will keep me out of Paris for a time, and so silence the objections of his family. However, he has asked me how I, loving Paris as I do, could make up my mind to bury myself in the country. I told him that I was ill, and that I wanted rest. He seemed to have some difficulty in believing me. The poor old man is always on the watch. We must take every precaution, my dear Armand, for he will have me watched while I am there; and it isn't only the question of his taking a house for me, but he has my debts to pay, and unluckily I have plenty. Does all that suit you?"

公爵观赏风景的时候，我问过阿尔努太太了，她是叫阿尔努太太吧？我问她有没有合适的房子可以租给我，恰好她有一套，带有客厅、会客室和卧室。每个月60法郎，整个房间里的装修风格都能让一个忧郁的人高兴起来。我把它租了下来，怎么样？"

我紧紧拥着玛格丽特，情不自禁地吻了她。

"这下就好啦，"她继续说，"小门上的钥匙给你，我答应把栅栏门的钥匙给公爵，不过他不会要的，因为他就算来也是在白天。我想他肯定很赞成我这个离开巴黎的突发奇想，这样他们家的人就不会再说什么了。但是他问我，我这么热爱巴黎，怎么舍得隐居乡下去了。我告诉他说，我身体不大好，需要去乡下休养，他似乎不太相信。这个可怜的老头儿总是对我不放心。我们可得多加小心。亲爱的阿尔芒，他会派人去那儿看着我的。他不单单要为我租房子，还得替我还债呢。很不幸，我身负巨债。这样安排你觉得合适吗？"

"Yes," I answered, trying to quiet the scruples which this way of living awoke in me from time to time.

"We went all over the house, and we shall have everything perfect. The duke is going to look after every single thing. Ah, my dear," she added, kissing me, "you're in luck; it's a millionaire who makes your bed for you."

"And when shall you move into the house?" inquired Prudence.

"As soon as possible."

"Will you take your horses and carriage?"

"I shall take the whole house, and you can look after my place while I am away."

A week later Marguerite was settled in her country house, and I was installed at Point du Jour.

Then began an existence which I shall have some difficulty in describing to you. At first Marguerite could not break entirely with her former habits, and, as the house was always en fete, all the women whom she knew came to see her. For a whole month there was not a day when Marguerite had not eight or ten people to meals. Prudence, on her side, brought down all the people she knew, and did the honours of the house as if the house belonged to her.

"可以。"我回答，尽量克制住内心不断涌上来的对这种生活的内疚感。

"房子我们细细查看过了，一切都很棒。公爵样样都想得很周到。啊！亲爱的，"她亲吻着我说，"你太幸运了，有一个百万富翁为你铺床呢。"

"那你什么时候搬过去？"普鲁登斯问道。

"越早越好。"

"要带着车马吗？"

"我把家里的东西都搬过去，我不在的日子请你替我看家。"

一星期后，玛格丽特搬进了乡下那座房子，我被安置在曙光饭店。

从此便开始了一种我很难向你描述的生活。刚开始，玛格丽特还不能完全摒弃以前的习惯，她家里天天像过节一样，她认识的所有的女伴都来看她。整整一个月，玛格丽特家里每天都有 8 到 10 个人在吃饭。而普鲁登斯也把所有她认识的人全带来了，得意洋洋的样子就像房子是她自己的。

The duke's money paid for all that, as you may imagine; but from time to time Prudence came to me, asking for a note for a thousand francs, professedly on behalf of Marguerite. You know I had won some money at gambling; I therefore immediately handed over to Prudence what she asked for Marguerite, and fearing lest she should require more than I possessed, I borrowed at Paris a sum equal to that which I had already borrowed and paid back. I was then once more in possession of some ten thousand francs, without reckoning my allowance. However, Marguerite's pleasure in seeing her friends was a little moderated when she saw the expense which that pleasure entailed, and especially the necessity she was sometimes in of asking me for money. The duke, who had taken the house in order that Marguerite might rest there, no longer visited it, fearing to find himself in the midst of a large and merry company, by whom he did not wish to be seen. This came about through his having once arrived to dine tete-a-tete with Marguerite, and having fallen upon a party of fifteen, who were still at lunch at an hour when he was prepared to sit down to dinner. He had unsuspectingly opened the dining-room door, and had been greeted by a burst of

就像你想象的那样,公爵为这一切埋单。但是普鲁登斯却常常以玛格丽特的名义来向我要走一张1000法郎的钞票。你知道我以前赌钱时小赚了一笔,我急忙把她为玛格丽特要的钱交给她。我怕手头的钱满足不了她的需要,就和以前一样去巴黎去借来一笔钱,数目上也和以前的一样。当然以前的债早就还清了。这样我手头又有了一万左右法郎,津贴费还不算在内。不过,当玛格丽特看到这种吃喝玩乐的日子开销巨大,尤其时不时还得向我伸手时,她招待朋友的热情便有所减缓。公爵是为了让玛格丽特好好休养才租下这个房子的,但他自己已经不怎么来了,他害怕这种一大群人嘻嘻哈哈的场面,不想被她们看到。他就遇上过这样的场面,有次他来和玛格丽特共进晚餐,却碰到有十四五个人正在玛格丽特家聚餐,他觉得该吃晚饭的时候这顿午饭都还没结束。当时他推开饭厅的大门,顿时爆发出一阵哄堂大笑,在这群女人肆无忌惮的笑声中,他不得不立即退出来。

laughter, and had had to retire precipitately before the impertinent mirth of the women who were assembled there.

Marguerite rose from table, and joined the duke in the next room, where she tried, as far as possible, to induce him to forget the incident, but the old man, wounded in his dignity, bore her a grudge for it, and could not forgive her. He said to her, somewhat cruelly, that he was tired of paying for the follies of a woman who could not even have him treated with respect under his own roof, and he went away in great indignation.

Since that day he had never been heard of.

In vain Marguerite dismissed her guests, changed her way of life; the duke was not to be heard of. I was the gainer in so, far that my mistress now belonged to me more completely, and my dream was at length realized. Marguerite could not be without me. Not caring what the result might be, she publicly proclaimed our liaison, and I had come to live entirely at her house. The servants addressed me officially as their master.

Prudence had strictly sermonized Marguerite in regard to her new manner of life; but she had replied that she loved me, that she could not live without me, and

玛格丽特从餐桌上离开，到隔壁房间看公爵。她想尽办法想让他忘掉这件事，但是这个老头儿的自尊心已经受到了伤害，他对此耿耿于怀，不肯原谅她。他近乎残忍地告诉这个可怜的姑娘，他不想再养着这样一个让自己在家里都得不到尊敬的女人。说完他怒气冲冲地走了。

从那天以后，我们再也没听到过他的任何消息。

后来虽然玛格丽特谢绝待客，也改变了原来的习惯，公爵还是杳无音信。如此一来倒让我坐收渔利，我的情妇完完全全属于我一个人了，终于我美梦成真了。玛格丽特再也不能没有我，她全然不顾后果，公然宣布我们的关系，我也就干脆住在她家里了。仆人们也正式称我为男主人。

对现在的这种新生活，普鲁登斯曾郑重地警告过玛格丽特，但是玛格丽特告诉她，她爱我，没有我她就活不下去，不论发生什么事她

that, happen what might, she would not sacrifice the pleasure of having me constantly with her, adding that those who were not satisfied with this arrangement were free to stay away. So much I had heard one day when Prudence had said to Marguerite that she had something very important to tell her, and I had listened at the door of the room into which they had shut themselves.

Not long after, Prudence returned again. I was at the other end of the garden when she arrived, and she did not see me. I had no doubt, from the way in which Marguerite came to meet her, that another similar conversation was going to take place, and I was anxious to hear what it was about. The two women shut themselves into a boudoir, and I put myself within hearing.

"Well?" said Marguerite.

"Well, I have seen the duke."

"What did he say?"

"That he would gladly forgive you in regard to the scene which took place, but that he has learned that you are publicly living with M. Armand Duval, and that he will never forgive that. 'Let Marguerite leave the young man,' he said to me, 'and, as in the past, I will give her all that she requires; if not, let her ask nothing more

都不会放弃和我在一起的朝朝暮暮。还说谁要是反对这种生活，大可不必再来。这些是有一天普鲁登斯对玛格丽特说她有一些重要事情要告诉她，她俩关在屋里窃窃私语时，我在门外偷听到的。

没多久，普鲁登斯又来了。她进来的时候，我在花园的另一头，她没看见我。从玛格丽特向她走去的样子中，我就能确定又会有一番和上次一样的谈话，我迫不及待地想听听她们在谈论些什么。两个女人关在一间小客厅里，我就躲在门外偷听。

"如何？"玛格丽特问。

"如何？我见到了公爵。"

"他说什么了？"

"至于他来看你的那天所发生的事情，他愿意原谅你。但是你公开和阿尔芒·迪瓦尔先生同居的事，他已经知晓，而且不会原谅你了。他告诉我：'只要让玛格丽特离开那个小伙子，那么一切和过去一样，她要什么我就给她什么，否则她就别想再从我这儿得到什么了。'"

from me.'"

"And you replied?"

"That I would report his decision to you, and I promised him that I would bring you into a more reasonable frame of mind. Only think, my dear child, of the position that you are losing, and that Armand can never give you. He loves you with all his soul, but he has no fortune capable of supplying your needs, and he will be bound to leave you one day, when it will be too late and when the duke will refuse to do any more for you. Would you like me to speak to Armand?"

Marguerite seemed to be thinking, for she answered nothing. My heart beat violently while I waited for her reply.

"No," she answered, "I will not leave Armand, and I will not conceal the fact that I am living with him. It is folly no doubt, but I love him. What would you have me do? And then, now that he has got accustomed to be always with me, he would suffer too cruelly if he had to leave me so much as an hour a day. Besides, I have not such a long time to live that I need make myself miserable in order to please an old man whose very sight makes me feel old. Let him keep his money; I will do without it."

"But what will you do?"

"你是怎么回答的？"

"我说我会把他的想法向你转达，并允诺让你明白事理。亲爱的孩子，好好想想吧，想想你失去的地位，这是阿尔芒永远也给不了你的。阿尔芒全心全意地爱着你，但是他没有什么财产，满足不了你的需要，总有一天他会离开你的，到那时候就一切都晚了。公爵再也不会为你付出什么了，需要我去和阿尔芒说吗？"

似乎玛格丽特在考虑什么，因为她没有答复，我的心狂乱地跳着，等待着她的回答。

"不用了，"她回答道，"我不会离开阿尔芒的，我也不会再隐瞒和他同居的事实。毫无疑问，这样做很傻，但是我爱他！你叫我怎么办？而且现在他已经习惯和我在一起了，哪怕有一个小时不在我身边，他也会痛不欲生的。再说我也活不了多久，不需要可怜兮兮地去讨好一个老头儿，一见他，我就觉得自己也变老了。让他把钱留着吧，没有他的钱我也会活得好好的。"

"但是你以后怎么办呢？"

"I don't in the least know."

Prudence was no doubt going to make some reply, but I entered suddenly and flung myself at Marguerite's feet, covering her hands with tears in my joy at being thus loved.

"My life is yours, Marguerite; you need this man no longer. Am I not here? Shall I ever leave you, and can I ever repay you for the happiness that you give me? No more barriers, my Marguerite; we love; what matters all the rest?"

"Oh yes, I love you, my Armand," she murmured, putting her two arms around my neck. "I love you as I never thought I should ever love. We will be happy; we will live quietly, and I will say good-bye forever to the life for which I now blush. You won't ever reproach me for the past? Tell me!"

Tears choked my voice. I could only reply by clasping Marguerite to my heart.

"Well," said she, turning to Prudence, and speaking in a broken voice, "you can report this scene to the duke, and you can add that we have no longer need of him."

From that day forth the duke was never referred to. Marguerite was no longer the same woman that I had known. She avoided everything that might recall to me the life which she had been leading when I

"我还不知道。"

普鲁登斯似乎还要说什么,可是我突然冲进去,扑倒在玛格丽特的脚下。我被一个人这样深地爱着,幸福的泪水忍不住流下来,滑落在她的手上。

"玛格丽特,生生死死我都是你的。你已经不需要那个老头儿了,我不是在你身边吗?我会离开你吗?我报答得了你给我的幸福吗?从此再也没有什么能阻挡我们了,我的玛格丽特,我们相亲相爱!其余的事,管他呢!"

"是呀,我爱你,我的阿尔芒!"她双手搂着我的脖子,柔声说道,"我从来没想到我会这么爱一个人。我们会幸福的,会静静地享受这份幸福的。那种令我脸红的不光彩生活,我要永远说再见。告诉我,你不会计较我的过去。好吗?"

泪水哽塞了我的声音,我只能把玛格丽特紧紧地抱在怀里,贴在心上作为回答。

"去吧,"她转身向普鲁登斯颤声说道,"你可以把这一幕告诉公爵,再告诉他我们不需要他了。"

从那一天以后,公爵再也没有被提起过。玛格丽特也不再是那个我过去认识的姑娘了。所有让我想起第一次见她时她过的生活的一切,她都尽量避免。玛格丽特给我

first met her. Never did wife or sister surround husband or brother with such loving care as she had for me. Her nature was morbidly open to all impressions and accessible to all sentiments. She had broken equally with her friends and with her ways, with her words and with her extravagances. Any one who had seen us leaving the house to go on the river in the charming little boat which I had bought would never have believed that the woman dressed in white, wearing a straw hat, and carrying on her arm a little silk pelisse to protect her against the damp of the river, was that Marguerite Gautier who, only four months ago, had been the talk of the town for the luxury and scandal of her existence.

Alas, we made haste to be happy, as if we knew that we were not to be happy long.

For two months we had not even been to Paris. No one came to see us, except Prudence and Julie Duprat, of whom I have spoken to you, and to whom Marguerite was afterward to give the touching narrative that I have there.

I passed whole days at the feet of my mistress. We opened the windows upon the garden, and, as we watched the summer ripening in its flowers and under the shadow of the trees, we breathed together

的爱是没有一个妻子或者姐妹能比得上的。她天性多愁善感。她和以前的朋友断绝来往，和过去的生活一刀两断，再也不像以前那样说话，不像以前那样挥霍了。那些看着我们从屋里出来，乘着我买的那只精巧小船在河里泛舟的人，永远也不会相信，这个一袭白裙裹身，戴着大草帽，肩上搭着一件再普通不过的绸外衣御寒的女人就是玛格丽特·戈蒂埃——4个月前曾因奢侈糜烂而名噪一时。

天哪！我们忙不迭地享受着幸福，似乎已经料到好景不长。

我们甚至已经有2个月没去巴黎了。除了普鲁登斯和我对你提过的那个朱莉·杜普拉，没有人来看过我们。现在在我这儿的那些令人肝肠寸断的日记，就是玛格丽特后来交给朱莉的。

我整天偎依在我情妇的身边。我们打开了朝着花园的窗户，欣赏着花团锦簇的夏景。我们在树荫下并肩享受着这种真切的生活，一种我和玛格丽特以前从未尝试过的生

that true life which neither Marguerite nor I had ever known before.

Her delight in the smallest things was like that of a child. There were days when she ran in the garden, like a child of ten, after a butterfly or a dragon-fly. This courtesan who had cost more money in bouquets than would have kept a whole family in comfort, would sometimes sit on the grass for an hour, examining the simple flower whose name she bore.

It was at this time that she read Manon Lescaut, over and over again. I found her several times making notes in the book, and she always declared that when a woman loves, she can not do as Manon did.

The duke wrote to her two or three times. She recognised the writing and gave me the letters without reading them. Sometimes the terms of these letters brought tears to my eyes. He had imagined that by closing his purse to Marguerite, he would bring her back to him; but when he had perceived the uselessness of these means, he could hold out no longer; he wrote and asked that he might see her again, as before, no matter on what conditions.

I read these urgent and repeated letters,

活。

她对一些小东西所表现出的欢欣就像个小女孩一样。有些日子她像 10 岁的小女孩儿那样，在花园里扑蝶或者捕蜻蜓。这个过去在鲜花上花的钱比维持一个舒适安逸的家庭还要多的烟花女子，常常在草坪上一坐就是一个小时，盯着她用来当做名字[1]的普通小花发呆。

就在那段日子里，她反反复复地读着《曼侬·莱斯科》。好几次我看见她在书上加注，而且总是告诉我，一个恋爱中的女人肯定不会像曼侬那样做的。

公爵给她写过两三封信，她认出是公爵的笔迹后，看都不看就把信交给了我。有几次信里的语气让我流下了眼泪。他原以为，断了玛格丽特的财源，就能让她再次回到他的身边。但是当他看到这个办法不奏效的时候，就再也坚持不下去了，他一再写信，请求像以前一样见她，不论什么条件他都可以答应。

我看完这些恳切、哀求的信以

and tore them in pieces, without telling Marguerite what they contained and without advising her to see the old man again, though I was half inclined to, so much did I pity him, but I was afraid lest, if I so advised her she should think that I wished the duke, not merely to come and see her again, but to take over the expenses of the house; I feared, above all, that she might think me capable of shirking the responsibilities of every consequence to which her love for me might lead her.

It thus came about that the duke, receiving no reply, ceased to write, and that Marguerite and I continued to live together without giving a thought to the future.

后，便把它们撕了，没有告诉玛格丽特信的内容，也没有劝她再去看看那位老人。尽管我对这个可怜的人动了恻隐之心，但是我不敢劝她，我怕她会以为我的希望不仅仅是见见公爵那么简单，而是要公爵负担这座房子的开销。她对我的爱给她带来的所有结果，我都会负责的，我现在最怕的就是她会以为我逃避承担后果。

最后公爵收不到回信也就不再来信了。玛格丽特和我还是像以前一样一起生活，没有想过以后的日子怎么办。

CHAPTER 18

第十八章

It would be difficult to give you all the details of our new life. It was made up of a series of little childish events, charming for us but insignificant to any one else. You know what it is to be in love with a woman, you know how it cuts short the days, and with what loving listlessness one drifts into the morrow. You know that forgetfulness of everything which comes of a violent confident, reciprocated love. Every being who is not the beloved one seems a useless being in creation. One regrets having cast scraps of one's heart to other women, and one can not believe in the possibility of ever pressing another hand than that which one holds between one's hands. The mind admits neither work nor remembrance; nothing, in short, which can distract it from the one thought in which it is ceaselessly absorbed. Every day one discovers in one's mistress a new charm and unknown delights. Existence itself is but the unceasing accomplishment of an unchanging desire; the soul is but the

我们新生活的点点滴滴是很难一一讲给你听的。这种由一系列孩子般的嬉笑构成的生活对我们来说十分有趣，但是对其他人来说却毫无意义。你知道和一个女人相爱是怎么一回事，你知道白天如何飞快地过去，晚上又是如何的缠绵温存，难舍难分。你不会不知道相互信赖、彼此付出的热烈爱情，可以让人忘乎所以。除了自己心爱的女人，其他一切似乎都是多余的。我后悔以前在别的女人身上浪费感情，我不知道除了自己握着的手以外，还有什么可能去握另一只手。我的头脑既不思考，也不回忆。总之，我现在只有一个念头，那就是，一切影响这个念头的东西都不能接受。每一天我都会在我的情妇身上发现一种新的魅力和一种未知的快感。活着本身就是为了满足不断变化的欲望，灵魂只不过是守护爱情圣火的女神。

vestal charged to feed the sacred fire of love.

We often went at night-time to sit in the little wood above the house; there we listened to the cheerful harmonies of evening, both of us thinking of the coming hours which should leave us to one another till the dawn of day. At other times we did not get up all day; we did not even let the sunlight enter our room.

The curtains were hermetically closed, and for a moment the external world did not exist for us. Nanine alone had the right to open our door, but only to bring in our meals and even these we took without getting up, interrupting them with laughter and gaiety. To that succeeded a brief sleep, for, disappearing into the depths of our love, we were like two divers who only come to the surface to take breath.

Nevertheless, I surprised moments of sadness, even tears, in Marguerite; I asked her the cause of her trouble, and she answered:

"Our love is not like other loves, my Armand. You love me as if I had never belonged to another, and I tremble lest later on, repenting of your love, and accusing me of my past, you should let me fall back into that life from which you have taken me. I think that now that I have tasted of

晚上，我们经常会坐在房子对面的高高的小树林里，静静听着夜的协奏曲，一起想着不久又可相拥至天明。有时我们一整天都躺在床上，甚至都不让阳光照进来。

窗帘一直合着，一时间，外面的世界似乎不存在。只有纳尼娜才有权打开我们的房门，但也只是来给我们送吃的。就算吃饭我们也在床上吃，还不停地嬉笑打闹。接着又小睡一会儿。我们就像两个潜水员一样，沉浸在爱河之中，只是在换气的时候才浮出水面。

但是，有几次玛格丽特显得很哀怨，甚至还流泪了，我很惊讶，问她原因，她回答我说：

"我们的爱情和别人的不一样，我亲爱的阿尔芒。你爱我就像我从来没有属于过别人一样，但是我很担心，我害怕过不了多久你就会后悔爱上我，指责我的过去。我怕你让我回到那种你已经让我摆脱了的生活。既然我已经尝到了新的

another life, I should die if I went back to the old one. Tell me that you will never leave me!"

"I swear it!"

At these words she looked at me as if to read in my eyes whether my oath was sincere; then flung herself into my arms, and, hiding her head in my bosom, said to me: "You don't know how much I love you!"

One evening, seated on the balcony outside the window, we looked at the moon which seemed to rise with difficulty out of its bed of clouds, and we listened to the wind violently rustling the trees; we held each other's hands, and for a whole quarter of an hour we had not spoken, when Marguerite said to me:

"Winter is at hand. Would you like for us to go abroad?"

"Where?"

"To Italy."

"You are tired of here?"

"I am afraid of the winter; I am particularly afraid of your return to Paris."

"Why?"

"For many reasons."

And she went on abruptly, without giving me her reasons for fears:

"Will you go abroad? I will sell all that I have; we will go and live there, and there

生活的滋味，如果要我再回到过去的生活，我宁愿死了。告诉我你永远不会离开我。"

"我向你发誓！"

听到这句话，她望着我的眼睛，似乎要从里面读出我的誓言是否真诚。随后她扑在我的怀里，把头埋在我的胸前，对我说："你不知道我是多么爱你啊！"

一天傍晚，我们坐在阳台外面的窗台上，望着云层中探出身影的月亮，听着风吹着树木沙沙作响。我们握着对方的手，沉默了好一阵子，突然玛格丽特对我说：

"冬天快到了，我们去国外吧？"

"去哪儿？"

"去意大利。"

"在这儿待腻了吗？"

"我怕冬天，我更怕你回到巴黎去。"

"为什么呢？"

"原因很多。"

她没有告诉我她在害怕什么，突然接下去说：

"你愿意去国外吗？我把我的东西统统卖掉，一起去国外生活，

will be nothing left of what I was; no one will know who I am. Will you?"

"By all means, if you like, Marguerite, let us travel," I said. "But where is the necessity of selling things which you will be glad of when we return? I have not a large enough fortune to accept such a sacrifice; but I have enough for us to be able to travel splendidly for five or six months, if that will amuse you the least in the world."

"After all, no," she said, leaving the window and going to sit down on the sofa at the other end of the room. "Why should we spend money abroad? I cost you enough already, here."

"You reproach me, Marguerite; it isn't generous."

"Forgive me, my friend," she said, giving me her hand. "This thunder weather gets on my nerves; I do not say what I intend to say."

And after embracing me she fell into a long reverie.

Scenes of this kind often took place, and though I could not discover their cause, I could not fail to see in Marguerite signs of disquietude in regard to the future. She could not doubt my love, which increased day by day, and yet I often found her sad, without being able to get any explanation

那儿没有任何我过去的痕迹。没有人会认出我是谁。你愿意吗？"

"玛格丽特，好，我们去吧，要是你喜欢的话，我们去旅行。"我对她说，"但是没有必要把所有东西都卖掉吧？你回来时看到这些东西不是很高兴吗？我没有足够的财产值得你做这样的牺牲，但是像样地作一次五六个月的旅行，我还是绰绰有余的，如果这能讨得你哪怕是半点欢欣的话，我们去吧。"

"那还是算了吧，"她说着离开窗台，走向房间另一端的沙发，"我们干嘛还要跑去国外花钱？我在这儿已经花了你不少钱了。"

"你在埋怨我，玛格丽特，这不公平啊！"

"请原谅，朋友，"她说着把手伸过来，"这种雷雨天气让我精神不好，我讲这些话不是有意的。"

随后她抱了我一下又陷入沉思。

类似的情景经常出现，虽然我不知道原因是什么，但是我不难发现，玛格丽特是在担忧未来。她不会怀疑我对她一日胜过一日的爱情。但是我经常看到她闷闷不乐，对此她除了身体不适之外，也没有做过其他的解释。我担心她厌倦了

of the reason, except some physical cause. Fearing that so monotonous a life was beginning to weary her, I proposed returning to Paris; but she always refused, assuring me that she could not be so happy anywhere as in the country.

Prudence now came but rarely; but she often wrote letters which I never asked to see, though, every time they came, they seemed to preoccupy Marguerite deeply. I did not know what to think.

One day Marguerite was in her room. I entered. She was writing.

"To whom are you writing?" I asked.

"To Prudence. Do you want to see what I am writing?"

I had a horror of anything that might look like suspicion, and I answered that I had no desire to know what she was writing; and yet I was certain that letter would have explained to me the cause of her sadness.

Next day the weather was splendid.' Marguerite proposed to me to take the boat and go as far as the island of Croissy. She seemed very cheerful; when we got back it was five o'clock.

"Mme. Duvernoy has been here," said Nanine, as she saw us enter. "She has gone again?" asked Marguerite.

"Yes, madame, in the carriage; she said

这种单调的生活，就提议回巴黎，但她总是一口回绝，并确切地告诉我没有地方能比乡下更能让她感到快乐。

普鲁登斯现在不怎么来了，但是她经常来信，虽然每次玛格丽特一收到信就心事重重的样子，但是我从未要求看过这些信，我猜不出写着些什么。

一天，玛格丽特在她的房间里，我进去的时候，她正在写信。

"在给谁写信呢？"我问她。

"给普鲁登斯，想看看我写了些什么吗？"

一切看似猜忌的事情我都很憎恶，我回答说，我并不想知道信的内容，但是我能肯定这封信能解释她忧郁的真正原因。

第二天，天气很好，玛格丽特提议乘船去克罗瓦西岛，她似乎很兴奋。我们回家时已经 5 点钟了。

"迪韦尔诺瓦太太来过了。"纳尼娜看见我们进来说道。"她走了吗？"玛格丽特问道。

"走了，夫人，坐着车子走的，

it was arranged."

"Quite right," said Marguerite sharply. "Serve the dinner."

Two days afterward there came a letter from Prudence, and for a fortnight Marguerite seemed to have got rid of her mysterious gloom, for which she constantly asked my forgiveness, now that it no longer existed.

Still, the carriage did not return.

"How is it that Prudence does not send you back your carriage?" I asked one day.

"One of the horses is ill, and there are some repairs to be done. It is better to have that done while we are here, and don't need a carriage, than to wait till we get back to Paris."

Prudence came two days afterward, and confirmed what Marguerite had said. The two women went for a walk in the garden, and when I joined them they changed the conversation. That night, as she was going, Prudence complained of the cold and asked Marguerite to lend her a shawl.

So a month passed, and all the time Marguerite was more joyous and more affectionate than she ever had been. Nevertheless, the carriage did not return, the shawl had not been sent back, and I began to be anxious in spite of myself, and as I knew in which drawer Marguerite put

她说这是讲好了的。"

"很好,"玛格丽特急切地说,"给我们准备晚饭。"

两天以后,普鲁登斯写信来了,接下来的两周里,玛格丽特似乎已经摆脱了那种莫名其妙的忧郁,而且不时地请我原谅她。

但是马车再也没有回来。

"普鲁登斯怎么还不把你的马车还回来啊?"有一天我问。

"有一匹马病了,车子也需要修理。现在我们在这里也用不着坐车子,不如趁我们还没有回巴黎就把它修好?"

两天后,普鲁登斯来了,证实了玛格丽特对我讲的话。两个女人在花园里散步,我走近她们时,她们就转移了话题。那天晚上,普鲁登斯走的时候,抱怨天气太冷,向玛格丽特借走了披肩。

这样过了一个月,其间玛格丽特比以往任何时候都要快乐,也更加爱我了。然而,马车没有回来,披肩也没有送来。我隐隐有些担忧。我知道玛格丽特把普鲁登斯的信放在哪个抽屉里,趁她在花园里的时候,我来到这个抽屉前,想打开看

Prudence's letters, I took advantage of a moment when she was at the other end of the garden, went to the drawer, and tried to open it; in vain, for it was locked. When I opened the drawer in which the trinkets and diamonds were usually kept, these opened without resistance, but the jewel cases had disappeared, along with their contents no doubt.

A sharp fear penetrated my heart. I might indeed ask Marguerite for the truth in regard to these disappearances, but it was certain that she would not confess it.

"My good Marguerite," I said to her, "I am going to ask your permission to go to Paris. They do not know my address, and I expect there are letters from my father waiting for me. I have no doubt he is concerned; I ought to answer him."

"Go, my friend," she said; "but be back early."

I went straight to Prudence.

"Come," said I, without beating about the bush, "tell me frankly, where are Marguerite's horses?"

"Sold."

"The shawl?"

"Sold."

"The diamonds?"

"Pawned."

"And who has sold and pawned them?"

看，但是抽屉锁着我打不开。然后当我打开她平常放首饰和钻石的抽屉时，这些抽屉一下就打开了，但是珠宝盒不见了，毫无疑问盒子里面的东西也没有了。

一阵恐惧猛然袭上心头。我本该去问玛格丽特这些东西到底去哪儿了，但是她肯定不会告诉我真相。

"我的好玛格丽特，"我告诉她说，"我想请你允许我去一趟巴黎。我的家人还不知道我住在这里呢，我想我父亲也该来信了，他一定很担心我，我得给他写封回信。"

"去吧，我的朋友，"她说，"但是早些回来。"

我径直去了普鲁登斯家里。

"快，"我开门见山地跟她说，"老实告诉我，玛格丽特的马车呢？"

"卖了。"

"披肩呢？"

"卖了。"

"钻石呢？"

"当了。"

"谁替她卖，替她当的？"

"I."

"Why did you not tell me?"

"Because Marguerite made me promise not to."

"And why did you not ask me for money?"

"Because she wouldn't let me."

"And where has this money gone?"

"In payments."

"Is she much in debt?"

"Thirty thousand francs, or thereabouts. Ah, my dear fellow, didn't I tell you? You wouldn't believe me; now you are convinced. The upholsterer whom the duke had agreed to settle with was shown out of the house when he presented himself, and the duke wrote next day to say that he would answer for nothing in regard to Mlle. Gautier. This man wanted his money; he was given part payment out of the few thousand francs that I got from you; then some kind souls warned him that his debtor had been abandoned by the duke and was living with a penniless young man; the other creditors were told the same; they asked for their money, and seized some of the goods. Marguerite wanted to sell everything, but it was too late, and besides I should have opposed it. But it was necessary to pay, and in order not to ask you for money, she sold her horses and her

"我。"

"你为什么不告诉我?"

"因为玛格丽特要我答应不告诉你。"

"那你为什么不向我要钱呢?"

"她不让。"

"这些钱用来干什么了呢?"

"还账。"

"她欠了很多钱吗?"

"3万法郎左右。啊!我亲爱的朋友,我不是早就告诉过你吗?你不相信,现在信了吧。以前由公爵应付的地毯商找公爵的时候吃了闭门羹,第二天公爵就写信告诉他戈蒂埃小姐的事别再找他了。这个人想要回他的钱,只好分期付给他,就是我向你要的那几千法郎。后来一些'好心人'警示他,他的债务人已经被公爵抛弃了,现在和一个身无分文的青年过日子。别的债权人也得到了同样的警示,纷纷来讨债,查封了玛格丽特的部分财产。玛格丽特本来想卖掉一切,但是来不及了,而且我也反对她那样做。但是账总归要还的,为了不向你要钱,她卖掉了马匹和披肩,当掉了珠宝。你要看看收据和当票吗?"

shawls, and pawned her jewels. Would you like to see the receipts and the pawn tickets?"

And Prudence opened the drawer and showed me the papers.

"Ah, you think," she continued, with the insistence of a woman who can say, I was right after all, "ah, you think it is enough to be in love, and to go into the country and lead a dreamy, pastoral life. No, my friend, no. By the side of that ideal life, there is a material life, and the purest resolutions are held to earth by threads which seem slight enough, but which are of iron, not easily to be broken. If Marguerite has not been unfaithful to you twenty times, it is because she has an exceptional nature. It is not my fault for not advising her to, for I couldn't bear to see the poor girl stripping herself of everything. She wouldn't; she replied that she loved you, and she wouldn't be unfaithful to you for anything in the world. All that is very pretty, very poetical, but one can't pay one's creditors in that coin, and now she can't free herself from debt, unless she can raise thirty thousand francs."

"All right, I will provide that amount."

"You will borrow it?"

"Good heavens! Why, yes!"

"A fine thing that will be to do; you will

于是普鲁登斯打开抽屉给我出示这些票据。

"啊！你以为呢，"她用一种幸灾乐祸的口气接着说，"嗯？你以为相爱就够了吗？你以为到乡下过梦一般的田园生活就够了吗？不够，我的朋友，远远不够。理想生活总是离不开物质生活的，最纯洁的决心都会被微不足道的小事压垮，而这些小事又都是铁一般的事实，逃脱不掉的。如果说玛格丽特从来没有做过对你不忠的事，那是因为她的性格与众不同。我真不忍心看到这个可怜的姑娘把自己弄得一穷二白，劝不住她不是我的错，她根本听不进我的话！她告诉我她爱你，她不会为了任何事情而欺骗你。听起来很美，很有诗意，但这些都不能当做钱来还债啊。眼下除非她能筹集到 3 万法郎，否则就会债务缠身。"

"好吧，我来负担这笔钱。"

"你要去借吗？"

"上帝啊，当然得借。"

"你可要干出好事来了，你会

fall out with your father, cripple your resources, and one doesn't find thirty thousand francs from one day to another. Believe me, my dear Armand, I know women better than you do; do not commit this folly; you will be sorry for it one day. Be reasonable. I don't advise you to leave Marguerite, but live with her as you did at the beginning. Let her find the means to get out of this difficulty. The duke will come back in a little while. The Comte de N., if she would take him, he told me yesterday even, would pay all her debts, and give her four or five thousand francs a month. He has two hundred thousand a year. It would be a position for her, while you will certainly be obliged to leave her. Don't wait till you are ruined, especially as the Comte de N. is a fool, and nothing would prevent your still being Marguerite's lover. She would cry a little at the beginning, but she would come to accustom herself to it, and you would thank me one day for what you had done. Imagine that Marguerite is married, and deceive the husband; that is all. I have already told you all this once, only at that time it was merely advice, and now it is almost a necessity."

What Prudence said was cruelly true.

"This is how it is," she went on, putting

和你父亲决裂的，自断财路。再说3万法郎也不是一天两天就能筹划得到的。相信我，亲爱的阿尔芒，我对女人的了解可比你多很多，别干蠢事，总有一天你会后悔的。理智一点儿吧，我并不是叫你离开玛格丽特，而是像以前那样和她生活，她的难题让她自己去解决好了。公爵不久就会回到她身边的。昨天N伯爵甚至还说，如果玛格丽特肯接待他的话，他会替她还清所有债务，不仅如此，还要每月给她四五千法郎。他每年有20万法郎的收入。对她来说这也算是个出路，而你迟早肯定是要离开她的。别等到破产了再这样做，更何况这位N伯爵是个傻瓜，你大可以继续做玛格丽特的情人。刚开始她会难过，但过不了多久她就会习惯的，按我说的去做吧，总有一天她会感谢你的。你就权当玛格丽特已经结婚了，你只是在欺骗她的丈夫，这样不就行了。这些话我已经对你讲过了，当时还只是一个建议，而现在已几乎是一种必需了。"

普鲁登斯讲的确实是残酷的事实。

away the papers she had just shown me; "women like Marguerite always foresee that some one will love them, never that they will love; otherwise they would put aside money, and at thirty they could afford the luxury of having a lover for nothing. If I had only known once what I know now! In short, say nothing to Marguerite, and bring her back to Paris. You have lived with her alone for four or five months; that is quite enough. Shut your eyes now; that is all that any one asks of you. At the end of a fortnight she will take the Comte de N., and she will save up during the winter, and next summer you will begin over again. That is how things are done, my dear fellow!"

And Prudence appeared to be enchanted with her advice, which I refused indignantly.

Not only my love and my dignity would not let me act thus, but I was certain that, feeling as she did now, Marguerite would die rather than accept another lover.

"Enough joking," I said to Prudence; "tell me exactly how much Marguerite is in need of."

"I have told you: thirty thousand francs."

"And when does she require this sum?"

"Before the end of two months."

"She shall have it."

"情况就是这样，"她一边收起刚才给我出示的票据，一边继续说道，"像玛格丽特这种女人就等着别人爱她们，而她们永远不会爱别人。除非她们攒钱，在30多岁的时候，找一个一无所有的情人养着。如果我以前就知道这些该有多好啊！总之，什么也别和玛格丽特说，带她回巴黎。你已经和她单独生活了四五个月了，这已经足够了。睁一只眼闭一只眼就行了。半个月以后她就会接待N伯爵的。一个冬天她会积攒一些钱，到了明年夏天你们还可以再过这种生活。事情就是这样，我亲爱的。"

看起来普鲁登斯对自己的一番劝谏很得意，可我愤怒地拒绝了。

不仅仅是我的爱和我的尊严不允许我这样做，而且我很确定玛格丽特死也不会再接受别的情人。

"够了，"我对普鲁登斯说，"告诉我玛格丽特到底需要多少钱？"

"我告诉过你了，3万法郎。"

"这笔钱什么时候要呢？"

"两个月以内。"

"她会有的。"

Prudence shrugged her shoulders.

"I will give it to you," I continued, "but you must swear to me that you will not tell Marguerite that I have given it to you."

"Don't be afraid."

"And if she sends you anything else to sell or pawn, let me know."

"There is no danger. She has nothing left."

I went straight to my own house to see if there were any letters from my father. There were four.

普鲁登斯耸了耸肩膀。

"我会把钱交给你的,"我继续说,"但是你必须发誓不告诉玛格丽特这钱是我给的。"

"放心吧。"

"如果她再托你变卖或是当什么东西,一定要让我知道。"

"别担心,她已经不剩什么了。"

我径直回到我的住处看是否有父亲写的来信。有 4 封。

CHAPTER 19
第十九章

In his first three letters my father inquired the cause of my silence; in the last he allowed me to see that he had heard of my change of life, and informed me that he was about to come and see me.

I have always had a great respect and a sincere affection for my father. I replied that I had been travelling for a short time, and begged him to let me know beforehand what day he would arrive, so that I could be there to meet him.

I gave my servant my address in the country, telling him to bring me the first letter that came with the postmark of C., then I returned to Bougival.

Marguerite was waiting for me at the garden gate. She looked at me anxiously. Throwing her arms round my neck, she said to me: "Have you seen Prudence?"

"No."

"You were a long time in Paris."

"I found letters from my father to which I had to reply."

A few minutes afterward Nanine

前3封信里，父亲询问我为什么不回信，在最后一封信里，他表示已经知晓了我生活上的变化，并告诉我不久就要来巴黎看我。

我向来都很尊敬我的父亲，并对我的父亲怀有一种真挚的感情。我回信告诉他我作了一次短期旅行，所以没看到他的信，并请他提前告诉我他什么时候来，我好接他。

我把乡下的地址留给了我的仆人，并嘱咐他接到印有C城邮戳的来信后第一时间给我送过去，然后我马上赶回布吉瓦尔。

玛格丽特在花园门口等我。她焦急地望着我，一下子搂住我，问道："你见到普鲁登斯了吗？"

"没有。"

"你在巴黎待了好久。"

"有几封父亲写来的信，我得回。"

几分钟后，纳尼娜气喘吁吁地

entered, all out of breath. Marguerite rose and talked with her in whispers. When Nanine had gone out Marguerite sat down by me again and said, taking my hand:

"Why did you deceive me? You went to see Prudence."

"Who told you?"

"Nanine."

"And how did she know?"

"She followed you."

"You told her to follow me?"

"Yes. I thought that you must have had a very strong motive for going to Paris, after not leaving me for four months. I was afraid that something might happen to you, or that you were perhaps going to see another woman."

"Child!"

"Now I am relieved. I know what you have done, but I don't yet know what you have been told."

I showed Marguerite my father's letters.

"That is not what I am asking you about. What I want to know is why you went to see Prudence."

"To see her."

"That's a lie, my friend."

"Well, I went to ask her if the horse was any better, and if she wanted your shawl and your jewels any longer."

Marguerite blushed, but did not answer.

进来了。玛格丽特起身走过去和她悄悄说了几句。纳尼娜出去后,玛格丽特重新坐回我身旁,握着我的手说:

"为什么要骗我?你去见普鲁登斯了。"

"谁告诉你的?"

"纳尼娜。"

"她怎么知道?"

"她跟踪了你。"

"是你叫她跟着我的吗?"

"是的。你已经和我形影不离地生活了4个月,我想你这次去巴黎肯定有什么重要原因。我怕你发生了什么事情,或是去看别的女人了。"

"孩子气!"

"现在我终于舒一口气了,我知道你做了些什么,但是我不知道别人对你说什么了。"

我把父亲的信给玛格丽特。

"我说的不是这个,我想知道你为什么要去普鲁登斯家里。"

"去看看她。"

"你在撒谎,我的朋友。"

"好吧,我去问她你的马病好了没有,你的披肩,你的首饰她还用不用了。"

玛格丽特的脸一下子就变红了,她并未作答。

"And," I continued, "I learned what you had done with your horses, shawls, and jewels."

"And you are vexed?"

"I am vexed that it never occurred to you to ask me for what you were in want of."

"In a liaison like ours, if the woman has any sense of dignity at all, she ought to make every possible sacrifice rather than ask her lover for money and so give a venal character to her love. You love me, I am sure, but you do not know on how slight a thread depends the love one has for a woman like me. Who knows? Perhaps some day when you were bored or worried you would fancy you saw a carefully concerted plan in our liaison. Prudence is a chatterbox. What need had I of the horses? It was an economy to sell them. I don't use them and I don't spend anything on their keep; if you love me, I ask nothing more, and you will love me just as much without horses, or shawls, or diamonds."

All that was said so naturally that the tears came to my eyes as I listened.

"But, my good Marguerite," I replied, pressing her hands lovingly, "you knew that one day I should discover the sacrifice you had made, and that the moment I discovered it I should allow it no longer."

"But why?"

"于是，"我继续说，"我才知道你的马匹、披肩和珠宝都被用来做什么了。"

"那么你怪我吗？"

"我怪你从来不向我索要你需要的东西。"

"像我们这种关系，如果那个女的还有一点点自尊心的话，她就应该作出所有可能的牺牲，也决不向她的情人要一分钱，否则就是对她的爱情的亵渎。你爱我，这我相信。但是你不知道对我这种女人的爱是多么的脆弱。谁知道呢？也许有一天你厌倦了，你就会把我们的爱情想象成一桩精心策划的交易。普鲁登斯真是个长舌妇，我还要这些马做什么？卖了它们更划算，我已经用不到它们了，也不需要再花钱养它们了。只要你爱我，别的什么我都不需要。即使我没有马，没有披肩，没有钻石，你也一定会和以前一样地爱我。"

她讲这些话的时候神情自若，听着听着我的眼眶湿润了。

"但是，我的好玛格丽特，"我深情地紧握着她的手回答说，"你知道，总有一天我会发现你所做的牺牲，那时我怎么受得了。"

"为什么受不了呢？"

"Because, my dear child, I can not allow your affection for me to deprive you of even a trinket. I too should not like you to be able, in a moment when you were bored or worried, to think that if you were living with somebody else those moments would not exist; and to repent, if only for a minute, of living with me. In a few days your horses, your diamonds, and your shawls shall be returned to you. They are as necessary to you as air is to life, and it may be absurd, but I like you better showy than simple."

"Then you no longer love me."

"Foolish creature!"

"If you loved me, you would let me love you my own way; on the contrary, you persist in only seeing in me a woman to whom luxury is indispensable, and whom you think you are always obliged to pay. You are ashamed to accept the proof of my love. In spite of yourself, you think of leaving me some day, and you want to put your disinterestedness beyond risk of suspicion. You are right, my friend, but I had better hopes."

And Marguerite made a motion to rise; I held her, and said to her:

"I want you to be happy and to have nothing to reproach me for, that is all."

"And we are going to be separated!"

"因为，我亲爱的孩子，我不允许你因为爱我而搭上你的哪怕一件小首饰。我同样也不希望你在无聊或者焦虑的时候想，如果现在是和别人同居，也不会沦落至此。我也不希望你在和我生活的日子里有哪怕一分钟的后悔。过几天，你的马匹、你的钻石和你的披肩都会回来。这些东西之于你，就像空气之于生命一样不可或缺。也许这很荒谬。但是我希望你过得奢华一点儿，而不要那么朴素。"

"看来你已经不爱我了。"

"胡说八道！"

"如果你爱我，那么就让我用我的方式来爱你，否则，你就只是把我看成了一个挥霍成性的姑娘，你老是觉得要在我身上花钱才踏实。对于我的爱情表白，你觉得很惭愧。而且你老想着总有一天会离开我，小心翼翼，唯恐被人怀疑。你是对的，我的朋友，但是我的希望还不只是这些。"

玛格丽特动了一下，想起身，我拉住她，对她说：

"我希望你幸福，希望以后你不会埋怨我，就这些。"

"那么我们就得分手了！"

"Why, Marguerite, who can separate us?" I cried.

"You, who will not let me take you on your own level, but insist on taking me on mine; you, who wish me to keep the luxury in the midst of which I have lived, and so keep the moral distance which separates us; you, who do not believe that my affection is sufficiently disinterested to share with me what you have, though we could live happily enough on it together, and would rather ruin yourself, because you are still bound by a foolish prejudice. Do you really think that I could compare a carriage and diamonds with your love? Do you think that my real happiness lies in the trifles that mean so much when one has nothing to love, but which become trifling indeed when one has? You will pay my debts, realize your estate, and then keep me? How long will that last? Two or three months, and then it will be too late to live the life I propose, for then you will have to take everything from me, and that is what a man of honour can not do; while now you have eight or ten thousand francs a year, on which we should be able to live. I will sell the rest of what I do not want, and with this alone I will make two thousand francs a year. We will take a nice little flat in which we can both live. In the summer we will go

"为什么，玛格丽特？谁能把我们分开？"我喊道。

"你！你不想让我和你站在同一个水平线上。你！你希望我过着以前的奢侈生活，来保持我们思想上的差距。你！你不相信我对你无私的爱情，不相信我和你同甘共苦的决心。尽管我们可以靠这笔财产幸福地生活，但是你宁愿把自己弄得倾家荡产，你的内心深处还是存在这种愚蠢的偏见。你真的以为我会把车子、首饰和你的爱情相比吗？你以为我的幸福就是这些无关紧要的奢侈品吗？一个没有爱的人或许很看重这些东西，但是对于一个心中有爱的人来说，这些东西毫无意义。你要替我还债，把自己的钱花完，最后养着我？你能养我多久？两三个月？那时候再按我的办法生活就太晚了，那时的你一切都得依靠我，而一个有声望的男人不会这样做的。现在你每年有8000到1万法郎的收入，我们完全可以靠这些生活。我把多余的东西卖掉，每年也会有2000法郎的收入。我们去租一套够两人住的精致公寓。夏天我们去乡下，不用住现在这种房子，有一间够两个人住的小房子就行。你无拘无束，我自由自在，我们都还年轻。看在上帝的分上，阿尔芒，不要让我再回到从前那种迫

into the country, not to a house like this, but to a house just big enough for two people. You are independent, I am free, we are young; in heaven's name, Armand, do not drive me back into the life I had to lead once!"

I could not answer. Tears of gratitude and love filled my eyes, and I flung myself into Marguerite's arms.

"I wanted," she continued, "to arrange everything without telling you, pay all my debts, and take a new flat. In October we should have been back in Paris, and all would have come out; but since Prudence has told you all, you will have to agree beforehand, instead of agreeing afterward. Do you love me enough for that?"

It was impossible to resist such devotion. I kissed her hands ardently, and said:

"I will do whatever you wish."

It was agreed that we should do as she had planned. Thereupon, she went wild with delight; danced, sang, amused herself with calling up pictures of her new flat in all its simplicity, and began to consult me as to its position and arrangement. I saw how happy and proud she was of this resolution, which seemed as if it would bring us into closer and closer relationship, and I resolved to do my own share. In an

不得已的生活中去吧。"

我无言以对。感激和爱的泪水溢出了我的眼眶，我扑在玛格丽特的怀抱之中。

"我原想，"她接着说，"瞒着你把一切安排妥当，把所有的债还清，租一个新居。等10月份我们回巴黎的时候，一切都已经齐备。不过既然普鲁登斯把一切都告诉你了，那么事先同意总比事后接受好。你能爱我到这般地步吗？"

如此情深意重的爱，让人无法抗拒。我热烈地吻着玛格丽特的手对她说：

"我一切都听你的。"

我们讲好按她的计划行事。于是她高兴得发疯，又唱又跳，描绘着她简朴的新居。她开始和我商量在哪儿找房子，里面又如何布置，等等。我能看得出她对这个主意有多么的高兴和骄傲，似乎这样我们就能长相厮守，对此我也决定出一份力。很快我今后的生活就定下来了，我把我的财产作了安排，把我母亲留给我的财产转赠给玛格丽

instant I decided the whole course of my life. I put my affairs in order, and made over to Marguerite the income which had come to me from my mother, and which seemed little enough in return for the sacrifice which I was accepting. There remained the five thousand francs a year from my father; and, whatever happened, I had always enough to live on. I did not tell Marguerite what I had done, certain as I was that she would refuse the gift. This income came from a mortgage of sixty thousand francs on a house that I had never even seen. All that I knew was that every three months my father's solicitor, an old friend of the family, handed over to me seven hundred and fifty francs in return for my receipt.

The day when Marguerite and I came to Paris to look for a flat, I went to this solicitor and asked him what had to be done in order to make over this income to another person. The good man imagined I was ruined, and questioned me as to the cause of my decision. As I knew that I should be obliged, sooner or later, to say in whose favour I made this transfer, I thought it best to tell him the truth at once. He made none of the objections that his position as friend and solicitor authorized him to make, and assured me that he would

特。当然这笔财产远不足以报答我所接受的牺牲。这样我还有我父亲留给我的每年 5000 法郎的津贴，不管发生什么事情，靠这笔钱足以过日子。这一切我都没有告诉玛格丽特，因为我深信她肯定会拒绝这笔赠予。这笔收入来自一座 6 万法郎的房屋抵押费。那座房子我至今也没见过。我只知道每一季度，我父亲的公证人——我家的一位世交——都会凭我一张收据交给我 750 法郎。

玛格丽特和我回巴黎找房子的那天，我找到这位公证人，向他咨询了要把这笔财产转让给另外一个人需要办哪些手续。这位好心人以为我破产了，问我为什么要做这个决定。我知道我迟早得告诉他这次转让的受益人是谁，我想还是立即把实情告诉他为好。作为一个公证人或者一个朋友，他有权利提出异议，但是他没有，只是向我保证他会尽量把事情办好。当然我请求他在我父亲那里严守秘密。从公证人那里离开后我立刻回到玛格丽特身

arrange the whole affair in the best way possible. Naturally, I begged him to employ the greatest discretion in regard to my father, and on leaving him I rejoined Marguerite, who was waiting for me at Julie Duprat's, where she had gone in preference to going to listen to the moralizings of Prudence.

We began to look out for flats. All those that we saw seemed to Marguerite too dear, and to me too simple. However, we finally found, in one of the quietest parts of Paris, a little house, isolated from the main part of the building. Behind this little house was a charming garden, surrounded by walls high enough to screen us from our neighbours, and low enough not to shut off our own view. It was better than our expectations.

While I went to give notice at my own flat, Marguerite went to see a business agent, who, she told me, had already done for one of her friends exactly what she wanted him to do for her. She came on to the Rue de Provence in a state of great delight. The man had promised to pay all her debts, to give her a receipt for the amount, and to hand over to her twenty thousand francs, in return for the whole of her furniture. You have seen by the amount taken at the sale that this honest man would

边，她在朱莉·杜普拉家里等我。她宁愿到朱莉家等我也不愿意去听普鲁登斯的说教。

　　我们开始找房子。所有我们看过的房子，玛格丽特觉得太贵，我觉得太简陋。不过我们最终在巴黎最清静的地方找到了一幢小房子，这个小房子从主题建筑中独立出来，后面还附有一个漂亮的小花园，花园的围墙高低适宜，既能把我们和邻居隔开来，又不妨碍视线。这出乎我们的意料。

　　我去退原来我那套房子的时候，玛格丽特去见一个经纪人了。她告诉我，这个人曾经为她的一个朋友办过她现在想请他办的事。她常高兴地来普罗旺斯街找我。这个经纪人答应清偿她的一切债务，把结清的账单给了她，同时还给了她2万法郎，作为所有家具的补偿。从这个售价你可以看到，这个老实人从他的客户那里赚了3万多法郎。

have gained thirty thousand francs out of his client.

We went back joyously to Bougival, talking over our projects for the future, which, thanks to our heedlessness, and especially to our love, we saw in the rosiest light.

A week later, as we were having lunch, Nanine came to tell us that my servant was asking for me. "Let him come in," I said.

"Sir," said he, "your father has arrived in Paris, and begs you to return at once to your rooms, where he is waiting for you."

This piece of news was the most natural thing in the world, yet, as we heard it, Marguerite and I looked at one another. We foresaw trouble. Before she had spoken a word, I replied to her thought, and, taking her hand, I said, "Fear nothing."

"Come back as soon as possible," whispered Marguerite, embracing me; "I will wait for you at the window."

I sent on Joseph to tell my father that I was on my way. Two hours later I was at the Rue de Provence.

我们又欢天喜地地回到布吉瓦尔去，继续筹划我们的未来。由于我们现在没有任何后顾之忧，特别是我们情深意切，我们觉得未来无限美好。

一个星期后的一天，我们正在吃午饭，纳尼娜跑来告诉我，我的仆人要见我。我让他进来说话。

"先生，"他说，"你父亲来巴黎了，他请你马上回家，他在那里等你。"

听到这个再平常不过的消息后，玛格丽特和我却面面相觑。我们猜想情况不妙。她正要开口说点什么，我把手伸给她，回答她说："别怕。"

"尽量早点回来，"玛格丽特抱着我喃喃地说，"我在窗口等你。"

我派约瑟夫告诉我父亲说我马上就到。两小时以后，我已经到了普罗旺斯街。

CHAPTER 20

第二十章

My father was seated in my room in his dressing-gown; he was writing, and I saw at once, by the way in which he raised his eyes to me when I came in, that there was going to be a serious discussion. I went up to him, all the same, as if I had seen nothing in his face, embraced him, and said:

"When did you come, father?"

"Last night."

"Did you come straight here, as usual?"

"Yes."

"I am very sorry not to have been here to receive you."

I expected that the sermon which my father's cold face threatened would begin at once; but he said nothing, sealed the letter which he had just written, and gave it to Joseph to post.

When we were alone, my father rose, and leaning against the mantelpiece, said to me:

"My dear Armand, we have serious matters to discuss."

我父亲穿着晨衣，正坐在我的客厅里写信。从他抬头看我的眼神里，我立即明白会有一场严肃的交谈。但是我装作没有看到，走上前拥抱了他。

"你什么时候到的，爸爸？"

"昨天晚上。"

"你还是和以前一样，一下车直接来我这里了吗？"

"是的。"

"我很抱歉没去接你。"

父亲的脸色阴冷，我等待着他训话。但是他什么也不说，封上他刚写好的信，让约瑟夫去寄。

当屋里只剩下我和父亲两个人的时候，他站起来，靠在壁炉上对我说：

"亲爱的阿尔芒，我们要谈一些严肃的事情。"

"I am listening, father."

"You promise me to be frank?"

"Am I not accustomed to be so?"

"Is it not true that you are living with a woman called Marguerite Gautier?"

"Yes."

"Do you know what this woman was?"

"A kept woman."

"And it is for her that you have forgotten to come and see your sister and me this year?"

"Yes, father, I admit it."

"You are very much in love with this woman?"

"You see it, father, since she has made me fail in duty toward you, for which I humbly ask your forgiveness today."

My father, no doubt, was not expecting such categorical answers, for he seemed to reflect a moment, and then said to me:

"You have, of course, realized that you can not always live like that?"

"I fear so, father, but I have not realized it."

"But you must realize," continued my father, in a dryer tone, "that I, at all events, should not permit it."

"I have said to myself that as long as I did nothing contrary to the respect which I owe to the traditional probity of the family I could live as I am living, and this has

"我听着，爸爸。"

"你保证告诉我实话吗？"

"我不是一直都这样吗？"

"你和一个叫做玛格丽特·戈蒂埃的女人同居，这是真的吗？"

"是真的。"

"你知道这个女人的来头？"

"一个妓女。"

"就是为了这个女人，今年你都忘了来看你妹妹和我？"

"是，爸爸，我承认。"

"你很爱这个女人吗？"

"是，你说对了，爸爸，正是由于她我没有尽到对你的孝心，所以我今天来请求你原谅。"

我父亲无疑没有料到我会这样干脆利索地回答他，他似乎考虑了一会儿，然后对我说：

"你应该意识到你不能一直这样生活下去吧？"

"我曾经担心过，爸爸，但是我没意识到。"

"可是你必须意识到，"我父亲用一种生硬的语气继续说，"我是绝不允许你这样做的。"

"我想只要我不辱没门风，败坏门庭，我就可以像现在这样生活，正是这些想法才使我安心了些。"

reassured me somewhat in regard to the fears I have had."

Passions are formidable enemies to sentiment. I was prepared for every struggle, even with my father, in order that I might keep Marguerite.

"Then, the moment is come when you must live otherwise."

"Why, father?"

"Because you are doing things which outrage the respect that you imagine you have for your family."

"I don't follow your meaning."

"I will explain it to you. Have a mistress if you will; pay her as a man of honour is bound to pay the woman whom he keeps, by all means; but that you should come to forget the most sacred things for her, that you should let the report of your scandalous life reach my quiet countryside, and set a blot on the honourable name that I have given you, it can not, it shall not be."

"Permit me to tell you, father, that those who have given you information about me have been ill-informed. I am the lover of Mlle. Gautier; I live with her; it is the most natural thing in the world. I do not give Mlle. Gautier the name you have given me; I spend on her account what my means allow me to spend; I have no debts; and, in

爱情和感情正作着激烈的斗争，为了保住玛格丽特，我准备作出一切反抗，甚至是我父亲。

"那么现在该是你改变生活方式的时候了。"

"为什么，爸爸？"

"因为你正在做败坏门风的事，而且你自己也认为是应该保持家庭声望的。"

"我不明白你的意思。"

"我来告诉你。你有一个情妇，这没什么。你像其他时髦的人那样包养一个妓女，这也无可非议。但是你居然为了她而忘记了最神圣的职责，你居然让你的丑闻流传到了我们洁净的家乡，玷污了我家的门楣，这还得了！以后不准这样。"

"请听我说，爸爸，不是你所听到的那样。我是戈蒂埃小姐的情人，我和她同居，这种事再平常不过了。我并没有把从你那儿得到的姓氏给戈蒂埃小姐，我花在她身上的钱是我的收入所能负担的。我没有欠债，总之我还没有堕落到要一个父亲向他儿子说你刚才对我说的

short, I am not in a position which authorizes a father to say to his son what you have just said to me."

"A father is always authorized to rescue his son out of evil paths. You have not done any harm yet, but you will do it."

"Father!"

"Sir, I know more of life than you do. There are no entirely pure sentiments except in perfectly chaste women. Every Manon can have her own Des Grieux, and times are changed. It would be useless for the world to grow older if it did not correct its ways. You will leave your mistress."

"I am very sorry to disobey you, father, but it is impossible."

"I will compel you to do so."

"Unfortunately, father, there no longer exists a Sainte Marguerite to which courtesans can be sent, and, even if there were, I would follow Mlle. Gautier if you succeeded in having her sent there. What would you have? Perhaps am in the wrong, but I can only be happy as long as I am the lover of this woman."

"Come, Armand, open your eyes. Recognise that it is your father who speaks to you, your father who has always loved you, and who only desires your happiness. Is it honourable for you to live like husband and wife with a woman whom

这番话。"

"父亲总是有权让自己的儿子悬崖勒马。你还没有做什么坏事，但你以后会做的。"

"爸爸！"

"先生，对于人生我的经验总比你多些。只有真正贞洁的女人才会有纯洁的感情。任何一个曼侬都会有一个德·格里欧的，时代变了，如果走错了路，那年纪再大也是白搭。离开你的情妇。"

"很抱歉我不能听从你，爸爸，这是不可能的。"

"我要强迫你同意。"

"很遗憾，爸爸，放逐妓女的圣玛格丽特岛已经没有了，即使有，你要是把她发送到那里，我也会跟着去的。你叫我怎么办？也许是我错了，但是只有在做这个女人的情人时我才有幸福可言。"

"啊，阿尔芒，睁大你的眼睛，要知道站在这里和你说话的人是你的父亲，他一直在爱着你，一心盼望你过得幸福。你觉得像丈夫一样跟一个和很多人睡过的女人同居是件荣耀的事吗？"

everybody has had?"

"What does it matter, father, if no one will any more? What does it matter, if this woman loves me, if her whole life is changed through the love which she has for me and the love which I have for her? What does it matter, if she has become a different woman?"

"Do you think, then, sir, that the mission of a man of honour is to go about converting lost women? Do you think that God has given such a grotesque aim to life, and that the heart should have any room for enthusiasm of that kind? What will be the end of this marvellous cure, and what will you think of what you are saying today by the time you are forty? You will laugh at this love of yours, if you can still laugh, and if it has not left too serious a trace in your past. What would you be now if your father had had your ideas and had given up his life to every impulse of this kind, instead of rooting himself firmly in convictions of honour and steadfastness? Think it over, Armand, and do not talk any more such absurdities. Come, leave this woman; your father entreats you."

I answered nothing.

"Armand," continued my father, "in the name of your sainted mother, abandon this life, which you will forget more easily than

"只要她以后不再和别人睡, 爸爸, 那又有什么关系? 只要这个姑娘爱我, 只要她的生活由于我们相互的爱慕而改变, 那又有什么关系呢? 只要她已经彻底从良, 那又有什么关系!"

"啊! 先生, 难道你以为一个有声誉的男人, 他的任务就是转变误入风尘的女子吗? 难道你认为上帝赋予人生的就是这么一个怪诞的使命吗? 一个人的内心里就只有那方面的热情吗? 你这了不起的医治最终会怎么样呢? 到你 40 岁的时候, 对你今天所说的一切又会有什么想法呢? 如果你的爱情没有在你的过往中留下太深的痕迹, 如果到时你还笑得出来的话, 你会觉得这种爱情很可笑。如果你的父亲以前也抱着和你一样的想法, 一生为情所控, 而不以荣誉和正派立身的话, 你现在又会是怎样呢? 好好想想, 阿尔芒, 别再讲这种蠢话了。去, 离开这个女人, 你的父亲恳求你。"

我保持沉默。

"阿尔芒,"我父亲接着说,"看在你圣洁的母亲的分上, 丢弃这种生活吧, 忘记这一切比你想象的容

you think. You are tied to it by an
impossible theory. You are twenty-four;
think of the future. You can not always
love this woman, who also can not always
love you. You both exaggerate your love.
You put an end to your whole career. One
step further, and you will no longer be able
to leave the path you have chosen, and you
will suffer all your life for what you have
done in your youth. Leave Paris. Come and
stay for a month or two with your sister
and me. Rest in our quiet family affection
will soon heal you of this fever, for it is
nothing else. Meanwhile, your mistress
will console herself; she will take another
lover; and when you see what it is for
which you have all but broken with your
father, and all but lost his love, you will tell
me that I have done well to come and seek
you out, and you will thank me for it.
Come, you will go with me, Armand, will
you not?"

I felt that my father would be right if it
had been any other woman, but I was
convinced that he was wrong with regard
to Marguerite. Nevertheless, the tone in
which he said these last words was so kind,
so appealing, that I dared not answer.

"Well?" said he in a trembling voice.

"Well, father, I can promise nothing," I
said at last; "what you ask of me is beyond

易多了。你的这种想法是行不通的。
你已经 24 岁了，想想你的将来吧。
你不可能永远爱着这个女人，她也
不会永远爱你的。你们彼此都把爱
情夸大了。你断送了你的前途。再
往前走一步，你就永远回不了头了，
年少时的一时冲动，会让你终生受
累。离开巴黎，来和你的妹妹还有
我一起住一段日子，在家静养一段
时间，你对爱情的狂热会很快冷却，
这又不是什么大不了的事。与此同
时，你的情妇自己会好起来的，她
会有别的情人，而当你发现你差一
点儿为这种女人和自己的父亲闹
翻，失去他的爱，你就会对我说，
我今天来找你，把你从深渊中拉回
来是对的，你会因此而感谢我的。
来吧，阿尔芒，跟我走，好吗？"

如果是对别的什么女人，我觉
得父亲的话是对的。但是我深信他
这样看待玛格丽特就错了。然而他
的最后几句话的语气是那么温和，
那么恳切，我都不敢回答他。

"怎么样？"他声音颤抖着问。

"这个……爸爸，我什么也不
能答应你。"我终于说道，"你的要

my power. Believe me," I continued, seeing him make an impatient movement, "you exaggerate the effects of this liaison. Marguerite is a different kind of a woman from what you think. This love, far from leading me astray, is capable, on the contrary, of setting me in the right direction. Love always makes a man better, no matter what woman inspires it. If you knew Marguerite, you would understand that I am in no danger. She is as noble as the noblest of women. There is as much disinterestedness in her as there is cupidity in others."

"All of which does not prevent her from accepting the whole of your fortune, for the sixty thousand francs which come to you from your mother, and which you are giving her, are, understand me well, your whole fortune."

My father had probably kept this peroration and this threat for the last stroke. I was firmer before these threats than before his entreaties.

"Who told you that I was handing this sum to her?" I asked.

"My solicitor. Could an honest man carry out such a procedure without warning me? Well, it is to prevent you from ruining yourself for a prostitute that I am now in Paris. Your mother, when she died, left you

求我办不到，相信我，"看见他做了一个很不耐烦的动作，我继续说道，"你把这种关系的后果想得太严重了。玛格丽特和你想象中的女人不一样。这种爱情非但不会把我推向深渊，相反它让我找到了正确的方向。爱情总是会让人上进，不管激起这种爱情火花的女人是谁。如果你认识玛格丽特，你就会知道我的处境没有任何危险。她和最高贵的女人一样高贵。其他的女人有多少贪婪，她就有多少无私。"

"这倒不妨碍她接受你的全部财产，你把你母亲留给你的 6 万法郎全部给了她。记住，这 6 万法郎是你仅有的财产。"

我父亲可能有意把这句威胁留在最后万不得已的时候讲出来。在威胁面前我的态度比在婉言恳求面前更加坚决。

"谁告诉你我要把这笔钱赠给玛格丽特的？"我问道。

"我的公证人。一个诚实正直的人会在没通知我的情况下办这种事吗？我之所以来巴黎，就是要防止你为一个妓女堕落。你母亲临死前给你留下这笔钱是为了让你体面地

enough to live on respectably, and not to squander on your mistresses."

"I swear to you, father, that Marguerite knew nothing of this transfer."

"Why, then, do you make it?"

"Because Marguerite, the woman you calumniate, and whom you wish me to abandon, is sacrificing all that she possesses in order to live with me."

"And you accept this sacrifice? What sort of a man are you, sir, to allow Mlle. Gautier to sacrifice anything for you? Come, enough of this. You will leave this woman. Just now I begged you; now I command you. I will have no such scandalous doings in my family. Pack up your things and get ready to come with me."

"Pardon me, father," I said, "but I shall not come."

"And why?"

"Because I am at an age when no one any longer obeys a command."

My father turned pale at my answer.

"Very well, sir," he said, "I know what remains to be done."

He rang and Joseph appeared.

"Have my things taken to the Hotel de Paris," he said to my servant. And thereupon he went to his room and finished dressing. When he returned, I went up to

过日子，而不是让你在情妇面前摆阔。"

"我向你发誓，爸爸，玛格丽特完全不知道这回事。"

"那么，你为什么要这样做？"

"因为玛格丽特，这个你很鄙视的女人，这个你要我抛弃的女人，为了和我在一起牺牲了她所有的一切。"

"而你接受了这种牺牲？你成什么人了？先生，你竟然接受那个玛格丽特为你做的牺牲？行了，够了。离开这个女人！刚刚我是在恳求你，现在我命令你。我不允许这样的丑事出现在我家里。收拾收拾东西，准备跟我走。"

"请原谅我，爸爸，"我说，"我不能走。"

"为什么？"

"因为我已经到了可以不服从命令的年龄。"

听到我的回答，我父亲的脸色霎时惨白。

"很好，先生，"他说，"我知道该怎么办了。"

他拉铃把约瑟夫叫进来。

"把我的东西收拾一下送到巴黎旅馆。"他对我的仆人说着，走进卧室穿好衣服。他出来时，我迎上

him.

"Promise me, father," I said, "that you will do nothing to give Marguerite pain?"

My father stopped, looked at me disdainfully, and contented himself with saying, "I believe you are mad." After this he went out, shutting the door violently after him.

I went downstairs, took a cab, and returned to Bougival.

Marguerite was waiting for me at the window.

去。

"爸爸，请答应我，"我说，"别做任何让玛格丽特痛苦的事，好吗？"

我父亲站定了，轻蔑地望着我说道："我想你疯了。"说完他重重地关上门走了。

我跟着下了楼，搭上一辆马车回布吉瓦尔去了。

玛格丽特正在窗口等我。

CHAPTER 21
第二十一章

"At last you have come," she said, throwing her arms round my neck. "But how pale you are!"

I told her of the scene with my father.

"My God! I was afraid of it," she said. "When Joseph came to tell you of your father's arrival I trembled as if he had brought news of some misfortune. My poor friend, I am the cause of all your distress. You will be better off, perhaps, if you leave me and do not quarrel with your father on my account. He knows that you are sure to have a mistress, and he ought to be thankful that it is I, since I love you and do not want more of you than your position allows. Did you tell him how we had arranged our future?"

"Yes; that is what annoyed him the most, for he saw how much we really love one another."

"What are we to do, then?"

"Hold together, my good Marguerite, and let the storm pass over."

"Will it pass?"

"你终于来了！"她一边喊着，一边张开双臂，搂着我的脖子，"天哪！你的脸怎么这么苍白！"

于是，我向她述说了与父亲之间发生的事。

"上帝啊！我就担心这样，"她说，"当约瑟夫告诉我你父亲过来的消息时，我就浑身乱颤，仿佛大难降临。我可怜的朋友！我是你所有苦难的根源。假使和我分开，或许会比让你因为我同父亲之间吵翻要好一些。他绝对明白你应该养一个情妇，同时，他也该为我作为你的情妇而欣慰，因为我不但深爱着你，还知晓你的家境，我不会提出让你承担不了的要求。你有向他提过我们以后的打算吗？"

"向他提过了，可让他最恼火的就是这个，正因为这一点，他才看出了我们之间是多么的相爱。"

"那我们怎么办？"

"一切照旧，善良的玛格丽特，就让我们一起看着这场狂风暴雨渐渐平息吧。"

"It will have to."

"But your father will not stop there."

"What do you suppose he can do?"

"How do I know? Everything that a father can do to make his son obey him. He will remind you of my past life, and will perhaps do me the honour of inventing some new story, so that you may give me up."

"You know that I love you."

"Yes, but what I know, too, is that, sooner or later, you will have to obey your father, and perhaps you will end by believing him."

"No, Marguerite. It is I who will make him believe me. Some of his friends have been telling him tales which have made him angry; but he is good and just, he will change his first impression; and then, after all, what does it matter to me?"

"Do not say that, Armand. I would rather anything should happen than that you should quarrel with your family; wait till after today, and tomorrow go back to Paris. Your father, too, will have thought it over on his side, and perhaps you will both come to a better understanding. Do not go against his principles, pretend to make some concessions to what he wants; seem not to care so very much about me, and he will let things remain as they are. Hope,

"能平息吗？"

"绝对能。"

"可你父亲就甘心这件事这样结束？"

"那你说他该怎么做？"

"我又怎能知道？为了让自己的儿子听从他的意志，他可能会想尽一切办法。比如，为了使你放弃我他会让你想到我从前的行径，甚至会对那些事情添油加醋。"

"可你明白我是那么的爱你。"

"的确如此，不过，我也明白总有一天你会被你的父亲说服，最终服从他的意志的。"

"不，玛格丽特，迟早我会说服他。他之所以会如此生气，是因为听了一些朋友的造谣。但他心地善良，公正不阿，最终一定会不计前嫌。况且，话又说回来，这些和我又有什么关系！"

"千万不能这么说，阿尔芒，我宁愿发生任何事都不希望因为我让你和你的亲人吵翻。等到明天，你立即赶回巴黎。同你一样，你的父亲也会以他的角度认真地想想的，说不定，你们能达成彼此双方的谅解。记住，不要再违背他的意志，你可以假装对他的要求作一些让步，同时，也别让他觉得你太在乎我，就这样，他就能使这件事风平浪静。想开一些，我亲爱的朋友，

my friend, and be sure of one thing, that whatever happens, Marguerite will always be yours."

"You swear it?"

"Do I need to swear it?"

How sweet it is to let oneself be persuaded by the voice that one loves! Marguerite and I spent the whole day in talking over our projects for the future, as if we felt the need of realizing them as quickly as possible. At every moment we awaited some event, but the day passed without bringing us any new tidings.

Next day I left at ten o'clock, and reached the hotel about twelve. My father had gone out.

I went to my own rooms, hoping that he had perhaps gone there. No one had called. I went to the solicitor's. No one was there. I went back to the hotel, and waited till six. M. Duval did not return, and I went back to Bougival.

I found Marguerite not waiting for me, as she had been the day before, but sitting by the fire, which the weather still made necessary. She was so absorbed in her thoughts that I came close to her chair without her hearing me. When I put my lips to her forehead she started as if the kiss had suddenly awakened her.

"You frightened me," she said. "And

你一定要坚信：无论如何，玛格丽特永远在你身边。"

"你发誓？"

"难道我需要对你发誓？"

能被来自爱人的声音所劝服该是多么甜蜜的一件事啊！这一整天，玛格丽特和我都在不断地讨论着我们对未来的计划，因为，就像我们已经明白：我们需要尽早实现这些计划。每时每分，我们都在期盼着能够发生什么。然而，一天过去，什么也没有发生。

次日上午 10 点，我离开此处，12 点时，我已赶到了旅馆，可我的父亲却出去了。

我想父亲可能是回自己家了，便又赶了过去。可那里却没人来过。我又奔向律师家，那里也没人。我又赶回旅馆，在这里一直坐到下午 6 点，还是没有见到父亲的影子。我只好又奔回布吉瓦尔了。

我发现，玛格丽特并没有像前天那样等着我，而是在炉边坐着，如今的天气的确需要火炉来取暖。她是那么全神贯注，以至于当我站到她的椅边时，她都没有任何反应。直到我用嘴唇贴上她的前额时，她才颤抖了几下，如同是被这片刻的温情惊醒了一般。

"你可把我吓了一跳。"她说，

your father?"

"I have not seen him. I do not know what it means. He was not at his hotel, nor anywhere where there was a chance of my finding him."

"Well, you must try again tomorrow."

"I am very much inclined to wait till he sends for me. I think I have done all that can be expected of me."

"No, my friend, it is not enough; you must call on your father again, and you must call tomorrow."

"Why tomorrow rather than any other day?"

"Because," said Marguerite, and it seemed to me that she blushed slightly at this question, "because it will show that you are the more keen about it, and he will forgive us the sooner."

For the remainder of the day Marguerite was sad and preoccupied. I had to repeat twice over everything I said to her to obtain an answer. She ascribed this preoccupation to her anxiety in regard to the events which had happened during the last two days. I spent the night in reassuring her, and she sent me away in the morning with an insistent disquietude that I could not explain to myself.

Again my father was absent, but he had left this letter for me:

"你父亲怎么没来？"

"我一天都没见到他。我不明白，无论是旅馆，还是其他任何可能的地方都无法找到他。"

"那么，明天你还得去。"

"我更倾向于在这里等他的消息。我觉得，该做的，我都已经做了。"

"别，朋友，这还差得远，你必须明天就去见你的父亲。"

"怎么偏偏是明天？其他的日子不行吗？"

听我这么一问，玛格丽特的脸色略微有些涨红，她说，"因为，你表现得越是急迫，他也就会越快地原谅我们。"

此后的这一整天，玛格丽特一直面无神色，焦虑不堪。每次我都得把话重复一遍，才能听到她的回复。她解释说，之所以一直忧心忡忡，是因为这两天发生的一些不幸的事情。我整整安慰了她一个晚上，可第二天一大早，她就急躁地催促我动身，这让我很不能理解。

父亲依旧不在，可他却留给了我以下这封信：

If you call again today, wait for me till four. If I am not in by four, come and dine with me tomorrow. I must see you.

I waited till the hour he had named, but he did not appear. I returned to Bougival.

The night before I had found Marguerite sad; that night I found her feverish and agitated. On seeing me, she flung her arms around my neck, but she cried for a long time in my arms. I questioned her as to this sudden distress, which alarmed me by its violence. She gave me no positive reason, but put me off with those evasions which a woman resorts to when she will not tell the truth.

When she was a little calmed down, I told her the result of my visit, and I showed her my father's letter, from which, I said, we might augur well. At the sight of the letter and on hearing my comment, her tears began to flow so copiously that I feared an attack of nerves, and, calling Nanine, I put her to bed, where she wept without a word, but held my hands and kissed them every moment.

I asked Nanine if, during my absence, her mistress had received any letter or visit which could account for the state in which I found her, but Nanine replied that no one

倘若今天你又来找我就等到下午4点，如果那时我没来，就等到明天晚上，我必须见你，咱们边吃边聊。

直到下午4点，父亲还是没来，我便奔回了布吉瓦尔。

昨天，我就发现玛格丽特一直心神不宁，焦躁不安，似乎是在发烧。一见我过来，她就猛扑进了我的怀里，在我的臂弯中抽泣了很久。我急忙问她为什么忽然如此。可她却哭得更厉害了，这让我觉得惊奇不已。然而，她并没有对此给我一个可以说得过去的理由，反倒是说了些女人们用来搪塞的借口。

在她略微冷静了一些之后，我便告诉了她此次往返的遭遇，并拿出父亲留下的信。我告诉她，按照信上的说法，这件事我们已能乐观面对了。看到了这封信，又听完了我这一天的遭遇，她立即痛哭起来，为了防止她的神经受到刺激，我急忙找来了纳尼娜。我们把她扶到床上，可她却只字不提，只是紧握着我的手不停地亲吻。

我问纳尼娜，我不在时是不是有什么来信给玛格丽特，抑或有哪位客人见过她，以至于她变成这样。可纳尼娜却说，这儿从没来过任何

had called and nothing had been sent.

Something, however, had occurred since the day before, something which troubled me the more because Marguerite concealed it from me.

In the evening she seemed a little calmer, and, making me sit at the foot of the bed, she told me many times how much she loved me. She smiled at me, but with an effort, for in spite of herself her eyes were veiled with tears.

I used every means to make her confess the real cause of her distress, but she persisted in giving me nothing but vague reasons, as I have told you. At last she fell asleep in my arms, but it was the sleep which tires rather than rests the body. From time to time she uttered a cry, started up, and, after assuring herself that I was beside her, made me swear that I would always love her.

I could make nothing of these intermittent paroxysms of distress, which went on till morning. Then Marguerite fell into a kind of stupor. She had not slept for two nights.

Her rest was of short duration, for toward eleven she awoke, and, seeing that I was up, she looked about her, crying:

"Are you going already?"

"No," said I, holding her hands; "but I

人，也没寄来过任何东西。

可昨天一定是发生了什么，她越是不告诉我，我就越觉得焦躁不堪。

到了晚上，玛格丽特好像变得冷静了些。她让我在床脚处坐下，并反复不断地絮叨着对我的坚贞不二的爱。而后，她冲我露出了一抹勉强的微笑，不管她如何克制，双眸里依然注满了泪水。

我用尽所有办法让她说出如此难过的真正原因，可她却始终是含糊其辞地给我说一些之前向你叙说过的毫不沾边的缘由。最后，她靠在我的臂弯上睡着了，可这样的睡眠，不但没有让她得到丝毫休息，反而会给她带来更深的摧残——她时不时会突然惊醒，然后尖叫一声。当确定我就在她身旁后，她就让我发誓要爱她一直到永远。

这时不时地突然发作的苦楚折磨着她直到第二天清晨，可我却完全不知根由。然后，玛格丽特就又昏昏沉沉地睡过去了，连续整整两夜她都没有安睡片刻了。

没睡多久，到了大约11点，她就又醒了，她发现我已站起来，便四处环顾，大喊道：

"你已经准备要走了？"

"不，"我紧握着她的手道，"不

wanted to let you sleep on. It is still early."

"What time are you going to Paris?"

"At four."

"So soon? But you will stay with me till then?"

"Of course. Do I not always?"

"I am so glad! Shall we have lunch?" she went on absentmindedly.

"If you like."

"And then you will be nice to me till the very moment you go?"

"Yes; and I will come back as soon as I can."

"You will come back?" she said, looking at me with haggard eyes.

"Naturally."

"Oh, yes, you will come back tonight. I shall wait for you, as I always do, and you will love me, and we shall be happy, as we have been ever since we have known each other."

All these words were said in such a strained voice, they seemed to hide so persistent and so sorrowful a thought, that I trembled every moment lest Marguerite should become delirious.

"Listen," I said. "You are ill. I can not leave you like this. I will write and tell my father not to expect me."

"No, no," she cried hastily, "don't do that. Your father will accuse me of

过我希望你能再躺会儿，还早呢。"

"你打算什么时候去巴黎？"

"4 点。"

"那么快就走？那你会一直陪我到 4 点吗？"

"那是当然，我不是一直都这样吗？"

"太好了！咱们一起吃午餐吧？"她有些茫然地说。

"听你的。"

"那么，你可以不停地抱着我，直到走为止吗？"

"没问题，并且，我一定会尽快赶来。"

"你会回来？"她一边说，一边用哀伤憔悴的眸子盯着我看。

"那是自然的。"

"哎，没错，今晚你会回来，我也会同往常一般盼着你。你依然会深爱着我，我们也会像刚认识时那样无比地开心与快乐的。"

玛格丽特结结巴巴时断时续地说着，就好像在竭力掩盖着什么万分痛苦的事情，这使得我不住地为她担心，以免她会突然精神错乱。

"听着，"我说道，"你一定是病了，我不会就这样把你丢下的，我会给父亲写信，让他先不要等我了。"

"别，别，"她急忙大喊着，"别

hindering you again from going to see him when he wants to see you; no, no, you must go, you must! Besides, I am not ill. I am quite well. I had a bad dream and am not yet fully awake."

From that moment Marguerite tried to seem more cheerful. There were no more tears.

When the hour came for me to go, I embraced her and asked her if she would come with me as far as the train; I hoped that the walk would distract her and that the air would do her good. I wanted especially to be with her as long as possible.

She agreed, put on her cloak and took Nanine with her, so as not to return alone. Twenty times I was on the point of not going. But the hope of a speedy return, and the fear of offending my father still more, sustained me, and I took my place in the train.

"Till this evening!" I said to Marguerite, as I left her.

She did not reply.

Once already she had not replied to the same words, and the Comte de G., you will remember, had spent the night with her; but that time was so far away that it seemed to have been effaced from my memory, and if I had any fear, it was certainly not of

那样，你父亲想要见你，我却阻碍你们相见，你父亲一定会怪罪我的。不！不！你必须走，一定要走！况且，我也没生病，我可健康着呢，只不过昨晚做了个噩梦，直到现在我都没完全缓过神呢！"

此后，她便开始强忍泪水，对我强颜欢笑。

到了分别的时候，我紧搂着玛格丽特，问她是否乐意送我到车站，希望能够通过散步使她稍微快慰一些，同时外面的新鲜空气也能让她尽量好受一点儿。我是多么希望能够让她多陪我一会儿啊！

她答应了，顺便裹了一件外套，同时，为了防止回家时孤单一人，就让纳尼娜陪她一同出去。有数次我都准备下决心不回去了，可是，由于担心会因此而冒犯父亲，同时，我也希望能够早去早回，我还是踏上了离别的火车。

"今晚我就回来！"离别前我这样对她说。

可玛格丽特却并没有吱声。

曾经有一次，她也对我的离别之前的话毫不吱声。你应该还记得，那天，她家中还有G伯爵陪她过夜，不过，那件事太早了，我都快要想不起来了。就算我现在有所担心，也绝不是担心她会失贞于我。一到

Marguerite being unfaithful to me. Reaching Paris, I hastened off to see Prudence, intending to ask her to go and keep Marguerite company, in the hope that her mirth and liveliness would distract her. I entered without being announced, and found Prudence at her toilet.

"Ah!" she said, anxiously; "is Marguerite with you?"

"No."

"How is she?"

"She is not well."

"Is she not coming?"

"Did you expect her?"

Madame Duvernoy reddened, and replied, with a certain constraint:

"I only meant that since you are at Paris, is she not coming to join you?"

"No."

I looked at Prudence; she cast down her eyes, and I read in her face the fear of seeing my visit prolonged.

"I even came to ask you, my dear Prudence, if you have nothing to do this evening, to go and see Marguerite; you will be company for her, and you can stay the night. I never saw her as she was today, and I am afraid she is going to be ill."

"I am dining in town," replied Prudence, "and I can't go and see Marguerite this evening. I will see her tomorrow."

巴黎，我便赶往普鲁登斯家，我想让她去陪陪玛格丽特，希望能够用她的轻松与活泼给玛格丽特解解闷。未经通报，我便进到普鲁登斯家中，而她正在化妆间里梳妆打扮。

"哎呀！"她有些焦躁地说，"玛格丽特没有和你一起过来？"

"没。"

"她最近身体怎样？"

"不大好。"

"也就是说她不会过来了？"

"你希望她过来？"

迪韦尔诺瓦夫人红着脸，矜持了一下，便道：

"我的意思是，你已经到巴黎了，她是不是也快要过来和你约会了？"

"不，她不会来了。"

我一直望着普鲁登斯，她垂着双眼，从她那面部表情足以看出，恐怕她担心我一直赖在她家。

"我亲爱的普鲁登斯，我正是来请你的，倘若今晚你不忙，那就请你去陪陪她吧，你去和她做个伴，也可以陪她睡在那儿。我真担心玛格丽特要生病了，她今天这个样子，我以前从未见过。""可是晚上我还得去城里吃饭，"普鲁登斯回答道，"恐怕今天我去不了了，明天我一

I took leave of Mme. Duvernoy, who seemed almost as preoccupied as Marguerite, and went on to my father's; his first glance seemed to study me attentively. He held out his hand.

"Your two visits have given me pleasure, Armand," he said; "they make me hope that you have thought over things on your side as I have on mine."

"May I ask you, father, what was the result of your reflection?"

"The result, my dear boy, is that I have exaggerated the importance of the reports that had been made to me, and that I have made up my mind to be less severe with you."

"What are you saying, father?" I cried joyously.

"I say, my dear child, that every young man must have his mistress, and that, from the fresh information I have had, I would rather see you the lover of Mlle. Gautier than of any one else."

"My dear father, how happy you make me!"

We talked in this manner for some moments, and then sat down to table. My father was charming all dinner time.

I was in a hurry to get back to Bougival to tell Marguerite about this fortunate change, and I looked at the clock every

定去。"

我只好告别了迪韦尔诺瓦夫人，她今天也是忧心忡忡，就像玛格丽特一样。我终于去了父亲那里，父亲一见我，就开始反复地打量着我，之后，才向我伸出双手。

"你这两次前来探望我，让我很开心，阿尔芒，"他接着说，"我能够预见，你已经像我一样，站在我的角度上考虑过这件事情了。"

"那么，爸爸，我能不能冒昧地问一句，你对这件事是如何考虑的？"

"我是这么想的，亲爱的儿子，看来我过分高估了那些流言蜚语的影响的严重程度，因此，我决定不再对你那么苛刻。"

"什么？爸爸！"我欣喜地叫着。

"亲爱的儿子，我说，年轻人个个都有情妇，同时，就我所了解的一些最新的消息而言，我更希望戈蒂埃小姐，而不是其他人，作为你的情妇。"

"亲爱的父亲！你让我欣喜万分！"

就这样，我们又聊了一会儿，然后，我和父亲一块儿吃了晚饭，整段时间父亲一直那么和蔼可亲。

由于急着想把这个令人惊喜的变故告知玛格丽特，我不时地留意

moment.

"You are watching the time," said my father, "and you are impatient to leave me. O young people, how you always sacrifice sincere to doubtful affections!"

"Do not say that, father; Marguerite loves me, I am sure of it."

My father did not answer; he seemed to say neither yes nor no.

He was very insistent that I should spend the whole evening with him and not go till the morning; but Marguerite had not been well when I left her. I told him of it, and begged his permission to go back to her early, promising to come again on the morrow.

The weather was fine; he walked with me as far as the station. Never had I been so happy. The future appeared as I had long desired to see it. I had never loved my father as I loved him at that moment.

Just as I was leaving him, he once more begged me to stay. I refused.

"You are really very much in love with her?" he asked.

"Madly."

"Go, then," and he passed his hand across his forehead as if to chase a thought, then opened his mouth as if to say something; but he only pressed my hand, and left me hurriedly, saying:

着钟表的指针。

"你一直在看表,"父亲说,"你急着要走。哎,孩子!你总是为了那些结果难料的爱情,而忽视了真挚的亲情!"

"话不能这么说,爸爸!我对玛格丽特的忠贞毫不怀疑。"

父亲默不做声,似乎对此既有赞同,又有怀疑。

父亲坚持让我留下来陪他,直到次日早上再走。可我告诉父亲,我离开时,玛格丽特正有病在身,我恳请他答应让我早点回去,同时,我允诺,明天一大早就回来。

今天天气真好。他一直把我送到了站台。我有生以来头一次这么开心,我所梦寐以求的生活总算要到来了。我自始至终都没有像现在一样深爱着我的父亲。

就在我即将离开时,他再次地想要挽留我,可我还是没有答应。

"你真的这么爱她?"他问道。

"若癫若狂!"

"去吧!"他伸手抚了抚额头,貌似是要驱除一些念头,而后,他又张着嘴,好像要说什么,可最终却只是拍了拍我的手,便匆忙离我远去了,同时大声道:

"Till tomorrow, then!"

"那好，我们明天见！"

CHAPTER 22

第二十二章

It seemed to me as if the train did not move. I reached Bougival at eleven.

Not a window in the house was lighted up, and when I rang no one answered the bell. It was the first time that such a thing had occurred to me. At last the gardener came. I entered. Nanine met me with a light. I went to Marguerite's room.

"Where is madame?"

"Gone to Paris," replied Nanine.

"To Paris!"

"Yes, sir."

"When?"

"An hour after you."

"She left no word for me?"

"Nothing."

Nanine left me.

Perhaps she had some suspicion or other, I thought, and went to Paris to make sure that my visit to my father was not an excuse for a day off. Perhaps Prudence wrote to her about something important. I said to myself when I was alone; but I saw Prudence; she said nothing to make me

我感觉火车像是在爬行似的，直到 11 点才抵达布吉瓦尔。

屋子的窗户都黑着灯，我按了按门铃也没有任何回应。这我可从来没遇见过。最后，园丁总算是给我开门了，我进了屋。纳尼娜拎着一盏灯走了出来。我则径直走向玛格丽特的房间。

"夫人不在？"

"夫人去巴黎了。"纳尼娜说。

"巴黎？！"

"没错，先生。"

"何时走的？"

"在你离开一小时后。"

"她没给我留下什么东西？"

"什么都没留下。"

纳尼娜也走开了。

独处时，我喃喃自语道："也许她怀疑着什么，或者，她去巴黎是为了验证我是否为了换得一天的自由而借口去巴黎看望父亲。又或者，普鲁登斯因为一些要事而致信给她。可是，在巴黎时我分明见过普鲁登斯，从她的话里我没有听出任

suppose that she had written to Marguerite.

All at once I remembered Mme. Duvernoy's question, "Isn't she coming today?" when I had said that Marguerite was ill. I remembered at the same time how embarrassed Prudence had appeared when I looked at her after this remark, which seemed to indicate an appointment. I remembered, too, Marguerite's tears all day long, which my father's kind reception had rather put out of my mind. From this moment all the incidents grouped themselves about my first suspicion, and fixed it so firmly in my mind that everything served to confirm it, even my father's kindness.

Marguerite had almost insisted on my going to Paris; she had pretended to be calmer when I had proposed staying with her. Had I fallen into some trap? Was Marguerite deceiving me? Had she counted on being back in time for me not to perceive her absence, and had she been detained by chance? Why had she said nothing to Nanine, or why had she not written? What was the meaning of those tears, this absence, this mystery?

That is what I asked myself in affright, as I stood in the vacant room, gazing at the clock, which pointed to midnight, and seemed to say to me that it was too late to

何给玛格丽特写过信的征兆。"

就在这时，我忽然想到，在我提及玛格丽特有些难受时，迪韦尔诺瓦夫人便问我："那今天玛格丽特不来了？"当她问完这句话之后，我仔细端详着她的脸色，我记得那时她的表情显得很窘迫，这似乎说明，她们之间有约会。我还记得，那一整天，玛格丽特的眼里都注满了泪水，可因为此后父亲热情地款待让我淡忘了这件事。此时，我觉得这所有的事情都在绕着之前的第一个疑虑团团打转，甚至包括父亲对我的热心款待，都让我越来越怀疑。

玛格丽特几乎是硬把我逼到巴黎的，我是不是中了她的计：我一说要陪着她，她就开始故作沉静。难道她要蒙骗我？难道她准备按时回来，以至于我没能察觉她曾外出过，然而因为出了什么意外导致她被迫耽搁了？可她为什么不告诉纳尼娜，也不给我留下任何书信？她的眼泪，她的不辞而别，她的这一系列诡秘的事情到底意味着什么？

我独自待在这个空无一人的屋子里，诚惶诚恐地思忖着上述问题，双眼紧盯着挂钟的指针：午夜了，已经太晚了，想要见到我归来的情

hope for my mistress's return. Yet, after all the arrangements we had just made, after the sacrifices that had been offered and accepted, was it likely that she was deceiving me? No. Itried to get rid of my first supposition.

Probably she had found a purchaser for her furniture, and she had gone to Paris to conclude the bargain. She did not wish to tell me beforehand, for she knew that, though I had consented to it, the sale, so necessary to our future happiness, was painful to me, and she feared to wound my self-respect in speaking to me about it. She would rather not see me till the whole thing was done, and that was evidently why Prudence was expecting her when she let out the secret. Marguerite could not finish the whole business today, and was staying the night with Prudence, or perhaps she would come even now, for she must know bow anxious I should be, and would not wish to leave me in that condition. But, if so, why those tears? No doubt, despite her love for me, the poor girl could not make up her mind to give up all the luxury in which she had lived until now, and for which she had been so envied, without crying over it. I was quite ready to forgive her for such regrets. I waited for her impatiently, that I might say to her, as I

妇好像不大可能了。就在前不久，我们刚刚才对今后的日子作了打算，为此她已经作出了牺牲，而我也接受了这些。可是，难道她所做的这些都是为了蒙骗我吗？不，不是的。我想要尽全力抛开之前的那种种猜忌。

也可能玛格丽特已经给她的那些家当觅得了买主，她奔往巴黎谈价钱去了。之所以不希望我提前知晓，因为她很明白，即便出售那些家当对我俩日后美满的生活来说是非常必要的，同时，我也认可了，可为了生计出售家当这种事情还是会令我相当尴尬的。她担心把这件事告诉我会诋毁我的尊严。因此，她宁可等把这些事情都解决了再见我。很显然，被我识破的普鲁登斯想要和她约会的事情也是为了这件事。今天，玛格丽特可能还无法谈成这笔买卖，也许她此时正睡在普鲁登斯家，也说不定她没过多久就过来了，因为她一定知道我正在为她担心，她决不愿意让我这样待在这儿的。可果真如此，她的那些眼泪又是怎么一回事？毫无疑问，无论她有多么爱我，想让这个可怜的女孩彻底抛弃这些已经习惯了的奢华的东西以及令人羡慕的生活还是很不情愿的。对于她的这种不舍之情我完全能够体谅。我急切地盼着

covered her with kisses, that I had guessed the reason of her mysterious absence.

Nevertheless, the night went on, and Marguerite did not return.

My anxiety tightened its circle little by little, and began to oppress my head and heart. Perhaps something had happened to her. Perhaps she was injured, ill, dead. Perhaps a messenger would arrive with the news of some dreadful accident. Perhaps the daylight would find me with the same uncertainty and with the same fears.

The idea that Marguerite was perhaps unfaithful to me at the very moment when I waited for her in terror at her absence did not return to my mind. There must be some cause, independent of her will, to keep her away from me, and the more I thought, the more convinced I was that this cause could only be some mishap or other. O vanity of man, coming back to us in every form!

One o'clock struck. I said to myself that I would wait another hour, but that at two o'clock, if Marguerite had not returned, I would set out for Paris. Meanwhile I looked about for a book, for I dared not think. Manon Lescaut was open on the table. It seemed to me that here and there the pages were wet as if with tears. I turned the leaves over and then closed the book, for the letters seemed to me void of

她的归来，我想一边狂吻她，一边对她说：她的这次不辞而别的原因我已经知晓了。

可是，夜已经很深了，而我的玛格丽特还是不见踪影。

我越发觉得焦躁了，满脑子里都是急切和压抑的想法。难道是她发生了什么意外？难道是她受伤了？生病了？抑或是死了？可能不久之后就会有一个信使前来告诉我一个噩耗，也可能直到第二天清晨，我还沉浸在这满腹的困惑与愁苦之中。

在她不辞而别的这段时间里，我一直是战战兢兢地等候着，可是，关于玛格丽特是否会背叛我这件事我却再也没有想过。肯定是发生了什么她无法应对的事情，导致她无法赶回这里。我越乱想，越觉得那件事一定是什么事故或者灾祸——哎，人自负的情结啊！你总是以各种不同的形式表现出来。

凌晨一点的钟声敲响了，我自喃着：如果再等一小时玛格丽特还没有回来，我就亲自赶往巴黎。在这期间，因为不敢多想，我找来一本书。《曼侬·莱斯科》正摊开放在桌上，似乎有许多书页都被泪水给浸湿了。由于此时我忧心忡忡，满腹疑虑，书中的文字对我来说几乎毫无意义，于是，我只是翻看了几

meaning through the veil of my doubts.

Time went slowly. The sky was covered with clouds. An autumn rain lashed the windows. The empty bed seemed at moments to assume the aspect of a tomb. I was afraid.

I opened the door. I listened, and heard nothing but the voice of the wind in the trees. Not a vehicle was to be seen on the road. The half hour sounded sadly from the church tower.

I began to fear lest some one should enter. It seemed to me that only a disaster could come at that hour and under that sombre sky.

Two o'clock struck. I still waited a little. Only the sound of the bell troubled the silence with its monotonous and rhythmical stroke.

At last I left the room, where every object had assumed that melancholy aspect which the restless solitude of the heart gives to all its surroundings.

In the next room I found Nanine sleeping over her work. At the sound of the door, she awoke and asked if her mistress had come in.

"No; but if she comes in, tell her that I was so anxious that I had to go to Paris."

"At this hour?"

"Yes.

下，就又把它给合上了。

时间缓缓流逝，满天乌云密布，一阵秋雨骤至，四处鞭笞着窗户，空空的床貌似一尊坟墓，使我不禁胆寒起来。

我推开门，竖起耳朵，可周围一片寂静，除了那瑟瑟的风扫过树枝的声音。路上丝毫看不见一辆马车，而教堂半点的钟声却凄凉地回响着。

此刻，我反倒担心会有什么人过来了，我想，大概只能是因为发生了什么糟糕的事，才会有人在这光景黯淡，一片灰沉的时候来找我。

两点的钟声响了，我又等了片刻。只有那不断的乏味的滴答声时不时地划破这四周的沉寂。

最终我还是从屋里走了出来，在我看来，屋内所有的物件都被我内心的忧愁与沮丧所感染，全被蒙上了一层阴影。

旁边的屋，纳尼娜趴在活计上睡着了。她被这推门声震醒，向我询问女主人是不是已经回来了。

"不，不过倘若她回来了，你告诉她，我太焦急已经赶去巴黎了。"

"现在就走？"

"没错。"

"But how? You won't find a carriage."

"I will walk."

"But it is raining."

"No matter."

"But madame will be coming back, or if she doesn't come it will be time enough in the morning to go and see what has kept her. You will be murdered on the way."

"There is no danger, my dear Nanine; I will see you tomorrow."

The good girl went and got me a cloak, put it over my shoulders, and offered to wake up Mme. Arnould to see if a vehicle could be obtained; but I would hear of nothing, convinced as I was that I should lose, in a perhaps fruitless inquiry, more time than I should take to cover half the road. Besides, I felt the need of air and physical fatigue in order to cool down the over- excitement which possessed me.

I took the key of the flat in the Rue d'Antin, and after saying good-bye to Nanine, who came with me as far as the gate, I set out.

At first I began to run, but the earth was muddy with rain, and I fatigued myself doubly. At the end of half an hour I was obliged to stop, and I was drenched with sweat. I recovered my breath and went on. The night was so dark that at every step I feared to dash myself against one of the

"可你如何去,连车都没有。"

"走去。"

"可是现在正下雨呢!"

"没什么大不了的。"

"夫人迟早会回来,即便她没回来,你明早再去看看究竟是什么事让她无法脱身也不晚啊。你就这样去可能会遭到歹人暗算的。"

"亲爱的纳尼娜,没什么危险的,咱们明天再见。"

这善良而又忠实的姑娘拿了件外套套在了我的肩上,并劝我去把阿尔努太太叫醒,看看是否能叫来一辆马车。可我却不想叫她,因为我深知,与其这样浪费时间,不如用来赶一半的路。况且,我认为我正需要用路上的清新空气和肢体上的劳累来缓解如今躁动不安的心情。

我拿起位于昂坦街上的那间住所的钥匙,向一直把我送到正门处的纳尼娜道了一声再见,便转身走了出去。

开始时我是在跑,可由于道路被雨水淋得泥泞不堪,我感到格外疲劳。跑了有半个小时,全身都已被雨水淋湿了,我只好停下来喘喘气,便又继续向前赶路。午夜的路上一片漆黑,道边的大树突兀无比,像是一个个向我冲来的恶魔,

trees on the roadside, which rose up sharply before me like great phantoms rushing upon me.

I overtook one or two wagons, which I soon left behind. A carriage was going at full gallop toward Bougival. As it passed me the hope came to me that Marguerite was in it. I stopped and cried out, "Marguerite! Marguerite!" But no one answered and the carriage continued its course. I watched it fade away in the distance, and then started on my way again. I took two hours to reach the Barriere de l'Etoile. The sight of Paris restored my strength, and I ran the whole length of the alley I had so often walked.

That night no one was passing; it was like going through the midst of a dead city. The dawn began to break. When I reached the Rue d'Antin the great city stirred a little before quite awakening. Five o'clock struck at the church of Saint Roch at the moment when I entered Marguerite's house. I called out my name to the porter, who had had from me enough twenty-franc pieces to know that I had the right to call on Mlle. Gautier at five in the morning. I passed without difficulty. I might have asked if Marguerite was at home, but he might have said "No," and I preferred to remain in doubt two minutes longer, for, as

每赶一步路，我都十分担心会冲撞上去。

我遇上了一两辆小货车，没过多久，我就被远远甩开了。一架马车朝布吉瓦尔奔驰而去，当它从我身边穿过时，我忽然寄希望于我的玛格丽特就坐在这辆车里。我停住脚步大声喊着："玛格丽特！玛格丽特！"可是，却没有回应，马车仍旧向前飞奔而去，我望着它在眼前逐渐消失，便又继续向前赶路。赶了有两个小时，我到了巴里尔星形广场。巴黎就在眼前，我又重新打起精神，顺着那条数次经过的巷道奔了过去。

整夜，路上都见不到半个行人。我就像是穿行在一座死去的城市中一般。夜色渐渐淡去，当我赶到昂坦大街的时候，巴黎这座大都市才从睡梦中醒来，开始蠢蠢欲动。当我踏入玛格丽特的房门时，塞因特罗奇教堂的大钟刚刚敲过 5 点。我向门卫通报了自己的姓名，我曾多次给他面值 20 法郎的金币，所以在凌晨 5 点我是有权进入戈蒂埃的家中的。我毫不费力地走了进去。原本我应当向他打听一下玛格丽特是否就在家中，可是想到他极有可能回复说："不在。"而我更愿意继续猜测，因为这样的话，我起码还有

long as I doubted, there was still hope.

I listened at the door, trying to discover a sound, a movement. Nothing. The silence of the country seemed to be continued here. I opened the door and entered. All the curtains were hermetically closed. I drew those of the dining-room and went toward the bedroom and pushed open the door. I sprang at the curtain cord and drew it violently. The curtain opened, a faint light made its way in. I rushed to the bed. It was empty.

I opened the doors one after another. I visited every room. No one. It was enough to drive one mad.

I went into the dressing-room, opened the window, and called Prudence several times. Mme. Duvernoy's window remained closed.

I went downstairs to the porter and asked him if Mlle. Gautier had come home during the day.

"Yes," answered the man; "with Mme. Duvernoy."

"She left no word for me?"

"No."

"Do you know what they did afterward?"

"They went away in a carriage."

"What sort of a carriage?"

"A private carriage."

一丝希望。

我将双耳紧贴着房门，试图听听房内的一些声响，一些动静。房里静得出奇，就如同在乡下田边一般。我推门进去，房内的一切都被窗帘严严实实地裹着。我掀开了餐厅的窗帘，又推开了卧室的门向里面走了进去。我忙蹿到窗前，猛地拉了一下帘绳。一抹淡淡的日光从拉开的窗子中透了进来。我冲到床边，可是，床上空空如也！

我将一道一道的门纷纷打开，排查了每一间屋子。还是没有一个人！我就要被逼疯了。

我闯进梳妆室，打开窗子朝外不停地喊普鲁登斯。可迪韦尔诺瓦夫人的窗子却一直紧闭着。

我又走到楼下去问门卫这一天戈蒂埃小姐是否曾经回来过。

"是，"门卫回答道，"她和迪韦尔诺瓦夫人一同来的。"

"她没留什么口信给我？"

"没。"

"那你知不知道她们之后又做了些什么？"

"她们又坐马车离开了。"

"那马车是什么样子的？"

"是一辆私家贵族马车。"

What could it all mean?

I rang at the next door.

"Where are you going, sir?" asked the porter, when he had opened to me.

"To Mme. Duvernoy's."

"She has not come back."

"You are sure?"

"Yes, sir; here's a letter even, which was brought for her last night and which I have not yet given her."

And the porter showed me a letter which I glanced at mechanically. I recognised Marguerite's writing. I took the letter. It was addressed, "To Mme. Duvernoy, to forward to M. Duval."

"This letter is for me," I said to the porter, as I showed him the address.

"You are M. Duval?" he replied.

"Yes.

"Ah! I remember. You often came to see Mme. Duvernoy."

When I was in the street I broke the seal of the letter. If a thunder-bolt had fallen at my feet I should have been less startled than I was by what I read.

"By the time you read this letter, Armand, I shall be the mistress of another man. All is over between us.

"Go back to your father, my friend, and to your sister, and there, by the side of a pure

可这究竟是怎么一回事？

我又拉响了邻居家的门铃。

"先生，你有何贵干？"门卫打开门，问道。

"我找迪韦尔诺瓦夫人。"

"她还没回来呢。"

"你确定？"

"是的，先生，我这儿有一封昨晚送来的寄给她的信，可到现在，我还没能递给她呢。"

门卫把那封信递给我看，我只是大概扫一眼，便认出这是玛格丽特的字迹。我接过信，只见信封上写道：劳烦迪韦尔诺瓦太太将这封信交给迪瓦尔先生。

"这封信是留给我的。"我指着信上的字对门卫说。

"你是迪瓦尔先生？"他问道。

"正是。"

"哎呀！我记起来了，你常常来这儿找迪韦尔诺瓦夫人。"

一回到大街，我便拆开这封信。现在，即便是老天在我的立脚之处来个晴天霹雳，恐怕都不如读这封信给我带来的惊恐更加剧烈。

"亲爱的阿尔芒，当你在读这封信时，我已经成为别人的情妇了，我们的一切都结束了。

"我的朋友，回到你父亲的身边去吧，顺便也去关心一下你的妹妹，

young girl, ignorant of all our miseries, you will soon forget what you would have suffered through that lost creature who is called Marguerite Gautier, whom you have loved for an instant, and who owes to you the only happy moments of a life which, she hopes, will not be very long now."

When I had read the last word, I thought I should have gone mad. For a moment I was really afraid of falling in the street. A cloud passed before my eyes and my blood beat in my temples. At last I came to myself a little. I looked about me, and was astonished to see the life of others continue without pausing at my distress.

I was not strong enough to endure the blow alone. Then I remembered that my father was in the same city, that I might be with him in ten minutes, and that, whatever might be the cause of my sorrow, he would share it.

I ran like a madman, like a thief, to the Hotel de Paris; I found the key in the door of my father's room; I entered. He was reading. He showed so little astonishment at seeing me, that it was as if he was expecting me. I flung myself into his arms without saying a word. I gave him Marguerite's letter, and, falling on my knees beside his bed, I wept hot tears.

她是那么的单纯，根本不明白我们所承受的痛苦。只要你陪着她，没过多久，你便会忘掉那个曾被你深爱过的，被你赋予了一生中仅有的幸福的叫做玛格丽特·戈蒂埃的姑娘，如今，她希望她的生命能够早些结束。"

念到末尾那句时，我感到自己就要精神崩溃了。刹那间我担心会忽然栽倒在大街上。我眼前一片模糊，汩汩热血在太阳穴里疯狂地涌动。最后，我稍微定了定神，向四周张望，惊奇地发现，周围的人居然漠不关心，依旧如往常一样生活着。

我的意志不是那么的坚强，恐怕承受不了这样的刺激。这时我想到了我的父亲，他也在这个城市，只消十分钟，我便能坐在他的身边，不管我是因为什么而痛苦，他都能和我分担。

我就像是疯子、小偷一般一路奔到了巴黎旅馆，我发现父亲的那间房门上插着一把钥匙，我走进屋里。他正在看书。当他看到我时，他似乎一点儿也不奇怪，就好像明知道我要来一样。我什么也没说便栽进了他的怀抱里，我把玛格丽特的那封信给了他，我再也控制不住自己的泪水，跪倒在他的床边大声恸哭起来。

CHAPTER 23
第二十三章

When the current of life had resumed its course, I could not believe that the day which I saw dawning would not be like those which had preceded it. There were moments when I fancied that some circumstance, which I could not recollect, had obliged me to spend the night away from Marguerite, but that, if I returned to Bougival, I should find her again as anxious as I had been, and that she would ask me what had detained me away from her so long.

When one's existence has contracted a habit, such as that of this love, it seems impossible that the habit should be broken without at the same time breaking all the other springs of life. I was forced from time to time to reread Marguerite's letter, in order to convince myself that I had not been dreaming.

My body, succumbing to the moral shock, was incapable of movement. Anxiety, the night walk, and the morning's news had prostrated me. My father profited

生活又如往常一样继续着，可我决不认为即将到来的一天和刚刚过去的那段时光能有什么不同。我有数次都在设想是发生了一些实在无法想起的事，以至于令我不能住在玛格丽特家中，可倘若我又赶回布吉瓦尔，我便会发现，她就如同当时的我一般，万分焦虑地在家中等我，她同样会问，究竟是什么让本应归来的我滞留了那么长的时间。

当诸如爱情此类的事物已经成为了生活习惯的一部分时，倘若要打破这种习惯的同时，又不打破其他生活中的种种联系，几乎是无稽之谈。于是我被迫一遍又一遍地读着玛格丽特留给我的信，以使自己相信，那的确不是一场梦。

我的身体被这来自精神层面的巨大震撼刺激得几乎不能动弹了。焦虑，夜里奔波的疲劳，以及清晨的信件，这种种不幸使我彻底瓦解

by this total prostration of all my faculties to demand of me a formal promise to accompany him. I promised all that he asked, for I was incapable of sustaining a discussion, and I needed some affection to help me to live, after what had happened. I was too thankful that my father was willing to console me under such a calamity.

All that I remember is that on that day, about five o'clock, he took me with him in a post-chaise. Without a word to me, he had had my luggage packed and put up behind the chaise with his own, and so he carried me off. I did not realize what I was doing until the town had disappeared and the solitude of the road recalled to me the emptiness of my heart. Then my tears again began to flow.

My father had realized that words, even from him, would do nothing to console me, and he let me weep without saying a word, only sometimes pressing my hand, as if to remind me that I had a friend at my side.

At night I slept a little. I dreamed of Marguerite.

I woke with a start, not recalling why I was in the carriage. Then the truth came back upon me, and I let my head sink on my breast. I dared not say anything to my father. I was afraid he would say, "You see I was right when I declared that this

了。趁我身心俱疲，接近崩溃之际，父亲要我明确答应和他一同离开巴黎。我完全答应了，因为在经历了这样的事情之后，我再也没有精力和他辩驳，同时，我也需要用一种真挚的情感来维系我的生活。在我受到如此不幸的创伤时，父亲前来安慰我，这使我感到万分欣慰。

我唯一还能记起的是：大约凌晨5点，他把我带上了一辆邮车。他让人帮我包裹好行李，并同他的行李一起堆在车后，什么也没有对我说，便将我从这里带走了。直到城市的影子在我的眼前渐渐消失，而旅途的孤寂与落寞又撩起了掩在胸中的无尽的空虚时，我才茫然地意识到，我要告别这里了。想到这儿，我又禁不住抽泣起来。

父亲明白，无论说什么都无法安慰我心中的凄苦，于是，他什么也不说，任凭我在那里抽泣。只是偶尔按住我的手，好像是想让我知道，有一个朋友永远陪在我身旁。

一夜里我只小睡了片刻，而在睡梦中我又见到了玛格丽特。

忽然，我惊醒过来，我完全不明白为什么会坐上这辆车子。可我很快就回想起了现实的情形，便把脑袋垂在了胸前。我之所以不敢同父亲说这件事，是因为担心他回答说："你看，我就知道那个女的对你

woman did not love you." But he did not use his advantage, and we reached C. without his having said anything to me except to speak of matters quite apart from the event which had occasioned my leaving Paris.

When I embraced my sister, I remembered what Marguerite had said about her in her letter, and I saw at once how little my sister, good as she was, would be able to make me forget my mistress.

Shooting had begun, and my father thought that it would be a distraction for me. He got up shooting parties with friends and neighbours. I went without either reluctance or enthusiasm, with that sort of apathy into which I had sunk since my departure.

We were beating about for game and I was given my post. I put down my unloaded gun at my side, and meditated. I watched the clouds pass. I let my thought wander over the solitary plains, and from time to time I heard some one call to me and point to a hare not ten paces off. None of these details escaped my father, and he was not deceived by my exterior calm. He was well aware that, broken as I now was, I should some day experience a terrible reaction, which might be dangerous, and,

不是真心吧。"可他却并没有揪着这点不放，直到 C 城，他都没有对我说过半句关于为什么要离开巴黎的话，反倒是扯了许多和此事毫无瓜葛的事情。

当我抱起我那妹妹的时候，我想到玛格丽特在那封离别信里的关于我的小妹妹的话。这时，望着我的如此清纯的小妹妹，我立即明白了，这仍难使我忘掉曾经的情妇。

狩猎的季节到了，父亲觉得这是天赐良机，正好可以让我分心不去想那些痛苦的事情。于是他召集了许多邻里故交一起参加了几次狩猎聚会。我没有反对，可也毫无热情，自打离开巴黎之后，我对所有聚会都是漠不关心、无精打采。

我们开始围猎，我待在安排好的位置上，我把猎枪的子弹全部卸掉放在一边，就又陷入了沉思之中。眼见朵朵白云飘过，任凭思维在孤寂茫然的旷野中驰骋。时不时地听见其他猎人喊着，有一只野兔正在我身旁不到 10 步远处蹲着。这种种细节都被父亲看在眼里，他绝对不会被我冷静的外表所蒙蔽。他非常明白，无论现在我遭受了什么沉重的打击，将来一定会孕育出一种可怕至极，抑或是危险至极的副作用。

without seeming to make any effort to
console me, he did his utmost to distract
my thoughts.

My sister, naturally, knew nothing of
what had happened, and she could not
understand how it was that I, who had
formerly been so lighthearted, had
suddenly become so sad and dreamy.

Sometimes, surprising in the midst of
my sadness my father's anxious scrutiny, I
pressed his hand as if to ask him tacitly to
forgive me for the pain which, in spite of
myself, I was giving him.

Thus a month passed, but at the end of
that time I could endure it no longer. The
memory of Marguerite pursued me
unceasingly. I had loved, I still loved this
woman so much that I could not suddenly
become indifferent to her. I had to love or
to hate her. Above all, whatever I felt for
her, I had to see her again, and at once.
This desire possessed my mind, and with
all the violence of a will which had begun
to reassert itself in a body so long inert.

It was not enough for me to see
Marguerite in a month, a week. I had to see
her the very next day after the day when
the thought had occurred to me; and I went
to my father and told him that I had been
called to Paris on business, but that I
should return promptly. No doubt he

一方面，他竭尽全力假装没有在安
慰我，另一方面，他又想尽最大的
努力使我能够缓解心中的忧愁。

自然，我的妹妹全然不知其中
的根由，她也绝对无法参透为什么
我会从原先的无忧无虑忽然变成了
一个整日忧心忡忡，愁苦不堪的人。

有时，在我郁郁寡欢之际，我
会惊奇地发现，父亲也在焦虑无比
地盯着我，我走过去按着他的手，
好像要通过这默然的行为来恳请他
的谅解，希望他能够原谅我因为无
法克制而让他承受的痛苦。

就这样，一个月过去了，可到
了最后，我还是无法继续忍受下去，
玛格丽特的形象持续不断地闪现在
我的眼前，不论是过去还是现在，
我都一直深爱着她。爱她也好，恨
她也罢，可我必须要见到她，而且，
越快越好。这个念头在我心头牢牢
地扎了根，我长久以来未曾出现过
的坚强的意志如今在我的血肉之躯
里又重新萌生了。

自我有了这个念头以来，我就
迫切地希望去见玛格丽特，不是一
个月之后，也不是一星期之后，而
是明天。于是我告诉父亲，在巴黎
有一些事情急需我去处理，不过我
一定会尽快赶回。父亲坚持不让我
去巴黎，毫无疑问他已经猜出了我

guessed the reason of my departure, for he insisted that I should stay, but, seeing that if I did not carry out my intention the consequences, in the state in which I was, might be fatal, he embraced me, and begged me, almost, with tears, to return without delay.

I did not sleep on the way to Paris. Once there, what was I going to do? I did not know; I only knew that it must be something connected with Marguerite. I went to my rooms to change my clothes, and, as the weather was fine and it was still early, I made my way to the Champs-Elysees. At the end of half an hour I saw Marguerite's carriage, at some distance, coming from the Rond-Point to the Place de la Concorde. She had repurchased her horses, for the carriage was just as I was accustomed to see it, but she was not in it. Scarcely had I noticed this fact, when looking around me, I saw Marguerite on foot, accompanied by a woman whom I had never seen.

As she passed me she turned pale, and a nervous smile tightened about her lips. For my part, my heart beat violently in my breast; but I succeeded in giving a cold expression to my face, as I bowed coldly to my former mistress, who just then reached her carriage, into which she got with her

去那里的真正原因。可看到我此时正怒气冲冲，情绪异常激动，倘若无法达成这个目的恐怕会造成巨大的灾祸，他只好泪流满面地抱着我，恳求我能够尽早归来。

在赶到巴黎之前，我一直都没合过眼。到了巴黎，我又该怎么办呢？我不清楚，不过，我只知道我所做的事情应该都是关于玛格丽特的。我到自己家中换了件衣服，外面天朗气清，时间尚早，我便先走向了香榭丽舍大街。半小时后，我从远处便可望见那架玛格丽特的马车从圆形广场向协和广场驶去。她已经赎回了自己的马匹，马车和原来没什么两样，可她却不在车上。一见她不在车上，我便立即环顾四周，却发现她正陪着另一个我完全陌生的女人向这里走来。

从我身边经过时，她的脸色立即变得苍白，紧抽了一下有些痉挛的嘴唇，露出一丝局促的微笑。至于我？我的整颗心都在疯狂地震颤，不断地敲打着我狭小的胸腔，可我还是故作沉静，满面漠然地冲我昔日的情人鞠了个躬，玛格丽特

friend.

I knew Marguerite: this unexpected meeting must certainly have upset her. No doubt she had heard that I had gone away, and had thus been reassured as to the consequences of our rupture; but, seeing me again in Paris, finding herself face to face with me, pale as I was, she must have realized that I had not returned without purpose, and she must have asked herself what that purpose was.

If I had seen Marguerite unhappy, if, in revenging myself upon her, I could have come to her aid, I should perhaps have forgiven her, and certainly I should have never dreamt of doing her an injury. But I found her apparently happy, some one else had restored to her the luxury which I could not give her; her breaking with me seemed to assume a character of the basest self-interest; I was lowered in my own esteem as well as in my love. I resolved that she should pay for what I had suffered.

I could not be indifferent to what she did, consequently what would hurt her the most would be my indifference; it was, therefore, this sentiment which I must affect, not only in her eyes, but in the eyes of others.

I tried to put on a smiling countenance, and I went to call on Prudence. The maid

则急忙走向了马车，同自己的朋友一道坐了进去。

我知晓玛格丽特的性格，这次与她碰面定然会让她局促不安。毫无疑问她知道我早已离开了巴黎，所以对我们感情决裂后的一切后果她都比较放心。可是，当她发现我又赶回巴黎，尤其是在街上和我面对面地相遇，看到了我的那张如此苍白的脸，她一定明白，我不会无故而返，现在，她一定是在设想这件事之后究竟还会发生什么。

倘若发现玛格丽特的生活并不怎么阔绰，我会去帮助她，从而报复她，同时，我也可能会因此原谅她，绝不想再让她遭受半点痛苦。可如今我发现，她看起来似乎很幸福，某个人已经重新为她提供了那种铺张浮华的生活。我俩感情的决裂全是因为她内心的卑劣与自私，我感到自己的尊严和爱情都遭到了极大侮辱，为此，她一定要付出惨痛的代价。

对于她的所作所为，我绝对无法漠然视之，同时，也许我对她的一切行为都不闻不问，才能给她带来最大的痛苦。因此，无论是在她面前，还是在别人面前，我都要假装置若罔闻。

我尽量佯装笑脸，奔向了普鲁登斯家中。女仆让我在客厅内稍候

announced me, and I had to wait a few minutes in the drawing-room. At last Mme. Duvernoy appeared and asked me into her boudoir; as I seated myself I heard the drawing-room door open, a light footstep made the floor creak and the front door was closed violently.

"I am disturbing you," I said to Prudence.

"Not in the least. Marguerite was there. When she heard you announced, she made her escape; it was she who has just gone out."

"Is she afraid of me now?"

"No. but she is afraid that you would not wish to see her."

"But why?" I said, drawing my breath with difficulty, for I was choked with emotion. "The poor girl left me for her carriage, her furniture, and her diamonds; she did quite right, and I don't bear her any grudge. I met her today," I continued carelessly.

"Where?" asked Prudence, looking at me and seeming to ask herself if this was the same man whom she had known so madly in love.

"In the Champs-Elysees. She was with another woman, very pretty. Who is she?"

"What was she like?"

"Blonde, slender, with side curls; blue

片刻，便跑去向普鲁登斯通报了。最终，迪韦尔诺瓦夫人出现了，并让我随她一起到她的卧室来。就在我就座之时，客厅里传来了一阵推门的声音，紧接着，听到一阵阵轻盈的脚步声从地板上响起，最后，便是一记重重的关门声。

"我是不是给你带来什么不便了？"我问普鲁登斯。

"怎么会。刚才那个是玛格丽特，一听通报说是你来了，她便立即跑了。"

"那么，她现在很怕我？"

"她也不是怕你，是担心让你见了之后你会讨厌她。"

"为什么？"我紧张得快要窒息了，猛吸了口气，呼吸畅通了一些，又漠然地说道，"为了她豪华的马车，奢侈的家具，名贵的钻石，这个如此可怜的姑娘抛弃了我，这样做没错，我没理由怪罪于她。今天，我和她已经见过面了。"

"在哪儿见的？"普鲁登斯一边问，一边仔细地打量着我，好像在思忖着如今的这个我是否就是昔日的那个痴情公子。

"在香榭丽舍大街，在她身旁还有一个十分动人的女人。她是谁？"

"她长什么样？"

eyes; very elegant."

"Ah! It was Olympe; she is really very pretty."

"Whom does she live with?"

"With nobody; with anybody."

"Where does she live?"

"Rue Troncliet, No. – . Do you want to make love to her?"

"One never knows."

"And Marguerite?"

"I should hardly tell you the truth if I said I think no more about her; but I am one of those with whom everything depends on the way in which one breaks with them. Now Marguerite ended with me so lightly that I realize I was a great fool to have been as much in love with her as I was, for I was really very much in love with that girl."

You can imagine the way in which I said that; the sweat broke out on my forehead.

"She was very fond of you, you know, and she still is; the proof is, that after meeting you today, she came straight to tell me about it. When she got here she was all of a tremble; I thought she was going to faint."

"Well, what did she say?"

"She said, 'He is sure to come here,' and she begged me to ask you to forgive her."

"I have forgiven her, you may tell her.

"她身材高挑，金发鬈曲，碧眼欲穿，漂亮至极。"

"噢，那是奥利姆，没错，她确实十分的漂亮。"

"有人包养她了？"

"还不确定。"

"她家住哪儿？"

"鲁—特隆克利街……号，哦，难道你是想追求她？"

"这事可不好说。"

"那你就不管玛格丽特了？"

"如果说我丝毫没有挂念玛格丽特，那绝对是骗你的。可我对于如何分手这种事情又非常的在意，而她居然那么随意地就把我给甩了，以至于让我觉得在她面前，我就是个傻瓜，之前我对她的感情实在是太投入了，因为我实在是太爱她了。"

你能想象得到我是用什么口气来说出以上这些话的，当时，我的前额布满了硕大的汗珠。

"你明白，直到现在，她依然是十分爱你。今天在外面碰到你之后，她便立刻前来告诉我，这已足以证明。而她赶来这里时，身体在不停地颤抖，就好像是得了什么重病。"

"她又对你说了些什么？"

"她说'他一定会来找你的'，她恳请我告诉你，请你原谅她。"

She was a good girl; but, after all, like the others, and I ought to have expected what happened. I am even grateful to her, for I see now what would have happened if I had lived with her altogether. It was ridiculous."

"She will be very glad to find that you take it so well. It was quite time she left you, my dear fellow. The rascal of an agent to whom she had offered to sell her furniture went around to her creditors to find out how much she owed; they took fright, and in two days she would have been sold up."

"And now it is all paid?"

"More or less."

"And who has supplied the money?"

"The Comte de N. Ah, my dear friend, there are men made on purpose for such occasions. To cut a long story short he gave her twenty thousand francs, but he has had his way at last. He knows quite well that Marguerite is not in love with him; but he is very nice with her all the same. As you have seen, he has repurchased her horses, he has taken her jewels out of pawn, and he gives her as much money as the duke used to give her; if she likes to live quietly, he will stay with her a long time."

"And what is she doing? Is she living in Paris altogether?"

"请你转告她，我早已原谅她了。她的确善良，不过，无论多善良，也只是个妓女。我本应提前预料到今天的遭遇。我也同样感激她，正是她，让我看到了把自己的情感全部投入一个妓女的怀抱会引发什么样的后果。那实在是荒唐至极。"

"倘若她发现你同她一样，已经意识到非这样做不可时，她定会倍感欣慰。我亲爱的朋友，她离开的时机正好。她曾提到过的那些准备购买她家具的流氓代理人，偷偷去找了她的债主，打听她的欠款金额。一听说她欠下的款项，那些浑蛋代理人就慌了，决定就在两天之内对其进行拍卖。"

"现在那些欠款还清了没？"

"大部分都还完了。"

"谁付的钱？"

"是 N 伯爵。哦，亲爱的朋友！专门有人干这种行当。简言之，N 伯爵给了他们 2 万法郎，当然，他也心满意足了。他十分明白玛格丽特根本不爱他，可尽管这样，他还是给了她很多好处。如你所见，他赎回了玛格丽特的马车，买回了她的珠宝首饰。像公爵一样，他也给了她那么多的钱。倘若如今玛格丽特想要过安稳的生活，这个一直痴心于她的伯爵倒是个不错的选择。"

"那她现在又在忙些什么？她

"She would never go back to Bougival after you went. I had to go myself and see after all her things, and yours, too. I made a package of them and you can send here for them. You will find everything, except a little case with your initials. Marguerite wanted to keep it. If you really want it, I will ask her for it."

"Let her keep it," I stammered, for I felt the tears rise from my heart to my eyes at the recollection of the village where I had been so happy, and at the thought that Marguerite cared to keep something which had belonged to me and would recall me to her. If she had entered at that moment my thoughts of vengeance would have disappeared, and I should have fallen at her feet.

"For the rest," continued Prudence, "I never saw her as she is now; she hardly takes any sleep, she goes to all the balls, she goes to suppers, she even drinks. The other day, after a supper, she had to stay in bed for a week; and when the doctor let her get up, she began again at the risk of her life. Shall you go and see her?"

"What is the good? I came to see you, because you have always been charming to me, and I knew you before I ever knew Marguerite. I owe it to you that I have been her lover, and also, don't I, that I am her

还住在巴黎？"

"自打你走后，她就再也不想回到布吉瓦尔了。我不得不自己回去收拾所有的东西，包括你的，我把那些东西打包，将来你也能差人到这里取。除了一个印有你姓名的首写字母的小皮包，所有的东西都在，玛格丽特很想留下那个小皮包，便将它带走了。如果你非要的话，我可以给你要过来。"

"让她留着吧。"我有些结巴地道，回想起当年在那个小村留下的幸福美好的记忆，又回想起玛格丽特非要将我的那件皮包留下当做纪念，我顿时泪如泉涌，满腹辛酸。倘若此时，她能够走到我身边，我恐怕会立即跪在她的脚下，顷刻间所有仇恨的情绪定会全部消失殆尽。

"另外，"普鲁登斯接着道，最近她几乎天天熬夜，参加所有舞会，到处吃夜宵，总是喝得昏天黑地，我从来都没见到过她像现在这样。有次，她吃完夜宵，不得不在床上躺了一周。可一旦医生同意她下床，她就又准备继续这种昏天黑地的日子，难道你就不想去探望探望她？"

"有必要吗？我是专程来探望你的，因为一直以来你都对我那么和善，况且，比起玛格丽特，我可是先认识的你。要不是你，我也做

lover no longer?"

"Well, I did all I could to get her away from you, and I believe you will be thankful to me later on."

I owe you a double gratitude," I added, rising, for I was disgusted with the woman, seeing her take every word I said to her as if it were serious.

"You are going?"

"Yes."

I had learned enough.

"When shall I be seeing you?"

"Soon. Good-bye."

"Good-bye."

Prudence saw me to the door, and I went back to my own rooms with tears of rage in my eyes and a desire for vengeance in my heart.

So Marguerite was no different from the others; so the steadfast love that she had had for me could not resist the desire of returning to her former life, and the need of having a carriage and plunging into dissipation. So I said to myself, as I lay awake at night though if I had reflected as calmly as I professed to I should have seen in this new and turbulent life of Marguerite the attempt to silence a constant thought, a ceaseless memory. Unfortunately, evil passion had the upper hand, and I only sought for some means of avenging myself

不了她的情夫，当然，也是因为你，我再也不想做她的情夫了，不是吗？"

"上帝啊！我费尽心机让她从你身边消失，如此一来，我肯定你日后会非常感激我的。"

我站起身接着说道："当然，这样一来，我会加倍感谢你的，因为我早就烦透了那个女人，她总是把我说的每一句话都看得那么重。"

"那你现在要走吗？"

"没错。"

这件事我了解得够清楚了。

"那我们何时能够再见？"

"用不了多久的，再见。"

"拜拜。"

普鲁登斯一直将我送到了大门口，我的眼中充满了憎恨的泪光，胸中满是复仇的欲望，气冲冲地回到了家里。

如此说来，玛格丽特和其他的妓女也没什么两样：如此真切又坚定的爱情看来还是无法使她放弃对先前的奢华生活，对曾经的车马香脂和纵欲狂欢的渴望。整整一夜我都无法入睡，不停地想着这些。不过，倘若我真的可以像伪装的那样，沉下心来想一想，我也许能够看出，玛格丽特是在试图靠这种新的混乱生活来摆脱这种持续不断的痛苦记忆。然而，不幸得很，这股邪恶的

on the poor creature. Oh, how petty and vile is man when he is wounded in one of his narrow passions!

This Olympe whom I had seen was, if not a friend of Marguerite, at all events the woman with whom she was most often seen since her return to Paris. She was going to give a ball, and, as I took it for granted that Marguerite would be there, I tried to get an invitation and succeeded.

When, full of my sorrowful emotions, I arrived at the ball, it was already very animated. They were dancing, shouting even, and in one of the quadrilles I perceived Marguerite dancing with the Comte de N., who seemed proud of showing her off, as if he said to everybody: "This woman is mine."

I leaned against the mantel-piece just opposite Marguerite and watched her dancing. Her face changed the moment she caught sight of me. I saluted her casually with a glance of the eyes and a wave of the hand.

When I reflected that after the ball she would go home, not with me but with that rich fool, when I thought of what would follow their return, the blood rose to my face, and I felt the need of doing something to trouble their relations.

After the contredanse I went up to the

情绪不断萦绕在心中，我挖空心思寻求报复这个可怜女人的办法。哎！当一个男人的欲望与自尊遭到迫害时，他会变得多么的卑微和狭隘啊！

我想，那天在大街上见到的和玛格丽特一起的奥利姆不是她的女伴，至少也是自玛格丽特回巴黎之后最为亲密的人。如今，她正在筹划一场舞会，我敢肯定玛格丽特也会到现场，于是，我便尽力搞到了一封请柬。

在我满怀辛酸，踏进舞场大门之时，里面已是热闹非凡了。人们在肆意跳舞、放纵欢呼。其中有一组四人舞蹈，我亲眼看见玛格丽特和她的 N 伯爵也在里面纵情欢跳。N 伯爵的神情就像是在向所有人炫耀："她是我的！"

我对着玛格丽特，倚在壁炉的靠板前，眼睛眨都不眨地望着她的舞姿。当她瞥见我的那一刹那，脸色变得煞白，我又瞅了她一眼，漫不经心地冲她挥手打了个招呼。

可是，当我联想到：舞会结束，将是那个愚蠢的伯爵，而不是我陪她一起回家；当我又想到等他们回家之后可能发生的事情时，血液顷刻间便把我的脸涨得通红，我开始下定决心破坏他们之间的爱情。

等 4 组舞跳完，我便走到女主人身边，向她致意。女主人那柔软

mistress of the house, who displayed for the benefit of her guests a dazzling bosom and magnificent shoulders. She was beautiful, and, from the point of view of figure, more beautiful than Marguerite. I realized this fact still more clearly from certain glances which Marguerite bestowed upon her while I was talking with her. The man who was the lover of such a woman might well be as proud as M. de N., and she was beautiful enough to inspire a passion not less great than that which Marguerite had inspired in me. At that moment she had no lover. It would not be difficult to become so; it depended only on showing enough money to attract her attention.

I made up my mind. That woman should be my mistress. I began by dancing with her. Half an hour afterward, Marguerite, pale as death, put on her pelisse and left the ball.

而圆硕的臂膀和她那半露着的丰满酥胸完全展露在全场嘉宾眼前，无人不为之折服。她的确很美，甚至，单说身材，她比玛格丽特还漂亮。我很清楚地意识到：当一个男人能够成为这样的女人的情人时，他所得到的自豪与满足绝对不亚于刚才那位炫耀的N伯爵，同时，这个女人的美貌也足够令我升起从玛格丽特身体上重获的情欲。如今，在我同这位奥利姆小姐讲话时，从玛格丽特间或投来的目光中足以证明以上我的这些想法。在这一刻奥利姆没有情夫。不过，想要做她的情夫并不难，只要你有足够的钱去装阔，能够引起她的注意即可。

我决定，让她做我的情人。于是，我借跳舞开始追求她。过了半个小时，玛格丽特便已满面铁青，毫无血色，如同死人一般，匆忙披上皮大衣，从舞会中离开了。

CHAPTER 24

第二十四章

It was something already, but it was not enough. I saw the hold which I had upon this woman, and I took a cowardly advantage of it.

When I think that she is dead now, I ask myself if God will ever forgive me for the wrong I did her.

After the supper, which was noisy as could be, there was gambling. I sat by the side of Olympe and put down my money so recklessly that she could not but notice me. In an instant I had gained one hundred and fifty or two hundred louis, which I spread out before me on the table, and on which she fastened her eyes greedily.

I was the only one not completely absorbed by the game, and able to pay her some attention. All the rest of the night I gained, and it was I who gave her money to play, for she had lost all she had before her and probably all she had in the house.

At five in the morning, the guests departed. I had gained three hundred louis.

All the players were already on their

本来这已经足够折磨她了，可我觉得还没有完。我明白，自己能够支配玛格丽特，于是，我便更加卑劣地利用了这种手段。

现在，我觉得她已经心如死灰了，我扪心自问：上帝能够饶恕我给她带来的痛苦吗？

夜宵之后，四处一片喧闹，大家纷纷开始赌钱。我不断地大把大把地下注，自然而然地引起了坐在一旁的奥利姆的注意。没过多久，我便赢下了一二百个路易，我将这些钱摊开放在了桌前，而她则是一眼不眨地盯着那些钞票，两眼迸射出贪婪的目光。

全场唯有我一人不是在全神贯注地赌钱，而是在不断地注意着她。一晚上我都在不停地赢钱。而奥利姆早把手中的钱全输光了，甚至可能已经把她的所有家当都输完了，于是，我便拿出一部分钱来让她赌。

到了凌晨 5 点，宾客们便已纷纷告辞。而我一共赢下了 300 路易。

赌客们都已走下了楼，可是，

way downstairs; I was the only one who had remained behind, and as I did not know any of them, no one noticed it. Olympe herself was lighting the way, and I was going to follow the others, when, turning back, I said to her:

"I must speak to you."

"Tomorrow," she said.

"No, now."

"What have you to say?"

"You will see."

And I went back into the room.

"You have lost," I said.

"Yes.

"All that you had in the house?"

She hesitated.

"Be frank."

"Well, it is true."

"I have won three hundred louis. Here they are, if you will let me stay here tonight."

And I threw the gold on the table.

"And why this proposition?"

"Because I am in love with you, of course."

"No, but because you love Marguerite, and you want to have your revenge upon her by becoming my lover. You don't deceive a woman like me, my dear friend; unluckily, I am still too young and too good-looking to accept the part that you

由于这里没有一个人认识我，因此，当我一个人留在上面时，没有任何人留意到。奥利姆提着灯在楼梯上给大家引路，就在我准备同宾客们一起下楼时，我突然转过身来对她说道：

"我觉得有必要和你聊聊。"

"明天再聊吧。"她回答道。

"不行，就这会儿。"

"那你想和我聊什么呢？"

"聊了就知道了。"

于是，我又折回到那个房间里。

"今晚你赌输了。"我说道。

"没错。"

"你输光了所有的家底吧。"

她支支吾吾，没有作答。

"你就实话实说吧。"

"是，确实输光了。"

"今晚我赢了 300，如果你同意让我留在这儿的话，这些就都是你的了。"

说着我把钱币丢在了桌上。

"你干嘛要这样？"

"毫无疑问，那是因为我爱上你了。"

"不对，你并不爱我，你依然深爱着玛格丽特，之所以选择做我的情夫，是为了借此向她报复。很不幸，我亲爱的朋友，你这样是骗不到像我这样的女人的，我还年轻得很，而且那么漂亮，我是不会接

offer me."

"So you refuse?"

"Yes.

"Would you rather take me for nothing? It is I who wouldn't accept then. Think it over, my dear Olympe; if I had sent some one to offer you these three hundred louis on my behalf, on the conditions I attach to them, you would have accepted. I preferred to speak to you myself. Accept without inquiring into my reasons; say to yourself that you are beautiful, and that there is nothing surprising in my being in love with you."

Marguerite was a woman in the same position as Olympe, and yet I should never have dared say to her the first time I met her what I had said to the other woman. I loved Marguerite. I saw in her instincts which were lacking in the other, and at the very moment in which I made my bargain, I felt a disgust toward the woman with whom I was making it.

She accepted, of course, in the end, and at midday I left her house as her lover; but I quitted her without a recollection of the caresses and of the words of love which she had felt bound to shower upon me in return for the six thousand francs which I left with her. And yet there were men who had ruined themselves for that woman.

受你这样的要求的。"

"你不同意我的请求？"

"没错，我不同意。"

"你愿意就这样不把我当回事？我可不同意。试想一下，我亲爱的奥利姆：倘若我让人送上这300路易，再附上我的那些条件，恐怕你会同意吧。但我更愿意像这样当面和你谈。不要再对我的什么动机而耿耿于怀，答应我吧。再说了，既然你自己都说你生来如此美丽动人，那么如今我爱上你这么个美人又有什么好奇怪的呢。"

尽管和奥利姆一样，玛格丽特也是一个妓女，但是当我第一次遇见她时，我是绝对不敢把刚才对奥利姆的那番话说给玛格丽特的。这就充分说明了我依然爱着玛格丽特，从她身上我发现一种其他妓女所不具备的气质。因此，即便在我和这位千娇百媚的奥利姆小姐谈生意时，我仍旧十分讨厌和憎恶她。

当然，最后她还是同意了。第二天中午从她家离开时，我已经是她的情人了。我又给她留下了6000法郎，作为回报，她同我讲一些情话，并和我亲热了一番。可一旦离开她，我便把那些都忘得一干二净了。然而，依然会有男人愿意为这样一个女人而毁了他们自己。

From that day I inflicted on Marguerite a continual persecution. Olympe and she gave up seeing one another, as you might imagine. I gave my new mistress a carriage and jewels. I gambled, I committed every extravagance which could be expected of a man in love with such a woman as Olympe. The report of my new infatuation was immediately spread abroad.

Prudence herself was taken in, and finally thought that I had completely forgotten Marguerite. Marguerite herself, whether she guessed my motive or was deceived like everybody else, preserved a perfect dignity in response to the insults which I heaped upon her daily. Only, she seemed to suffer, for whenever I met her she was more and more pale, more and more sad. My love for her, carried to the point at which it was transformed into hatred, rejoiced at the sight of her daily sorrow. Often, when my cruelty toward her became infamous, Marguerite lifted upon me such appealing eyes that I blushed for the part I was playing, and was ready to implore her forgiveness.

But my repentance was only of a moment's duration, and Olympe, who had finally put aside all self-respect, and discovered that by annoying Marguerite she could get from me whatever she

这天以后，我便开始时刻不断地蹂躏玛格丽特的神经。你也能够料到，奥利姆再也不和她见面了。我给新结交的情妇买了豪华马车和许多珠宝首饰。正如所有爱上类似奥利姆这样的女人的男人一样，我开始赌钱，不断地挥霍。没过多久，我重结新欢的消息便迅速传开了。

最终，普鲁登斯也被我骗了，她也相信我早已把玛格丽特抛到脑后了。而玛格丽特呢，或者是因为洞悉了我的动机，或者是已经同其他人一样，被我骗了。对于我每日不断地对她精神的蹂躏，她仍怀着极高的尊严予以应对。可看上去她却异常心痛，不管何时何地遇见她，我都会发现，她的神色日渐憔悴，心智也变得日渐惆怅。我对她爱得近乎发狂以至于演变为现在的憎恨，每次见她这般痛苦，我都会感到异样的舒心。有好几次，当我过分下流地残害她的神经时，她便睁着可怜巴巴的眼睛望着我，以哀求我停止对她的折磨。当时，我甚至想恳求她能够饶恕我的所作所为。

可是，我的这种羞愧内疚之情只持续了片刻，而到最后奥利姆则将自己的尊严完全撇开不顾，她只要继续折磨玛格丽特，不论她想要得到什么都能够兑现。她常常挑拨

wanted, constantly stirred up my resentment against her, and insulted her whenever she found an opportunity, with the cowardly persistence of a woman licensed by the authority of a man.

At last Marguerite gave up going to balls or theatres, for fear of meeting Olympe and me. Then direct impertinences gave way to anonymous letters, and there was not a shameful thing which I did not encourage my mistress to relate and which I did not myself relate in reference to Marguerite.

To reach such a point I must have been literally mad. I was like a man drunk upon bad wine, who falls into one of those nervous exaltations in which the hand is capable of committing a crime without the head knowing anything about it. In the midst of it all I endured a martyrdom. The not disdainful calm, the not contemptuous dignity with which Marguerite responded to all my attacks, and which raised her above me in my own eyes, enraged me still more against her.

One evening Olympe had gone somewhere or other, and had met Marguerite, who for once had not spared the foolish creature, so that she had had to retire in confusion. Olympe returned in a fury, and Marguerite fainted and had to be carried out. Olympe related to me what had

离间，一有机会便去侮辱诋毁玛格丽特，使我的愤恨更加强烈，当一个女人有了靠山时，她们耍出的手段真是异常的卑鄙与恶劣。

最终，由于害怕再次遇到我和奥利姆，玛格丽特再也不去任何舞会或是去看戏了。于是，我便不再当面侮辱她，而是换作写一些匿名信来继续践踏她的心灵。无论是让奥利姆，还是由我亲自向外散布，我们都尽力把所有下流可耻的事情全部扯到玛格丽特身上。

恐怕也只有那些神志癫狂的人才会干出上述的行为来，当时我的神经异常兴奋，如同被劣酒大灌特灌的醉汉似的，甚至可能都完全没有意识到自己的双手正在犯下极大的罪行。在这期间，我的内心在不断地承受着巨大的痛苦。对于我的那些侮辱与诋毁，玛格丽特镇定而不蔑视，保持尊严而不表现鄙夷，这就让我感到她比我更加高尚，同时，也让我对她的火气越来越大。

有一天夜里，奥利姆无意间遇到了玛格丽特，这次，玛格丽特并没能放过这个曾经不断诋毁她的傻姑娘，直到奥利姆被迫退让她才肯罢休。奥利姆满脸愤怒地赶回来，而玛格丽特却因气晕被抬回了家。到家之后，奥利姆把刚才的整件事

happened, declared that Marguerite, seeing her alone, had revenged herself upon her because she was my mistress, and that I must write and tell her to respect the woman whom I loved, whether I was present or absent.

I need not tell you that I consented, and that I put into the letter which I sent to her address the same day, everything bitter, shameful, and cruel that I could think of.

This time the blow was more than the unhappy creature could endure without replying. I felt sure that an answer would come, and I resolved not to go out all day. About two there was a ring, and Prudence entered.

I tried to assume an indifferent air as I asked her what had brought her; but that day Mme. Duvernoy was not in a laughing humour, and in a really moved voice she said to me that since my return, that is to say for about three weeks, I had left no occasion untried which could give pain to Marguerite, that she was completely upset by it, and that the scene of last night and my angry letter of the morning had forced her to take to her bed. In short, without making any reproach, Marguerite sent to ask me for a little pity, since she had no longer the moral or physical strength to endure what I was making her suffer.

都告诉了我，并说，由于她做了我的情妇，因此，只要见到她独自一人玛格丽特便想要对她报复。奥利姆让我给玛格丽特致信说：以后，无论我是否在场，玛格丽特都必须对我的情人——奥利姆保持尊敬。

毫无疑问，我答应了，不但如此，我甚至用了几乎所有的肮脏、下流、挖苦、羞辱的词汇，当天，我便将信寄到了她的住所。

这封信对于不幸的玛格丽特的打击实在是太沉重了，以至于她再也无法默言以对了。我想这次她必定会有所回复。于是，我决定一天都待在家里。下午2点时，有人按门铃，我发现是普鲁登斯来了。

我尽量假装什么事情都没有发生，问她因为何事前来找我。可是，今天迪韦尔诺瓦夫人再也不像往常一样满脸笑容，而是一脸严肃，非常激动地冲我喊道：自打我赶回巴黎的将近3个礼拜以来，我就没有放过任何一个能够侮辱、蹂躏、折磨玛格丽特的机会，她已经被气得生病了。而昨晚的奥利姆和她的那场争执再加上今天清晨我寄去的那封诋毁的信终于将她气得卧床不起了。总而言之，玛格丽特仍旧没有怪罪于我，只是托她来向我恳求，能否不要再那样折磨她了，无论是她的心智还是肉体都再也无法承受

"That Mlle. Gautier," I said to Prudence, "should turn me out of her own house is quite reasonable, but that she should insult the woman whom I love, under the pretence that this woman is my mistress, is a thing I will never permit."

"My friend," said Prudence, "you are under the influence of a woman who has neither heart nor sense; you are in love with her, it is true, but that is not a reason for torturing a woman who can not defend herself."

"Let Mlle. Gautier send me her Comte de N. and the sides will be equal."

"You know very well that she will not do that. So, my dear Armand, let her alone. If you saw her you would be ashamed of the way in which you are treating her. She is white, she coughs – she won't last long now."

And Prudence held out her hand to me, adding:

"Come and see her; it will make her very happy."

"I have no desire to meet M. de N."

"M. de N. is never there. She can not endure him."

"If Marguerite wishes to see me, she knows where I live; let her come to see me, but, for my part, I will never put foot in the Rue d'Antin."

我的那些侮辱与诽谤了。

我对普鲁登斯夫人说道："将我赶出房门，那是戈蒂埃小姐的自由，可是，倘若她借口奥利姆是我的情妇，便要侮辱她，这一点我是绝对无法容忍的。"

"我的朋友，"普鲁登斯回答道，"现在你受到了一个没心没肺的女人的驱使；没错，你的确爱她，可是，你也不能因为爱她而去折磨一个根本无法自卫的女人啊。"

"倘若戈蒂埃小姐能够答应我和她的 N 伯爵分手，我便就此罢休。"

"你心里清楚得很，让她那样做是不可能的。所以，我亲爱的阿尔芒，让她静静吧。倘若你见到她，你一定会为之前对她的种种手段而深感羞愧。她满面苍白，她还咳嗽不止，恐怕她已经活不了多久了。"

普鲁登斯一边向我伸出了手，一边补充道：

"去看看她吧，倘若你能去探望她，她一定会十分欣慰的。"

"可我不想看见 N 伯爵。"

"N 伯爵从来没在她家待过，她根本受不了他。"

"如果玛格丽特真希望见到我的话，就让她来找我吧，反正她知道我住哪儿，总之，我是不会再踏

"Will you receive her well?"

"Certainly."

"Well, I am sure that she will come."

"Let her come."

"Shall you be out today?"

"I shall be at home all the evening."

"I will tell her."

And Prudence left me.

I did not even write to tell Olympe not to expect me. I never troubled much about her, scarcely going to see her one night a week. She consoled herself, I believe, with an actor from some theatre or other.

I went out for dinner and came back almost immediately. I had a fire lit in my room and I told Joseph he could go out.

I can give you no idea of the different impressions which agitated me during the hour in which I waited; but when, toward nine o'clock, I heard a ring, they thronged together into one such emotion, that, as I opened the door, I was obliged to lean against the wall to keep myself from falling.

Fortunately the anteroom was in half darkness, and the change in my countenance was less visible.

Marguerite entered.

She was dressed in black and veiled. I could scarcely recognise her face through the veil. She went into the drawing-room

入昂坦大街一步了。"

"你能够好好地招待她吗？"

"我保证。"

"好，我确信她会来找你的。"

"那就让她过来找我吧。"

"你今天有空吗？"

"今天一晚上我都待在家里。"

"我这就去告诉她。"

普鲁登斯告辞了。

我甚至没有写信告诉奥利姆不去她家了。我对她一向漠不关心，每周能去见她一晚就不错了。我十分确信，一定会有不知哪家剧院的某个男演员能够去抚慰她的心灵。

我只是出去吃晚餐，此后，便立即奔了回来。我命令下人把屋内的炉火烧旺，还打发约瑟夫回家了。

现在，我已经无法形容，在那段等待的时光中，我的内心是多么的焦急，多么的烦躁不安。9点整时，当我听到门铃被按响的那一刹那，我几乎手足无措，焦虑无比，以至于当我去开门的时候，为了防止跌倒，我被迫将身体倚靠在墙上。

还好，客厅里一片昏暗，对方很难窥见我如此窘迫的面容。

玛格丽特走了进来。

她一身黑衣，蒙着纱，以至于我几乎无法认出她那遮在布纱下的面目。她进了客厅，掀开了布纱。

and raised her veil. She was pale as marble.

"I am here, Armand," she said; "you wished to see me and I have come."

And letting her head fall on her hands, she burst into tears.

I went up to her.

"What is the matter?" I said to her in a low voice.

She pressed my hand without a word, for tears still veiled her voice. But after a few minutes, recovering herself a little, she said to me:

"You have been very unkind to me, Armand, and I have done nothing to you."

"Nothing?" I answered, with a bitter smile.

"Nothing but what circumstances forced me to do."

I do not know if you have ever in your life experienced, or if you will ever experience, what I felt at the sight of Marguerite.

The last time she had come to see me she had sat in the same place where she was now sitting; only, since then, she had been the mistress of another man, other kisses than mine had touched her lips, toward which, in spite of myself, my own reached out, and yet I felt that I loved this woman as much, more perhaps, than I had ever loved her.

面容如同大理石一般毫无血色。

"阿尔芒，我已经来了，"玛格丽特说道，"如你所愿，我过来了。"

话音未落，她便垂下了脸，双手遮住颜面，失声痛哭起来。

我走到她身边。

"发生什么事情了？"我的声音也有些低沉阴郁。

由于早已泣不成声了，因此，她并没有回答，只是紧紧地握住了我的手。过了片刻，她略微冷静了一些，便说道：

"阿尔芒，你把我折磨得好苦，可我并没有做任何伤害你的事情。"

"难道你真的没有做过丝毫伤害我的事情？"我苦笑着辩解道。

"除了那些现实状况不得已的事情之外，我真的没有做过什么。"

不知道你是否曾经经历过，或者是将来可能会经历如今目睹玛格丽特的窘境之后我内心所产生的这种感受。

如今她所坐的位置正是上次她来到我家里时坐下的地方。不过，自打那次之后，她已变成了他人的情妇。而她的双唇，也不再是被我，而是被另外一个人亲吻着了，可如今我还是情不自禁地将双唇迎了上去。我感觉，如今，我依然像往常一样，深爱着她，甚至，比当时的爱来得更加强烈与迫切。

It was difficult for me to begin the conversation on the subject which brought her. Marguerite no doubt realized it, for she went on:

"I have come to trouble you, Armand, for I have two things to ask: pardon for what I said yesterday to Mlle. Olympe, and pity for what you are perhaps still ready to do to me. Intentionally or not, since your return you have given me so much pain that I should be incapable now of enduring a fourth part of what I have endured till now. You will have pity on me, won't you? And you will understand that a man who is not heartless has other nobler things to do than to take his revenge upon a sick and sad woman like me. See, take my hand. I am in a fever. I left my bed to come to you, and ask, not for your friendship, but for your indifference."

I took Marguerite's hand. It was burning, and the poor woman shivered under her fur cloak.

I rolled the arm-chair in which she was sitting up to the fire.

"Do you think, then, that I did not suffer," said I, "on that night when, after waiting for you in the country, I came to look for you in Paris, and found nothing but the letter which nearly drove me mad? How could you have deceived me,

可是，我还是无法说出找她来到我家的缘由，毫无疑问，玛格丽特也意会到了这一点，于是，她又继续说道：

"阿尔芒，很抱歉打扰你，我这次来是为了两件事情：首先，希望你原谅昨天我对奥利姆小姐所说的那些过分的话。其次，恳请你放过我。不管你是否故意而为，自打你回到巴黎，已经折磨我够久了，即便只是类似今天上午让我承受的痛苦的1/4，我也无法再忍受了！你一定会怜悯我的，对吗？同时，你清楚，像你这样心地善良的绅士，一定有相当多的比报复我这么个可怜又凄楚的女人更崇高的事要做。你摸摸我的手，我还在发高烧，之所以离开卧床前来探望你，不是为了博得你的友情，而是祈求你忘了我，不要再挂念我了。"

我握着玛格丽特的手，的确烫得吓人，即便裹着厚厚的羊毛大衣，这可怜的女人依旧浑身乱颤。

我将玛格丽特所坐的那把扶手椅移到了火炉的旁边。

"难道你觉得我过得快活？"我继续说道，"那个晚上，我先是在乡下的住所等你，然后又亲自跑到巴黎来找你，可是，在巴黎，唯一被我找到的却是一封近乎让我疯狂的信。玛格丽特，我曾经那么疯狂

Marguerite, when I loved you so much?

"Do not speak of that, Armand; I did not come to speak of that. I wanted to see you only not an enemy, and I wanted to take your hand once more. You have a mistress; she is young, pretty, you love her they say. Be happy with her and forget me."

"And you. You are happy, no doubt?"

"Have I the face of a happy woman, Armand? Do not mock my sorrow, you, who know better than any one what its cause and its depth are."

"It only depended on you not to have been unhappy at all, if you are as you say."

"No, my friend; circumstances were stronger than my will. I obeyed, not the instincts of a light woman, as you seem to say, but a serious necessity, and reasons which you will know one day, and which will make you forgive me."

"Why do you not tell me those reasons today?"

"Because they would not bring about an impossible reunion between us, and they would separate you perhaps from those from whom you must not be separated."

"Who do you mean?"

"I can not tell you."

"Then you are lying to me."

Marguerite rose and went toward the door. I could not behold this silent and

地爱着你，你为什么要欺骗我呢！"

"阿尔芒，别说这个了，我来这里不是为了和你谈这个。我仅仅是期望今后见面时别像仇人一样。我想再次握一下你的手。你已经有了位年轻又漂亮的情妇，既然你爱她，那就祝你们幸福，忘了我吧。"

"那你呢，过得很快活吧？"

"阿尔芒，我如今的面孔看起来像个快活的女人？你比任何人都明白我痛苦的缘由和程度。请不要再拿我的痛苦当做嘲笑的资本了。"

"倘若确如你所言，你为何不改变这一切的不快乐的状况？"

"不，朋友，现实远超出了我的意志，好像你觉得我不过是服从了妓女的本性。其实，我是服从了严酷的现实，这一切你终有一天能够明白，到那时，你也一定会为此而原谅我的。"

"那么，今天，你何不把那个原因告诉我呢？"

"因为倘若今天我向你述说了那个原因，我俩说不定能够重新在一起，不过，你也可能会被迫疏远一个你决不应当疏远的人。"

"那个人是谁？"

"我恐怕不能告诉你。"

"那你一定是在欺骗我。"

玛格丽特起身径直向正门走去。我的内心深处将如今面容憔悴、

expressive sorrow without being touched, when I compared in my mind this pale and weeping woman with the madcap who had made fun of me at the Opera Comique.

"You shall not go," I said, putting myself in front of the door.

"Why?"

"Because, in spite of what you have done to me, I love you always, and I want you to stay here."

"To turn me out tomorrow? No; it is impossible. Our destinies are separate; do not try to reunite them. You will despise me perhaps, while now you can only hate me."

"No, Marguerite," I cried, feeling all my love and all my desire reawaken at the contact of this woman. "No, I will forget everything, and we will be happy as we promised one another that we would be."

Marguerite shook her head doubtfully, and said:

"Am I not your slave, your dog? Do with me what you will. Take me; I am yours."

And throwing off her cloak and hat, she flung them on the sofa, and began hurriedly to undo the front of her dress, for, by one of those reactions so frequent in her malady, the blood rushed to her head and stifled her. A hard, dry cough followed.

泣不成声的可怜女人同当初在巴黎歌剧院大声取笑我的美丽姑娘一番对比之后，我再也无法眼睁睁看着她沉郁痛苦的表情而无动于衷了。

"我不能让你走。"我堵在门口对她说。

"为什么不让我走？"

"因为，不论你曾经如何对我，我始终深爱着你，今天我希望你能待在我家。"

"为了明天早上再把我赶走？不，不可能的！我俩缘分已尽，不要再妄想重归旧好了。如果我答应你的话你可能会更加的鄙视我，而如今你却只能憎恨我。"

"不是的，玛格丽特，"我大声喊着，当我再次面对这个女人时，曾经浓烈的爱火又一次燃起，"不，我一定会忘掉这一切的，我们也一定会像曾经许诺过的那样幸福的。"

玛格丽特怀疑地摇摇头，说道：

"这样一来我和你的奴仆、你的狗有什么两样呢？好吧，随你所愿吧，占有我吧，我就是你的。"

她一边说一边脱掉了外套和帽子，将它们抛到了沙发上，她开始迅速松开连衣裙的搭扣，由于顽疾引来了一系列的惯性反应，鲜血涌上面门，闷得她几乎要窒息，紧接着，便是一连串撕心裂肺的干咳。

"Tell my coachman," she said, "to go back with the carriage."

I went down myself and sent him away. When I returned Marguerite was lying in front of the fire, and her teeth chattered with the cold.

I took her in my arms. I undressed her, without her making a movement, and carried her, icy cold, to the bed. Then I sat beside her and tried to warm her with my caresses. She did not speak a word, but smiled at me.

It was a strange night. All Marguerite's life seemed to have passed into the kisses with which she covered me, and I loved her so much that in my transports of feverish love I asked myself whether I should not kill her, so that she might never belong to another.

A month of love like that, and there would have remained only the corpse of heart or body.

The dawn found us both awake. Marguerite was livid white. She did not speak a word. From time to time, big tears rolled from her eyes, and stayed upon her cheeks, shining like diamonds. Her thin arms opened, from time to time, to hold me fast, and fell back helplessly upon the bed.

For a moment it seemed to me as if I could forget all that had passed since I had

"找人打点一下我的车夫，"她又说道，"让他自己把车送回家。"

我亲自动身，走到楼下，让那个车夫自己回去了。可当我赶回房间时，玛格丽特正在壁炉前躺着，浑身冻得瑟瑟发抖。

我将她紧紧搂在怀里，除去她身上的衣物，她只一动不动，我将这个浑身冰冷的女人抱上床。然后，坐在她身旁，试图用我双手的抚摸来给她带来温暖。她微笑着，静静地注视着我的举动。

这个夜晚实在太美妙了，玛格丽特近乎将她生命中的一切完全倾注在她浓烈的双唇中。我太爱她了，以至于当我处在这样一种异常亢奋的爱的欲火之中时，甚至幻想着是否应该让她永远长眠于此，这样，她就再也不会属于其他男人了。

一个人能够如此死心塌地地爱上一个月的话，他也就只剩下一具干枯的皮囊了。

第二天清晨，我俩同时醒来。玛格丽特的脸死灰一般苍白。可她还是只字不提，唯有那一颗颗的晶莹闪亮如钻石般的泪珠不时地滚落出眼眶，滑向她的面颊，她不断地伸出疲软的双臂来搂着我，却又十分无力地垂到了床边。

有那么一段光景，我似乎觉得可以将自离开布吉瓦尔以来的所有

left Bougival, and I said to Marguerite:

"Shall we go away and leave Paris?"

"No, no!" she said, almost with affright; "we should be too unhappy. I can do no more to make you happy, but while there is a breath of life in me, I will be the slave of your fancies. At whatever hour of the day or night you will, come, and I will be yours; but do not link your future any more with mine, you would be too unhappy and you would make me too unhappy. I shall still be pretty for a while; make the most of it, but ask nothing more."

When she had gone, I was frightened at the solitude in which she left me. Two hours afterward I was still sitting on the side of the bed, looking at the pillow which kept the imprint of her form, and asking myself what was to become of me, between my love and my jealousy.

At five o'clock, without knowing what I was going to do, I went to the Rue d'Antin.

Nanine opened to me.

"Madame can not receive you," she said in an embarrassed way.

"Why?"

"Because M. le Comte de N. is there, and he has given orders to let no one in."

"Quite so," I stammered; "I forgot."

I went home like a drunken man, and do you know what I did during the moment of

不幸一笔勾销，我对玛格丽特说道：

"我们一起离开巴黎吧？"

"不，绝不，"她近乎恐惧地回答道，"我们不会幸福的。只要还有一口气，我就能够任你摆布，我能随你支配。不论白天还是晚上，只要你愿意，你都可以过来，那时，我是你的。不过，请别再把你的前途同我的联系到一起，那样的话，你会十分苦恼，也会让我苦恼的。眼下我依然美貌，那就尽情享用吧，可是，千万别再提其他的要求了。"

她走之后，我孤寂难耐，异常凄楚。直到她走后整整两个小时，我依然原封不动地坐着，双眼紧盯着刚才她躺过的枕头，以及枕头上她的印迹，不断思忖着，在经受如此的爱与嫉妒之下的我，究竟将会变成什么样子。

5 点，虽然说不清目的，但我又奔向了昂坦大街。

纳尼娜为我打开了房门。

"恐怕现在玛格丽特夫人无法见你。"她局促不安地说道。

"为什么？"

"因为 N 伯爵在里面，他之前已经吩咐过，任何人都不许进入。"

"哦，"我支吾道，"我忘记了。"

我像个醉汉一般回到家中。你可曾预料到，在被嫉妒逼得亢奋到

jealous delirium which was long enough for the shameful thing I was going to do? I said to myself that the woman was laughing at me; I saw her alone with the count, saying over to him the same words that she had said to me in the night, and taking a five-hundred-franc note I sent it to her with these words:

"You went away so suddenly that I forgot to pay you. Here is the price of your night."

Then when the letter was sent I went out as if to free myself from the instantaneous remorse of this infamous action.

I went to see Olympe, whom I found trying on dresses, and when we were alone she sang obscene songs to amuse me. She was the very type of the shameless, heartless, senseless courtesan, for me at least, for perhaps some men might have dreamed of her as I dreamed of Marguerite. She asked me for money. I gave it to her, and, free then to go, I returned home.

Marguerite had not answered.

I need not tell you in what state of agitation I spent the next day. At half past nine a messenger brought me an envelope containing my letter and the five-hundred-franc note, not a word more.

"Who gave you this?" I asked the man.

"A lady who was starting with her maid

癫狂之时，我能干出怎样卑鄙下流的事情吗？我不断暗示自己，这个女人一定正在耻笑我，我幻想着，她一定在和那位伯爵欢颜嬉笑，不断地对伯爵重复昨晚她对我说过的话，以博得伯爵的欢心。于是，我掏出一张 500 法郎的钞票，连同以下的字条一并送到她家：

这是你的过夜费，今天早上你匆匆忙忙就离开了，我忘了把这些钱给你了。

字条送出后，我立即出走了，似乎要逃避这种异常低劣的行为所带来的愧疚。

我到奥利姆家，她正在试衣，房里别无他人后，她开始唱低俗的曲子来调情。这个女人真是个典型的完全没廉耻、没心没肺、淫荡下贱的妓女，至少我这么认为，因为，就像我与玛格丽特那样，恐怕也有不少的男人也同她做过那种春宵美梦。她问我要钱，我给了她一些就自由了，我又回到自己家中。

玛格丽特并无答复。

已经不用向你详细说明，接下来的那天我是怎样亢奋度过的。9点半，信差递给我一封信，里面除了此前我寄去的字条以及那张 500 法郎的钞票外，再没有任何一个字。

"谁让你给我的？"我问道。

"一位夫人，她同侍女一起坐

in the next mail for Boulogne, and who told me not to take it until the coach was out of the courtyard."

I rushed to the Rue d'Antin.

"Madame left for England at six o'clock," said the porter.

There was nothing to hold me in Paris any longer, neither hate nor love. I was exhausted by this series of shocks. One of my friends was setting out on a tour in the East. I told my father I should like to accompany him; my father gave me drafts and letters of introduction, and eight or ten days afterward I embarked at Marseilles.

It was at Alexandria that I learned from an attache at the embassy, whom I had sometimes seen at Marguerite's, that the poor girl was seriously ill.

I then wrote her the letter which she answered in the way you know; I received it at Toulon.

I started at once, and you know the rest.

Now you have only to read a few sheets which Julie Duprat gave me; they are the best commentary on what I have just told you.

上了赶往布伦的邮车。她嘱咐我必须等到邮车驶出后再交给你。"

我立即奔向了昂坦大街。

"6 点时，夫人就起身前往英国了。"门卫告诉我说。

没有恨，也没有爱，没有任何事情可以将我留在巴黎了。一系列的打击早已把我弄得精疲力竭。我听说一位友人想去东方旅游，我便告诉父亲希望能和他一同前去。父亲给了我一些支票，还为我写了一封介绍信。大约 10 天之后，我便抵达了马赛港上，准备远行。

在亚历山大[1]，我遇到了一位在玛格丽特家中曾有过几面之缘的大使馆的随员，从他口中得知，玛格丽特已经病入膏肓了。

我便给她写了一封信，当我在土伦[2]时，收到了她的一封回信，这封回信，想必你已经目睹过了。

我马上起身返回，而在这之后的事情，你也都知晓了。

如今，你只需通读一遍那本由朱莉·杜普拉交给我的日记就明白了，而这正是对我此前给你讲述的这个故事的必不可少的补充。

---

[1] 亚历山大，埃及著名港口。
[2] 土伦，法国地中海沿岸城市。

CHAPTER 25
第二十五章

Armand, tired by this long narrative, often interrupted by his tears, put his two hands over his forehead and closed his eyes to think, or to try to sleep, after giving me the pages written by the hand of Marguerite. A few minutes after, a more rapid breathing told me that Armand slept, but that light sleep which the least sound banishes.

This is what I read; I copy it without adding or omitting a syllable:

Today is the 15th December. I have been ill three or four days. This morning I stayed in bed. The weather is dark, I am sad; there is no one by me. I think of you, Armand. And you, where are you, while I write these lines? Far from Paris, far, far, they tell me, and perhaps you have already forgotten Marguerite. Well, be happy; I owe you the only happy moments in my life.

I can not help wanting to explain all my conduct to you, and I have written you a letter; but, written by a girl like me, such a

阿尔芒疲惫的大段叙述常被泪水打断。当他将玛格丽特给他的亲笔信交付于我后，便紧闭双眼，双手支着额头，似沉思，或想小憩片刻。没多久，就从他那里传来了一阵快速而急促的喘息声，很明显，阿尔芒又睡过去了，可是，他却睡得很轻，哪怕是一丝的声响都会将他重新从睡梦中惊醒。

以下便是玛格丽特的信中的内容，我将其一字不差地抄了出来：

今天是 12 月 15 日，我已经卧床不起三四天了。整个上午一直在床上躺着，天色昏暗如我沉郁的心境。此时无人在我身边陪伴。亲爱的阿尔芒，我想你。现在，在我执笔之时，你在何方呢？有人对我说，你正在一个离巴黎很远的地方，可能你已经将玛格丽特抛在脑后了吧。祝你活得快乐，因为我这辈子所仅有的快乐时光正是你赐予的。

我实在忍不住了，要向你彻底解释一番，我曾经给你写过一封信，可

letter might seem to be a lie, unless death had sanctified it by its authority, and, instead of a letter, it were a confession.

Today I am ill; I may die of this illness, for I have always had the presentiment that I shall die young. My mother died of consumption, and the way I have always lived could but increase the only heritage she ever left me. But I do not want to die without clearing up for you everything about me; that is, if, when you come back, you will still trouble yourself about the poor girl whom you loved before you went away.

This is what the letter contained; I shall like writing it over again, so as to give myself another proof of my own justification.

You remember, Armand, how the arrival of your father surprised us at Bougival; you remember the involuntary fright that his arrival caused me, and the scene which took place between you and him, which you told me of in the evening.

Next day, when you were at Paris, waiting for your father, and he did not return, a man came to the door and handed in a letter from M. Duval.

His letter, which I inclose with this, begged me, in the most serious terms, to keep you away on the following day, on some excuse or other, and to see your father,

是，由于是出一个像我这样的女人之手，极可能被认为是谎言连篇；要么是我死去，借助死的庄严变得些许神圣与诚恳；要么，非同一般，是来自于我内心的忏悔与供认不讳的虔诚，这才能使人相信它的真实。

现在我已病入膏肓，恐怕会因此撒手人间。我一直感觉自己肯定不会长寿。因为我的母亲就是得肺结核死的，这病根是她遗留于我的唯一财产，同时，我平时花天酒地的生活习惯，加重了病情。可是，我不忍心就这样不明不白地死去，而你依旧被蒙在鼓里。这样一来，当你归来之时，你还会为那个曾经深爱着的可怜姑娘而留恋万分。

下面是这封信的所有内容，我十分乐意再将其书写一遍，就当是为我的辩驳提供另外一个例证吧。

你没忘记吧，阿尔芒，当得知你父亲赶到布吉瓦尔时我有多么惊慌失措吧，你没有忘记你父亲的到来使我情不由衷产生的恐慌吧，你也没有忘记那个夜里你对我讲的关于你和你父亲之间的那些事情吧。

此后的第二天，在你赶赴巴黎苦苦等候你的长久未能归来的父亲之时，有个男人来到了我家，递给我一封来自迪瓦尔先生的信件。

现在，我将这封信的内容为你奉上，你父亲说有话和我谈谈，便以极

who wished to speak to me, and asked me particularly not to say anything to you about it.

You know how I insisted on your returning to Paris next day.

You had only been gone an hour when your father presented himself. I won't say what impression his severe face made upon me. Your father had the old theory that a courtesan is a being without heart or reason, a sort of machine for coining gold, always ready, like the machine, to bruise the hand that gives her everything, and to tear in pieces, without pity or discernment, those who set her in motion.

Your father had written me a very polite letter, in order that I might consent to see him; he did not present himself quite as he had written. His manner at first was so stiff, insolent, and even threatening, that I had to make him understand that I was in my own house, and that I had no need to render him an account of my life, except because of the sincere affection which I had for his son.

M. Duval calmed down a little, but still went on to say that he could not any longer allow his son to ruin himself over me; that I was beautiful, it was true, but, however beautiful I might be, I ought not to make use of my beauty to spoil the future of a young

其严厉的措辞强烈要求我在第二天务必要找个理由把你支开，以使他能够和我碰面。同时，他再三嘱咐我千万不能把这件事告诉你。

你现在一定还记得吧，那天，我是如何强烈地逼迫你再次奔赴巴黎的吧。

你刚走了大约一小时，他便赶来了。他那严酷的面孔给我留下什么样的印象我不愿再提了。你的父亲已经被那些保守的观念弄得冥顽不灵了，在他看来，所有的妓女都是一群没心没肺、没有理性、只为金钱而活的钢铁机器，她们时刻都可能绝不留情、不分是非地将曾经给过她们一切好处的双手碾得粉碎，把那些曾经包养的人驱逐出去。

为了求得我同意接见他，他甚至给我写了一封十分体面的信。可之后，等他来同我相见时，却不再像信中所言的那么客气了。谈话之初，他便口气生硬，咄咄逼人，甚至摆出恐吓的言辞，到后来我只好尽量让他知道，他这是在我家里，若不是因为我是真心实意地爱着他的儿子，我根本不会将自己的私生活向他和盘托出。

迪瓦尔先生略微恢复了沉静，然而，他继续对我说道，他还是不会同意让他的儿子因为我而搞得倾家荡产。迪瓦尔先生说，我的确十分漂亮，

man by such expenditure as I was causing.

At that there was only one thing to do, to show him the proof that since I was your mistress I had spared no sacrifice to be faithful to you without asking for more money than you had to give me. I showed him the pawn tickets, the receipts of the people to whom I had sold what I could not pawn; I told him of my resolve to part with my furniture in order to pay my debts, and live with you without being a too heavy expense. I told him of our happiness, of how you had shown me the possibility of a quieter and happier life, and he ended by giving in to the evidence, offering me his hand, and asking pardon for the way in which he had at first approached me.

Then he said to me:

"So, madame, it is not by remonstrances or by threats, but by entreaties, that I must endeavour to obtain from you a greater sacrifice than you have yet made for my son."

I trembled at this beginning.

Your father came over to me, took both my hands, and continued in an affectionate voice:

"My child, do not take what I have to say to you amiss; only remember that there are sometimes in life cruel necessities for

可是，不管我长得多么美丽动人，我也不能靠自己的姿色去迫害一个年轻人的未来，去挥霍一个年轻人的前程。

因此，对于这样的威胁我只好用铁证来辩解：为了保持自己的忠实与诚恳，同时，也不向你提出超出经济承受能力之外的要求，自打我做你的情人后，我做出了所有可能的牺牲。我给你父亲拿出了那些售卖家具的当票，还拿出了一些因为无法典当而卖掉的东西的买主的收据。同时，我还告诉迪瓦尔先生，为了和你一起生活，又不使你承担过分沉重的负担，我已下决心变卖我的那些家具来还债。我向迪瓦尔先生讲述了我们的幸福以及相对平静生活的憧憬。听到这些，他终于想通了，并向我伸出双手，要我谅解他先前的粗暴的态度。

接着，他又继续说道：

"既然这样，夫人，我只好不用抱怨或是威胁的口吻，而是虔诚地恳求你，希望你能够为我的儿子做出比你先前做出的更大的牺牲。"

一听到你父亲的这些话，我的全身便已开始震颤不已。

迪瓦尔先生走到我身边，握住了我的双手，十分和蔼地对我说道：

"我的孩子，不要把我接下来的话往坏处想。可是，你一定要明

the heart, but that they must be submitted to. You are good, your soul has generosity unknown to many women who perhaps despise you, and are less worthy than you. But remember that there is not only the mistress, but the family; that besides love there are duties;that to the age of passion succeeds the age when man, if he is to be respected, must plant himself solidly in a serious position. My son has no fortune, and yet he is ready to abandon to you the legacy of his mother. If he accepted from you the sacrifice which you are on the point of making, his honour and dignity would require him to give you, in exchange for it, this income, which would always put you out of danger of adversity. But he can not accept this sacrifice, because the world, which does not know you, would give a wrong interpretation to this acceptance, and such an interpretation must not tarnish the name which we bear.

No one would consider whether Armand loves you, whether you love him, whether this mutual love means happiness to him and redemption to you; they would see only one thing, that Armand Duval allowed a kept woman (forgive me, my child, for what I am forced to say to you) to sell all she had for him.

Then the day of reproaches and regrets

白，生活对于心灵有时就是残酷的，但这是一种需要，因此，你没有选择，只能顺从。你那么善良，你心中蕴涵着很多女人不具备的慷慨，或许她们瞧不起你，但是，她们却也根本比不上你。然而，夫人，请你再想想，除了情人，一个人还应当有家庭。而除了爱，一个人还应当负有责任。当经历了激情昂扬的光辉岁月之后，他就应当去经历一段有固定地位的令人敬仰的时光。可如今我的儿子却是前途未卜，同时，他又要把来自他母亲的遗产过户给你。倘若他选择接受你为他所作的牺牲，那他不得不为你付出名誉与自尊，以作为对你牺牲的回报。而一旦你拥有了这些财富，你的生活也就再也不会充满危机与磨难了。然而，现实社会对你的真爱毫不知情，人们会认为他之所以选择接受你做出的牺牲也许是基于一个不光彩的原因，从而使我们家的声誉遭到极大损害，因此，他绝对不能接受你的牺牲。

没人会关心阿尔芒对你是否出自真爱，你又是否对他痴情到底，你们的爱情是否预示着真正的幸福生活，你将要改过自新。人们只会认清一点：阿尔芒·迪瓦尔心甘情愿地包养着一个妓女（请原谅，亲爱的孩子，我不得这样说），包养

would arrive, be sure, for you or for others, and you would both bear a chain that you could not sever. What would you do then? Your youth would be lost, my son's future destroyed; and I, his father, should receive from only one of my children the recompense that I look for from both.

"You are young, beautiful, life will console you; you are noble, and the memory of a good deed will redeem you from many past deeds. During the six months that he has known you Armand has forgotten me. I wrote to him four times, and he has never once replied. I might have died and he not known it!

"Whatever may be your resolution of living otherwise than as you have lived, Armand, who loves you, will never consent to the seclusion to which his modest fortune would condemn you, and to which your beauty does not entitle you. Who knows what he would do then!

He has gambled, I know; without telling you of it, I know also, but, in a moment of madness, he might have lost part of what I have saved, during many years, for my daughter's portion, for him, and for the repose of my old age. What might have happened may yet happen.

"Are you sure, besides, that the life hich you are giving up for him will never

个为了他而变卖家产的妓女。

请相信，倘若你们真的这么做，谴责和悔恨之日便会接踵而来，不论对你还是对其他人都是这样，你们俩都将会被一条无法打破的枷锁禁锢。你们将如何面对呢？你们的青春一去不复返，我儿子的光明前程也断送了。至于做父亲的我，原本期盼着能有两个孩子来报答我，也将仅仅剩下一个了。

"你那么年轻美丽，未来的幸福生活一定会使你得到安慰。你的精神是崇高的，你若能做一件善事，定能将之前的那些不好的行为统统抹去。阿尔芒仅仅和你相处了6个月，便已把我完全抛在脑后了。我曾4次致信给他，可他却没给我一封回信，恐怕我死了他都不知道！

"阿尔芒如此深爱你，你的不像先前那样铺张奢侈的决心再坚决，他也决不会因自己的窘迫境况而让你过凄苦贫困的生活的，同时，你的绝美身姿和这种清贫的生活也是格格不入的。等到那时，上帝才会知晓他又会耍出什么名堂！

"我知道他开始赌钱了，也知道他没告诉你。可是，一旦他冲动起来，极有可能会将我多年为女儿置办嫁妆和儿子婚礼酒宴的积蓄，还有让我享受一个平静的晚年的积蓄赔进去。当然，我还需要应对任

again come to attract you? Are you sure, you who have loved him, that you will never love another? Would you not-suffer on seeing the hindrances set by your love to your lover's life, hindrances for which you would be powerless to console him, if, with age, thoughts of ambition should succeed to dreams of love?

Think over all that, madame. You love Armand; prove it to him by the sole means which remains to you of yet proving it to him, by sacrificing your love to his future. No misfortune has yet arrived, but one will arrive, and perhaps a greater one than those which I foresee.

Armand might become jealous of a man who has loved you; he might provoke him, fight, be killed. Think, then, what you would suffer in the presence of a father who should call on you to render an account for the life of his son!

"Finally, my dear child, let me tell you all, for I have not yet told you all, let me tell you what has brought me to Paris. I have a daughter, as I have told you, young, beautiful, pure as an angel. She loves, and she, too, has made this love the dream of her life. I wrote all that to Armand, but, absorbed in you, he made no reply. Well, my daughter is about to marry. She is to marry the man whom she loves; she enters

何其他可能出现的意外情况。

"另外，难道你能确定不再眷恋过去的那种奢华生活？你能确定，你深爱着阿尔芒，今后绝不移情别恋？随着时间的推移，你们对事业的壮志雄心逐渐取代了曾经的对美好爱情的翘首企盼，你们之间的这种情人的关系便会成为极大的障碍，一种绝对无法逾越的障碍，等你们遇到了那种障碍之时，你不为之难过吗？

"夫人，请你好好思量一下。你的确深爱着阿尔芒，可当下你却只能用这种为了他的前程而牺牲自己的方式来证明你对他的忠贞与虔诚。如今，糟糕的事情还没发生，可早晚会的，甚至将远远超过我的预料。

也许，阿尔芒会为了一个曾经深爱你的人而争风吃醋，他可能会冲他寻衅，和他厮打，甚至被杀死。请试想一下，到那时，当你站在一个允诺过为其儿子的生命以及幸福负责的父亲面前时，你又会承受多么巨大的痛苦与悲伤啊！

"总而言之，我亲爱的孩子，我把一切都告诉你吧，之前我还有一些隐瞒，我告诉你我赶赴巴黎的真正原因。正如先前提到的，我还有一个女儿，她年轻，也很漂亮，纯洁得像个天使。她也在恋爱，她

an honourable family, which requires that mine has to be no less honourable. The family of the man who is to become my son-in-law has learned what manner of life Armand is leading in Paris, and has declared to me that the marriage must be broken off if Armand continues this life.

The future of a child who has done nothing against you, and who has the right of looking forward to a happy future, is in your hands. Have you the right, have you the strength, to shatter it? In the name of your love and of your repentance, Marguerite, grant me the happiness of my child."

I wept silently, my friend, at all these reflections which I had so often made, and which, in the mouth of your father, took a yet more serious reality. I said to myself all that your father dared not say to me, though it had come to his lips twenty times: that I was, after all, only a kept woman, and that whatever excuse I gave for our liaison, it would always look like calculation on my part; that my past life left me no right to dream of such a future, and that I was accepting responsibilities for which my habits and reputation were far from giving any guarantee. In short, I loved you, Armand.

The paternal way in which M. Duval had

和你一样将爱情视为生活中最甜蜜的梦想。我将这些写在给阿尔芒的信中了，可他将所有的精力都放在你这里，根本没有回复我。如今，我的小女儿即将出嫁，嫁入她爱恋的、体面的家庭。当然，他们也希望能够门当户对。可是，我未来女婿的家人已经知晓了阿尔芒在巴黎的所作所为，他们冲我施压，倘若阿尔芒执迷不悟，他们将取消婚约。

如今，一个未曾损害你半分、一个渴望拥有幸福生活的小女孩的命运已经掌握在你的手中。你有什么权利，你忍心使她美好的未来遭到迫害呢？亲爱的玛格丽特，既然你深爱着我的儿子，既然你对你先前的生活深感愧疚，那就让我的孩子重新过上幸福的生活吧。"

我亲爱的朋友，当面对这种种结果，以及你父亲的颇为现实的言辞，我也只能欲哭无泪了。我在内心深处不停地想着以下这番话，尽管你父亲曾经数次想要对我说，可还是憋到了心里的话：无论我所说的是否有凭有据，我也不过是个妓女，这个身份使我所说的所有话语听起来都更像是一种为自己生活的谋划与打算。我经历过的那种生活早已让我失去了憧憬美好未来的权利，因此，我将不得不全力承担因我过去的行为与名声所酿成的结

spoken to me; the pure memories that he awakened in me; the respect of this old man, which I would gain; yours, which I was sure of gaining later on: all that called up in my heart thoughts which raised me in my own eyes with a sort of holy pride, unknown till then. When I thought that one day this old man, who was now imploring me for the future of his son, would bid his daughter mingle my name with her prayers, as the name of a mysterious friend, I seemed to become transformed, and I felt a pride in myself.

The exaltation of the moment perhaps exaggerated the truth of these impressions, but that was what I felt, friend, and these new feelings silenced the memory of the happy days I had spent with you.

"Tell me, sir," I said to your father, wiping away my tears, "do you believe that I love your son?"

"Yes," said M. Duval.

"With a disinterested love?"

"Yes.

"Do you believe that I had made this love the hope, the dream, the forgiveness – of my life?"

"Implicitly."

"Well, sir, embrace me once, as you would embrace your daughter, and I swear to you that that kiss, the only chaste kiss I

果。最后，我只想说，阿尔芒，我永远爱你。

迪瓦尔先生向我讲述这些话时的父亲般的口吻，使我萌生了一种超然的感情，我将得到这位老人的敬意，我有信心将来也能从你身上得到。正是这种油然而生的情感，使我从内心深处产生了一股神圣而又崇高的念头，这种思想让我体会到自身的价值，并感到一种从未经历过的神圣的自豪感。我憧憬着，未来的某天，这个曾经为了孩子的前程而请求我的老人，要他的小女儿把我作为帮助他们实现梦想的一个神秘的友人来祷告时，我的灵魂升华了，一股自豪之情油然而生。

当时的那种激进的想法恐怕是有些夸张了，不过，那正是我实实在在的想法。亲爱的朋友，这种想法将我那些渴望和你一起享受幸福的生活的憧憬全部抛在脑后了。

于是，我擦干了眼泪向你的父亲说道："先生，请回答我，你相信我对你儿子的爱是忠诚的吗？"

"是的。"迪瓦尔先生答道。

"我的爱是无私的吗？"

"是的。"

"那么，杜瓦尔先生，你相信我曾经把对你儿子的爱当做是我生活的憧憬，理想和慰藉吗？"

"我全都相信。"

have ever had, will make me strong against my love, and that within a week your son will be once more at your side, perhaps unhappy for a time, but cured forever."

"You are a noble child," replied your father, kissing me on the forehead, "and you are making an attempt for which God will reward you; but I greatly fear that you will have no influence upon my son."

"Oh, be at rest, sir; he will hate me."

I had to set up between us, as much for me as for you, an insurmountable barrier.

I wrote to Prudence to say that I accepted the proposition of the Comte de N., and that she was to tell him that I would sup with her and him. I sealed the letter, and, without telling him what it contained, asked your father to have it forwarded to its address on reaching Paris.

He inquired of me what it contained.

"Your son's welfare," I answered.

Your father embraced me once more. I felt two grateful tears on my forehead, like the baptism of my past faults, and at the moment when I consented to give myself up to another man I glowed with pride at the thought of what I was redeeming by this new fault.

It was quite natural, Armand. You told me that your father was the most honest man in the world.

"既然如此，先生，正如你对女儿那样，吻我一下吧，我敢向你保证，这将是我有生以来仅有的纯真的吻，这一定能战胜我爱情的力量。同时，我保证，一周之内，你的儿子会重新回到你身边，也许，一段时间内，他会相当痛苦，可从这以后，他便真正地解脱了。"

杜瓦尔先生一边吻着我的前额一边说道："你太高尚了。上帝也会对你将做的事情大为称赞，可是，我十分担心，你无法说服我儿子。"

"哦，你放心，先生，他会憎恨我的。"

因此，不论是为了你，还是为了我，我都不得不在我俩之间竖起一道永远无法逾越的屏障。

于是，我写信给普鲁登斯，说我已答应了 N 伯爵的请求，让她替我转告 N 伯爵，晚上我将同他们一起吃夜宵。封好后，我并没有告诉你父亲信的内容，而是直接请他在到巴黎后派人送往指定的地址。

他还是向我追问信中的内容。

"你儿子的幸福。"我答道。

最后，杜瓦尔先生又一次吻了我。我感觉前额有两滴传递着他无尽感激的泪珠，这泪珠正是对我曾经犯下的罪行的洗礼。而当我想到，在不久之前，我才答应了另一个男人的请求，做他的情妇，可是，倘

M. Duval returned to his carriage, and set out for Paris.

I was only a woman, and when I saw you again I could not help weeping, but I did not give way.

Did I do right? That is what I ask myself today, as I lie ill in my bed, that I shall never leave, perhaps, until I am dead.

You are witness of what I felt as the hour of our separation approached; your father was no longer there to support me, and there was a moment when I was on the point of confessing everything to you, so terrified was I at the idea that you were going to bate and despise me.

One thing which you will not believe, perhaps, Armand, is that I prayed God to give me strength; and what proves that he accepted my sacrifice is that he gave me the strength for which I prayed.

At supper I still had need of aid, for I could not think of what I was going to do, so much did I fear that my courage would fail me. Who would ever have said that I, Marguerite Gautier, would have suffered so at the mere thought of a new lover? I drank for forgetfulness, and when I woke next day I was beside the count.

That is the whole truth, friend. judge me and pardon me, as I have pardoned you for all the wrong that you have done me since

若能用这样的新的错误去救赎先前的种种错误，我依然无比的自豪。

阿尔芒，这再正常不过了。你过去对我说过，你父亲是当今世上最公正而耿直的人。

你的父亲重新坐上马车，奔赴巴黎去了。

我只是个女人，当在巴黎再次相遇，我还是情不自禁地流下了眼泪，可是，这绝不会改变我的决心。

"我这样做对吗？"我躺在床上，不停地思考这个问题，恐怕除非真的死去，我再也不能起身了。

你似乎是注视着我一点点逼近死亡的，你父亲不在身边支持我，当我想到你将要万分憎恨、鄙视我时，我又是那么的恐惧，差一点儿就要把这所有的事情都告诉你了。

阿尔芒，恐怕你万万不会相信，我曾祷告上天请他赐予我力量。最终，上天还是把那股力量赐予了我，这就足以说明，他已经接受了我所做出的牺牲。

晚餐时我依然需要一些帮助，因为我根本不知道应该做些什么，我非常担心会失去勇气来面对你！还会有谁肯相信我，玛格丽特·戈蒂埃，在想着即将得到一个新情夫之时，居然会如此痛苦？为了能忘记一切，我酩酊大醉，直到第二天醒来之时，我正躺在 N 伯爵的床上。

that day.

亲爱的朋友，这就是前因后果，请你做出一番评判吧，也恳请你能够原谅我，正如我能够原谅你自回巴黎的那天之后给我带来的一切痛苦一样。

CHAPTER 26

第二十六章

What followed that fatal night you know as well as I; but what you can not know, what you can not suspect, is what I have suffered since our separation.

I heard that your father had taken you away with him, but I felt sure that you could not live away from me for long, and when I met you in the Champs-Elysees, I was a little upset, but by no means surprised.

Then began that series of days; each of them brought me a fresh insult from you. I received them all with a kind of joy, for, besides proving to me that you still loved me, it seemed to me as if the more you persecuted me the more I should be raised in your eyes when you came to know the truth.

Do not wonder at my joy in martyrdom, Armand; your love for me had opened my heart to noble enthusiasm.

Still, I was not so strong as that quite at once.

Between the time of the sacrifice made

你和我一样清楚，在那个决定我命运的晚上后将会发生什么事，可是，你一定无法设想预料，当我俩分别之后，我将承受多大的痛苦。

我听说杜瓦尔先生已经带你离开那里了，可是，你肯定你不会这样长久地离我而去。因此，当那天我在香榭丽舍大街和你相遇时，尽管我的情绪异常激动，但我却一点儿也不觉得吃惊。

这之后就是那一段令人痛心的岁月，几乎每天，你都会耍出些新点子来折磨我，我之所以欣然接受，是因为，我觉得，那些侮辱不但能够证明你依然深爱我，还让我隐约感到，你把我折磨得越狠，当真相大白之时，我在你心中的地位也就越高不可攀。

阿尔芒，别对我这种心甘情愿为爱牺牲的情操而吃惊，你对我炽热的爱火早已将我心中高尚而激情的大门给烧开了。

当然，我也不是忽然之间就变得如此毅然决然的。

for you and the time of your return a long while elapsed, during which I was obliged to have recourse to physical means in order not to go mad, and in order to be blinded and deafened in the whirl of life into which I flung myself. Prudence has told you (has she not?) how I went to all the fetes and balls and orgies. I had a sort of hope that I should kill myself by all these excesses, and I think it will not be long before this hope is realized. My health naturally got worse and worse, and when I sent Mme. Duvernoy to ask you for pity I was utterly worn out, body and soul.

I will not remind you, Armand, of the return you made for the last proof of love that I gave you, and of the outrage by which you drove away a dying woman, who could not resist your voice when you asked her for a night of love, and who, like a fool, thought for one instant that she might again unite the past with the present. You had the right to do what you did, Armand; people have not always put so high a price on a night of mine!

I left everything after that. Olympe has taken my place with the Comte de N., and has told him, I hear, the reasons for my leaving him. The Comte de G. was at London. He is one of those men who give just enough importance to making love to

在我选择为爱牺牲和你重返巴黎之间，有一段异常难熬的光景，为了不使自己被痛苦逼得发疯，也为使我能够沉浸在曾经过往的生活中，我只好借助肉体的堕落来自我麻醉。正如普鲁登斯对你说的（不是吗？），我整天泡在狂欢派对里，不断跳舞，纵情畅饮。我多么希望能纵欲而死，而且，我也相信，像我这样，迟早要死的。毫无疑问，我的身体状况越来越差了。当我让迪韦尔诺瓦夫人向你请求不要再折磨我的时候，我已经完全虚脱了，无论是精神上还是肉体上，都已经彻底枯竭了。

我本不想提的，阿尔芒，当我最后一次对你证明我炽热而忠贞的爱情时，你是采取怎样的侮辱手段将这个临死的女人赶走的。当她听到你所提出的一夜情的要求后，她顿时感到无法回绝，如同白痴一般，居然妄想能够让你因为那一夜的温柔将过去的美好和现在的惨淡重新联系起来。你的确有权像以往那样做。可是，阿尔芒，其他人在我这儿过夜，可没出过像你这么高的价钱！

这之后，我便放弃了一切，而奥利姆也替代了我在N伯爵身边的地位。我听其他人说，她已经将我离开巴黎的原因告诉了N伯爵。至

women like me for it to be an agreeable pastime, and who are thus able to remain friends with women, not hating them because they have never been jealous of them, and he is, too, one of those grand seigneurs who open only a part of their hearts to us, but the whole of their purses. It was of him that I immediately thought. I joined him in London. He received me as kindly as possible, but he was the lover there of a woman in society, and he feared to compromise himself if he were seen with me. He introduced me to his friends, who gave a supper in my honour, after which one of them took me home with him.

What else was there for me to do, my friend? If I had killed myself it would have burdened your life, which ought to be happy, with a needless remorse; and then, what is the good of killing oneself when one is so near dying already?

I became a body without a soul, a thing without a thought; I lived for some time in that automatic way; then I returned to Paris, and asked after you; I heard then that you were gone on a long voyage. There was nothing left to hold me to life. My existence became what it had been two years before I knew you. I tried to win back the duke, but I had offended him too

于远在伦敦的 G 伯爵，他不过是把与类似我这样的女人的情人关系当做是一种纯粹的寻欢作乐罢了。因此，他总能同那些和他有过情人关系的女伴保持着友好的关系，他从不憎恨她们，也从不因她们而醋意大发，像他们那种阔佬，虽然从不以真心对待那些情人，却总会对她们敞开自己的金库。于是，我即刻便想到了 G 伯爵，就赶往伦敦找他，他对我相当地慷慨和善，可是，他在伦敦已经有了一个身处上流社会的情人。他担心和我相处的事情导致他的名声遭到损害，便把他的朋友们介绍给我。他的朋友们便请我吃了夜宵，夜宵过后，其中一位就带我离开了。

亲爱的朋友，我还能怎么办呢？难道自尽？那样可能会毁了你本应快乐的一生，也会给你带来无尽的不必要的自责。况且，像我这样本来就濒临死亡的人，自尽又有什么意义呢？

于是，我变成了一个丧失灵魂并且迷失了意识的躯壳，那段日子，我如行尸走肉一般，此后，我赶回了巴黎打听你的消息，我听说你早已同父亲一起远游了。由于没有任何依靠，我不得不像两年前刚刚结识你时那样生活了。我想去找公爵，可是我曾经让他伤透了心，而像他

deeply. Old men are not patient, no doubt because they realize that they are not eternal. I got weaker every day. I was pale and sad and thinner than ever. Men who buy love examine the goods before taking them. At Paris there were women in better health, and not so thin as I was; I was rather forgotten. That is all the past up to yesterday.

Now I am seriously ill. I have written to the duke to ask him for money, for I have none, and the creditors have returned, and come to me with their bills with pitiless perseverance. Will the duke answer? Why are you not in Paris, Armand? You would come and see me, and your visits would do me good.

December 20.

The weather is horrible; it is snowing, and I am alone. I have been in such a fever for the last three days that I could not write you a word. No news, my friend; every day I hope vaguely for a letter from you, but it does not come, and no doubt it will never come. Only men are strong enough not to forgive. The duke has not answered.

Prudence is pawning my things again.

I have been spitting blood all the time. Oh, you would be sorry for me if you could see me. You are indeed happy to be under a

那样的老年人是不会对我那么有耐心的，因为，毫无疑问，他们知道自己不是永远都那么年轻的。我的病情越来越糟，脸色苍白，心情沉重，身体也变得消瘦。那些购买爱情的男人们总会先看看货色再取货的。而在巴黎，比我更加健康丰满的女人多得是，于是，我便就这样被大家些许遗忘了。以上这些便是截止到今日所发生的事情。

如今，我疾病缠身了。我曾给公爵致信希望他能给我一些钱，因为我一无所有了。债主们接踵而至，他们没有丝毫同情心，绷着铁面，拿着借据向我逼债。公爵会回信吗？阿尔芒，为什么你现在不在巴黎啊！倘若你在，你一定会来看我的，你过来了，一切都会好转的。

12月20日

外面大雪纷飞，天气糟糕透了，我孤单一人待在家中。由于持续高烧，过去的三天我半个字也没写。亲爱的朋友，没什么新消息传来，基本上每天我都会期望着你能够给我来封信，可是，从来没有，恐怕以后也不会有了。只有男人才会这么铁石心肠，从不宽恕别人。公爵依然没有回信。

普鲁登斯又替我典当东西了。

我一直在咳血。哦！倘若你见到

warm sky, and not, like me, with a whole winter of ice on your chest. Today I got up for a little while, and looked out through the curtains of my window, and watched the life of Paris passing below, the life with which I have now nothing more to do. I saw the faces of some people I knew, passing rapidly, joyous and careless. Not one lifted his eyes to my window. However, a few young men have come to inquire for me. Once before I was ill, and you, though you did not know me, though you had had nothing from me but an impertinence the day I met you first, you came to inquire after me every day. We spent six months together. I had all the love for you that a woman's heart can hold and give, and you are far away, you are cursing me, and there is not a word of consolation from you. But it is only chance that has made you leave me, I am sure, for if you were at Paris, you would not leave my bedside.

December 25.

My doctor tells me I must not write every day. And indeed my memories only increase my fever, but yesterday I received a letter which did me good, more because of what it said than by the material help which it contained. I can write to you, then, today. This letter is from your father, and this is what it says:

我这个样子，一定会难过的。现在，这个满是冰霜的严冬灌在我的胸腔，几乎喘不过气，而你，一定快活地待在某个充满阳光的地方。今天我下床待了会儿，透过窗帘，注视着外面的巴黎的生活，恐怕我将永远告别这种生活了。我看见几张熟悉的面孔匆匆而过，个个洋溢着愉悦的笑容和无忧无虑的神情。然而，竟没有一个会仰起脸看看我的窗扉。偶尔也有一两个年轻人过来探望我。记得曾经，那次我也是在生病，虽然你那时并不认识我，只是在我们初次相识时从我这里遭到了一次十分失礼的接待，可自从那次之后，几乎每天，你都会过来探望我。我俩曾经相处了6个月之久，我把一个女人所能承受和付出的所有爱意都献给了你。如今你身在远方，不停谩骂我，没能给我一句宽慰的话。然而，我坚信，你将我抛弃不闻不问，是命运的安排，倘若你现在就在巴黎，你绝对会一刻不离地陪伴在我左右的。

12月25日

医生不允许我天天写信。确实，总是浮想联翩只会使病情加剧。可是，昨天，一封来信让我的心情顿时好了许多，信中文字所蕴涵的情感远远要比它给予我的物质援助更让我欣慰。因此，今天我又能够写信给你

"MADAME: I have just learned that you are ill. If I were at Paris I would come and ask after you myself; if my son were here I would send him; but I can not leave C., and Armand is six or seven hundred from here; permit me, then, simply to write to you, madame, to tell you how pained I am to hear of your illness, and believe in my sincere wishes for your speedy recovery.

One of my good friends, M. H., will call on you; will you kindly receive him? I have intrusted him with a commission, the result of which I await impatiently. "Believe me, madame,

"Yours most faithfully."

This is the letter he sent me. Your father has a noble heart; love him well, my friend, for there are few men so worthy of being loved. This paper signed by his name has done me more good than all the prescriptions of our great doctor.

This morning M. H. called. He seemed much embarrassed by the delicate mission which M. Duval had intrusted to him. As a matter of fact, he came to bring me three thousand francs from your father. I wanted to refuse at first, but M. H. told me that my refusal would annoy M. Duval, who had authorized him to give me this sum now, and later on whatever I might need. I accepted it, for, coming from your father, it could not be

了。那封信是你的父亲寄来的。以下则是那封信的内容：

夫人：我刚刚听说你身染重病，倘若我身在巴黎，一定会亲自过来看望，假使阿尔芒在我身边，我也会让他立即去你那里。可是，如今我远在C城无法离开，而阿尔芒又在六七百里之遥。请允许我简简单单给你写封信吧。听到你生病的消息，我相当难过，请不要怀疑我的诚意，我真心希望你能早日康复。

我的好朋友——H先生，想到你家中拜访，不知道你是否乐意。我请他来替我办一件事，现在我正十分迫切地期盼着那件事的结果。

在此致以我最诚挚的问候。

以上便是那封信的内容，我亲爱的阿尔芒，你的父亲拥有一颗高尚的心灵，你一定要好好地敬爱他，因为这世上值得我们去爱的人实在太少了。这张留有他签名的信纸给我带来的舒适远远多于那些卓越的名医所开出的任何药方。

这天上午，H先生过来拜访我，对于迪瓦尔先生所托付的那个微妙的请求，他看起来有些尴尬。事实上，他专程来是为了替迪瓦尔先生给我3000法郎。开始我不好意思收下，可是H先生告诉我，倘若我拒绝，迪瓦尔先生会不高兴的。迪瓦尔先生已经授权他将这些钱给我，随后，他还

exactly taking alms. If I am dead when you come back, show your father what I have written for him, and tell him that in writing these lines the poor woman to whom he was kind enough to write so consoling a letter wept tears of gratitude and prayed God for him.

January 4.

I have passed some terrible days. I never knew the body could suffer so. Oh, my past life! I pay double for it now.

There has been some one to watch by me every night; I can not breathe. What remains of my poor existence is shared between being delirious and coughing.

The dining-room is full of sweets and all sorts of presents that my friends have brought. Some of them, I dare say, are hoping that I shall be their mistress later on. If they could see what sickness has made of me, they would go away in terror.

Prudence is giving her New Year's presents with those I have received.

There is a thaw, and the doctor says that I may go out in a few days if the fine weather continues.

January 8.

I went out yesterday in my carriage. The weather was lovely. The Champs-Elysees

会满足我的任何需求。我之所以接受，是因为它并非来自施舍，而是来自于你父亲的真心关怀。倘若在你赶回时，我已经不在这世上了，请将我写下的这些关于他的话让他看看，请你告诉他，他对这个可怜女人的无比仁慈与关怀，深深地打动她，她的无尽感激之情完全流露在这篇日记的字里行间，她愿意为你的父亲向上天祷告。

1月4日

我经历了痛苦不已的岁月。我从没想过肉体竟然能遭受如此折磨。哎，我现在双倍奉还我曾经的那段荒淫生活啊！

每个晚上都会有人来照顾我，可我还是几乎无法喘息。我这可怜一生中仅存的光阴恐怕将在这不断的咳嗽与精神错乱中挨过。

客厅里到处都是好友送来的糖果以及五花八门的礼品。我敢保证，在这些人中，一定有人巴望着将来能成为我的情夫。倘若他们亲眼目睹我被疾病折磨得苦不堪言的样子，肯定早就被吓得躲得远远的了。

普鲁登斯拿我收到的礼品当做她新年的赠礼。

天气转暖了，医生告诉我，倘若这好天气能够持续下去，说不定，过些日子我便能出去散散步了。

was full of people. It was like the first smile of spring. Everything about me had a festal air. I never knew before that a ray of sunshine could contain so much joy, sweetness, and consolation.

I met almost all the people I knew, all happy, all absorbed in their pleasures. How many happy people don't even know that they are happy! Olympe passed me in an elegant carriage that M. de N. has given her. She tried to insult me by her look. She little knows how far I am from such things now. A nice fellow, whom I have known for a long time, asked me if I would have supper with him and one of his friends, who, he said, was very anxious to make my acquaintance. I smiled sadly and gave him my hand, burning with fever. I never saw such an astonished countenance.

I came in at four, and had quite an appetite for my dinner. Going out has done me good. If I were only going to get well! How the sight of the life and happiness of others gives a desire of life to those who, only the night before, in the solitude of their soul and in the shadow of their sick-room, only wanted to die soon!

January 10.

The hope of getting better was only a dream. I am back in bed again, covered with

1月8日

昨天，我坐上马车到外面逛了逛，天气相当的好，如同早春一般明媚和煦。香榭丽舍大街上挤满了人，到处都是一派热闹欢腾的景象。我从来都不知道，这柔和的春光居然能够给人们带来那么多的愉悦、甜蜜和欣慰。

我几乎遇到了所有的朋友，都是那么喜笑颜开，沉浸在欢乐的海洋。唉，这世上有许多人身在福中不知福啊！奥利姆从我这里经过，坐在N伯爵送她的精美的马车上，她试图用犀利的眼光嘲笑我。可她全然不知，如今的我已经再也没有那种无聊的虚荣心了。一位相识已久十分好心的朋友，他问我是否愿意和他及他的朋友一同晚餐，他告诉我，他的朋友十分渴望能结识我。我苦笑了一下，向他伸出烧得滚烫的手，他的脸色变得异常诧异，这是我从未见过的。

下午4点钟回到家中，晚餐时食欲旺盛。这次出门真是大有裨益啊。要是我的病情能够彻底好转那该多好啊！一个人待在渺小又空荡荡的房间里，孤苦伶仃、无尽抑郁，整天巴望着能尽早撒手人间，可是，一旦他窥见了别人幸福快乐的生活之后，竟然也会顿时萌生了继续活下去的渴望。

plasters which burn me. If I were to offer the body that people paid so dear for once, how much would they give, I wonder, today?

We must have done something very wicked before we were born, or else we must be going to be very happy indeed when we are dead, for God to let this life have all the tortures of expiation and all the sorrows of an ordeal.

January 12.

I am always ill.

The Comte de N. sent me some money yesterday. I did not keep it. I won't take anything from that man. It is through him that you are not here.

Oh, that good time at Bougival! Where is it now?

If I come out of this room alive I will make a pilgrimage to the house we lived in together, but I will never leave it until I am dead.

Who knows if I shall write to you tomorrow?

January 25.

I have not slept for eleven nights. I am suffocated. I imagine every moment that I am going to die. The doctor has forbidden me to touch a pen. Julie Duprat, who is looking after me, lets me write these few

1 月 10 日

然而，对大病康复的渴望只不过是一场空洞的梦。我又病倒了，浑身涂满了那种令我烫得发痛的药膏。曾经人们一掷千金都难求一见的身体，现在，恐怕一文不值了！

我想，我们的前生一定是犯下了什么巨大的罪孽，或者是曾经过分享乐，以至于如今上天让我们在一生中经历如此多的痛苦折磨来赎罪。

1 月 12 日

我仍被病痛折磨得苦不堪言。

昨天，N 伯爵来送钱给我，我没有接受他的援助。我才不会接受他的施舍，因为正是他才使得你无法陪在我的身旁。

唉！当初在布吉瓦尔的光阴多么美妙啊！可现在，你又身在何方？

倘若我还能活着走出屋子，我一定会到当初我俩住过的那所房子处虔诚朝拜，可是，看现在的情形，我恐怕只有被人抬出去的份了。

天知道明天我是否还能活着给你写信？

1 月 25 日

我已有整整 11 个晚上都没能合眼了，我无法呼吸，无时无刻不在想着，是不是就要死了。医生再三叮嘱

lines to you. Will you not come back before I die? Is it all over between us forever? It seems to me as if I should get well if you came. What would be the good of getting well?

January 28.

This morning I was awakened by a great noise. Julie, who slept in my room, ran into the dining-room. I heard men's voices, and hers protesting against them in vain. She came back crying.

They had come to seize my things. I told her to let what they call justice have its way. The bailiff came into my room with his hat on. He opened the drawers, wrote down what he saw, and did not even seem to be aware that there was a dying woman in the bed that fortunately the charity of the law leaves me.

He said, indeed, before going, that I could appeal within nine days, but he left a man behind to keep watch. My God! what is to become of me? This scene has made me worse than I was before. Prudence wanted to go and ask your father's friend for money, but I would not let her.

I received your letter this morning. I was in need of it. Will my answer reach you in time? Will you ever see me again? This is a happy day, and it has made me forget all the days I have passed for the last six weeks. I

我，千万不能再拿笔了。朱莉·杜普拉一直照顾着我，她同意让我给你简单写几句。在我死之前，你不会回来吗？难道我俩缘尽于此了吗？我潜意识里感到，一旦你能赶来，我的病情便会马上好转。然而，病好了又能怎样呢？

1月28日

今天早上，一阵极大的声响把我吓醒了。在我屋内睡着的朱莉急忙跑向了客厅。之后，我便听到了朱莉和一些男人的争吵声，可是，毫无作用。朱莉又哭着跑了回来。

那些人是前来查封房产的。我告诉朱莉让他们去做他们所谓的合法的事情吧。执法官员们头顶高帽粗鲁地走进来，将抽屉都打开，并把所见的一切记了下来，他似乎根本就没有发现，他身旁的床上还躺着一个濒临死亡的女人，多亏了仁慈的法律，那张床总算没被封掉。

临走之时，他终于蹦出一句话，允许我在9天内提出异议，然而，他们必须派一人在这里留守！上帝啊，他们把我当成什么了！这件事情的打击使我的病情变得更加严重了。普鲁登斯希望去找你父亲的朋友寻求经济援助，可我不同意那么做。

今天上午终于收到了你的信，我是多么期待啊，你是否能立即收到我

seem as if I am better, in spite of the feeling of sadness under the impression of which I replied to you.

After all, no one is unhappy always.

When I think that it may happen to me not to die, for you to come back, for me to see the spring again, for you still to love me, and for us to begin over again our last year's life!

Fool that I am! I can scarcely hold the pen with which I write to you of this wild dream of my heart.

Whatever happens, I loved you well, Armand, and I would have died long ago if I had not had the memory of your love to help me and a sort of vague hope of seeing you beside me again.

February 4.

The Comte de G. has returned. His mistress has been unfaithful to him. He is very sad; he was very fond of her. He came to tell me all about it. The poor fellow is in rather a bad way as to money; all the same, he has paid my bailiff and sent away the man.

I talked to him about you, and he promised to tell you about me. I forgot that I had been his mistress, and he tried to make me forget it, too. He is a good friend.

The duke sent yesterday to inquire after me, and this morning he came to see me. I do

的回信？是否能够再见到我？这真是无比快乐的一天，它已经将我这6周以来经历的所有不幸全部从脑海中驱除出去了，尽管当我给你写这封回信之时，依然相当的沉郁，可还是感到欣慰了许多。

毕竟，一个人不会总是不幸吧。

我甚至想到若我能逃过死劫，可能你还会回到我身边，可能我还会看到春天，可能你依然深爱着我，可能我们还能像去年那样重新幸福地生活！

我简直是疯了！我甚至已经连笔都握不稳了，现在，我正用它将我的胡言乱语写给你。

可是，无论将来会发生什么，亲爱的阿尔芒，我依然那么爱你，倘若不是过往爱情的美妙回忆以及和你重归旧好的渴望支撑着我，也许我早就撒手人间了。

2月4日

G伯爵又回来找我了。他被情妇骗了，这让他伤心万分，他曾经那么爱她。这个同样可怜的先生的事业同他的爱情一样，也很糟糕，可是，即便如此，他依然给了那些执法干员一笔钱，并将那个在我家留守的干警也打发走了。

我把你的事情告诉了他，他也同意我向你说说我现在的状况。我居然

not know how the old man still keeps alive. He remained with me three hours and did not say twenty words. Two big tears fell from his eyes when he saw how pale I was. The memory of his daughter's death made him weep, no doubt. He will have seen her die twice. His back was bowed, his head bent toward the ground, his lips drooping, his eyes vacant. Age and sorrow weigh with a double weight on his worn-out body. He did not reproach me. It looked as if he rejoiced secretly to see the ravages that disease had made in me. He seemed proud of being still on his feet, while I, who am still young, was broken down by suffering.

The bad weather has returned. No one comes to see me. Julie watches by me as much as she can. Prudence, to whom I can no longer give as much as I used to, begins to make excuses for not coming.

Now that I am so near death, in spite of what the doctors tell me, for I have several, which proves that I am getting worse, I am almost sorry that I listened to your father; if I had known that I should only be taking a year of your future, I could not have resisted the longing to spend that year with you, and, at least, I should have died with a friend to hold my hand. It is true that if we had lived together this year, I should not have died so soon.

忘了，我曾经当过他的情人，而他也希望我将那忘得一干二净！他真是个好朋友。

昨天，公爵差人去探望我，今天上午，他亲自过来了。我真不清楚这位老公爵是如何支撑到现在的。他陪了我大约3个小时，却几乎没说几句话。毫无疑问，望见如今憔悴又虚弱的我时，他一定联想到死去的女儿了，两颗硕大的泪珠从苍老的眼眶里滚落下来。如今，他似乎要目睹她再次死亡了，他脊背弯曲，脑袋下沉，唇角毫无生气地低垂着，两眼毫无神色。支离破碎的身体担负着老迈和伤痛这两层重负，他丝毫没怪罪我。他好像在偷偷庆幸病痛带给我的折磨呢。他看起来对依然能够站在我面前而深感自豪，可是，虽然我还这么年轻，却早已被疾病彻底压垮了。

天气又变得糟糕了，没人来看望我了，朱莉尽她最大的努力照顾着我。由于我无法像过去那样给普鲁登斯那么多钱，她便也开始找理由不到这里来了。

无论医生们怎么说，如今我还是快要死了。我的好几个医生都已断定，我的病情依然进一步加剧。我现在真后悔当时听从了杜瓦尔先生的要求，倘若当时能预知我只能再占据你一年的时间，恐怕我会坚持和你在一起的，最起码，在我临死前，会有

God's will be done!

February 5.

Oh, come, come, Armand! I suffer horribly; I am going to die, O God! I was so miserable yesterday that I wanted to spend the evening, which seemed as if it were going to be as long as the last, anywhere but at home. The duke came in the morning. It seems to me as if the sight of this old man, whom death has forgotten, makes me die faster.

Despite the burning fever which devoured me, I made them dress me and take me to the Vaudeville. Julie put on some rouge for me, without which I should have looked like a corpse. I had the box where I gave you our first rendezvous. All the time I had my eyes fixed on the stall where you sat that day, though a sort of country fellow sat there, laughing loudly at all the foolish things that the actors said. I was half dead when they brought me home. I coughed and spat blood all the night. Today I can not speak, I can scarcely move my arm. My God! My God! I am going to die! I have been expecting it, but I can not get used to the thought of suffering more than I suffer now, and if –

After this the few characters traced by Marguerite were indecipherable, and what followed was written by Julie Duprat.

一个挚爱的人握着我的双手。毫无疑问，倘若我俩真的这样又生活了一年，我也一定不会像现在这样，这么早就要死去的。

上帝的意志是不可违背的！

2月5日

天哪！我亲爱的阿尔芒，回来吧，快回来吧，我太痛苦了，我就要死了，上帝啊！昨晚实在太难受了，我宁愿去任何地方也不愿待在家里，像以前一样熬过那样漫长的夜晚。上午，公爵来看我了，当这个几乎被死神忘却的老年人出现在我面前时，我似乎觉得他的到来是在催促着我能够早些死去。

虽然我还在饱受高烧的摧残，可我还是让人帮我穿好衣服，坐马车到了轻歌舞剧院。要不是朱莉帮我擦些脂粉，我的容貌真同死尸没什么两样。我订了和你首次约会的那个包厢。我的双眼始终注视着当时你坐的那个位置，可是，坐在那里的是个乡巴佬，每每听到演员们讲到段子，便迸发出夸张的大笑。朋友将我送到家时，我几乎要昏死过去了。那一夜我一直咳血。今天已经不能说话了，我的手臂也不能动了。上帝啊！我的上帝啊！我真的要死了。虽然我早已预料到，可根本没想到竟是如此的痛苦，如此令人无法忍受，倘若……

February 18.

Monsieur Armand:

Since the day that Marguerite insisted on going to the theatre she has got worse and worse. She has completely lost her voice, and now the use of her limbs. What our poor friend suffers is impossible to say. I am not used to emotions of this kind, and I am in a state of constant fright.

How I wish you were here! She is almost always delirious; but delirious or lucid, it is always your name that she pronounces, when she can speak a word.

The doctor tells me that she is not here for long. Since she got so ill the old duke has not returned. He told the doctor that the sight was too much for him.

Mme. Duvernoy is not behaving well. This woman, who thought she could get more money out of Marguerite, at whose expense she was living almost completely, has contracted liabilities which she can not meet, and seeing that her neighbour is no longer of use to her, she does not even come to see her. Everybody is abandoning her. M. de G., prosecuted for his debts, has had to return to London. On leaving, he sent us more money; he has done all he could, but they have returned to seize the things, and the creditors are only waiting for her to die in order to sell

玛格丽特勉强拼写出的那些单词已经模糊得无法辨认了。接下来是由朱莉·杜普拉代写的。

2月18日

亲爱的阿尔芒:

自打玛格丽特执意要去轻歌舞剧院的那天后，她变得越来越糟糕了，嗓子彻底无法发声了，后来，双手和双脚也无法动弹了。我实在无法向你叙述这位凄惨的朋友所遭受的折磨。我从没经历过如此沉重的打击，一直又担心又害怕。

我多么渴望你能在这里！她在不停地胡言乱语，可是，不管精神错乱或是清醒，一旦嘴唇能蹦出几个音节，那便一定是你的名字。

医生告诉我她撑不了多久了。自打玛格丽特病情严重后，那位老公爵再也没来过。他曾告诉医生，这个场面让他难以接受了。

那位迪韦尔诺瓦夫人实在太差劲了。她完全依靠玛格丽特维持生活，她曾经认为能继续从玛格丽特身上得到更多的钱，便背上了许多她根本无法还清的债务。当她发现邻居再也没什么利用价值后，便不再过来探望她了。玛格丽特被所有人遗忘了。G伯爵由于自己的债务原因而不得不重新赶赴伦敦。在他即将离开之时，又差人送来许多钱，他能做的都

everything.

I wanted to use my last resources to put a stop to it, but the bailiff told me it was no use, and that there are other seizures to follow. Since she must die, it is better to let everything go than to save it for her family, whom she has never cared to see, and who have never cared for her. You can not conceive in the midst of what gilded misery the poor thing is dying.

Yesterday we had absolutely no money. Plate, jewels, shawls, everything is in pawn; the rest is sold or seized. Marguerite is still conscious of what goes on around her, and she suffers in body, mind, and heart. Big tears trickle down her cheeks, so thin and pale that you would never recognise the face of her whom you loved so much, if you could see her. She has made me promise to write to you when she can no longer write, and I write before her. She turns her eyes toward me, but she no longer sees me; her eyes are already veiled by the coming of death; yet she smiles, and all her thoughts, all her soul are yours, I am sure.

Every time the door opens her eyes brighten, and she thinks you are going to come in; then, when she sees that it is not you, her face resumes its sorrowful expression, a cold sweat breaks out over it, and her cheek-bones flush.

已经做了。但是，债主们都在巴望着她早点死去，以便变卖她的家当。

我本希望用我最后的积蓄阻止他们，但是执法干员告诉我这么做根本没有意义，同时，他有别的判决等待执行。既然她活不了多久了，倒不如放弃眼前这一切，没有必要为那些她未曾关心过，也根本不关心她的家人留下什么财产。你绝对无法想象这个看起来富丽堂皇，事实上却穷困潦倒的姑娘是如何一步步走向死亡的。

昨天我们彻底破产了。餐具、珠宝、衣物等所有的东西都被典当完了，剩下的不是被卖，就是被查封了。玛格丽特依然清楚她的一切境况。她的肢体、心灵以及精神被折磨得支离破碎了，硕大的泪珠滚出眼眶，流过双颊，她如此憔悴消瘦，你绝对无法辨认出眼前的这个女人就是你曾经那么挚爱的人。她恳请我在她无法为你写日记后，要我代笔，如今我就在她身旁为其执笔。她双目紧盯着我，可是，她却根本看不到我，她的双瞳已经被即将到来的死神挡住了，可她依然在微笑，我绝对相信，她的所有思绪、全部心智都紧紧围绕着你。

每当屋门被推开之时，她的双瞳便会绽放出光芒，她总以为你要来了，可是，当她认出那个人不是你的时候，面容上便又重现出先前的苦涩，脸上渗出了一层层冷汗，两颊也

February 19, midnight.

What a sad day we have had today, poor M. Armand! This morning Marguerite was stifling; the doctor bled her, and her voice has returned to her a while. The doctor begged her to see a priest. She said "Yes," and he went himself to fetch an abbe' from Saint Roch.

Meanwhile Marguerite called me up to her bed, asked me to open a cupboard, and pointed out a cap and a long chemise covered with lace, and said in a feeble voice:

"I shall die as soon as I have confessed. Then you will dress me in these things; it is the whim of a dying woman.

Then she embraced me with tears and added:

"I can speak, but I am stifled when I speak; I am stifling. Air!"

I burst into tears, opened the window, and a few minutes afterward the priest entered. I went up to him; when he knew where he was, he seemed afraid of being badly received.

"Come in boldly, father," I said to him.

He stayed a very short time in the room, and when he came out he said to me:

"She lived a sinner, and she will die a Christian."

A few minutes afterward he returned with

被血涨得通红。

2 月 19 日 深夜

我可怜的阿尔芒先生，今天是个悲惨的日子。清晨，玛格丽特断气了，医生帮她放血后，她又能稍微地发出一些声音了。医生劝告她去请神甫来办理后事，她答应了，于是，医生便亲自赶到圣罗克教堂去请神甫过来。

就在这时，玛格丽特把叫我到她的床边，恳请我去把她的衣橱打开，她用手指着一顶帽子以及一件镶满花边的长袖衬衣，声嘶力竭地说道：

"等我完成忏悔恐怕就要死了，请你为我穿戴上这些衣物，这便是这个濒临死亡的女人的验妆。"

此后，她便满面泪光地和我拥抱在一起，又说道：

"我还能说话，可是感到气闷得要死，我快窒息了！空气啊！"

我泪如泉涌，立即打开窗子。不久神甫就来了。我向他走了过去。可是，当他得知自己目前身处何地时，他好似非常担心不被盛情款待。

"神甫，请放心过来吧。"我对他说道。

他只在这间病房里待了片刻便出来了，他告诉我说：

"她一生充满罪孽，但她仍能如虔诚的基督徒一般升入天堂。"

没多久神甫便回来了，同时，一

a choir boy bearing a crucifix, and a sacristan who went before them ringing the bell to announce that God was coming to the dying one.

They went all three into the bedroom where so many strange words have been said, but was now a sort of holy tabernacle.

I fell on my knees. I do not know how long the impression of what I saw will last, but I do not think that, till my turn comes, any human thing can make so deep an impression on me.

The priest anointed with holy oil the feet and hands and forehead of the dying woman, repeated a short prayer, and Marguerite was ready to set out for the heaven to which I doubt not she will go, if God has seen the ordeal of her life and the sanctity of her death.

Since then she has not said a word or made a movement. Twenty times I should have thought her dead if I had not heard her breathing painfully.

February 20, 5 P.M.

All is over.

Marguerite fell into her last agony at about two o'clock. Never did a martyr suffer such torture, to judge by the cries she uttered. Two or three times she sat upright in the bed, as if she would hold on to her life, which was

个手擎耶稣受难十字架的唱诗班的孩子以及一个教堂的侍役陪他一起,侍役手摇圣铃,表示上帝已经降临到了这位临终者的家中。

他们三人一同进入卧房,这个曾经充满奇怪言语的小房间,现在竟变成了布满圣灵气息的神坛。

我双膝跪下,不清楚这样的景象能在眼帘中维持多久;可是我确信,世上再也不会有什么事情能够在我心中留下更深刻的印象了。

神甫往玛格丽特的脚上、胳膊上以及额头上都擦了一层圣油,又诵读了一段简短的祷告词,此时,这位濒死者已经准备升天了,倘若上帝亲眼目睹了玛格丽特在世时所遭受的种种苦难,以及临别前的神圣,她一定能够顺利升天的。

打这以后,玛格丽特没有说过一个字,也没有任何动静,有好多次,当我听不到她声嘶力竭的喘气声时,我都认为她已经升天了。

2月20日下午5点

一切都过去了。

凌晨2点,玛格丽特已经快支撑不住了。她不断发出痛苦的呻吟,恐怕再也没有任何临终的人遭受过如此痛苦的折磨了。有好几次她笔直地从床上坐起来,似乎是想抓住即将升

escaping toward God.

Two or three times also she said your name; then all was silent, and she fell back on the bed exhausted. Silent tears flowed from her eyes, and she was dead.

Then I went up to her; I called her, and as she did not answer I closed her eyes and kissed her on the forehead.

Poor, dear Marguerite, I wish I were a holy woman that my kiss might recommend you to God.

Then I dressed her as she had asked me to do. I went to find a priest at Saint Roch, I burned two candles for her, and I prayed in the church for an hour.

I gave the money she left to the poor.

I do not know much about religion, but I think that God will know that my tears were genuine, my prayers fervent, my alms-giving sincere, and that he will have pity on her who, dying young and beautiful, has only had me to close her eyes and put her in her shroud.

February 22.

The burial took place today. Many of Marguerite's friends came to the church. Some of them wept with sincerity. When the funeral started on the way to Montmartre only two men followed it: the Comte de G., who came from London on purpose, and the

入天国的她的生命。

也有那么几次，她呼唤着你的名字，此后又是一片沉寂，她重新浑身无力地摔在床上，泪珠静静地从她的眼眶中滑了出来，随后，她去世了。

我立即走到她的身边，呼唤她，可是，她再也没有回应了。我合上她的双眼，在她的前额亲吻了一下。

我亲爱的、悲惨的玛格丽特啊，我真希望自己是一个圣女，这样，我的吻就能将你送到上帝身边了。

随后，我遵照她在世时的嘱咐，为她穿戴整齐，到圣罗克教堂请来神甫，替她点上两支蜡烛，又在朝拜室里为她做了1个小时的祷告。

我还将她留下的钱施舍给了一些穷苦的人。

我不太了解宗教，可是，我确信仁慈的上帝一定会洞悉我真挚的泪水，由衷的祈祷以及诚心的施舍。上帝一定会怜悯这么一位年轻漂亮却在死前唯有我一个人前来为其合上双目并为其入殓的女人。

2月22日

今天下葬。玛格丽特的许多好友都赶到教堂了，其中有一些还流出了真挚的热泪，当殡仪队载着玛格丽特走向蒙马特公墓时，却唯有两个人紧紧跟在后面：一位是专程从伦敦赶来的G伯爵；另一位则是由两位仆人搀

duke, who was supported by two footmen.

I write you these details from her house, in the midst of my tears and under the lamp which burns sadly beside a dinner which I can not touch, as you can imagine, but which Nanine has got for me, for I have eaten nothing for twenty-four hours.

My life can not retain these sad impressions for long, for my life is not my own any more than Marguerite's was hers; that is why I give you all these details on the very spot where they occurred, in the fear, if a long time elapsed between them and your return, that I might not be able to give them to you with all their melancholy exactitude.

扶着的公爵。

我正在她家给你叙述整件事情，眼泪不住地滑落，伤感而昏暗的灯火旁还摆着一份由纳尼娜亲自为我做的晚餐，我已经连续 24 个小时没有吃任何东西了。你一定想象得到，此时的我一点儿胃口也没有。

我的生命终究不总是属于我一个人，就如同玛格丽特一样，因此，这些惨淡而痛苦的景象恐怕不会持续停留在我的思绪中，可是，我担心时间久了，当你赶回这里时，我就无法将这些惨淡的景象完全而又确切地告诉你了，于是，我决定在发生这些事情的地方将这些事情记录下来并转交于你。

CHAPTER 27

第二十七章

"You have read it?" said Armand, when I had finished the manuscript.

"I understand what you must have suffered, my friend, if all that I read is true."

"My father confirmed it in a letter."

We talked for some time over the sad destiny which had been accomplished, and I went home to rest a little.

Armand, still sad, but a little relieved by the narration of his story, soon recovered, and we went together to pay a visit to Prudence and to Julie Duprat.

Prudence had become bankrupt. She told us that Marguerite was the cause of it; that during her illness she had lent her a lot of money in the form of promissory notes, which she could not pay, Marguerite having died without having returned her the money, and without having given her a receipt with which she could present herself as a creditor.

By the help of this fable, which Mme. Duvernoy repeated everywhere in order to

"你全部看完了吗？"读完这些手稿之后，阿尔芒问道。

"我的朋友，倘若这些都是真的，我能够理解你现在所承受的是怎样的煎熬！"

"我父亲的信也能够证明。"

关于这个刚刚结束了的凄惨的一生，我们又畅谈了一会儿，此后，我便到家中休息了片刻。

讲述完这整件事情时，阿尔芒依然很痛苦，不过现在，他的情绪已经恢复了平静，我俩便一同去探望了普鲁登斯和朱莉·杜普拉。

普鲁登斯已经破产了，她告诉我们，是玛格丽特将她害成这样的。玛格丽特病重之时，曾向她借了一大笔钱，可是，她还没还钱便死了，因此，她相当于开出许多空头支票而没有问玛格丽特要收据，所以，她也不算是债权人。

作为经济破产的原因，迪韦尔诺瓦夫人将这些肆意造谣的谎言四

account for her money difficulties, she extracted a note for a thousand francs from Armand, who did not believe it, but who pretended to, out of respect for all those in whose company Marguerite had lived.

Then we called on Julie Duprat, who told us the sad incident which she had witnessed, shedding real tears at the remembrance of her friend.

Lastly, we went to Marguerite's grave, on which the first rays of the April sun were bringing the first leaves into bud.

One duty remained to Armand – to return to his father. He wished me to accompany him.

We arrived at C., where I saw M. Duval, such as I had imagined him from the portrait his son had made of him, tall, dignified, kindly.

He welcomed Armand with tears of joy, and clasped my hand affectionately. I was not long in seeing that the paternal sentiment was that which dominated all others in his mind.

His daughter, named Blanche, had that transparence of eyes, that serenity of the mouth, which indicates a soul that conceives only holy thoughts and lips that repeat only pious words. She welcomed her brother's return with smiles, not knowing, in the purity of her youth, that far

处散播。她向阿尔芒讨了一张 1000 法郎的钞票，尽管阿尔芒绝对不相信她编造的那些故事，可是，他还是愿意假装去相信她，这是出于他对任何曾经与玛格丽特有过交往的人的尊重。

我们又拜访了朱莉·杜普拉，她叙说了她亲身经历的那段凄惨的故事，当她回忆起玛格丽特时，双瞳里流露出了真挚的热泪。

最后，我们赶往玛格丽特所在的公墓，此时，四月的第一缕春光正轻轻爱抚着周围的一切，绿叶萌生，到处洋溢着一片春意。

阿尔芒还有最后一件事情，那便是赶到老家看望他的父亲。他还盼望着我能够和他一同前去。

于是，我们便一同赶往 C 城，在那里我终于结识了迪瓦尔先生，正如阿尔芒所描述的那样：他高大，威严，可亲。

他满含激动的热泪迎接阿尔芒，并和我热情握手。很快我便感到，在如今的这位迪瓦尔先生心中，父爱比其他的都要崇高。

他的小女儿叫布兰齐，有着一双透亮的眼睛，那宁静的双唇已经证明她心灵里的圣洁思想，嘴中满是诚挚的话语。一见她哥哥从远方归来，便露出笑容，可是，这个如此单纯的女孩却全然不知，就是为

away a courtesan had sacrificed her own happiness at the mere invocation of her name.

I remained for some time in their happy family, full of indulgent care for one who brought them the convalescence of his heart.

I returned to Paris, where I wrote this story just as it had been told me. It has only one merit, which will perhaps be denied it; that is, that it is true.

I do not draw from this story the conclusion that all women like Marguerite are capable of doing all that she did – far from it; but I have discovered that one of them experienced a serious love in the course of her life, that she suffered for it, and that she died of it. I have told the reader all that I learned. It was my duty.

I am not the apostle of vice, but I would gladly be the echo of noble sorrow wherever I bear its voice in prayer.

The story of Marguerite is an exception, I repeat; had it not been an exception, it would not have been worth the trouble of writing it.

了维护她的姓氏的庄严与纯正，有个远方的妓女已经放弃了自己一生的幸福。

我又在这个洋溢着幸福的家庭里待上了一段日子，他们一家人都为治愈阿尔芒的心病而无所不至地辛劳着。

我赶回巴黎后，便将我所听到的这个故事记录了下来。这个故事仅有的可以推崇的，便是它的真实性，尽管，这恐怕会遭来一些争议。

通过这个故事，我并没能得出结论说，几乎每个如同玛格丽特一般的女人都可以经历她那样的事迹，而事实恰恰相反。可是，我十分清楚在这些女人中有这么一个姑娘，她经历了一系列的庄重爱情，甚至，为此忍受痛苦的蹂躏，直到被折磨至死。而我的责任便是将我所听说的这个故事讲给读者听。

在此，我无意倡导荒淫与邪佞，可是，不管我身处何方，只要能够听到类似这样的崇高的苦难人在虔诚祷告，我都会欣然为其宣扬。

在此，我再重申一遍，玛格丽特的故事只是一个特例，可是，倘若所有的故事都是这样，那大概也就没有必要将它记录下来了吧。

（完）